The Diary of Horace Wilt

Part 1

The W-w-wonder Years

By John Money

A Horace Tale

Text copyright © 2015, 2019 John Money

Published by Regency Rainbow Publishing

Cover by Maria Spada Design at www.mariaspada.com

Introduction

What follows is a story originally inspired by a song, the Diary of Horace Wimp by the Electric Light Orchestra. It grew and grew just like Alice after *that* bottle of Mr Dodgson's imagination, and it became a fictional biography of the life of a potential loser.

The emphasis there should be on 'potential'.

This is part one of two, trailing our... *hero*, Horace Wilt, in his years through college and his discovery of the opposite gender's charms and troubles, and of his own talents – leaving him poised on the verge of a new future with a raft of new characters.

And talking of the characters, none of them are based entirely on real people (heaven forfend), but all of them contain traits that I have witnessed over the years. They became real people to me, which would no doubt please a psychologist, and even the lives and places they inhabit took on that mantle as well. Their 'reality' between my ears meant that they needed, for me, to endure the joys and strife of the real world and for all that they laugh – and cry – their fictional lives are peppered with the truths of life back then in the early eighties.

One scene, for example, features a rock concert, and that really did happen (not the characters coming to life and attending, but the concert and my attendance) – and is included as part of the story simply so I could share that extraordinary experience. It fits with the tale, as well, I hope.

One reviewer of *this* part of the tale remarked that it made him 'laugh like a drain, cry like a baby, and jump on his wife'. I rather liked that review.

None of the characters here are real, or at least real outside of their actual situations. Their management companies wouldn't let me and perhaps I can't blame them too much.

This is a fictional story of the lives of a hardy band of souls and is written to entertain, not educate. Mind you, I learned a few things when writing it and who knows? Maybe you will as well as you read. Most of all, though, I hope you enjoy reading it as much as I enjoyed writing it.

And at least you don't have to edit and proof the… thing.

John Money, 2015

And now in 2019 I just want to add that I am so happy to see this story, above all of my others, being republished. The Diary was so much fun to write, and no matter what I say above about editing and proofing, it was great fun to go back through everything – as one reviewer said, it's a 'charming' story and one that draws you in. I thought so as well, and I hope you do too.

I remember very clearly that as I was writing Horace's story he and the other characters steadfastly refused to follow my planned storyline. They were developing in their own ways to such an extent that I very rarely knew what was going to happen next – and for all that this sort of independence (or bloody mindedness) could be a planning pain, it was also quite fantastic for me as the author. I just hope the high highs and low lows (not to mention sudden sideways jumps) of Horace's roller-coaster of a story bring you as much pleasure as they brought me!

John Money, 2019

Chapter 1

1

Horace gazed helplessly at the massive notice board and tried to locate his name among the dozens posted there. The new intake at the recently expanded polytechnic exceeded four hundred, split among four campuses and he was beginning to think that he might well have turned up at the wrong site. He pressed forward, peering closer at the printed lists.

"Ow! Mind who you're treading on, plonker!"

Horace took a moment or two to locate the source of the complaint. Finally, he looked down, "Oh, er, I'm really sorry, I, er, didn't see you down there."

A short, blonde girl was staring malevolently up at him, "Not a 'eightist remark, I 'ope?"

"'eye-tist'?"

"Yeah. As in 'ow tall I am."

"'Ow tall?" Light dawned, "Oh, er, I see. Heightist. No, really, it's just that I w-w-was trying to find my name and I guess I didn't notice you down… I mean, in front of me."

"Well, just watch it, okay?"

Horace nodded. Despite the girl's aggressive words she was smiling and her blue eyes twinkled with humour, "As I said, I'm really sorry and I promise I w-w-will w-w-watch it. By the w-w-way, w-w-what did you call me?"

The smile turned into a full-blown grin, "Plonker, as it 'appens."

"I w-w-wouldn't mind betting I don't w-w-want to know w-w-what wh-wh-wh-one of those is, I suppose?" He tried to return the smile.

"You don't know much for a student, do you?"

"Do you always answer a question w-w-with a question?" She was really rather pretty, Horace thought.

"Doesn't everyone?"

He laughed, the first feeling of relief he'd experienced since he'd got out of bed that morning, "Isn't it obvious?"

"Touché, big guy, and, no, you probably don't want to know what plonker means. Sorry, but broken toes often bring out the worst in me."

"I'm really sorry-" he began but she interrupted him.

"Don't fret, I wasn't really looking where I was going either. And I reckon that board's 'eightist as well. 'Ow am I s'posed to find my name without the aid of a telescope?" she peered up at the board.

"Tell you w-w-what? You look for my name down there... I mean, on the lower part of the board and I'll search for yours higher up." He regretted the suggestion as soon as he'd made it.

"Fair enough. My name's Fields, 'Arriet Fields, what's yours?"

Horace hesitated.

"And why're you blushing?"

"It's, er, Horace."

"'Orris? Just 'Orris?"

"Bugger," he muttered, then bit the bullet, "'Orris, I mean *Horace* W-w-wilt."

"No kidding?" she giggled. "Almost like in that ELO song?"

Horace nodded miserably, only to be surprised by Harriet's response, "That's really cool, no-one's gonna forget a name like that, are they?"

"I suppose not. Harriet's pretty unusual too, though."

"Tell me about it. Anyway, my friends usually call me 'Arry," she stopped and giggled again, "I nearly asked you whether you were named after the song, but I guess you're older than three months, right? Who's the plonker now then?"

Horace laughed, "Not knowing w-w-what wh-wh-wh-one is I can't really say but I'm a very mature toddler though, I shall find out."

"Anyway, it was an easy mistake for me to make. See, you'd just said that 'Arriet was an unusual name, and I was about to tell you that I'd been named after a pop-star. Got the link?"

Horace thought for a moment, "W-w-well, yes, but I can't think of any pop stars called Harriet."

"It's after Cliff Richard."

"Er, Cliff?"

"Yeah, my mum was dead keen on 'im. Bit disappointed I was a girl and couldn't think of a female name that matched Cliff."

"I get it. She named you after his real name, right?"

"Clever guy," Harriet agreed, "After Harry Webb."

"Very resourceful, your mother."

Harriet giggled, "Thank Christ I wasn't born ten years later when she was into Elton John, though-"

Before she could explain Horace interrupted her, "Real name, Reginald Dw-w-wight, w-w-which w-w-would have probably lumbered you with Regina, yeah?"

"Okay, I take it back. You're definitely student material. Pity about that stammer of yours, though."

Horace grimaced, "Comes w-w-with this bloody silly surname," Emboldened by her friendliness and remembering his self-assertiveness course, he added, "You seem to have a little problem of your own."

"What?" she looked perplexed for a moment before grinning, "Oh, you mean the haitches, yeah? And, yeah I do know that's s'posed to be "aitch" but it's pretty daft isn't it? I mean the word for aitch not 'aving a haitch? It's just where I was brought up. Haitches were laid off in the sixties and no-one's seen 'em since. Anyway, regional accents are well cool now."

"So I've heard," Horace was relieved that she hadn't taken offence, "Anyw-w-way, perhaps with your surname w-w-we could call you "Elision", you know, as in "Elision Fields"?"

Harriet laughed delightedly, "Very w-w-witty. Smartarse."

Horace barely stopped himself from replying that hers was both smarter and prettier, and blushed instead.

"What?" Harriet asked.

"Er, nothing."

His blushed deepened when Harriet looked from his face and then over her shoulder and downwards, "You could 'ave said it, you know," she teased, "I'm not one of those raging feminists, despite the jeans."

"I'm, er, not really, er, like that…"

"So I see. Lovely shade of pink, that," she indicated his glowing cheeks. "Oops," she added, when pink deepened to crimson, "Sorry, big guy, I shouldn't tease, should I? It's just me mouth running away with itself. Always does when I'm nervous."

Nervous was the last description Horace would have applied to her but he guessed you didn't have to stammer and blush just to be nervous.

Harriet giggled again, a sound that was beginning to appeal to him, "Anyway, I think blushing is a cute thing in a guy."

"Must make me very cute, then," Horace said and blushed, involuntarily, even deeper.

Her giggle turned to outright laughter, "I think you're okay," she said when she had control of herself, "What course are you taking?"

The unexpected question momentarily fazed him, "Er…"

"Tell me it's business studies."

"Okay," he replied then added, "It is. I mean, it *really* is."

"Great! Me too. At least I'll know one person when we get into the lectures."

Horace agreed. He'd been dreading the whole process of getting to know a new bunch of contemporaries and although he doubted they would all be as nice as Harriet, he was relieved to have broken the ice with at least one of them. *And* she hadn't taken the mickey out of his name, "Yeah, it's good to know. And talking of lectures, if w-w-we don't find out w-w-where our induction room is, w-w-we may never have to get to know anywh-wh-wh-one." The crowd around the notice board had thinned considerably.

"You're not wrong, big guy," Harriet said, "Let's get looking." She pushed forward to the board and began to scan the lower reaches, "Let's see, Wilt, Wilt."

"Harriet!"

She giggled again, "Sorry. Okay, Horace, Horace."

"That's not much better!"
"Oops. Right. Pink guy, pink guy..."
"Harriet!" Horace's voice rose in amused despair.
"Ah, here we go!"
"You've found out w-w-where w-w-we're supposed to go?"
"No, but I have found a guy called Guy Pink. Apparently he's our senior tutor. "
"You're kidding, right?"
Harriet shook her long blonde hair and pointed to the name at the head of one of the lists, "Some coincidence or what?"
Horace could only agree, "Totally."
"And here we are," Harriet added, pointing further down the list. To Horace's surprise, she grabbed his hand. "Come on, big guy, let's find our future." She led him away from the notice board towards a map that had been pinned by the entrance doors.
She looked up to see him blushing furiously once again, "Now what?" she asked in mock-exasperation. Following his glance at their joined hands she laughed, "Pink and shy. The guy just gets cuter and cuter. Don't worry, I won't bite."
"Er, good."
"Disappointed?" she teased.
"You know?" he replied in total confusion, "I really haven't got a clue."
"I'll let go if you want?"
"No, it's, er, okay."
Harriet raised one eyebrow and shrugged, "Okay. Come on then, we're probably already late."
Five minutes later they arrived outside the right door. A brass plate bore the legend *G.PINK*, the name followed by a seemingly random selection of letters and punctuation marks.
"Must be the place," Horace said, and rapped the door.

"Come!" a voice called.

Harriet opened the door and they crossed the threshold.

"My first new intake," the red-haired tutor welcomed them, "Amazing," he went on, ignoring their quizzical stares, "I normally don't see any of you for the first week or two. Sit down, sit down," he gestured towards two chairs then bent down underneath his desk muttering something about finding their reading lists.

"So much for being late," Harriet said.

"All that nervous energy w-w-wasted," Horace agreed.

Harriet gave his hand a quick squeeze as they seated themselves, "I don't think this is going to be so bad after all,"

"Quite right," Guy Pink agreed, emerging from beneath the desk. "Anyway, let's get the formalities over with." He handed them each a sheaf of papers. "First off, welcome to the North East London Polytechnic, or whatever we're called this year, and I hope your stay with us will be pleasant. What I've just given you is the syllabus and the reading lists. Mostly very boring stuff, I'm afraid, except, possibly for the first book on the list."

"'Modern Practices and the Role of the Computer in Business'" Harriet read aloud, "'Author:Guy Pink'. Sounds very, er, interesting."

"No it's not," Guy smiled, "However, since I set the examinations for all course work, it's fair to say that I tend to have a slight bias towards those who seem to have read the boring old thing. Just a little tip to help you on your way since you two were decent enough to turn up at the start of the term."

Horace laughed, "Thanks, er, Sir... Mr?"

"Just Guy will do. And now, of course, let's see who you are." He held up a hand to stop them introducing themselves, "You must be Horace Wilt, yes? And you, young lady, would be Harriet Fields, correct?"

They stared back at him, amazed.

"That's incredible," Harriet said.

"Actually, I was standing behind you both at the notice board," Guy laughed. "Sorry, I would have helped you find your way, but I had to get back here and clear out last term's coffee cups before you arrived. Quite remarkably furry they were. On that subject, can I get you two a coffee?"

Horace and Harriet declined as politely as possible.

"Probably a wise choice," Guy said, "And besides, it's much better in the Student Union. If you like, I'll show you the way?"

"That's very kind," Harriet replied after first checking with Horace. "Is there anything else we should know for now?"

The tutor thought for a moment and then shook his head, "I don't think so my young friends. First lecture is next Monday at eleven – the lecture hall is marked on the map tucked into the syllabus – and I suggest you locate the library and the bookshop in the meantime and start familiarising yourselves with what we'll be discussing this term." He paused and regarded their looks of surprise, "All a bit different from the school room, yes?"

Horace nodded.

"I hope you both enjoy yourselves," Guy went on, 'And it seems like you're doing okay so far.' Horace blushed and Harriet giggled. "Come on then, let's find the union."

Guy led them through a maze of corridors and they arrived at the large cafeteria-cum-bar, overlooking the sports fields at the rear of the main college building. He insisted on buying them coffee and left them almost immediately – "In the probably vain hope that someone else would turn up today".

"I think I'm going to like it here," Horace said.

"I think I already do," Harriet agreed, and brought another blush to Horace's over-worked cheeks by taking hold of his hand once again.

From The Diary of Horace Wilt

"Monday, September 18th 1979

Dear Diary,

First day at college today. Can't really take it all in. But get this! *I met a really nice girl; Harriet Fields - Harry to her friends, and she insists that* I *call her* Harry! *She's about five foot tall, blonde-haired, blue-eyed and she has the most amazing giggle. I met her at the notice board and we sort of chatted for a while and then found out we were on the same course. But most importantly, we* held hands! *I've only known her for a few hours but I can't seem to think of anything else! Mother guessed something was up when I came home but I didn't tell her anything, I mean, it's not as if Harriet's - Harry's! - my girlfriend or whatever, but.... I can always hope can't I? I've decided to ask her out - if I can pluck up the courage. She really is very pretty.*

Oh yes, college seems okay. Really relaxed. No lecture until next Monday and the tutor, Guy, said we should spend the week genning up on the books and stuff we'll be needing. Harry said she'd be at the college library tomorrow so I'm going to make sure I'm there really early in case I miss her."

2

The prospect of asking Harriet out petrified Horace, but, he reasoned, if *he* didn't ask her out as soon as possible, someone else would. He also tried hard not to think about the possibility of her already *having* a boyfriend. From what she'd said this didn't seem to be the case but Horace and chicken counting had never got along well.

The night passed in slow agony. He couldn't seem to drift off to sleep for more than ten minutes at a time and even then, the little lady haunted his dreams. By the time his alarm clock went off at the unusually early hour of six-thirty, he was more exhausted than when he'd climbed into bed.

An hour's worth of thorough ablutions later, he returned to his bedroom to decide what to wear. Forty more minutes passed before he arrived in the kitchen where his mother was cooking pulses and humming along, off-key, to Cliff Richard.

She looked up when he came into the room, "Could be us," she said, "We don't seem to talk anymore." She paused. Horace was staring off into space and smiling, "Horace?"

"Oh! Hi, mother." *Cliff Richard. Harry Webb. Harriet Fields*. "Sorry, I w-w-was w-w-wool gathering."

"Hmm, I'm sure there's a girl at the root of this weirdness," his mother observed.

He blushed and hurried to the coffee machine, "Not at all. It's just the new college and all that."

His mother laughed, "We'll see. And that reminds me. Have you thought anymore about moving into dugs?"

He sighed, "That's *digs*, mother. And w-w-we've already been through that. I mean, the college is only a fifteen minute bus ride aw-w-way. W-w-what's the point?"

"What about your privacy? Especially with a new girlfriend."

"Mother!"

"Well you do keep saying that you need a new image," his mother persisted. "Perhaps your own place will help you develop one."

"I get the feeling, that you're trying to get rid of me."

"Well, at least your sense of perception's improving. But it's not just *your* privacy I'm talking about here."

"Oh? Do I detect the imminent arrival of a boyfriend in your life?"

His mother's smile broadened, "Not at all, son of mine. But, like you, I've just met my first girlfriend."

"W-w-what!?" For the first time in twenty-two hours, Harriet slipped temporarily from Horace's fevered mind.

"Don't look so shocked. And, before you ask, I do mean girlfriend in the sexual sense of the word."

"I w-w-wasn't going to ask!"

"After all," his mother said, "I'd be a hypocrite if I told you that I didn't mind if you were homosexual and then denied myself the pleasure."

Horace felt she was relishing his discomfiture, "I..." he began, "W-w-well..." he tried again. Finally he said lamely, "Er, I, er, hope that you'll be very happy." He *would* have to think about the idea of a flat again.

"Good," his mother said, "And I'm sure you'll like her. Her name's Starchild." Horace groaned. "Don't be like that. And please take that grimace of shock off your face. You look like something in Mrs Tussaud's."

"That's 'Madame'," Horace corrected her automatically. He shook his head, "I guess it's just such a surprise."

"To me as well. Although why children always seem to think that their parents' sex lives stopped at the time of their conception is beyond me. Anyway, you said you wanted to leave early this morning and it's already eight-fifteen. Hadn't you better be off to meet your girlfriend?"

His mother was right; he had planned to have left by now, "Oh, right. Yes, thanks."

"I thought so."

Horace groaned again, "I'll tell you about her later," he promised, grabbing his coat and heading for the back door.

"Have fun," his mother called after him.

His mother's shocking revelation didn't occupy his mind for nearly as long as it would have in other circumstances and he was already picturing his meeting with Harriet when the bus arrived. Twenty five minutes later he was standing outside the still-closed college library and scanning the hallway for her diminutive figure.

At nine the library doors opened and a young woman looked out into the corridor, "We're open now."

"Oh, er, thanks. I'm just w-w-waiting for someone if that's okay?"

"It's a free world." She retreated back into the library.

As the minutes ticked by Horace could feel himself becoming more flustered. What if she didn't come today? She had *said* she would, but what if she changed her mind? What if he waited out here all day and she never turned up? The butterflies in his stomach had been taking steroids; he was sure he could see his shirt front rippling as they battered against his insides. He checked his watch for the fortieth time and raised a despairing look to the heavens.

"Something interesting up there, or are you just ignoring me?"

He started and looked down quickly. Harriet was grinning up at him.

"Wotcha, Orris."

"W-w-wotcha, I mean, Hi. I w-w-was just, you know?"

"Ignoring me?"

"No!" he exclaimed, sharper than he intended, "I mean, no." Relief was flooding out of every pore.

She laughed, "Thanks for waiting for me."

"I did say I w-w-would," Horace replied, delighted with her gratitude, blushing.

"Shy, turns pink at the drop of a hat, and keeps his promises. Lucky me."

Horace snorted, "Turns pink at the drop of an aitch, maybe."

She giggled in the way that had tortured Horace's dreams the previous night, "Okay, big guy. Fair's fair. Shall we?" Harriet gestured towards the library doors.

"Good idea." He was about to blurt out something along the lines of "the sooner we start, the sooner we can go for a beer afterwards" but stopped himself just in time. *Don't rush it! Relax!* He realised that Harriet was staring at him and he feigned a cough, "Yeah, let's get to it."

Harriet offered him her hand and he took it with only the briefest hesitation. He was in seventh heaven.

They walked together into the cavernous room and stared around. While Horace had been waiting outside, more than two dozen students had entered and there was a bustle of activity, chatter and the occasional burst of laughter all around.

"Beats the public library," Harriet said.

Horace nodded, "It's kind of nice to have a bit of background noise." He had been hoping that they would be allowed to chat in here since it was part of the master plan.

They crossed the room and found a vacant table opposite the main doors where they set down Harriet's drawstring bag and Horace's genuine imitation leather attaché case, "Let's 'ave a look at the reading list and grab some of 'em before the others arrive," Harriet suggested.

"Good idea. And w-w-we mustn't forget Guy's book."

"Good observation, Sherlock," Harriet grinned, "We might as well get off on the right foot with 'im."

They took their reading lists to the desk where a woman was idly flicking through a card index. She looked up as they approached and smiled, "Decided to join us after all?" she asked Horace.

"Er, yeah. This is Harriet, the wh-wh-wh-one I w-w-was w-w-waiting for."

"I can see why," the librarian said, causing Horace's blush to deepen appreciably, "Now," she went on, politely ignoring his embarrassment. "How can I help you? I take it you're with this year's new intake."

"That's right," Harriet said, "And we thought we'd get a 'ead start on the reading list."

"Very keen," the librarian fished two sheets of paper out of a drawer and picked up a pen. "Okay, this is the procedure; I'll need to take your details – name, address and so on – and then your course requirements and the name of your senior tutor." She looked up to see who wanted to go first. The young man, she noticed, was blushing even more than before.

Harriet giggled beside him, "I'm 'Arriet Fields."

The woman smiled, "With an aitch?"

Harriet nodded, "Yeah, as in 'Ackney."

"You're not *from* Hackney by any chance?"

"Nah, I'm Barking, me."

"You can say that again," Horace muttered and was rewarded with a hefty swat on his arm.

The librarian turned her attention to Horace, "And you are?"

With his usual sigh Horace told her.

"There's only one double-yoo in that," Harriet commented helpfully.

"Thanks a bunch," Horace gave her a mock-scowl.

"Great name," the librarian said, smiling, "It's a bit like that character from the ELO song. I love ELO."

"I used to as w-w-well."

The two women laughed. "And your address?"

"Number five, Plantation W-w-way, Leyton, E10."

"Okay, be sure to let us know if you move," she said, "Like, if you move into digs a bit more local."

Horace remembered his mother's revelation and resolved to buy a local newspaper later on, "I w-w-was just thinking about that."

Harriet nodded, "Me too," she turned to Horace. "Perhaps we can go searching together?"

Horace's blush had almost disappeared. It now returned with a vengeance, and he gulped loud enough for a couple of student heads to turn at a nearby table.

Harriet gave her customary giggle, "I meant search out *two* places. I wasn't asking you to shack up with me."

Horace breathed a sigh of relief and nearly choked on it when Harriet whispered, "Yet, anyway." He stared at her, delighted, embarrassed and totally confused.

The librarian laughed loudly, "Happy hunting. Now, what course are you on?"

Harriet, still giggling, couldn't answer and Horace, happy to be on firmer ground, answered. "Guy Pink's"

"Oh, the Red Setter's group."

"The Red Setter?" Horace asked.

The librarian nodded, "That's what the students call Guy. Even the other tutors do. You see, his name's Pink, his hair's red, and he sets all the course examinations."

"Makes sense," Harriet said, her giggling fit under control.

"So I guess you'll both want copies of *Modern Practice* for a start," the librarian went on, handing them each a copy from a stack below the desk. "And you'll find most of the other stuff in aisle D. There's still plenty of copies left; you two are the first of this year's crop to show up." She handed them each a large plastic carrier bag, "You'll need these. When you've done, just leave a list of the titles you've taken in the tray there, and if there's anything you can't find, give me a yell."

"Thanks," Harriet took her carrier bag and turned to Horace. "Shall we?"

"Good idea."

They spent half an hour poring through the shelves and returned to their table loaded down with dog-eared texts on subjects as fascinating as *Corporate Accounting for Beginners* and *Contract Law; A Definitive Guide* which weighed in at three and a half pounds on its own.

"Looks like fun," Horace said, setting down his heap of books and beginning to pack them into the carrier bag.

"I could think of more entertaining reading," Harriet grumbled.

"It'd be hard not to. W-w-what sort of stuff do you really like?"

"All sorts," Harriet said, "But my favourites at the minute are 'Arry 'Arrison and 'Erman

'Esse. And, no, I'm not kidding." She gave him a disapproving look as he grinned at her.

"Ever read Mein Kampf?" he asked innocently.

"No," she replied slowly. "Okay, then," she sighed, "Who's it by?"

"Hadolph 'Itler."

Harriet laughed, "Very funny, rat. I'll get you for that," Horace dodged her attempted smack, "I s'pose your favourites are John Wyndham and Winston Churchill, then?"

Horace laughed, "They might be if I could ever ask somewh-wh-wh-one for a copy." For the first time in his life he was happy to take the mickey out of his own speech impediment.

"Nice one. Anyway, do us a favour and look after my things, will you? I've gotta find the Ladies."

"Great! I mean, okay, fine, I'll just, er, w-w-wait here then," Horace stammered. As soon as Harriet returned, he'd make his move.

She gave him a quizzical look, and with a smile and a shake of her head, turned and left him at the table.

Horace fumbled the last of the books into his bag and took a few deep breaths. *Relax,* he told himself. His heart rate had soared and he was trembling all over. He hoped fervently that Harriet wouldn't be too long; if she was, he would either suffer a coronary or rattle himself into his component pieces.

While they had been harvesting their books Horace had noted down all of the titles on their borrower's forms, and he took them over to the tray that the librarian had indicated earlier – anything to distract his mind from the forthcoming event. He paced nervously back to the table and sat down. How long had she been gone? Unlike the nervous waiting outside the library, at least he knew that she *would* be coming back and he tried to use this thought to calm his high-tension nerves. He glanced at his watch and then decided to concentrate instead on the open doorway opposite. He didn't want her to think that he might be ignoring her again.

His mouth was as dry as a desert by the time Harriet reappeared in the doorway. Horace took a large gulp of air and returned the wave she gave him. *Here goes nothing*, he thought, steeling his resolve. In his mind, the simple sentence that he was going to say next took on monumental proportions. He cleared his throat and let the first words into his mouth, ready to be spoken.

Harriet took two steps into the room and then stopped, her head swivelling back to the corridor. The smile that had adorned her face turned into a broad grin as Horace watched, mystified. Harriet turned, the smile becoming even broader. She took a step back towards the corridor, and to Horace's horror, he saw a young man their own age step into the room.

Harriet's voice was all too clear; "'Unk!" she cried and rushed into the young man's open arms.

Horace's world collapsed around him. Here he had been, worrying about whether he would pluck up sufficient courage to ask her out before someone else did, and his worst fear had been confirmed; she *already* had a boyfriend. She even called him by a pet name – Hunk. And, Horace was even more horrified to see, he *was* a hunk. He looked on despairingly as the two embraced, his Harry and the Hunk. The Hunk looked like a younger version of Fonzie off *Happy Days*, all slicked-back, perfectly coiffured hair, tight blue jeans, motorcycle boots and leather jacket.

Why had he been stupid enough to think that Harriet might even be willing to date him? Horace the Wilted? What had he been thinking of?

Worse followed. Harriet and The Hunk hugged each other again, and then Harriet took his hand and led him towards the table where Horace sat, grief-stricken.

"Hey, big guy," she greeted Horace, oblivious to the sound of his heart shattering into a thousand pieces, "This is 'Unk, and guess what? 'E's made it on to our course!"

Horace was dumbstruck, but gave his best impression of a smile. There was no way could he speak just then.

"Orris, meet 'Unk – or should I say Phil – and 'Unk, meet Orris," she beamed at them both.

"Hi, guy, how's it hanging?" Phil the Hunk greeted the still dumbstruck Horace.

Horace mustered the last of his reserves, "Great."

"What's up, big guy?" Harriet asked, concerned.

"N-n-nothing." He tried to put on a smile. It didn't fit.

The Hunk didn't notice anything wrong, "I see you two have already done the book collecting thing. And judging by the looks of those bags I think I'll give it a miss for now. Anyone know where the Student Union is? I could murder a coffee."

Harriet, still with a concerned frown on her face, looked around at him, "I was just gonna suggest me and H go down there ourselves. We'll show you the way."

Horace shook his head. Seeing Harriet and her boyfriend together at close quarters here was bad enough. He didn't think he could stand to watch them chatting happily together over a coffee, "Actually," he began, realising to his horror that he was close to tears, "I'd better be getting home. Things to do." He grabbed his attaché case and the bulging carrier bag.

"Orris?" Harriet protested, "What's up? What about the flat hunting later?"

Horace didn't trust himself to speak. He rose quickly before anyone could see the level of his misery and made for the door.

"Orris!" Harriet made to go after him, but something about his body language suggested that it was the last thing he wanted. She looked back at The Hunk, confused, "What's bitten 'im?"

"Dunno. Weird kid, though. What did you say his name was?"

"Orris. Orris Wilt."

"Wilt by name, wilted by nature, huh?" The Hunk grinned.

Harriet scowled, "Uncle Phil, you can be a real pain at times. Orris is great. I thought we was getting on really well, you know? He's been real nervous all morning and I thought he might even ask me out," she stopped and sniffed. "We was gonna go flat 'unting together!"

"Hey, little niece," Phil put his arm around her shoulders, "Go easy there. It's okay."

"It's *not* okay! What's so bad about me?"

"Absolutely nothing," Phil said, squeezing her trembling shoulders, "You're the nicest niece an uncle could ever have. But less of the 'Unk' and 'Uncle' business here. After all we're at college now."

Harriet sighed and brushed a tear from the corner of her eye, "His loss, right?"

"Absolutely. Now, let me grab your books and you can show me the way to the coffee."

She sighed again and nodded, "I could use one." She picked up her bag and trailed disconsolately out of the library after her uncle.

3

Horace kept his head down and made his way out of the college as quickly as he could. By the time he reached the main doors he was running. He clattered through them into bright sunshine and almost ended up in the ornamental fountain outside. "Stupid, stupid, stupid," he muttered to himself.

Despite the weight of the books and the fact that the handle of the carrier bag was already stretching alarmingly, he decided to walk the three miles home. He needed time to think, time to compose himself.

The walk took him over two hours and he was forced to stop at an Asian general store to buy a replacement for the carrier bag which had given up the ghost while he was crossing a main road.

When he arrived at the end of Plantation Way he looked towards his house and saw a strange car in their driveway. He groaned. It must be the new woman's car; Starstruck, or whatever stupid name she called herself. He decided he couldn't face his mother and her new friend just yet, and passed by, making for his local, the Copperfield. By six, after several hours of illicit, out-of-hours, drinking, Horace had consumed seven pints of Guinness and re-read the first five pages of *Modern Practice* a dozen times. Despite the alcohol, Horace didn't feel at all drunk but when he made to leave he was decidedly unsteady.

He swayed back towards Plantation Way feeling numb, both physically through the beer, and mentally through being Horace the Wilted.

He set down the bags on his front doorstep and fumbled his key into the lock at the fourth attempt. Holding the door open with his foot as he bent to retrieve the bags, he succeeded in banging his head against the door jamb. He had determined to make straight for his room and lock himself inside –

possibly for good – but his mother intercepted him at the foot of the staircase.

"Hi, darling!" She welcomed him, her nose wrinkling at the smell of beer on his breath. "Been celebrating, I see."

"Oh, yeah." Horace's voice dripped sarcasm.

If his mother noticed this, she ignored it, "Come into the parlour for a minute. I want you meet Starchild."

"Mum, I'm really tired and I'm not in the mood."

She took the bags out of his hands and set them on the floor, "Nonsense! Now come along."

Heaving a mammoth sigh, Horace followed her into the front room.

"Horace, this is Starchild, and Starchild, this is my beloved son Horace," she declared.

Horace tried to ignore the irony of 'beloved' and looked past his mother at "Starchild". He hadn't really any idea of what to expect, but a frumpy-looking woman of about fifty certainly didn't fit the bill.

"Hello, Horace," Starchild said, "I'm so pleased to meet you, Moonflower has told me so much about you."

Horace's patience had worn too thin, "Likew-w-wise I'm sure," he muttered in the woman's general direction, then turned to his mother, evidently the Moonflower. "Mum," he said slowly, "She's old enough to be *your* mother."

He ignored his mother's plaintive howl and walked out of the room. He also ignored her entreaties to 'come back here and apologise', Starchild's directions for his mother 'not to fret, dear', the bags of books, and the telephone, which began ringing as he entered the hallway. He took the stairs three at a time, crossed into his room and locked the door behind him.

From The Diary of Horace Wilt

"Tuesday, September 19th 1979

Dear Diary,

Can't write much just now. It's hard enough just to write 'she already has a boyfriend' and I'm definitely not going to write down the bastard's name.

How stupid can I get?

Met mum's new girlfriend (yes, that's right) and insulted the old bat. I mean to say, though, wouldn't you have done in my position? It's not exactly very funny when everyone but me seems to have a girlfriend - EVEN MY OWN MOTHER!

Bed now."

4

If Horace thought that his first term at college had started badly, worse was to come. There were thirty two students beside himself on Guy Pink's Business Studies course; twenty-eight seemed to be paired off and going steady, two were male and gay, one never seemed to appear at all (although his course work did) and then there was Godfrey.

Godfrey was really Sean O'Hanlon. He'd attended a Catholic boarding school before college and was known as Godfrey because he was a devout atheist. He was also the only one of the class that Horace could term "friend". While Horace was undoubtedly wilted by name and nature, Godfrey out-wilted him in all but the name department. It was *inevitable* that they would become friends.

Horace avoided Harriet and Phil the Hunk whenever possible, despite their increasingly desperate attempts to involve him in their activities, and it was early October before he could even bear to look in their direction. At his first lecture he found an envelope on his desk but threw it away without reading it. It was clearly from Harriet (no-one else, he assumed, would address an envelope to "Orris") and he had decided that he wouldn't allow his already fragile nerves to be exposed to any more suffering.

Life at home had been distinctly chilly for a while after his introduction to Starchild (who was really Maisie Briggs, a semi-retired accountant) but his mother gradually came round and even began to cook for him again. The flat-hunting was put on hold, despite the increasingly intimate behaviour of his mother and the accountant, since he couldn't search for somewhere without being reminded of Harriet.

Horace had first got talking to Godfrey in, of all places, the gymnasium. In the first week of October Horace embarked on his latest "lose the wilted-iness" campaign and had joined the gym club. The instructor had assessed his general level of fitness and physique and, to Horace's surprise, told him that he had potential. The fact that he must have said the same to Godfrey, who was six feet six inches tall and weighed around nine stone dripping wet, did not occur to him.

After his first gruelling session with a variety of weighted devices straight out of an inquisition chamber, Horace had been sitting on a bench in what was termed the rec. The rec, short for "recovery", was a wide corridor which ran between the gym and the two changing rooms. It was lined with benches, and a table was kept constantly stacked with fresh towels. To reach the rec, part of the wall of the gym was pulled outwards and slid sideways to form a sheltered doorway. Horace was waiting until he could summon sufficient energy to take a shower, when a head appeared round the doorway. Horace recognised Godfrey immediately from the couple of lectures they had both taken, and from his hair, which was a similar colour to Horace's face whenever he was nervous.

"Er, hi," Godfrey said. "You're Horace, right?"

"Sure am," Horace wheezed.

"Do us a favour and throw me a towel, would you?"

Horace struggled upright and crossed to the table. Despite the incredible weight, he managed to lift one and crossed painfully to the doorway where Godfrey was concealed, "There you go."

Godfrey snatched the towel, disappeared back into the cover of the door-cum-wall and then reappeared with it wrapped around him, "Thanks, Horace."

"W-w-what's w-w-with the towel?"

Godfrey grunted, "One of those bloody machines ate my gym kit."

"W-w-what?"

"It got tangled up in the weights or something," Godfrey said, "And it was one of those new lightweight Lycra jobs. Ripped clean off me."

Horace laughed, "In the middle of the gym?"

"To be exact, in the middle of a gym packed full with female students."

"Ouch! Rather you than me; some of those females look a bit fierce."

"They certainly laugh pretty fiercely," Godfrey grumbled. "It had to be me, of course!"

Horace didn't think even *he* could manage to embarrass himself in quite such a spectacular fashion, "Bad luck, Godfrey."

"Stop grinning," Godfrey smiled, "But thanks anyway. From what I hear, it's bound to be your turn next."

"Oh, no! I'm taking extra care these days. Anyw-w-way, see you later, I think I can just about manage the shower now."

"Fancy a beer afterwards?"

Horace shrugged, "To tell the truth, I don't go down the Union often."

"Me neither, but I found a great pub ten minutes from here. If you don't mind paying the full whack, the beer's pretty good."

Horace initially had no intention of taking up Godfrey's offer, but now that it appeared that he wouldn't have to face the gauntlet of the Union – and the chance of running into Harriet and the Hunk – the proposition was far more attractive. "Yeah, okay then. W-w-why not?"

"Good man," Godfrey said, "I'll meet you at the main gate in about fifteen minutes. I need a sit down before showering and then

I've gotta collect my books from the laundry room where they're drying out."

Horace raised a quizzical eyebrow as Godfrey picked up another towel and settled on a bench.

"Don't ask," Godfrey instructed.

Horace laughed and made for the changing rooms and showers, content in the knowledge that there was at least one student who was more unfortunate than himself. At the doorway he looked back to where Godfrey was grinning and waving madly at him. Horace shook his head and returned the wave. *What a wimp*, he thought, walking into the changing room, making sure he didn't trip on his towel which was wrapping itself around his ankles.

"Oi!"

Horace's head snapped up. That voice had not sounded particularly male. "Oh bugger," he muttered as his eyes took in the scene. Prominent in the foreground was the figure of Stephanie Jameson, another Business Studies student. More important was the fact that, apart from a towel wrapped turban-like around her head, Stephanie was completely naked. His eyes rapidly took in the background where a number of other female students were in various stages of undress.

"Oh, I'm s-s-sorry," he stuttered, beginning to back out of the room.

Stephanie, making no attempt to cover herself (Horace couldn't help noticing), advanced angrily towards him, "Get the fuck out of here, Wilt!"

"Yeah, r-r-right, absolutely!" His back bumped into the wall beside the door. Before the angry and quivering Stephanie could reach him, he turned and bolted.

Outside, Godfrey was hanging onto the wall, laughing hysterically.

"W-w-why didn't you w-w-warn me?"

Between fits of laughter, Godfrey struggled out a few words, "I t-t-tried," Snort, giggle, "R-r-really. That's why I was…" Giggle, snort, "waving."

"Oh, very funny," Horace was trying hard not to laugh himself. A combination of acute embarrassment and the high-pitched giggles emanating from Godfrey was a potent brew on the road to hysterics.

"See anything interesting?" Godfrey asked, his voice returning to something resembling normal, "I thought I heard Stephanie's dulcet tones."

"Oh, that w-w-was Stephanie, alright," Horace shook his head, "And not a stitch on." He groaned – yet another female that he dare not look at in future.

"Wow, man! What's she like under those dungarees she always wears?"

Horace cast his mind back and shuddered, "A lot bigger than I'd have guessed. And she's not a natural blonde, either." Embarrassing or not, that episode was likely to supply plenty of material for night-time fantasies for some time to come. He hadn't seen that much bare female flesh before outside of a magazine.

Godfrey was still enthralled, "Nice timing. If it weren't for the facts that it'll be all round the place by tomorrow morning, I'd almost envy you."

"Don't remind me," Horace groaned.

The door of the women's changing rooms began to open and Horace dived across the corridor into the sanctuary of the men's room.

He had stripped and was standing under a steaming shower when Godfrey joined him, "If I were you, Horace," Godfrey advised, "I'd stay out of Stephanie's way for a while. I told her about the natural blonde thing."

"You did w-w-what!?"

"Just kidding. In fact, she thought it was quite a hoot."

Horace looked over doubtfully.

"Really," Godfrey said. "She said that she knew you were a klutz before and this just confirmed her opinion."

"Oh, w-w-wonderful!"

"Besides," Godfrey went on, "She doesn't mind much if anyone sees her in the raw. Apparently she models for the life-class for some extra cash."

With a figure like hers, Horace could well believe it. To his horror, the memory of her naked body not three feet from him began to have an arousing effect.

"She's that good, huh?" Godfrey commented amiably.

Horace covered his rapidly growing erection with one hand and quickly shut the shower jet off, "I'm out of here before some of the guys come in and see this. One humiliation is enough for one day."

"Good idea, Horace. Our reputations are pretty much shot already."

Horace dashed out with his towel clutched over his groin and dressed without even bothering to dry himself properly. To his immense relief, no-one had found him in the showers with both Godfrey and a hard-on. Rather than wait at the gates for his new friend, Horace decided that there was safety in numbers and went with him to the laundry room, where Godfrey's soggy books had now become rather stiff.

"How did you manage that?" Horace asked.

"Dropped them in the Red Setter's fish tank."

Horace laughed, "I bet he liked that."

"Actually, he doesn't know about it. I managed to fish them out before he arrived."

Horace picked up a somewhat dehydrated guppy that had fell from a copy of *Modern Practice*, "If I w-w-were you," he advised, "I'd check those books for novelty bookmarks before you hand any of them in."

"Yuck!" Godfrey grimaced, "Good idea, methinks."

They left the college as quickly as possible, making only one detour to avoid the now dungaree-clad Stephanie Jameson and a group of other female students who were laughing uproariously at whatever Stephanie was telling them. Horace was pretty certain he knew what the topic was.

The pub was vast. The Crown and Parliament boasted three ground floor bars, a snooker room on the first floor and a function hall on the second. In each room there was a different juke box, each thundering out the music of choice for the clientele of that particular bar. The one at the rear of the ground floor bars was given over to a rather eclectic mixture of punk, new wave and currently popular tracks. *Don't Bring Me Down*, the latest ELO hit flooded the room as they entered.

"Good track," Godfrey said, "Although I guess you've gone off ELO recently?"

Horace grinned, despite himself, "At least *The Diary of Horace W-w-wimp* gets me sort of recognised."

"Hard to forget," Godfrey agreed after ordering two pints of Guinness, "And I wouldn't mind betting that Stephanie's gonna feature in today's entry."

"How did you know I keep a diary?"

Godfrey looked surprised, "I didn't. It was just a joke. Do you really?"

Horace groaned and nodded, "Please? W-w-whatever you do, don't mention it in class. I've got enough problems as it is."

"Don't worry. I know only too well how tough it can get. The secret's safe with me. Seriously though, will you mention Stephanie in today's entry?"

Horace, feeling safer now that they were away from the college, smiled, "Too right! Not that I think I need to write it down to remember that particular scene."

"If she's that cute, I think I might attend a few art lessons."

"I don't think I'd be able to hold the brush steady."

"Brush?" Godfrey grinned, "I only said I'd attend."

"Good idea." To change the subject (memories of a certain someone's mammaries were beginning to make his jeans uncomfortable), he pointed to a large machine in the corner of the room, currently surrounded by a group of suspiciously young-looking punks, "W-w-what's that?"

"You never see one before? It's the latest craze. Space Invaders it's called."

"No. W-w-what's it do?"

"Hard to explain. I'll demonstrate it later when the crèche has gone home."

They spent the entire evening in the bar, the last two hours dedicated to zapping the alien hordes. When the last-orders bell rung, Horace looked at his watch in amazement, "Addictive stuff," he said.

Godfrey grunted through clenched teeth. He was determined to make it to level three before they were forced out into the night, "You don't say."

Despite Godfrey failing in his goal, they took their leave happily, and wandered into the still-warm night, "Seems like summer's lasted forever," Godfrey said.

"Yeah, I guess I'll w-w-walk home tonight."

"Where do you live?"

"Leyton," Horace replied.

"Long walk. Why don't you stay over at my place? It's only round the corner."

Horace shrugged. It might be nice to get away from home for a night; the happy couple were getting on his nerves, "W-w-won't your parents mind?"

Godfrey looked surprised, "Uh, huh," he shook his head, "It's *my* place. Just a couple of rooms, but it beats home. I'm the oldest of the eight kids and that place is bedlam."

"I'm thinking of getting my own place soon too," Horace said, "But, yeah, I wouldn't mind sleeping over. As long as I call home first."

"Mummy likely to miss you?"

"Probably not."

Godfrey laughed, "I don't think my ma's even *noticed* I've left home."

They walked back to Godfrey's bedsit and Horace called his mother. To his surprise, she wasn't in the least bit put out by him staying out all night and, in fact, seemed to think it a marvellous idea. She hoped that he and Godfrey would be happy. Together. Horace hung up groaning.

From The Diary of Horace Wilt

"Monday, 2ⁿᵈ October, 1979

Dear Diary,

More humiliation at college today. Went into wrong changing rooms by mistake and ended up face to face with Stephanie Jameson - who wasn't wearing a stitch! Despite all the embarrassment, can't help but remember what she looked like; really nice figure and, as I said, totally naked! Guess it's about time I actually saw a real live female without clothes on (my mother doesn't count). Apparently she models like that for the art class. If only I could pluck up the courage, I'd go along...

Got talking to Godfrey and went to Crown with him after college. Played fantastic new game called Space Invaders. G reckons it's addictive, but I'm pretty sure I won't get hooked on it. Stayed the night at G's bedsit - maybe I should consider getting a place of my own. Especially with that Maisie around home all the time."

6

Life followed a similar pattern during the next couple of weeks and Horace stayed over at Godfrey's on ever more frequent occasions. Three days before his nineteenth birthday he arrived back at his mother's house ostensibly to see her, but in reality to grab a couple more changes of clothes.

"Oh, Horace," she enthused when he located her alone, for a change, in the kitchen, "Just the little man I wanted to see."

Horace was automatically wary, "Er, yes?"

"Well, it's your birthday on Sunday," she said, "And I thought you might like this." She dried her hands absent-mindedly on the shirt Horace had laid on the kitchen table and handed him a thick envelope.

"Er, thanks. W-w-we w-w-were going to have a bit of a party on Saturday at Godfrey's so I'd better take this w-w-with me."

"Oh, no need. Open it now."

He shrugged and tore open the envelope. Inside was a thick stack of crisp twenty pound notes, "W-w-what's this for?" Horace asked, mentally calculating how many games of Space Invaders the money could buy.

"Well, seeing how you enjoy yourself so much away from home, I thought you could use it to find a place of your own."

"It's not that I don't like being at home-"

"Of course not, dear," she said, "But I think it will do you good, you know? A little respondability."

"Responsibility," he corrected her absently, "It's very kind of you, but..." he trailed off as Maisie 'Starchild' Briggs came bustling into the room like a hyperactive version of Hattie Jacques' Carry On matron.

"Oh, hello, Horace," she muttered. She still hadn't forgiven him over their first meeting, and Horace compounded the problem by insisting on referring to her as Maisie.

"On the other hand," he said to his mother, "Maybe I w-w-will have a look around for something."

"Wonderful!" She handed him the local free paper, "I've already circled a few likely looking places."

Horace smiled and shook his head, "I guess I know w-w-when I'm not w-w-wanted."

"Nonsense," his mother said, both she and Horace ignoring Maisie's stage-whispered 'Good'. "Oh, and by the way," she added, "This came in the post for you." She handed Horace an envelope that obviously contained a birthday card. He studied the address and postmark looking for clues to the identity of the sender but the address was typewritten on a label, and the postmark was absent; the card had been hand-delivered.

"Did you see who delivered it?"

His mother shook her head, "No, it was on the mat when we got home last night, sorry. Were you not expecting one?"

Horace and his mother had no close relations and the few friends he had made at school before he left for college were not into cards at birthdays, "No. But I guess I'll find out who it's from on Sunday." He opened the holdall he had taken from his bedroom, and slid the card into his diary.

Ten minutes later, Horace found himself in the street, waving half-heartedly to his mother who was on the doorstep waving *very* enthusiastically. He grinned to himself and made for the bus stop.

Checking his watch, he realised that he had already missed the lecture he had planned to attend that morning and decided to take the rest of the week off as his present to himself.

He got off the bus four stops short of the college and made his way directly to Godfrey's flat where, to his surprise, Godfrey had just returned.

"Skip the lecture?" he asked.

"Yeah," Godfrey nodded. "You too?"

"Contract Law isn't my favourite subject."

"How about a bit of Space Invaders study instead?"

"Now w-w-we're talking!"

The rest of Thursday and Friday passed in a blur of Guinness and little green men, interrupted only by a couple of curries at the local Indian restaurant, and a few hours of sleep (where the little green men seemed to have invaded Horace's dreams). Saturday started late and they met up with a few of the other students in the Crown and Parliament to celebrate both Horace's and Paul 'Snoopy' Fellows' birthdays. They were so celebrated by nine o'clock that both of them found it hard to walk in a straight line back to the flat.

They arrived eventually having detoured through a number of hedges and gardens and Horace collapsed onto the sofa, "Helluva day," he burped. This had been a great birthday, he thought, even if the real thing wasn't until the next day.

"Too true Horrish. Pity about so much booze though in one way."

Horace thought about this for a moment, "W-w-what pity?"

"I thought you were gonna pull there this evening."

"Pull?" Horace snorted laughter, "Me?"

43

"She seemed eager to talk to you."

Horace tried to remember any female that had been interested in talking to him. To be honest, he couldn't even remember many of the males. "Who you talking about?"

"Wass-her-face," Godfrey, swaying, thought for a moment, "Harry, Harriet Fields"

"She w-w-was there?"

Godfrey nodded, "She seemed pretty pissed off when you didn't talk to her, though."

"Oh bugger," Horace moaned. Perhaps this wasn't such a great birthday after all. "You sure she w-w-wanted to talk to me?"

"Oh yeah. Seemed pleased to find you there at first."

"Oh bugger, bugger, bugger. Then w-w-what?"

"You told her to be quiet 'cos you was about to get onto level five."

Horace couldn't remember any of this, "Oh bugger!"

Godfrey giggled, "One for the books, that was. The Wilted turning down a chance like that."

Horace scowled, "Don't call me W-w-wilted," he muttered absently, "W-w-what am I gonna do?"

"Buy a crash helmet."

Horace lay back on the sofa and closed his eyes. "Oh buggeration" were his last words before he drifted off into a thankfully dream-free alcoholic slumber.

7

The sunlight woke Horace at ten-thirty the next morning and he groaned loudly. Godfrey was still snoring in the armchair. Horace's head felt as if it were about to explode and his bladder was in a similar state. He groaned his way upright and staggered into the mercifully dark bathroom. After urinating for a century or two, he fumbled four life-savers from the Paracetamol jar on the shelf above the sink and washed them down his fur-lined throat from the tap.

He made for the small breakfast bar that constituted Godfrey's kitchen and switched on the kettle. After raking through the crockery in the sink, he located two relatively clean and fur-free mugs and spooned coffee and sugar into both. Godfrey passed him on the way to the bathroom, groaning the briefest of 'mornings' as he went. It wasn't until after their coffee mugs had been drained that either spoke.

"Happy birthday, Horace," Godfrey said, "But if you ask me, you look ten years older than you did yesterday, not one."

"Charming, but thanks," Horace grinned. "As it happens, I feel ten years older." A memory of the previous evening surfaced, "Do I remember you telling me that I'd ignored a certain lady last night?"

"Too true."

"Oh bugger," Horace muttered.

"I do seem to recall you expressing that sentiment last night," Godfrey nodded carefully.

"Stupid!"

"No arguments here."

"W-w-what am I going to do?"

Godfrey shrugged, "You're not exactly asking the expert, here, but if I was you, I'd just be honest with her."

"Oh, yeah," Horace mumbled.

"Anyway, you don't have to face her until tomorrow. Forget it for now."

Horace sighed, "Fat chance, but I'll give it a go." He grabbed his holdall and rummaged in it before extracting his diary, "I'd better write all this down before I forget w-w-what a moron I can be."

"Good idea. You've gotta be clear about these things."

"Ho, ho, ho," Horace muttered, and opened the diary. The envelope containing a birthday card fluttered to the floor. "Oh, yeah," he said, wincing as he retrieved the errant missive, "I'd forgotten about that."

"What is it?"

"Thereby hangs a tale. It was delivered to my mother's place by hand last w-w-week." He had received only one other card, a hand-drawn effort from Godfrey, purportedly depicting a naked Stephanie on the front and the message "Happy Birthday Suit" on the inside.

"Any idea who it's from?"

Horace shook his head. He was far too depressed to be interested. It was probably just from his bank manager.

"Come on them, open it!"

Horace had been about to return it to the holdall, but shrugged and tore open the seal. He pulled out the card and smiled at the illustration. It was another hand-drawn effort, this time depicting himself wearing a dunce's hat and the caption "Best W-w-wishes".

"Well," Godfrey persisted, "Who's it from?"

Horace opened the card and frowned deeply. Gradually his face cleared and he began to smile.

"Fess up, Horace," Godfrey said impatiently.

"It's from Harriet Fields," he said slowly, "And her UNCLE Phil."

"But you said…"

"She called him 'Unk'," Horace explained as realisation dawned on him. "You know w-w-what she's like with aitches-"

"You said she called him a Hunk and she really called him 'Unc'?"

"As in short for 'Uncle'," Horace nodded.

"You know what you are, don't you?"

"Yep - a pillock." He suddenly remembered the previous evening, "Oh bugger," he groaned, "And now, after last night…"

"Double pillock," Godfrey nodded.

"I've gotta explain things," Horace said decisively, then paused. "On second thoughts, *you've* gotta explain things to her."

Godfrey held up his hands, "Slow down there, chief."

"Really! I mean, please?"

"I don't know…"

Horace rummaged through his rucksack and extracted the envelope his mother had given him, "Here's tw-w-wenty quid." He offered the banknote to Godfrey, "Think of the number of games of Space Invaders you can play w-w-with that!"

Godfrey grinned and plucked the note from Horace's outstretched hand, "What are friends for? Let's see if the *Crown* is open for business, shall we?"

Horace plucked the note back, "After w-w-we w-w-work out how to explain things to Harriet."

"Can't it wait until tomorrow?"

Horace shook his head, "After last night, tomorrow might be too late. Even *now* might be too late. I mean, there w-w-were loads of guys there last night," he pleaded.

Godfrey sighed. He had never seen Horace so animated, "Okay then, what's her phone number?"

"Dunno."

"Alright, where does she live? We can call Directory Enquiries."

"Er, not sure exactly but it's somewh-w-where in Barking."

"I suppose you don't know her father's name?"

Horace looked miserable, "I don't even know if she *has* a father. W-w-what are w-w-we gonna do?"

Godfrey sat thoughtfully for a moment and then stood up and made for the telephone, "Relax, Horace. I know someone who can help us."

Horace gave him a round of applause a couple of minutes later when he hung up, "Very clever."

"They don't call me Godfrey the Genius for nothing," Godfrey beamed.

"They don't ever but I'll make sure everybody does now," Horace said. Godfrey had simply phoned the student union representative who had supplied the number after recognising the caller. "Come on, make the call," Horace urged.

Godfrey grinned at his near-frantic friend, "Don't get your knickers in a knot, pal." He began dialling. Horace groaned in despair when Godfrey began to say "No reply" but was then waved into silence.

"Hello, is that the Fields' residence?" he gave Horace the thumbs up as he listened to the reply. "Can I speak to Harriet, please?" Horace held his breath, "Thanks."   Horace had to endure the torture of hearing just one side of the conversation.

"Hi, Harriet? It's Godfrey... Yeah, that's me. Listen, I've have got the most amusing little tale I need to tell you. It's about Horace." Godfrey winced, a gesture that Horace involuntarily imitated. "I can't say I disagree with you, but there were, shall we say, extenuating circumstances... No, don't hang up!"

Horace winced again. Harriet apparently allowed Godfrey the benefit of the doubt and he told her what had occurred in far greater detail than Horace really appreciated.

"No, I promise," he finished, "Cross my heart as an atheist," he grinned at Horace as he listened to Harriet's reply, "Okay, will do. See you tomorrow," he held the received out towards Horace. "All yours pal. But, please, no cock-ups this time?"

Horace stared at the apparatus and then at Godfrey, "I...I c-c-can't!"

Godfrey shrugged and put the receiver to his ear once more, "Hi, Harriet, it's still me, Horace says-"

"No!" Horace took a deep breath and let it out slowly. He crossed to where Godfrey was once more holding the receiver towards him. He took it and gingerly put it to his ear, "Um, er, Harriet?"

"You are the most ridiculous, idiotic rat I have ever met!"

49

He groaned and then, to his amazement, he heard her giggle, "But I forgive you just this once."

Horace's heart leapt so high in his chest that he thought he was about to choke, "Really?!"

"Really."

"Oh, that's w-w-wonderful," he babbled. "Really, thank you. I'm so sorry about all that-"

"Enough, already," Harriet chided. "No more apologies, these things 'appen."

"Okay, sorry," Horace tried to get himself under control.

"I hope that was meant to be funny?"

"W-w-what? Oh, yeah, w-w-well-"

Harriet giggled again, "Relax, big guy."

Horace started to sweat. It was now or never. All he had to do was ask her if she fancied a drink sometime. But when? Where? What if he stumbled over all the words and ended up saying something totally ridiculous? What if-

Harriet interrupted his frantic thoughts, "How about we have a drink and patch things up?"

"W-w-what?!"

"Whatever am I going to do with you? 'Ow about I see you in that place we were in last night? You can tell me why you find a bunch of space aliens more interesting than me."

"I don't... I mean, yes please, that'd be great." He beamed at Godfrey who was sniggering in the armchair, "How about six o'clock?"

"Since they don't open until seven on Sunday's," Harriet said, "'Ow about seven?"

Horace couldn't stop smiling, "Actually, the Crown opens its back bar at six, but if you'd rather w-w-wait until seven-"

"Six it is then," Harriet interrupted, "And by the sound of you, it won't be a moment too soon."

After another couple of minutes of apology from Horace, and repeated threats from Harriet, Horace put down the phone. "She's meeting me at seven," he told Godfrey.

Godfrey groaned, "Horace, don't even *think* about cocking this one up. She's meeting you at six."

Horace looked confused and then realised his error. He gave Godfrey the twenty pound note and then another from the envelope, "Thanks, I owe you at least this much."

"I doubt it, but thanks anyway. Now, can we have that beer my head so desperately needs?"

Horace beamed from ear to ear, "Race you there!"

8

The pair stayed at the Crown until closing time celebrating
Horace's birthday with a couple of pints of Guinness. Neither of
them was in any state for alcoholic excess, and Horace wanted to
remain sober in advance of his meeting with Harriet. Godfrey bore
his friend's constant babbling about her with a fortitude born out of
the remains of his hangover and his own natural generosity of nature.

They returned to Godfrey's flat after collecting a celebratory
McDonald's take-out, and Horace spent the next two hours pacing
the limited confines of the living room. At five, the telephone rang
and Horace looked at in alarm. He knew, deep down inside, who this
was; Harriet had found some reason to cancel.

Godfrey, who had been sitting on the sofa wondering how much
it would cost to replace the carpet which was wearing rapidly under
Horace's constant pacing, grabbed the receiver, "O'Hanlon's house
of ill-repute."

Horace stared, panic rising in his throat. It accelerated rapidly as
Godfrey turned towards him and gestured that the call was for him.
Horace sighed and took the receiver from the solemn-looking
Godfrey, "It's Horace," he muttered.

"Happy birthday, darling," his mother's voice came.

"Oh, thank God for that!" Horace sighed in relief.

"Pardon?"

"Oh, er, nothing! I w-w-was thinking it might be bad news.
Thanks for calling."

He chatted to his mother for ten minutes and ended by promising
her that he would be hunting for a flat of his own in the morning, and

fending off her ribald suggestions about the nature of his relationship with Godfrey. This he achieved by mentioning his 'date' with Harriet which brought another set of ribald suggestions. He rang off, happy that there was only three quarters of an hour to go before his meeting with Harriet.

"I'd better get going," he told Godfrey, and then reluctantly, "Are you joining us?"

Godfrey reached for his jacket. He watched Horace's horrified look before settling back, "Just kidding. Of course I'm not joining you. Maybe see you in there later though."

Another sigh of relief from Horace, "W-w-was it that obvious?"

Godfrey laughed, "No more obvious than leaving forty minutes earlier than you need to."

"I don't w-w-want to risk being late."

"Horace," Godfrey gave him a long-suffering look, "Even *you* couldn't get lost on the way to the Crown. Come to that, even I couldn't."

"I guess so. I'll leave it another five minutes then."

Godfrey groaned and returned his attention to the newspaper, "If I weren't an atheist, I'd be praying for someone to give me strength."

He eventually persuaded Horace to take the risk and leave only leave twenty minutes too soon, and Horace dashed out of the flat at the sort of pace that would guarantee selection to the squad for the forthcoming Moscow Olympics.

He arrived at the Crown and took up position by the door leading to the back bar, his heart rate racing as much from his nervousness as from the sprint that had brought him there. He spent the next fifteen minutes rehearsing what he would say when – *if*, his subconscious kept reminding him – Harriet arrived. Should he just say "Hi, Harriet, glad you could make it"? At least there weren't any doubleyoos, but should he call her Harriet or Harry? After all, she had told him that her friends called her Harry and asked him to call her that. But that, of course, was before he'd been so stand-offish. 'Harry, Harriet,' he muttered to himself.

"That's me," a voice behind him confirmed.

He spun round. She was actually there! "Oh, er, er…" he stammered. So much for the fifteen minutes of rehearsals.

"Close yer gob, there's a bus coming," Harriet grinned, "Am I that 'orrible to look at?"

"Er, okay. I mean, I'll close my mouth. Not you're horrible to look at."

Harriet giggled, "Guess I made you jump? Never mind, I'll make it up to you by buying you a birthday beer. "'Appy birthday, by the way."

Horace's confusion was being replaced by pure relief, "Thanks. And it's definitely a happy birthday now," he reddened as he realised that was both true and a compliment.

Harriet smiled, "Love that colour."

Horace groaned, a smile on his face, "It seems to be permanent these days."

"At least it suits you. Anyway, that sounded like a pub door being unbolted," she offered Horace her hand, "Shall we?"

He looked down delightedly. It seemed that she'd forgiven his behaviour, "Okay," he took a deep breath, "Harry," he added, taking her hand. Together, they walked into the Crown and Parliament.

9

Horace had been worried that they'd have nothing to talk about, but to his relief Harriet chatted away at ninety-to-the-dozen, and he realised that she was probably as nervous as him. Not that he could work out what *that* might indicate.

Halfway through their second drinks, Harriet excused herself and made for the ladies. As she disappeared from the room Horace tried to work things out. He still wasn't sure that this evening represented a date, and come to that he still didn't know for sure whether Harriet already had a boyfriend. Should he ask her for a proper date? Could he even pluck up the courage without twenty four hours of fevered preparation?

He was deep in troubled contemplation when her voice startled him again, "Penny for 'em."

Horace jumped and looked around at Harriet, "Er, w-w-what?"

Harriet grinned, "Penny for 'em. Yer thoughts."

"Oh, er, I w-w-was just w-w-wondering…" he stopped, aware that he had nearly said what he'd been thinking.

"What?" Harriet grinned at his rapidly reddening features.

"I, er, oh, nothing."

Harriet's grin turned into a quizzical stare, "Methinks the boy doth protest too much."

Horace smiled weakly back at her.

"Anyway," Harriet went on, seeming to read his mind, "I've got a question for you…" she too trailed off, and to Horace's surprise, he saw a blush rise on her cheeks. She took a deep breath and continued, "I was sorta wondering. That is…" she paused again for another deep breath, "Is tonight, like, you know, us being 'ere together… Well, I mean, does this count as a date?" she finished in a rush.

Horace gazed down at her, dumbstruck. Had he heard right? "I, er…"

"It's okay, like, if you don't think so, er, or whatever," Harriet's blush deepened.

"No." He saw her face fall, "I mean, yes! Absolutely. It's okay. No," he stammered on, "It's better than okay. Really."

Harriet breathed a sigh of relief, her radiant grin returning, "Great! A date it is then. God, that was 'orrible. I'm really not good at this stuff."

"You're not!" Horace felt as if his smile stretched all the way round his head, "I w-w-was trying to pluck up the courage myself. And failing."

They stared at each other for a few seconds and then burst out laughing. The mutual relief turned to near hysterics, and before long their snorts and laughter was bringing amused looks from other customers. Before Horace realised what was happening, he was somehow hugging the still-giggling Harriet. Still snorting laughter himself, he looked down at her. Their laughter quietened and Horace received the most wonderful birthday present of his life as Harriet stretched up and kissed him gently.

"W-w-wow," he breathed as they parted.

"Yeah," Harriet agreed.

Horace reached for his beer and drained his glass, "This calls for a celebration!"

"Good idea, big guy."

She insisted on paying for the two pints of Guinness and Horace reluctantly agreed after she threatened to tell anyone within earshot about his excursion into the women's changing rooms at the college.

"How did you find out about that?" he asked, grimacing at the memory.

Harriet laughed, "Stephanie told all the girls. She thought it was really funny."

"Really?"

"Yep, she reckoned you looked as if you didn't know where to look… next"

"I didn't really look at all! I w-w-was just shocked."

Harriet laughed again, "Stephanie says she's surprised you 'aven't taken up art lessons yet. She poses there, you know?"

"I had been told. That's w-w-why I haven't been over to the arts block. Can w-w-we change the subject?"

"I guess so," Harriet teased, "We don't want you getting too excited, do we?"

"Harriet!"

"'Arry,"

"Harry, then. Subject change?"

"Good idea once again, big guy. Tell you what, you can show me how to play that silly game over there," she pointed at the hulking Space Invaders machine.

Horace groaned at the hazy memory of the previous night when he had apparently ignored Harriet, "I'm really sorry about last night."

Harriet grinned, "Don't fret, pet. It all made sense after Godfrey explained it. Just don't do it again, okay?"

Horace snorted, "No chance of that."

"Good enough, H." She reached up and gave him a quick peck on the cheek and took his hand. "Let's zap some aliens."

It took ten minutes before Horace realised that Harriet had played the game before. "You're actually rather good at this, aren't you?"

Harriet nodded, "Leastwise, I agree now that you've explained it to me. You've made it sound so much 'arder than I thought it was."

"Charming," Horace scowled at her and then smiled. He couldn't remember being so happy in all his life.

10

For Horace, the rest of the evening passed in a delirious daze. Godfrey arrived at nine to find the pair giggling away, and couldn't suppress a smile.

"Someone looks happy! I take it Horace's stupidity has been forgiven then?"

Horace gave him a mock scowl, "Very observant, W-w-watson."

Harriet protested that 'Er Orris' wasn't stupid.

Godfrey gave them a knowing look, "I take it from that comment that you two are an item now?"

They both nodded happily, "Amazing but true," Horace agreed, an 'I-can't-believe-it' look on his dumbfounded features.

"Amazing it *is*," Godfrey agreed, "But congratulations anyway. Who popped the question?"

"Orris!" Harriet said, "'E came straight out with the question as soon as we were here."

Horace stared happily at her. As far as he could remember, the only question he had asked was "w-w-what?", but if Harriet wanted to boost his credibility, that was fine by him.

"Amazing, again," Godfrey looked impressed. "From Horace the Wilted, to Horace the Love God in one day."

"Er, I think you might be exaggerating a little," Horace protested feebly.

"Don't bet on it," Harriet teased. She was rewarded with a trademark blush from Horace and a conspiratorial laugh from Godfrey.

"This calls for a celebratory drink," Godfrey said, "Then I'll leave you two love birds alone."

Neither Horace nor Harriet protested when Godfrey did exactly that twenty minutes later. In fact, when Godfrey left at the appointed closing time, neither of them noticed his departure. The manager of the Crown, a Scot named Iain McHay, normally allowed a few of the better behaved regulars to stay after hours in the secluded back bar, but only on the condition that they asked him politely and could prove themselves to be relatively sober. That night, he let the two young students stay on, despite the fact that they hadn't asked. He had got to know Horace during the previous few weeks and thought the kid was okay, if a bit of a wimp. Tonight he saw a new side to him, and – although he wouldn't breathe such a sentiment to a single soul – he was delighted to see the lad so happy, and he had no intention of cutting short what was a quite obviously a fun evening for the pair.

It was just after midnight when Horace glanced at the pub's clock, a hideous neon-lit advertising hoarding for Truman Ales, and realised with a shock what the time was. "You're not going to believe this," he told Harriet, "But it's turned tw-w-welve."

"Good God! Must be true what they say about time flying when you're 'aving fun."

"I w-w-was hoping you w-w-were."

"Well, yeah, I am," Harriet smiled, "But I guess we'd better get moving. Old sour Puss over there," she nodded in the direction of the manager, "looks as if 'e's ready to chuck us out anyway."

"I'm amazed he let us stay anyw-w-way. He normally insists in people asking him beforehand."

"I guess it's just our lucky day, then."

60

Horace smiled, "Never a truer w-w-word. At least from my point of view."

"Mine too, big guy."

They finished the last of their drinks and made their way into the cool of the night, Horace thanking the manager profusely on the way. Outside they stopped and gazed at each other, neither wanting the evening to end.

"Well…" Harriet sighed.

"Yes thanks," Horace grinned.

She swiped him gently, "So, was it a 'appy birthday then?"

"In the end, the best."

"Good," Harriet said, and hugged him, the top of her head nestling under his chin. After a couple of minutes she wriggled free. "Better not 'ang around too long. We do 'ave a lecture in the morning."

Reluctantly, Horace agreed, "I guess so. Let's find a cab for you."

"No need."

"You live round here now?"

Harriet smiled ruefully, "No, I'm still in Barking. I just meant that I'd get the night-bus."

Horace shook his head firmly, "No w-w-way. Get a cab. I'll pay. It's the least I can do for you making me so happy."

"But it'll cost a fortune this time of night."

"Don't w-w-worry. My mother's a money magnet and I'm loaded at the minute. She gave me a small fortune to try to get me to find a place of my own." They began to make their way towards the taxi rank outside the Grenada cinema.

"And 'ave you?"

Horace shook his head and hoped Harriet couldn't see his blush, "No, I didn't seem to have the heart after… w-w-well, you know?"

Harriet looked at him, amazement spreading across her features, "You too, huh?"

"W-w-well…" Horace began, stammering to a halt. Harriet could probably have seen his blush in pitch darkness.

She grinned and squeezed his hand, "Reckon we should pick up where we left off back in the library, then?"

"If you w-w-want to."

"Sure do."

"I'll pick up a local paper on the w-w-way in tomorrow. Are you free to start hunting then?"

Harriet nodded happily, "As soon as the Red Setter's finished."

They arrived at the taxi rank and Horace was disappointed to see two cars waiting there, "I guess this is "goodnight" then?"

Harriet's happy smile slipped, "Guess so, big guy."

He handed her a twenty pound note.

"That's way too much," Harriet protested, but Horace refused to take it back. "Well, thanks," she finally relented, "And thanks for a great night."

"It really, really, really, w-w-was a pleasure. Thanks Harry"

The driver of the first car, who had opened the rear door for them, gave a polite cough, "When you're ready, guys?"

"Better make this quick," Harriet told a delighted Horace, "'cos if it takes too long I'm not sure I could stand to leave." She reached up, hugged and kissed him. After half a minute and another polite cough from the driver, they parted, breathless, "See you tomorrow, big guy," Harriet said quietly.

"Oh yes. You most definitely w-w-will."

Harriet gave him a quick peck on the cheek and then dived into the waiting taxi, closing the door behind her. The taxi pulled away from the kerb and they waved to each other until it turned onto the main road.

Horace made his way slowly back to Godfrey's flat, a permanent grin pasted across his face.

From The Diary of Horace Wilt

"Sunday, October 22nd 1979

Dear Diary,

What a day! Started with a hangover and ended with a kiss!

The mystery birthday card was from Harriet(!) and I've finally got a girlfriend after Godfrey told Harriet all about the mix up last night (actually, the night before - it's three o'clock Monday morning now - I'm too excited to sleep). We spent the night in the Crown and didn't leave until after midnight. Played Space Invaders and talked and talked and talked.

We're going to go flat hunting tomorrow (i.e. Today) after Guy's lecture, which'll be so cool (the flat hunting, not his boring lecture!). Must remember to get a local newspaper on the way in tomorrow (not that I think I could forget!).

Better try to get some sleep now - don't want to be too tired for anything tomorrow. Can't describe how happy I am.

Lucky me!

P.S. Must phone mother tomorrow and tell her the good news. Perhaps she'll stop suggesting that Godfrey and me are an item!"

Chapter 2

1

For the first time in as long as Horace could remember, he woke on a Monday morning feeling enthusiastic. He made the coffee despite it being Godfrey's turn and took Godfrey's mug through to the bedroom, ignoring the agonised early-morning groans emanating from somewhere under the duvet.

Horace showered and dressed before Godfrey emerged, and left the flat whistling happily. At the nearest newsagent he bought all three of the local newspapers and stuffed them into his attaché case. He arrived at the college at nine, two hours early for the lecture, and retreated to the library to complete the previous week's assignment. Each week of the term so far, he seemed to have a little more left to do on Monday mornings, but this particular Monday he didn't mind at all - at least it kept his mind off the forthcoming events.

A couple of the others from his class were also feverishly scribbling at another table. Peter Davies, the unofficial class clown, sat with his head resting almost on his table and Horace wondered how anyone could write in that position. By contrast, Mick Temple, the official class idiot, sat bolt upright, his tongue protruding as he concentrated on his work. As far as Horace knew, these guys didn't have girlfriends; his earlier impression of everyone being paired off having proved far from accurate, and he gave himself a smug, congratulatory, smile. Perhaps he might get some respect from these guys now.

He finished the assignment with a quarter of an hour to spare and made his way to the lecture hall, daydreaming of the afternoon to come. His dream was brought to an abrupt halt when a large hand clapped him on the back, "Hi, Wilted, how's it hanging?"

Horace groaned, "Hi, Snoopy. And please stop calling me that." They might have shared birthday celebrations on the Saturday, but that was the only thing the two had in common. If he was to be believed, Snoopy had already slept with three of the girls in their year, and was busily working his way through the art class.

"You were well out of it at the Crown, weren't you?" Snoopy said somewhat unnecessarily.

Horace shrugged, "It's w-w-what birthdays are for."

"You're telling the expert, man. Anyway, I couldn't believe it when you gave that little Harriet the cold shoulder. She might not have much up front," he held his hands in front of his chest, "But I wouldn't kick her outta bed to get to you."

"Just a lover's tiff, Snoops," Horace said nonchalantly.

Snoopy stopped dead in his tracks, "Woah, what's all this? You mean to tell me that you and the little blonde are, like, *together*?"

Horace's smile broadened, and he crossed the first two fingers of his free hand, "It's a fact."

"You're shitting me, right?"

"Nope."

Snoopy let out a whistle, "That's incredible. I mean, there's gonna be a couple of really pissed off guys when they hear about this."

Horace puffed his chest, "W-w-well, I know she's really cute and that they missed the boat, but they'll have to live w-w-with it," Horace said airily. "It's just that w-w-we really get along, you know?"

"Not what I meant, Wilted. It's just that a few of the guys have got a book running on who turns out to be gay, and you were second favourite."

"W-w-what?" Horace's pride deflated.

"Guess you're outta the running now, though."

"Hiya, big guy," a voice behind him said.

Harriet walked up and, to Horace's immense delight, put her right arm round his waist – in front of Snoopy.

"Hi, Harry," he smiled.

She grinned, "Quite a night, huh?"

He happily ignored Snoopy's look of shock, "You bet. Shall w-w-we?" he nodded towards the lecture hall.

"Let's get it over with," Harriet said. "We've gotta lot of flat 'unting to do afterwards."

They left the stunned Snoopy and made their way into the lecture.

By the time the ninety minutes of boredom was over, all of their class knew the news and the responses to it were uniform; the guys shook their heads in disbelief (and Horace now knew which pair had backed him as a closet gay), and the girls either shrugged as if to say Harriet could do better, or gave her the thumbs up. Horace was interested to see that Stephanie Jameson was one of those who seemed to approve – perhaps what Godfrey and Harriet had told him about her was true. He might even be able to meet her eyes from now on.

After the lecture they lunched together in the Union, and to the still-disbelieving looks of a number of the students, left the college hand-in-hand.

"Let's 'ope we can find a couple of places really close together," Harriet said, "If nothing else, it'll leave some of the moronic guys on our class in doubt."

Horace laughed, "W-w-what about your reputation?"

Harriet grinned, "Don't care, 'cos I've gotta secret. Want me to share it?"

"If you're sure?"

She looked at him for a moment, "I guess I'd better tell you anyway. I don't want you getting your 'opes up too 'igh." She paused and laughed when she saw a worried frown on Horace's face, "Don't panic, big guy. It's like this. Whatever they might think about me, I'm still a virgin and intend to stay that way until college is done."

Horace relaxed, "Saving yourself until you get married?"

Harriet laughed, "No. I don't think so anyway. It's just that me mum fell with me when she was at college and never completed her course. I don't wanna waste my chance."

"Makes sense to me," Horace agreed, remembering that his own mother had not even reached college age when she became pregnant with him, courtesy of person unknown.

"Not disappointed?" Harriet asked shyly.

"Of course not. W-w-what kind of a guy do you think I am?"

She laughed, "I'm not sure that that was the perfect answer, but I thought I'd better let you know. Might save some bother later."

"Come on, my little nun. Let's find some accommodation."

The task proved much easier than they'd expected. Two hundred yards from the *Crown*, they came across a newly renovated property above an estate agency. Although the flats hadn't been advertised, Harriet spotted a woman putting up a notice inside the agency. They went inside and, after some initial confusion about how many flats the two of them wanted, they were shown upstairs. On each of the two floors above the shop there were two flats facing each other across the hallway. They went into the one on the left on the first floor and fell in love with it.

The rooms were freshly painted, bright and airy. There were two bedrooms, a living room, bathroom and separate, fitted kitchen. Each room was fully furnished. The rent, they were told, was ninety pounds per month, and the agency would require a three month deposit. The estate agent, a young woman wearing a very short skirt and, Horace couldn't help noticing as he followed her up the stairs, stockings and suspenders, left them to 'make their minds up' and retreated downstairs.

"These are perfect," Horace enthused when the woman had gone.

Harriet sighed, "In all but one respect."

Horace frowned, "W-w-what's that?"

Harriet looked miserable, "I can't afford one."

He laughed, drawing a frown from her.

"What's so funny?"

"Don't worry about the money. I said last night that my mother's loaded, and that she would probably mortgage her place to get me out of there. I'll cover you."

Harriet looked shocked, "I can't take money from you! Look, maybe we *could* share one of them. I mean, there're two bedrooms after all?"

Horace stared at her. He would happily give his right arm to share a flat with Harriet, but guessed it might not be such a good idea. Or, at least, not yet, anyway. He shook his head, "No, honestly. These places are really great. In fact they are just w-w-what w-w-we w-w-were looking for. I really can afford it, you know?"

"But, H, I might not ever be able to pay you back!"

"Pay me back?" Harriet nodded, "Harry, it's not a loan." She began to protest again, but he waved her to silence, "I can afford it; it's a gift. Hell, I'd pay every last penny to be living this close to you..." he trailed off blushing scarlet. Sometimes he could be too honest for his own comfort.

Harriet was staring at him with a half-smile on her face, "You really mean it, don't you?"

Horace nodded firmly, "Do you like the place?"

"I love it, but-"

"No more buts, then. Come on, let's go sign the papers or w-w-whatever w-w-we have to do. Which wh-wh-one do you w-w-want?"

"Are you really sure?" she asked again, her resolve weakening.

"I'm not alw-w-ways a w-w-wimp you know."

Harriet smiled back, "Not ever," she hugged him tightly.

He surprised himself and hugged her back, kissing the top of her head. He could feel her small, firm breasts pressing into the lower part of his chest, and that, accompanied by a flowery scent from her hair, began to create a reaction.

Harriet giggled, "Is that a ferret in your pocket, or are you just pleased to see me?"

Blushing furiously, Horace disengaged himself, "Naughty ferret," he chided the bulge in his jeans. "Perhaps w-w-we'd better w-w-wait a minute before w-w-we go downstairs?"

"Good idea," Harriet agreed, still giggling.

"And your giggle isn't helping much," Horace's blush deepened further.

"I do 'ope it's a tame ferret," Harriet dissolved into fits of laughter. Horace joined in.

They were still drying the tears from their faces when they made their way back to the agency ten minutes later. Twenty minutes after that they left, the proud new occupants of flats one and two, Church Hill Buildings.

From The Diary of Horace Wilt

"Monday, 23ʳᵈ October, 1979

Dear Diary,

If yesterday was fantastic, then there's no word to describe how good today was!

Harriet and me went flat hunting and found the most marvellous place not far from the Crown. We're moving in next door to each other! A place of my very own at last and a beautiful girlfriend (love that word!) living right next door!!!!

Everyone at college was really shocked when they saw me and Harry together and I've never felt more proud in my whole life. Harry's really, really cute; lovely blonde hair, big blue eyes. When we hugged in the flat, I could even feel her breasts pressing into me! I wonder if I'll ever get to see them? Come to that, I really wish I knew more about dating and stuff; this is all so new!

Must thank my mother for the money. I still can't believe how my luck's changed! A flat of my own and a real, honest to goodness girlfriend!"

2

They had both moved into their new flats by the end of the week and held a joint flat-warming party the following Tuesday, Halloween. Most of their class turned up during the course of the evening, and Horace even found himself dancing with Stephanie Jameson. It was dawn before the last of the revellers left and Thursday before the flats were returned to some semblance of order. Life for Horace and Harriet drifted into a pleasant pattern of study, drinks and Space Invaders in the Crown, and takeaway meals eaten together listening to their favourite groups; ELO (Horace's favourites), Queen (Harriet's), Blondie, the Stranglers, Elvis Costello and dozens of New Wave bands.

Horace had imagined that his new found status as someone's boyfriend might enhance his reputation with the guys in his class, and to a small degree it did seem to help. Snoopy Fellows, though, seemed to find Horace an even easier target than before and delighted in trying to embarrass him at every turn. Things reached a head early in December. Horace had risen late that Monday morning and had just spent ten minutes explaining to Guy Pink the reasons for his weekly assignment being incomplete. He left the Red Setter's office with a stern warning still ringing in his ears and was making his way to the library to attempt some cramming when he bumped into Snoopy in the corridor.

"Hey, Wilted, watch where you're going, man!"

"Sorry, Snoops. Guess I w-w-was daydreaming. And please don't call me W-w-wilted."

Snoopy grunted, "Yeah, whatever. I suppose you were dreaming about getting a girlfriend who actually has a pair of tits, right?" He leered at Horace.

Horace stared at his obnoxious class-mate. Normally he would have said nothing, years of practice lending him the ready ability to ignore the barbs of others, but when it came to Harriet a vague impression of a backbone materialised. "Not funny, Snoops."

"Ooh, the Wilted speaks," Snoopy jeered as Mick Temple and Peter Davies emerged from the library behind them. He addressed his next comment in their direction, "I was just telling Wilted here that it was about time he got a girlfriend with a proper set of knockers."

Mick laughed dutifully and even the normally polite Peter gave a chuckle.

Horace kept his gaze level on Snoopy as he turned back to face him, "Do you really believe that someone's looks are the most important thing about them?"

Snoopy nodded, "When it comes to the chicks, man, the bigger the tits the more attractive the meat."

Horace smiled, "Funny you should say that. Only I w-w-was reading just yesterday about research into young men. Apparently, there's a direct relationship betw-w-ween their preference in w-w-women's bust measurement and the size of the man's intellect."

"Guess that must make me a genius then."

"Not exactly," Horace was still smiling. "The relationship is inversely proportional. I guess that puts you somewh-w-where in the moron category"

Snoopy looked at him in disbelief as Mick and Peter roared laughter. "What did you say Wilted?"

"And too much masturbation makes you deaf, not blind," Horace said to more laughter from their audience. "I've finally w-w-worked out w-w-why you have such an active sex-life. It must be all that practising you do on your own. Shame really, though, isn't it? Loads and loads of sex, but no-wh-wh-one to share it w-w-with?" Satisfied that he had made his point and defended Harriet's honour, but trembling like a leaf in a gale, he turned on his heel and marched into the library before Snoopy could respond.

3

If Horace had thought that his uncharacteristic outburst would deter Snoopy he had seriously underestimated his class-mate. On the following Monday evening he was leaving the Student Union when he met Peter Davies.

"Hiya, Horace," Peter grinned, "Just the man."

"Hi, Peter. W-w-what's up?"

"Can you do me a favour?"

"Don't see w-w-why not."

"It's like this," Peter said, he held up a small file labelled '16th Century Italian Artists – Test Paper 1c', "I was supposed to take this over to the art block, but I just remembered that I promised to meet up with Mick for a pool tournament in the Union. You know what a dumbo he is, if I don't meet him there pretty soon, he'll probably wander off and get lost again."

Horace laughed. Mick Temple's sense of direction – or rather, lack of it – was becoming legendary, "You're probably right. I suppose you w-w-want me to take it there for you?"

"Got it in one, Horace, my man. Just put it on the workbench in Room 21. If you don't mind that is?"

Horace shrugged again, "I w-w-was just leaving anyw-w-way. It's not far out of my w-w-way."

"That's great! I owe you a beer for that." Peter handed Horace the file.

"No w-w-worry. See you later."

Peter coughed and tried not to laugh, "Sure will, Horace. Thanks man."

Horace set off towards the art block. He had promised to meet Harriet at the Crown at six and it was now ten-to. If he rushed, he could just make it.

He hurried down the corridor, not even bothering to check on the strange snorts of laughter that were emanating from the first room he passed, reached room 21 and quickly turned the door handle. He marched into the room, the door swinging shut behind him.

Standing in front of him, in the process of removing her panties, was Stephanie Jameson. She let out a squeal and stood upright, the panties falling to the floor. Once more Horace was standing face to face with the completely naked Stephanie.

"You again!" Stephanie roared.

Horace found it extremely hard to find his tongue, "I, er, s-s-sorry," he stammered, trying not to look at Stephanie's bare breasts which seemed to be pointing accusingly at him.

"What the fuck are you doing in here of all places?"

"I, er, I w-w-was asked to d-d-drop this off," Horace showed her the file. He threw it onto the nearest desk and spun on his heels, desperate to get out of the room.

"Hold it, Horace!"

Horace stopped, "W-w-what?"

"Who gave it to you?"

"P-p-peter."

Stephanie grunted, "That explains it."

"W-w-what?" Horace prayed that she would let him leave soon.

Stephanie gave a laugh, "You've been had. This is the room I change in when I'm posing for the art class. Normally I can lock the door but tonight for some "mysterious" reason the key wasn't in the door. And I saw Snoopy Fellows on my way here, which is a bit odd since he doesn't take art classes, just the students. They set you up, Horace."

He groaned. It all made perfect sense, "I thought I heard someone laughing back down the corridor."

Stephanie gave another laugh, "I bet it's them just down the corridor right now. Waiting to give you an even rougher time than usual. You reckon so, too?"

"Yep, I'm doomed."

"I don't think so… It's about time that jerk Snoopy got a bit of payback. I heard about what you said to him the other day and I guess that's why this has been set up. Good on you, by the way."

"Probably," Horace said, still facing the door. "And, w-w-well, he w-w-was insulting Harriet."

"Well, I reckon we can fix him this time."

"How?" he asked despairingly.

"For one thing, you've already been in here about three minutes – which would probably be two minutes and fifty-five seconds longer than they were expecting."

"They probably think you're beating me up," Horace was disconsolate.

"Quite. And when you don't reappear, their curiosity is going to get the better of them. They'll leave it another couple of minutes and then come to investigate."

"So?"

"Turn round and come here."

"W-w-what!?"

"Don't fret, just do it."

"But you're n-n-naked!"

"I had noticed," Stephanie commented, archly. "Come on Horace."

"But w-w-what about Harriet?"

"I'll square all this with her. She can't stand Fellows anyway; she'll think this is a riot."

"I d-d-don't-"

"Oh, Horace!" Stephanie groaned. "Trust me, okay?"

Horace's shoulders slumped and he slowly turned round, his eyes fixed on the floor.

"Come here," she demanded.

He shuffled forward until he could see her feet and stopped.

"Horace! If we're going to do this, we've got to make it look good. Look at me."

Horace's eyes shot up to hers, trying not to focus *en route*, still wondering what she had in mind.

Stephanie was smiling, "We're getting there," she said, more to herself than him. She moved back a pace and perched on the edge of the desk behind her, "Come right over here."

Horace moved forward again until he was a foot away.

"Right over, I said," Stephanie grinned. She reached out and took his right hand, pulling his reluctant form up against her, "Better. Now, put your hands on my tits."

"W-w-what!? I can't d-d-do that!"

"Just do it!" Stephanie said in a quiet but firm voice, "I think I heard someone outside and we've gotta make this look good when they come in. And when they do, kiss me and groan a bit."

"But-"

"Horace! We've gotta look as if we're making out."

"But w-w-what about Harriet! They're bound to tell her!"

"Stop fretting. I told you I'd square it with Harry." She was still holding his right hand and to Horace's mixture of horror and reluctant excitement, she lifted it onto her left breast.

"Oh God," Horace moaned. He had never touched a woman's bare breast before, and he had never imagined the first time would be like this – not even in his wildest nocturnal fantasies.

"And the other," Stephanie grinned. "Try not to enjoy it too much, though," she teased.

With deflating reluctance he followed her instruction and found himself with his hands full of naked, firm breasts. He could feel her nipples, hard and erect, pressing into his palms, "Oh God," he moaned again.

As another noise from the corridor filtered into the room, Stephanie pulled him hard against her, their groins at the same level, "I did say try not to enjoy it too much," she grinned.

Horace groaned as his erection pressed firmly into Stephanie's belly.

"Good groan," she whispered through another giggle, "Keep it up. The groan I mean."

His hands were trapped between his own chest and Stephanie's bare breasts and he suddenly realised that he was actually fondling her. He made to pull back but the sound of the door handle turning stopped him. Stephanie put one hand on the back of his neck and pulled his head forward. Her lips found his and she began to groan loudly, writhing against him.

Horace gave up but tried not to enjoy it too much. His own groaning was quite genuine.

There was a muffled "What the-" from behind him and Stephanie broke this kiss. "What the fuck do you think you're doing in here?" she yelled over Horace's shoulder.

"We were just... I mean..." Snoopy Fellows stammered.

"Just get the fuck out!"

She burst out laughing as the door slammed behind Fellows, "Got 'em!"

For the first time since he had entered the room, Horace smiled, "Thanks, Stephanie," he said, sincerely.

"Tell you what, Horace. There is *something* you can do if you really want to thank me."

"Anything you w-w-want."

Stephanie glanced down, "You could let go of my tits."

Horace gasped and snapped his hands to his sides, moving back a step, "I'm s-s-sorry," he stammered, the flush of excitement in his face changing to an even deeper blush.

Stephanie laughed, "Don't worry, Horace," she said gently, "It might not have been the way I would have chosen to get one over on Fellows, but I'm sorta glad it was you. Harry's a lucky girl."

Horace stared at her in amazement.

Stephanie laughed again, "Go on. No doubt you're meeting the lucky lady?"

Horace, dumbstruck, could only nod.

"Tell you what. If you're gonna be in the Crown at about ten, I'll meet you both and tell Harry all about this," she gestured down at her naked body, Horace's eyes involuntarily following.

He snapped his gaze back to her eyes, "I, er….D-d-do you think that's a good idea?"

"Trust me, Horace."

He shrugged, out of his depth. He resolved that Harriet would hear his version of things before Stephanie arrived, "W-w-well, okay then. And, you know, thanks again."

"Anytime."

"I hope not!"

Stephanie laughed and made shooing gestures, "Go on, now. Or I'll come over there and kiss you again."

Horace raised his hands in self-defence.

"Just joking. See you later, then?"

Horace breathed a sigh of relief, "Yeah, okay. Thanks again."

"If you see Fellows on the way out, tell him that I want his balls for earrings, would you?"

"W-w-with pleasure." He started suddenly as he realised that his eyes had drifted down to Stephanie's naked body. Blushing, and with a final "sorry", he stumbled out of the room to the accompaniment of her laughter. As he bustled along the corridor he could swear that he could feel the imprints of Stephanie's nipples in his palms. He was also wondering what Harriet looked like naked and his erection was threatening to burst through the denim of his jeans.

4

He arrived at the Crown, breathless and panting, fifteen minutes late.

"What kept you, H?" Harriet greeted him, kissing him deeply on the lips – the second time a girl had done that in the past hour, Horace couldn't help but remember.

"Sorry," he said when they parted, "But it's quite a story." He ordered drinks and after a long swallow of Guinness, he told her what had happened in Room 21.

On the way to the Crown he had been fretting over Harriet's reaction – and desperately hoping that she would believe him. He guessed she might be annoyed, and was dependent on her normal sense of understanding and fair play to get him through this unscathed. To his delight, she roared with laughter as he told her how Stephanie had ordered him around, and punched the air when he described how Snoopy Fellows had fled from the room.

"Got the bugger!" she said. She was grinning from ear to ear, "My poor Orris," she said, genuinely sympathetic. "Anyway, did you enjoy it too much?" she teased.

Horace groaned; it was the one question he didn't really want to hear – he had sworn to be honest with Harriet at all costs, "I, w-w-well…"

Harriet's smile broadened, "Bet ya did!"

"She *w-w-was* naked! And I did have to make it look good."

Harriet laughed, "Steph is pretty cute, isn't she?"

"I guess. But you're cuter."

"So, how come you never fondle my tits?" she asked, mock-stern.

"I, er, w-w-what!?" Horace stammered, totally flustered and blushing magnificently.

Harriet laughed again, quieter this time, "Frightened you won't be able to find them?"

"N-n-no! It's just, w-w-well... I didn't think you w-w-were sort of, you know, like that?"

"H," she whispered to be sure that no-one could overhear, "I said I don't intend to, you know, do *it*, until after college. I never said we couldn't, like, fool around a little."

Horace's mouth dropped open, "You mean..."

"Yeah, I mean! I really like you, H, you know that?"

"And me you," Horace nodded, his blush at full strength.

"We can always leave 'ere a bit earlier tonight," Harriet suggested, grinning at his discomfort.

"I, er, yeah. That'd be, er, great," he stammered. He suddenly remembered Stephanie's promise to join them later. "Oh."

"What?"

"Er, w-w-well..."

"Out with it, big guy."

"It's just that Stephanie said she'd meet us here about ten to tell you w-w-what happened," Horace explained in a rush. Harriet's eyebrows shot up and he thought she was about to take back all the nice things she'd said about the incident.

"Meet both of us here to tell us what 'appened?"

Horace nodded miserably, "Er, yeah."

Again, to his surprise, Harriet laughed. She leaned forward and kissed him, "You mean to tell me that Steph told you *she'd* tell me everything, and you put yourself through all that embarrassment to do it yourself?"

"W-w-well, yeah. I mean, I did say that I w-w-wouldn't keep any secrets from you."

"You know something, big guy? You're really rather wonderful." She kissed him again, "Anyway, I guess we *should* wait for Steph; after all she did 'elp you get one over on Fellows."

"Yeah," Horace's smile returned. "And anyw-w-way, w-w-we haven't got any lectures tomorrow," he added, blushing again.

"True," Harriet grinned. "Just one thing though?"

"W-w-whatever."

"Just don't start fondling 'er tits in 'ere, okay?"

Stephanie turned up just after ten, "Sorry I'm a bit late, but I'm sure you don't mind too much."

Harriet laughed, "We didn't 'ave anything else to do, did we Orris?"

Horace blushed, which raised a quizzical look from Stephanie, "N-n-not really."

Stephanie, deciding that she wasn't going to get an explanation, chose to get some drinks instead. She returned and set them on the table, "Has Horace told you what happened?" she asked Harriet with a grin.

Harriet laughed loudly, a few heads turning in her direction, and Horace's head turning puce, "Oh, yeah."

Stephanie recounted the tale from her point of view, and Horace was both surprised and pleased that she toned it down a bit; it made his own version seem even more honest.

"It's about time Fellows 'ad something backfire on 'im," Harriet said when Stephanie had finished.

"Too true," Stephanie agreed, laughing. "You should have seen his face when he clocked what we were doing. I thought he was going to have a coronary."

"I'd like to 'ave seen it myself," Harriet said.

"Me too," Horace agreed.

"But you were too busy not enjoying yourself too much, weren't you?" Harriet teased.

"W-w-well, er, yes."

"One bit of him seemed to be having fun, anyway," Stephanie grinned.

Horace blushed as Harriet giggled, "Friendly little ferret 'e's got there, isn't it?"

"Ferret?" Stephanie looked nonplussed. "Oh," she added when Harriet pointed down at Horace's groin, "I get it. And, yeah, very friendly."

"W-w-will you two *please* stop it?"

"'Ard to stop ferrets when they're that friendly," Harriet said.

Horace rose quickly, "I'm gonna get some more drinks," he said, mid-blush, as they dissolved into fits of laughter. He returned a couple of minutes later to find them still giggling.

"Please?" he begged, setting down the drinks.

After a few more snorts and giggles, they quietened, "I wish Fellows could see us all cosy and happy in here," Stephanie said. "Now that would *really* blow his mind."

As if on cue, the bar door opened and Fellows and Peter Davies walked in. Harriet and Stephanie burst into peals of laughter and Horace joined in when he turned to see what had happened. Fellows stared at his them, his jaw hanging somewhere around the bottom of his rib cage. He turned to look at Peter, standing just as surprised beside him, "I really don't fucking *believe* this," he muttered, and then stalked back outside. After a moment or two, shaking his head, Peter followed him.

"Perfect," Stephanie said when she had control of her voice.

The three of them left the Crown together shortly before midnight, and Stephanie insisted on walking with them as far as Church Hill Buildings, in the hope that Fellows and Davies would see them and jump to even further wrong conclusions. She left them at their front door after refusing the obviously reluctant offer of a coffee.

Horace and Harriet made their way upstairs in near silence and stopped outside their front doors.

"Whose turn is it to make the coffee?" Harriet asked after clearing her throat. This was their nightly ritual; each taking turns to make coffee, which they would drink slowly before a kiss and cuddle, and the reluctant departure of one of them to their own flat.

"I, er, g-g-guess it's yours."

"Yeah, I think so. Come on then, big guy." She fumbled in her bag for her door-key.

Horace noticed that it took her three attempts before she could get it into the lock and realised that he wasn't the only highly agitated person present.

Once inside, Harriet switched on the lamps in the living room and dropped her jacket over the back of an armchair. She cleared her throat again, "Actually, I'm not so sure coffee's a good idea."

He looked at her questioningly.

"Only... For some strange reason my 'ands seem to be trembling a bit. Don't want to scald myself, do I?"

"N-n-not a good idea."

Harriet sat on the sofa and held out a hand to Horace. The hand was, indeed, trembling. He took it and sat beside her, his body angled towards her. They leant into each other a kissed deeply. After a minute or two, Horace let his left hand drift from her right shoulder blade, over her collar bone and rested it lightly on the top of her chest.

"Sure you can find them?" Harriet whispered into his mouth.

Horace didn't trust himself to speak, but let his hand move slowly down her chest, finally settling it gently over the small, firm mound of her breast.

Harriet groaned and sighed, "I guess that answers my question."

For the second time that day, Horace could feel the pressure of a nipple in the palm of his hand; this time, though, one he had dreamed of feeling. He could tell that Harriet was wearing nothing under her customary denim blouse. He wondered what she would look like naked, as exposed to his eyes as Stephanie had been a few hours before. As if reading his mind, Harriet reached between them and undid the top button of the blouse.

She had pulled her head back a little and gazed into his eyes from the closest of ranges, "I really adore you, big guy," she whispered.

"And I you." He could feel her hand working its way down the front of her blouse; feel each tiny jerk as another button popped open. When it reached the waistband of her jeans, he felt the tug as she pulled the blouse free. Leaning back further, she shrugged her shoulders, and he watched, mesmerised, as the blouse slid down her arms, finally settling behind her on the sofa.

Horace gazed, awe-struck, at her bared breasts. They were small, perfectly formed mounds, tipped by deep pink, rigid nipples. He took a deep, shuddery breath, "You're beautiful."

Harriet smiled, biting gently on her lower lip, "You're not so bad yourself," she whispered. "And, big guy?" she added, "You're the first to get this view."

Horace lifted his eyes to her face, smiling crookedly. Once more he let his left hand slip slowly down her chest. He settled it gently over her bare breast and, once more, Harriet groaned softly. Horace thought that something inside him was probably going to explode. He didn't care. Ten minutes later, Horace's own shirt was lying on the sofa and he was holding Harriet tight against him, the pressure of her small, firm breasts a joy as they nudged into his ribs. They kissed again for a while before Harriet pulled back.

"I think maybe that I could manage to make the coffee now," she said. She didn't really want to break their embrace, much less move from the sofa, but a little warning bell was ringing inside her head. The way she was feeling right then, she was only too aware of where things could lead.

Horace smiled, "I guess that's a pretty good idea." His own warning bell had been ringing for the past five minutes.

Harriet made to pull her blouse back on, but stopped as Horace whispered, "Don't."

It was hard to tell who was the most surprised by his comment, but despite his blush he managed to add, "I m-m-mean, if you don't mind. It's j-j-just, you're so beautiful."

Harriet stared in delight, "Shy as well. But I find you 'ard to refuse, big guy." She stood up, leaving the blouse where it was. "Just one thing, though?"

Horace was pretty sure what she meant, "Don't worry, Harry. I w-w-won't forget your vow."

Harriet seemed about to say something and then changed her mind, "Yet another reason to adore you." She smiled and self-consciously went into the kitchen.

Horace took the opportunity to cover the front of his jeans with his shirt. A small damp patch had appeared next to his fly. He had really meant it when he had told her how beautiful she was – what he hadn't mentioned was just how much she turned him on.

He left her flat after two when it was clearly the only sensible thing to do. Harriet, the blouse back on but unbuttoned, walked him to the door.

"Thanks for a wonderful evening," she said.

Horace smiled, "The pleasure w-w-was all mine."

"Don't bet on it." Again she seemed about to say something else but stopped herself.

"See you in the morning," he said and kissed her forehead.

She surprised him by hugging him tightly. She released him and stepped back, the blouse flapping open to reveal her left breast. She didn't bother to cover herself. "Scoot! Before I lock the door with you still this side of it."

He nodded and sighed deeply, "Okay, beautiful." He opened the front door and turned back to face her, "You're really w-w-wonderful, you know?"

She grinned, "Whatever you say big guy. Now scoot! I'm running out of resolve, 'ere."

He laughed and stepped backwards across the corridor. Harriet watched him all the way, a half-smile on her lips. When he fumbled in his jeans pocket for his keys she began to swing her door closed, although from Horace's point of view, this appeared to be a massive effort. Just before it closed she whispered "Love you". The door clicked shut, leaving Horace, staring open-mouthed, at its brilliant white surface.

From The Diary of Horace Wilt

"Monday, 11th December, 1979

Dear Diary,

Where the hell do I start? What a day!!!!

Snoopy tried to set me up by sending me into the room Stephanie was changing in, and I found her in there completely naked again!!!! Instead of throwing me out, we set up Snoopy and when he came in I was kissing her and - get this! - fondling her breasts!!!! A real first!!!! AND I t

Told Harry all about it and she thought it was great. Which leads on to....

She actually asked me, in the pub, why I hadn't fondled her! When we got back, we went into her place and started kissing and cuddling and then she slowly took off her blouse. She's really, really beautiful. Her breasts are pretty small, but absolutely perfect. I thought I was going to explode when I actually got to touch them (must wash jeans in morning!!!!), and we were both topless after a while. I can't believe how good it felt (they felt!!!!).

Must get to bed now - bound to have some wonderful dreams!!!!!!!!!"

6

After that night, Horace and Harriet became completely inseparable. At college, Horace was delighted to find that the incident in room 21, coupled with Fellows' and Davies' visit to the Crown, had altered everyone's perception of him. For Horace, that was fine – no-one seemed to bother him anymore and most people (Fellows being the most obvious exception) stopped calling him Wilted. Harriet thought it was a hoot, and was grateful that her boyfriend was no longer tormented at every turn.

During the last week of term the subject of Christmas came up. Harriet had promised to attend her own family's traditional gathering – an idea she dreaded, since there would be more than thirty of them there. Likewise, Horace was dreading the occasion. Although his mother was now something of a Zen Buddhist or possibly Druid (he could never remember which, or was that witch?), she had decided that both the Winter Solstice and Christmas itself should be celebrated. This, he gathered, would involve a cosy dinner or two, with himself, his mother and her girlfriend, the matronly Maisie.

Neither Harriet nor Horace could bear the thought of being apart at such a special time of the year – even for a single day – and after much bargaining with their respective relatives, agreements were reached and they would only have to spend the Christmas Day itself apart.

Harriet would visit the Fields clan for their traditional dinner and return the next day with Horace (only uncle Phil knew him, and they were all fascinated to find out what her boyfriend was like). Likewise, Horace would only need to suffer one cosy dinner alone with Maisie and his mother on Christmas Day, as long as both he and Harriet attended the Solstice celebrations. Privately, Horace thought that his mother's insistence on meeting Harriet was more because she still harboured a suspicion that "Harry" would turn out to be male.

The Longest Night, which Horace could well believe to have more than one connotation this particular year, fell on the Thursday after they broke up for the Christmas recess. The night before, Horace and Harriet were lounging on his sofa having just demolished a takeaway from the local Kentucky Fried Chicken, and Horace was telling Harriet what to expect from his mother and Maisie. Privately he was praying that the pair didn't flaunt their new-found sexuality in front of Harriet, but he wouldn't have bet against it.

"Last time I w-w-was there, they w-w-were both w-w-wearing kaftans and spent an hour in silent meditation," he told her, "W-w-with a bit of luck, since it's the Solstice, they might spend three hours this time. Talk about wh-wh-one born again every minute. And w-w-why is it that born again people make you w-w-wish so fervently that they hadn't been born the first time?"

Harriet laughed, "I bet they're not nearly as bad as you make out."

"Don't count on it. W-w-when I told her you w-w-were coming w-w-with me, my mother promised that she w-w-wouldn't try to convert you to her alternative lifestyle."

"So, that's good isn't it?"

"Not w-w-with my mother. If she promises not to do something, she almost alw-w-ways does it anyw-w-way."

Harriet laughed, "Don't worry, big guy. If any of 'er beliefs include compulsory lesbianism I can promise you that this girl's not gonna be converted."

"I sincerely hope not."

"Anyway, I think it's great that your mum's got someone to share 'er life with. I mean, you don't object to *you* 'aving a girlfriend, do you?"

"Only w-w-when you tease me," he smiled.

94

"Moi!?"

"Yeah! Come here."

An hour later, they were sitting back on his sofa, sipping coffee. "I 'ope you don't count this as teasing?" Harriet asked.

Horace smiled. Harriet had put her blouse back on, and, as usual when they were alone in one of the flats it was still unbuttoned after their latest bout of heavy-ish petting. From his position beside her, Horace could see the swell of her right breast, "Not at all. How could I w-w-when you already told me about your vow."

"Sure?"

Horace set down his coffee, swept back the side of her blouse and gently kissed her nipple, something that Harriet found tremendously sensual, "I wouldn't torture myself like this if I w-w-wasn't sure, w-w-would I?"

"I guess not, rat," she said, covering herself and shivering. Privately, she was beginning to think that she *was* teasing. Herself.

They finished their coffee in companionable silence and then Harriet sighed, looking at her watch, "What time did you say we'd better leave tomorrow?"

He groaned, "I'd forgotten about that for a w-w-while."

"Glad to 'ear it."

"About eleven, I s'pose."

"Better get some kip then. It's after two."

Horace sighed. Their nightly parting of the ways was becoming increasingly difficult, "Guess so."

Harriet took their empty mugs into his kitchen and returned with her blouse buttoned. She had lost her shyness in front of Horace, but didn't fancy being caught by one of their two upstairs neighbours on the short journey back to her own flat, "Okay, then. Let's get this over with." She made for his front door.

Horace followed and stopped her in the short hallway, his hands on her shoulders, "Can I ask you something?"

Harriet turned under his hands, barely having to duck to do so, "Sure thing, big guy."

"W-w-would you mind if I…"

"What, H?"

Horace took a deep breath, "W-w-would you mind if I…"

"I got that bit," Harriet grinned.

"If I told you I think I… I-I-love you?"

"I'd love it," she said quietly. "The feeling's mutual, after all."

They kissed for a long time before Harriet finally found enough fortitude to scamper back to her own flat. They stood in their open doorways for what seemed like an hour, before they eventually blew each other a kiss and quietly closed their doors.

7

At half past ten the next morning, Harriet knocked on Horace's door and he let her in. The smell of last night's chicken hung in the air together with Horace's aftershave.

"Up for it?" she asked after a perfunctory kiss. They were neither very tactile people in the morning.

"Not in the least, but I guess w-w-we'd better get going soon."

"Stop fretting. I'm sure it'll be fun."

"Oh, yeah," Horace muttered.

He telephoned for a taxi and, despite his most fervent prayers, it arrived quickly. Ten minutes later he was paying off the driver outside his mother's house.

"Posh area," Harriet said.

"I s'pose it is. For this neck of the w-w-woods, anyw-w-way." He checked his watch, wondering whether the Copperfield was open yet; whether they could grab a drop of Dutch courage for the ordeal ahead.

Before he could suggest as much, the front door opened and his mother appeared on the doorstep. She waved enthusiastically and came dashing down the long drive towards them, a vision (of some sort) in a long, white, flowing kaftan, her long, black hair a startling contrast as it billowed behind her. Horace wondered when she'd had it dyed.

"Darling," she trilled as she arrived at the pavement, "Or should I say darlings. So glad you could come and help us celebrate such a special day," she burbled, a picture of delight. "And you must be the delightful Harriet," she said, giving her an unexpected and, in Horace's opinion, rather too intimate hug.

"Er, yeah," Harriet confirmed when she had extricated herself and got some air back into her lungs, "And you must be Mrs Wilt."

"Moonflower, darling, just Moonflower. Stop that groaning, Horace."

"Sorry," he muttered.

His mother gave him a baleful look, and then turned her attention back to Harriet, She took her hand and began tugging her towards the house, "Come on inside, dears. You must come and meet Starchild; she's my significant other, if you know what I mean?"

Horace grinned as Harriet glanced back at him, a mixture of horror and humour vying for supremacy on her face, "Delighted to," she managed.

Horace followed at a more leisurely pace, praying that things wouldn't become too silly.

In the event, the lunchtime and afternoon passed pretty easily for Horace. His mother and Maisie fussed around Harriet like two over-zealous mother hens, keeping up a constant stream of compliments, telling Harriet how beautiful she was, how 'naturally of the earth' (whatever that meant), and how Horace was the luckiest son alive to have found such a wonderful girl.

"A rare and beautiful thing," Horace's mother told Harriet after they had cleared away the last of the lunch (a vegetarian lasagne which Harriet had described as pulsing with flavour, the pun being appreciated by Horace and completely missed by the two older women), "I shall call you 'Orchid'. It seems so fitting, somehow."

Horace giggled quietly, ignoring his mother's baleful stare and Maisie's snort of contempt. He was also delighted to see that Harriet kept a pretty much permanent blush in place throughout the onslaught.

"That's, er, very kind of you," Harriet had responded to her new name.

Horace's mother beamed, "And she's so polite, with it. I hope you're taking notes here, son."

"Oh, definitely," Horace grinned.

At four o'clock, his mother asked them whether they would excuse Starchild and herself so that they could meditate for an hour or two on the coming celebration, and having agreed readily, Horace and Harriet managed to hold in their sighs of relief until after the two women had left the room.

"I did w-w-warn you, Orchid," Horace said.

"Oh, please," Harriet groaned, smiling, "I promise I'll listen to you next time. And, by the way, I don't envy you 'ere on your own on Christmas Day."

Horace shuddered, "Don't remind me."

They sat together on the sofa in companionable silence, interrupted only by the occasional 'Om' permeating through the ceiling. Exhausted by their ordeal, they were both drowsing when the door opened and the two women walked back in, beatific smiles on their faces.

"How sweet," Horace's mother said, with utmost sincerity, as the young ones shook themselves fully awake.

"Have a good meditate?" Horace yawned.

His mother frowned at him but gave him the benefit of the doubt, "Wonderful. You know, Orchid? It's amazing what you can learn from your children – how much patience you have, for a start. But now to the celebration!"

"W-w-which is?"

His mother beamed, "The celebration of the return of the light. After tonight, the days will get longer once again," she explained unnecessarily. Horace and Harriet sat quietly, "And the celebration we shall perform is the ancient Druidic rite which welcomes the return of the daylight. Of course, as you young ones are not ordained – not yet anyway – you will not be allowed to take part directly," she ignored her son's muttered 'thank God', "But you are welcome to witness the rite. Would you like to?"

"That's very kind of you," Harriet maintained her veneer of politeness.

"Guess so," Horace's veneer had worn down to the grain.

"Come along then, darlings."

They rose stiffly and followed his mother and Maisie through to the living room at the back of the house. Maisie opened the French windows and stepped onto the patio outside, his mother following. Horace and Harriet took positions in the open doorway, where the warmth of the room behind them helped to keep out the chill of the evening.

His mother turned so that she and Maisie were facing each other. She uttered some words in a language neither Horace nor Harriet recognised, and Maisie seemed to reply in the same strange tongue. Horace turned, grinning towards Harriet who was watching intently. He nudged her gently, hoping to catch her eye. He frowned as Harriet's eyes first widened in surprise and then frowned harder as she appeared to stifle a snort of laughter.

He turned back towards the patio and froze in horror. His mother was in the process of setting her kaftan carefully behind her having taken it off. Maisie was following suit. He stared aghast. The kaftans had been their only items of clothing.

"M-m-mother!"

She turned and shushed him, "Now, don't be so silly, Horace. This is all part of the ritual, a very natural rite. Don't get all prunish with me."

"Prudish," he said, just managing to avoid commenting that Maisie was, indeed, prunish. He shook his head in disbelief, "I think I'll just w-w-wait inside."

"As you wish, dear," his mother said, "I hope you'll stay though, Orchid?"

Harriet was finding it extremely difficult not to burst out laughing – both at the faintly ridiculous sight of the two women and more so at the look of pure, unadulterated horror on Horace's face , "Until I get too cold," she managed.

"Such a nice girl," Maisie 'Starchild' Briggs said.

Horace dashed for the shelter of the front room.

The three women joined him twenty minutes later, the two older ones thankfully now wearing their kaftans, and all of them looking slightly blue.

"That was really rather wonderful, don't you think?" his mother asked Harriet, studiously ignoring her son.

"Truly amazing," Harriet said, one corner of her mouth twitching.

"And now, to warm us up, I'll get some of our home-made brandy," she informed them.

The brandy duly arrived (Horace decided not to ask how they had managed to distil it) and they sipped the potent brew.

"Nice?" his mother asked them.

Horace, who had the impression that he had just swallowed some paint stripper mixed with hydrochloric acid, could only nod. Harriet, whose eyes were watering, followed suit.

Horace wondered when this would all end.

To his surprise, fifteen minutes later, his mother yawned extravagantly, "All this celebrating has quite tired me out."

"I guess w-w-we'd better leave you in peace then?" Horace suggested eagerly.

"It's quite alright if you'd prefer to stay for a while."

"Absolutely not! W-w-wouldn't dream of it. I'll go call a taxi." He shot out of the sofa before anyone could gainsay him.

The taxi arrived promptly, cutting short the incessant stream of compliments directed at Harriet by the two women. With the admonishment that Horace 'must take every care of his beautiful Orchid' ringing in their ears, they sprinted down the driveway and into the waiting car.

"Where to?" the driver enquired as the door slammed shut behind Horace.

"Planet Earth," Harriet managed before dissolving into gales of laughter.

From The Diary of Horace Wilt

"Thursday, 21st December, 1979

Dear Diary,

My mother's done it again. I just can't believe how embarrassing she can be at times, but this was extreme, to say the least. Went to her place with Harry for the Solstice celebration and everything was pretty much okay until the evening when they (my mother and Maisie) performed the rite - out in the back garden, naked! God, it was horrible; Maisie looks like a giant pink prune. Couldn't believe that they actually did that in front of Harry - or should I say, Orchid.

Glad to get back here. Also very glad to get back here 'cos we spent another hour on the sofa, half undressed. I'm really beginning to hope that Harry changes her mind about her vow; she's so beautiful and she really gets me aroused (note: more jeans washing in the morning)."

8

During the next three days, Harriet and Horace managed to reach an agreement over their Solstice visit to the House of Weird (as Horace now termed his mother's place); Harriet promised not to mention the incident in the garden to anyone, as long as Horace stopped calling her Orchid.

With no college to attend, they spent all their time together, with the exception of a couple of hours on the Friday when each of them disappeared to the market to buy gifts.

For Horace this was a very stressful experience. If you didn't count his mother he had never bought a single gift for a female, and even then, since his mother's conversion to the weirder faiths of the age, she no longer accepted gifts of any sort. But after a visit to Godfrey's where his friend's new girlfriend, Mandy, offered him some useful advice, he finally found the items he needed.

He carefully stowed the wrapped gifts (Mandy had told him to insist on this being done for him by the shop owners) into his wardrobe at a height where Harriet wouldn't be able to see them – about half way up (not that she came into his bedroom very often anyway). He checked his watch, seeing that it was six, and grabbed his jacket. He had promised to meet Harriet in the Crown at six sharp and dashed from the flat.

Harriet, ever-punctual, was already there, sitting with Stephanie Jameson and a tall, blonde-haired guy, who she introduced as Matt, Stephanie's boyfriend. He was back from Durham for Christmas.

"Hi, Horace," he greeted him, "Great name."

Horace smiled ruefully, "So people keep telling me. Nice to meet you, Matt. Can I get anywh-wh-wh-one a drink?"

Matt shook his head, "No, let me. I just got a couple in for the girls."

"Thanks. A Guinness w-w-would be perfect." He sat down next to Harriet as Matt headed for the bar, "Sorry I'm late, Harry."

"No sweat, big guy," Harriet smiled and kissed him, "As long as you're 'ere. Anyway, enough small talk," she glanced at the bar where Matt was trying to attract the attention of a barman, "I'm pretty certain that you wouldn't anyway but, H, whatever you do, don't mention those incidents with you and Stephanie."

"Yeah, please, Horace," Stephanie added, "Only Matt doesn't like that sort of thing, you know? He's really pretty jealous. And don't mention the modelling, either."

Horace shrugged, "No problem. I'm hardly likely to bring it up myself, am I?"

"Good boy, Fido," Harriet grinned.

"Yeah, thanks, Horace," Stephanie said.

Horace wondered whether he'd be jealous in Matt's position – if it were Harriet doing the posing, and if it had been Harriet that had set up Fellows with some other guy. To his own surprise – he hadn't given such concepts a moment's thought – he found that he wasn't sure about the set-up but, by and large, he wouldn't mind about the modelling. He was too proud of her for that. His musings were cut short by Matt's return, and the evening passed without any slip-ups.

The next two days passed in much the same fashion, a few drinks, more takeaways, and lively company. On Christmas Eve there was a party in the Crown, and Harriet and Horace didn't get back to their flats until after two o'clock, giggling about something neither could remember the next day.

After giving up trying to work out whose turn it was to make the coffee, they opted for Horace's flat and collapsed onto the sofa. The giggles eventually subsided, and they cuddled quietly.

"I'm not looking forward to tomorrow," Harriet sighed.

Horace grunted, "Me neither."

"Or Boxing Day."

"Ditto."

"Tell you what. 'Ow about we keep our presents until the day after and 'ave our own celebration then?"

"Yeah, w-w-why not?"

Harriet gave a sigh and a giggle, "Good!" she hugged him tighter.

The next thing either of them knew, the alarm clock in Horace's bedroom was buzzing excitedly. Christmas Day, the day of their enforced separation had arrived.

9

Horace waited with Harriet until her Aunt Brenda arrived to pick her up, and then called a taxi for himself. While he waited, he poured himself a large measure of whisky and drained it in one; if this was going to be the day from Hell, he wanted to make sure that he knew as little about it as possible. He was in the bathroom spitting mouthwash into the basin when the taxi driver rang his buzzer. Twenty minutes later, the considerably richer driver was pulling away from his mother's house.

"Here goes," Horace sighed as the front door opened. He double-checked to make sure his mother was actually wearing some clothes, and then made his heavy-footed way up the drive.

Things went better than he had imagined. This was largely thanks to Harriet (or Orchid, depending on which side of the dinner table you were sat on). Despite her absence, Horace's mother and the surly Maisie kept on complimenting her and fussing around Horace, telling him that he was a very lucky young man, that he should look after such a precious product of Mother Nature, that she was the most beautiful and charming young woman on the planet. Although Horace actually agreed with these sentiments, the barrage gradually wore him down.

While Maisie cleared away the lunch things (meatloaf *sans* meat), he asked his mother if he could try some more of her home-made brandy.

"Why of course you may, darling," his mother agreed, "I'm so pleased you like it."

If nothing else, Horace thought, at least it would kill the taste of the meat-free meatloaf, "Thanks, mother."

She hustled out of the room, kaftan billowing, and returned with a full bottle of the "organic" brandy and two glasses. She poured him a large measure and he sipped it carefully, mindful of the fact that he might like to hold a conversation in the near future. "How on earth did you manage to get the cat to sit on the bottle?"

"What was that, darling?"

"Nothing."

"Horace, my darling" she whispered conspiratorially, "One little thing, dear."

He gazed at his mother, dreading what would come next. With that woman, you never could tell, "Yes?"

"I had to wait until Starchild was out of the room, because I know how easily you get embarrassed."

Horace nearly choked on his next sip of brandy. After the Solstice rite he couldn't quite believe his ears.

"Well," his mother went on, "I do hope you're being careful with Orchid. You are, aren't you?"

Horace took a moment before he realised what his mother was inferring, "Mother!"

"Oh, don't be so bashful! She's a very pretty little thing and you're both young and in love. It's the most natural thing in the world. I just hope you're taking the necessary precautions."

Horace groaned. It was bad enough when his mother went on about her own sex life, but to have his own discussed was too much, "Must w-w-we really talk about that?"

"Absolutely. I don't want to be seen to shirk my parental responsibilities."

"Look, it's really our business. But if you insist," Horace could see that she would, "W-w-we don't have that sort of relationship." He was blushing but determined to end the conversation as soon as possible.

"Oh, my poor darling! Why didn't you tell me? I've got just the thing."

"W-w-what!?"

His mother smiled, "It's a special herbal ointment," she explained to Horace's mounting horror, "Starchild picked it up when she and her husband were in Singapore," she paused and looked at her son's confused, horror-struck expression, "Starchild used to be married," she went on, "He was a bit of a pig really. Starchild believes that she married beneath herself, but of course, all women do. Anyway," she ignored her son's feeble protests, "Whenever the pig couldn't, you know? Rise to the occasion? She just rubbed a little bit onto his beef sword and it perked him up no end, so to speak."

Horace didn't know where to look. "That's pork sword, mother. And w-w-where on earth did you learn that expression?"

His mother laughed, "Typical offspring. You all seem to think that us parents' sex lives ended at conscription, don't you?"

"Conception," he muttered. "And anyw-w-way, I don't have any problems in that area." Or, at least, nothing a larger size of jeans wouldn't cure, he thought privately.

"It's nothing to be ashamed of."

"Honestly, mother."

"Well, if you're absolutely sure, darling, but it really is excellent stuff."

"Mother, if you really must know, every time Harry w-w-walks into the same room as me I feel as if I've got a stick of rock down my trousers!"

"Such a crude way to talk about your girlfriend," Maisie's voice came from the doorway, "And Orchid's such a nice girl!"

He groaned loudly, "Beam me up, Scotty," Horace took a large swallow of the brandy.

After the coughing fit had died down, and his mother had explained to Maisie that, despite his normal chauvinistic behaviour, this time her son wasn't actually being a typical male, things returned to some semblance of normality. Or at least, what passed for normality in his mother's house. The three of them sat in the living room, sipping brandy, while a disembodied voice repeating the word 'Om' over and over again emanated from a speaker that Horace couldn't locate.

Horace awoke from a light doze when his mother gently prodded him in the ribs, "W-w-what is it?" he asked through a yawn.

"It's seven o'clock," his mother smiled, "I really think you should be getting home to Orchid. You did say she'd be back about now."

"Oh, er, right." In fact, Harriet had said that she wouldn't be getting home until ten, and he couldn't actually remember what he'd told his mother, "If you think so?"

"Definitely. I'll call a taxi for you, shall I?"

"Please," he said, grateful that the ordeal was nearly over.

His mother returned to tell him that the car would be arriving in ten minutes and then presented him with a large carrier bag, "Just a few things for you and Harriet."

He raised a surprised eyebrow, "I didn't think you believed in Christmas gifts and all that?"

His mother smiled indulgently at him, "Just because I don't, it doesn't mean to say that I think you don't either. Anyway, just think of it as a few little gifts to welcome Orchid into our lives."

That sounded more like his mother, Horace thought, "W-w-well, thanks." He peered into the depths of the bag.

His mother tapped the back of his hand, "No peeking, darling. Wait until you are back home with your Orchid."

He shrugged and closed the bag.

"And I thought you might like one of these," Maisie spoke up, offering him a bottle of homemade brandy.

"W-w-why, thank you, Starchild," he said (it was Christmas after all), "That'll come in very useful," he added, honestly. He had bought an old desk the previous week and he needed something to strip the paint off it.

All in all, the three of them parted on relatively good terms, and Horace settled happily into the back of the taxi. The worst of the Christmas ordeals was firmly behind him now.

10

Harriet arrived back at Church Hill Buildings, completely exhausted, at ten and tapped on Horace's door. He opened it quickly (having been gazing out into the street for the last half hour, watching for Harriet's aunt's car) and grinned, "Have fun?"

"Yes, please," Harriet managed a tired smile, "I'd forgotten just what these family gatherings are like," she followed him into the living room and collapsed onto the sofa.

"How many did you say w-w-were going to be there?" Horace poured Harriet a generous measure of his mother's home made brandy.

"There were supposed to be thirty-seven, but it seemed like damn near fifty turned up. The 'ouse was in total chaos."

Horace grinned, "At least with a crowd you can sorta fade into the background," he said as Harriet coughed and wheezed after her first sip of the brandy.

Harriet snorted, "Orris, 'alf my family's Irish. They don't let anyone 'ave a background to fade into. Anyway, you'll see for yourself tomorrow," she grinned mischievously, "'Ow was your lovely mum, the streaker?"

"A bit less w-w-weird than usual, I suppose. Did you know that you can have a meatloaf w-w-without meat? Apparently it's one of Maisie's specialities."

Harriet laughed, "Well it'll be quite different tomorrow. I was still digesting the dinner when me mum started laying out the tea things."

"Good. I'm starving and not one of the takeaways is open tonight." All in all, he was quite looking forward to the final Christmas visit.

"What's in the bag?" Harriet pointed at the carrier bag Horace had set on his desk.

Horace glanced over to it and noticed that a dribble of the brandy was already cutting through the desk's ancient varnish. "I hate to think. My mother gave it to me w-w-when I w-w-was leaving. Apparently there're some gifts in there for us."

"That's nice. Especially as she doesn't really believe in Christmas and all that stuff."

"I w-w-wouldn't bet on it. Anyw-w-way, it'll give us something else to open the day after tomorrow."

Harriet smiled, "Yeah. I'm looking forward to that."

11

Tired by her ordeal, Harriet left Horace's flat before midnight for once, and Horace decided an early night would probably be a good idea. He wanted to be as fresh as possible for his visit to the Fields. He slept contentedly and woke at the unusually early hour of seven, well-rested and, despite his usual nervousness when he had to meet strangers, quite relaxed. He carried out his morning ablutions to the accompaniment of ELO and then made a large pot of coffee. He was just about to wander over to Harriet's flat to see if she was up, when she knocked on his door.

"Hiya, big guy," she greeted him with a kiss. "Is that coffee I can smell?"

"Hiya, Harry. You seem to have the most remarkably sensitive nose. I w-w-was just coming over to see if you w-w-wanted any."

"Let me at it."

They drank their coffee in relative silence – if Rainbow belting out "Since You've Been Gone" at one hundred and ten decibels can be considered silence. By the time Horace had refilled their mugs, Harriet was wide awake.

"'Ow about a little test?" she suggested.

"W-w-what kind of test?"

Harriet grinned, "Me family tree. It'll be a real 'elp to you if you knew which ones were which."

"Oh?"

"Really. The Irish 'alf are over from Dublin for just a week, and they try to cram the other fifty-one weeks' worth of news in as well. It can get like the Spanish Inquisition."

"If you say so, but it's only for a few hours, isn't it?"

"It'll seem like weeks."

"Okay. I'm in your hands."

"Oh, that's another thing," Harriet said, "No kissing and cuddling. They don't approve of that sort of thing, especially me mum."

"I w-w-wouldn't dream of kissing your mum," Horace grinned.

Harriet gave him a disapproving look, "Are you gonna take this seriously?"

"As long as I can have a kiss and cuddle w-w-when w-w-we get back."

"Deal. Okay, then. 'Ere goes."

Horace didn't think that he would be able to remember more than a handful of the seemingly endless stream of names that Harriet poured out. A few salient facts did seem to lodge though; Harriet was the eldest of six children and the only girl (which would explain her tomboyish-ness, Horace thought) and likewise, her mother was the eldest of six, all girls but one, Phil, who was the youngest. Her maternal grandparents would be there, and Horace was to remember to address her grandmother as 'Gran' at all times. The Irish contingent, who made up the family on her paternal side, numbered twenty alone and Horace couldn't even pronounce some of the names he was told. Together with various cousins, second cousins and in-laws, Horace thought that Harriet's estimate of fifty seemed well short of the mark.

Harriet's aunt Brenda arrived to take them to Barking, and she greeted Horace like a long lost friend. "You must be the wonderful Horace," she beamed at him, "Harry's told us so much about you."

Horace smiled, "Yes, I'm Horace. And I hope Harry hasn't exaggerated."

"If you really are the greatest lover on the planet, then she 'asn't," Brenda smiled.

"Auntie!" Harriet squealed, and then to the furiously blushing Horace, "Really, H, take no notice. I said no such thing," she gave her giggling aunt a baleful stare; "You can be a right cow at times, auntie."

Her aunt laughed happily and Horace could see a strong resemblance between the two women, aided by the fact, he recalled, that Brenda was only five years older than her niece, "It's what aunties are for," she told Harriet, "And I'm sorry if I embarrassed you, Horace. I can't seem to 'elp meself at times."

"Most of the time," Harriet said. "She's the black sheep of the family."

Horace had regained some of his composure, "It's okay," he told Brenda, "I'm getting used to it from Harry, here."

Brenda laughed as Harriet swatted him on the arm, "They do say she's a lot like me."

This wasn't going to be so bad, Horace thought, "You certainly look it."

"I 'ope not," Harriet muttered.

Brenda laughed again, "Come on then, we'd better get a move on. You know what your mum's like, Harry."

They climbed into Brenda's battered Escort, Brenda insisting that they sat together in the back so that they could "have a last cuddle" before they arrived in the no-cuddling zone that was the Fields house. On the drive there Brenda kept up a constant stream of chatter, much of it questions to Horace about his background, hobbies, tastes in music and so on. Horace answered happily, glad that his innate shyness wouldn't be allowed to show at this rate, and only blushed slightly when answering questions about his own family.

They arrived at a cul-de-sac thirty minutes later and Brenda parked the car on the main road at its entrance, "No chance of parking in there," she explained, "Everyone seems to 'ave come by car this year. Even Feargal."

"That's one of me uncles from Dublin," Harriet said, "Drove 'is entire brood all the way over 'ere."

They walked the three hundred yards to the end of the cul-de-sac which resembled a car park shortly after an earthquake, cars pointing at all angles. Horace wondered how on earth they could have managed to park them in such a haphazard fashion.

The Fields' house stood at the very end of the cul-de-sac and seven or eight children were playing football on the patchy lawn in front of it. The front door stood open despite the chill air and a woman appeared in the doorway, waving to the three of them.

"'Ere we go," Harriet squeezed Horace's hand briefly before returning the wave. She led them up the pathway.

"Well, hello there," the woman greeted them, "Happy Christmas!"

Horace smiled at her. She seemed just like a very much older, and rather plumper, version of Harriet, "Hello! You must be Gran?"

The woman's smile slipped from her face in an instant and he could feel Harriet pinching the back of his arm.

"I'm Harriet's mother," she said frostily, "I would ask you to call me Doris, but I think Mrs Fields will do for now." She turned and marched back into the house.

Horace groaned, "Oh bugger." He turned to Harriet, his eyes full of remorse, "S-s-sorry."

Brenda laughed loudly, "Don't worry, Horace, it'll make for a fine story around the table at dinner."

"That's not much comfort," Horace said helplessly.

Harriet was grinning, "Another case of 'open mouth, insert foot'. At least it wasn't me for a change."

"That's not much comfort, either. I'd better go and apologise."

"Good idea, big guy. I'd better come with you though. I don't want you meeting me dad and you saying, 'Oh, you must be old father time' or something."

"Gee, thanks."

Things improved greatly after Horace managed to stammer his apologies and Harriet insisted that it was just his nerves getting the better of him. Much as Harriet had suffered the onslaught of compliments and questions at the Solstice meeting with Horace's mother, so Horace came under a barrage. Other than for two of the younger relations insisting on singing 'The Diary of Horace Wimp" at every mention of his name, Horace had little to blush about.

Harriet's uncle Feargal seemed to have inherited the entire family's share of wit, and was just proving to Horace how there could be no life on Mars (it wasn't listed on his teenage daughter's phone bill) when Harriet's mother reappeared. Two o'clock was the traditional dining hour in the Fields' residence, and she announced that dinner was served. She led Harriet and Horace into the kitchen where a table was groaning under the weight of food of every conceivable festive variety. "I've put you two in here away from the young ones," she explained, "They're in the dining room where we can keep an eye on them."

She went on to explain that the sheer numbers meant that the meal was spread over three rooms and that, what with the unexpected arrival of several Dublin relatives, the table in the kitchen was actually two tables and a pasting trestle, "I've sat you at the end of the table," she told Horace, "So be very careful, because it's not all that steady."

Horace sat carefully and tested the strength of the table in front of him. It seemed perfectly stable to him. There were eleven other place settings and these filled quickly as various relatives joined them. Harriet's mother had sat Harriet on Horace's left and Phil on his immediate right for which he was enormously grateful. At least he knew this pair.

When everyone was seated, Phil turned to Horace, "As our newest guest, you have the privilege of carving."

Horace stared at the enormous turkey in the middle of the table, "Er, I'm not sure that I really know how."

"No worries," Phil grinned, "Just hack it apart. It all goes down the same way in the end."

Shrugging, Horace stood up and leant over the table. Beside the bird were a number of lethal looking knives and he picked up one of the longest and, hopefully, sharpest. He carefully began to carve the breast of the turkey and, to his relief, found that the meat more or less fell off the bird. When he had cut a couple of dozen reasonably neat-looking slices he looked around, wondering what to do next.

"Well done, big guy," Harriet applauded.

"Yeah, good job," Phil agreed. "Now if you can just hack me off one of the legs, we'll help ourselves."

Pleased by the praise, Horace bent over the bird once again, his confidence blossoming. Unlike the breast meat, the leg was proving more recalcitrant and Horace moved to one side so that he could apply a little more leverage.

"'Aving trouble, H?" Harriet asked.

"No, I think it's coming."

119

With a pop, the leg finally parted company from the rest of the carcass. Unfortunately, it parted at considerable velocity, bouncing just once before plunging into the cleavage of Harriet's aunt Sandra, who was wearing a somewhat revealing blouse. For a moment or two, every eye around the table focussed on the faintly ridiculous sight of the turkey leg pointing up at the ceiling from its comfortable new resting place.

Phil was the first one to burst out laughing, just as Horace began to stammer his apologies. Everyone else soon joined in, including Harriet and Sandra. Blushing furiously, Horace grabbed a napkin and rushed around to Sandra's side of the table.

"I'm ever s-s-so s-s-sorry," he stammered and made to pluck the contented leg from the top of her blouse.

Still laughing, Sandra recoiled, "Don't fret, I'll get it," she tried to tell Horace.

Unable to stop his momentum, her backward movement put Horace off his aim and instead of liberating the offending limb, he grabbed the collar of Sandra's blouse. The top two buttons popped open as his hand jerked backwards, and the rest of the table were treated to the sight of Sandra's black, lacy bra, clearly struggling to retain its contents.

The laughter rose in volume, and Horace's blush became nearly audible. He was still stammering apologies when Harriet's mother came in to see what all the hilarity was about.

"Well, at least he's getting to know the family a little better," she commented, before walking back out of the room.

Horace groaned loudly and let his shoulders slump.

"Never mind, big guy," Harriet consoled him, trying not to laugh too much, "Now that you've finished getting all the breast off the turkey, and letting us all compare it to aunt Sandra's you can sit down."

Horace gave her a black look, and retreated to his chair, trying to make himself as small as possible.

As the hilarity died down, people began helping themselves to the meat, vegetables and other delicacies that were arrayed on the table. Despite his embarrassment, Horace's stomach growled at the thought of all that food, especially after the previous day's meagre offerings. Very, very carefully, he loaded his plate with some of everything that was on offer and finally set it on the table in front of him. When everyone was happy with their table-top harvesting, Phil called for a moment's silence in order that another uncle (Peter, Horace thought, but it could have been Paul) could say grace.

Unaccustomed to such rituals, Horace looked around to see what everyone else was doing. Happy that he could at least get this right, he copied their gestures, placing his elbows either side of his heaving plate, locking his hands together above it, bowing his head, and closing his eyes.

"Lord, may we thank you for your bounteous blessing-" the uncle began.

He was interrupted by the unmistakable sound of wood suddenly giving way under pressure. Horace's forehead nearly hit the table as the end of it folded under his elbows. The heaped plate dropped smartly into his lap, turning upside down as it made the short journey. He nearly screamed as the still-steaming gravy quickly soaked through his chinos and shot bolt upright, the plate crashing to the floor where, remarkably, it landed right-side up and didn't break. Grabbing a napkin, he shot into the corner of the room and began to frantically rub at his groin.

The laughter around the table was even louder this time, as both Harriet and Phil rushed to Horace's aid. They both began to dab at the dark stain with their own napkins although this was less effective than it might have been because they were laughing so hard.

"It's, r-r-really kind of you," Harriet snorted, giggling fit to bust.

Despite his discomfort and the obvious embarrassment to come, Horace's curiosity got the better of him, "W-w-what?"

"Sharing your d-d-dinner with the f-f-ferret," Harriet managed before collapsing on the floor and giggling even harder.

Her mother came into the room again to find out what was going on. She was confronted by her daughter literally rolling on the floor in hysterics and her daughter's boyfriend and her youngest brother standing in the corner of the room frantically wiping at Horace's groin with her best napkins. "I really don't think I'd better ask," she told the room in general and made her way out, smiling and shaking her head.

Phil persuaded Horace to accompany him upstairs where they managed to find trousers and underpants to fit. Horace was grateful that Phil waited for him while he changed – he didn't think he could possibly face anyone if he had to walk back into the kitchen alone.

"Thanks, Phil," he said when he was dressed.

"No problem, man. Everything okay down there?" he nodded in the direction of Horace's groin.

"Fortunately," Horace said and then sighed, "Oh God! How am I ever going to face them again?"

Phil laughed, "Don't fret, man. When you've got a family this size, there's all sorts of family folk tales that do the rounds. At least you've joined the lore with a bang."

Horace grinned ruefully, "More with a soggy splash."

Phil led the brilliantly blushing Horace back to the kitchen where, he was relieved to see, everyone was now busily tucking into their dinners. Apart from Phil's comment about Horace having a little more than the traditional meat and two veg, the remainder of the meal passed in relative comfort for Horace.

The rest of the afternoon was less tortuous for him as well, apart from the inevitable re-telling of the events in the kitchen to the many relatives who had been unfortunate enough not to see things first hand. At seven o'clock, after yet another sumptuous meal, Horace and Harriet were sitting in the front room listening to Feargal's tales from Dublin. He was just telling them about his neighbour who had come home shortly before Christmas accompanied by a live deer which he had intended as Christmas dinner but didn't have the heart to kill, when Brenda came into the room.

"Hi, everyone. I've been sent in to see if I can persuade Horace and Harriet to leave before Horace demolishes the greenhouse or something."

"Auntie!" Harriet protested, grinning as Horace blushed.

"Just kidding, kids. Seriously though, are you ready for the off?"

Harriet looked surprised, "It's a little bit early to leave for a Fields' do, isn't it?"

Brenda's smile broadened, "I would've thought that two youngsters in love like you pair would be grateful to 'ave a little of the 'oliday on your own."

Horace decided not to comment; he was sure that he'd contracted foot-in-mouth disease recently as it was.

Harriet shrugged, "I guess so. If no-one else minds?"

"To be sure, I was rather hoping for another floor-show from young Horace," Feargal grinned, "What with missing the first one and all."

"Don't you start, uncle Feargal!" Harriet complained. She turned to the others scattered around the room. "Well, if you're all sure?"

No-one had any objections and so she and Horace made their farewells and trailed out of the room after Brenda.

Her mother met them at the front door as they were putting on their jackets, "Thank you both for coming," she said. Horace began to apologise for what seemed like the thousandth time that day, but she waved him into silence. "No need, Horace. You seem like a very nice young man... If a little clumsy. Anyway, next time you visit, be sure to call me Doris, will you?"

Horace nodded in surprised relief, "Y-yes, I w-w-will. And thank you for a lovely day."

Harriet's mother gave her daughter a perfunctory kiss on the cheek and a large carrier bag filled with food. "I know how you youngsters don't care too much about food what with everything else on your minds, so it's just a few odds and ends so that you won't starve yourselves over the rest of the holidays."

Neither Harriet nor Horace was about to protest, "Ta, mum," Harriet said and took the heaving bag, almost dropping it at the unexpected weight. She straightened and offered it to Horace, "Reckon you can manage not to drop it?" she grinned.

"Now who's starting?" he complained, grinning back.

They followed Brenda out into the frosty night, relieved that the last of their ordeals was over and, thirty minutes later, were waving goodbye as the Escort departed from the front of Church Hill Buildings.

"Well, that wasn't so bad, was it?" Harriet asked Horace cheerfully, "I mean, everyone had a real good laugh."

He gave her a mock-scowl, and swatted her rump playfully, "Very funny."

She grinned, "'Ow about you put that food upstairs and we go get a drink. I think you deserve one."

"Good idea. And yes, I think I really do deserve at least one. I've had enough embarrassment for one day."

Ten minutes later they were sitting in the Crown with Stephanie and Matt, Horace blushing furiously as Harriet recounted the events of the day to them.

12

The next morning was to be Horace and Harriet's own personal celebration. They had left the Crown relatively early the previous night, the tortuous events of the day taking their toll (particularly on Horace) and they had even foregone their normal nightly coffee for fear of falling asleep face down in their mugs. So it was another relatively early start to the day for both of them, and Harriet knocked on Horace's door at eight, just as he was about to call on her to tell her the coffee was ready.

"Morning, big guy. Waif suffering from caffeine deprivation 'ere." She kissed Horace and followed him into his flat.

"Morning Harry, and Happy Christmas," he returned, pouring the coffees.

As was customary, they drank their first mugs in a comfortable silence, this time to the background of *Another Brick in the Wall*, an unusual Christmas number one which they both loved. When both the track and their coffees were finished, Horace got them a refill and Harriet went back to her flat to collect Horace's card.

She returned quickly, grinning from ear to ear, and handed Horace a large envelope, "Happy Christmas, H."

He took the card from her and gave her his own, "And a Happy Christmas to you, too."

They opened the cards and then stared open-mouthed at each other before bursting out laughing. "Amazing," Harriet said as she compared the identical cards.

Horace nodded, "W-w-what are the odds? It'll be matching anoraks next."

"'Eaven forbid, but I couldn't rule it out."

Horace put the cards side-by-side on his desk and brought the carrier bag his mother had given him back to where Harriet was sitting, cross-legged, in the middle of the room, "I think w-w-we should get these out of the w-w-way first. And if w-w-we survive, then w-w-we can open our own."

Harriet giggled, "Don't be mean. Anyway, I think your mother's lovely."

"That w-w-worries me," Horace emptied the contents of the bag onto the carpet, "You keep saying I'm lovely, too."

"A very different sort of lovely."

Horace sat beside her and picked up the first of the five packages. It was wrapped in something like hessian and a small card attached to the top of it bore the legend 'For Orchid, with love and the blessings of the land, Moonflower and Starchild'. Horace groaned and shook his head, "Presumably for you," he said, passing the lightweight package to Harriet.

She took it and read the message, "They're really into this Zen Druidism thing, aren't they?"

"Into w-w-what?"

Harriet swatted his thigh, "Don't you ever listen to what your mother is saying? She explained all about it the other day."

Horace grinned, "Not if I can help it. Anyw-w-way, w-w-what's in it?"

"Just like a big kid." She carefully untied the cord which held the coarse wrapping material in place and pulled out a clear plastic box, "Oh, it's gorgeous!"

Horace stared at the box. Inside was a single delicate orchid. Its manifold fronds and petals were a riot of delicate pastel shades ranging from the palest yellow to a deep blue. Horace nodded, surprised by his mother, "Yeah. Nearly as gorgeous as the real one sitting next to me."

Harriet smiled and kissed his cheek, "Thank you. See, I told you your mum's lovely." She got up and crossed to the desk where she placed the orchid carefully in front of their matching cards. She hurried back and dropped into her customary cross-legged position, "What's next?"

Horace grinned, "Now who's the big kid?" He picked up the next package and scanned the message, "Another one for you," he said, handing Harriet the gift.

"Lucky me. I must 'ave been a very good girl this year."

"Don't tempt me to say anything."

Harriet carefully unwrapped the present. "Wow!" She pulled the contents free. Standing up to let the present unravel, she grinned as Horace groaned, "And again, it's gorgeous."

The kaftan was in a delicate shade of blue, embroidered with strange symbols, and with ties at the front. "Very nice," Horace commented archly, "But promise me you w-w-won't w-w-wear it down to the Crown?"

"Probably not. But I will wear it. It feels gorgeous."

Horace touched the material and was surprised to find that it felt like silk, though quite a bit heavier. He wondered what it would feel like to caress Harriet through the delicate fabric and found himself blushing.

Harriet looked down and laughed, "It's my guess that even if you don't like it that much, a certain pocket rodent quite fancies it."

Horace coughed and tried to look as innocent as possible, "Don't know w-w-what you're talking about."

"Want me to try it on then?" Harriet wore a mischievous smile on her face.

"M-m-maybe later," Horace said, still trying to maintain an air of indifference and failing miserably, "W-w-we've got some more things to open yet."

Harriet giggled again and put the kaftan on the sofa before re-joining him on the floor, "Okay, it must be your turn next."

Horace picked up the next present which weighed considerably more than the previous two. Reading the attached message, he shrugged and said, "This one's apparently for both of us." He made to hand it to her, but she insisted that it was his turn to open one.

He pulled the wrappings apart with considerably less care than Harriet had taken. Reaching inside, he pulled out two massive, identical, candles. Even unlit, they could both smell the unmistakable aroma of Jasmine, a smell which permeated every corner of Horace's mother's house. "Just like home," he said with a half-smile. He actually rather liked the scent.

Harriet had fished around in the torn wrappings and retrieved a small piece of notepaper. She read it aloud, 'Two candles to symbolise the light in each of you. Light them to remember each other by when you are apart. Light them when you are together to bind the lights of your lives.'

"Pass the bucket."

"Don't be mean," Harriet chided, grinning, "I think it's a lovely idea."

"You're not going all weird and Druidic on me, are you?"

"I don't really fancy the idea of running around starkers in the middle of winter, so I don't think you need to worry too much."

"That's not the bit I'm w-w-worried about," he replied with a guilty smile, "*That* bit I quite like the idea of."

Harriet gaped at him in astonishment, "Orris Wilt!"

"S-s-sorry."

Harriet laughed, "Don't be. It's kind of a nice thought. I was just a bit surprised."

"M-m-me too. Let's see w-w-what else there is," he said quickly.

Harriet kissed the top of his head, "Go on then, I'll let you off this once."

The next gift was also labelled "To Orchid", and he passed it to her, "Another for you. I get the impression that my mother really likes you."

Harriet shrugged, feeling guilty, and accepted the small package, "Perhaps it's because I listen to 'er. Sure you don't mind?"

"Don't be daft. Anyw-w-way, I'd look silly in kaftan."

"You can say that again," Harriet agreed. She opened the wrapping and pulled out a small jar with a note attached.

"W-w-what is it?"

"No idea," Harriet replied, unscrewing the top of the jar. Inside was what appeared to be some kind of ointment. She took a tentative sniff and recoiled sharply, "Whatever it is, it's pretty potent. 'Ang on, I'll read the note."

"No!" Horace exclaimed. A very loud alarm bell was ringing inside his head.

Harriet looked at him in surprise, one eyebrow raised, "W-w-what's up, big guy?"

"N-n-nothing," Horace shrugged, trying to come up with some excuse to stop Harriet reading what, he felt sure, he didn't want her to read. When no ideas appeared he acted in desperation and tried to snatch the note from her.

130

She recoiled and rolled over on to her front, keeping the note under her nose, "Oh no you don't. This has really got my curiosity going."

Horace groaned and sat back, wincing as Harriet began to read.

"'Dearest Orchid'," she began, "'I know Horace has told me there are no problems but we women know best, don't we darling?'" Harriet rolled over and raised a quizzical eyebrow to Horace. He, however, appeared to be taking an inordinate interest in the ceiling, "'The ointment is called Tiger Balm, and a little, used sparingly when he's somewhat, shall we say, limp, will soon put things straight!'" Harriet stopped reading and burst out laughing. When she regained some semblance of control she poked the ceiling-gazing Horace in the ribs, "You been telling your mum tales?" she asked, still giggling.

Horace's blush was almost off the scale, "N-n-no! You know w-w-what she's like. She w-w-was going on about, w-w-well, you know, that sort of thing," he explained desperately, "And I just said that w-w-we w-w-weren't, sort of, like that."

Harriet laughed loudly, "Not many mums would be so concerned."

"Yeah," Horace agreed, darkly, "That's just my luck."

Harriet screwed the cap back on the jar and set it to one side, "I really must remember to thank 'er... for everything."

He groaned again, "P-p-please don't be too specific. I'd never hear the last of it."

"That might be quite a good bargaining tool. Anyway, what's in the last one?"

Relieved that the subject had changed, Horace picked up what appeared to be a very thick envelope and read the label, "For me," he shrugged, and tore the envelope open. He lifted it up and shook it. A single sheet of notepaper fell out, rapidly followed by countless, crisp new banknotes.

They both stared amazed at the heap of currency on the floor between them. Horace gave the envelope another shake and a few more notes joined their counterparts on the carpet.

"There must be 'undreds of quid there," Harriet said, awe-struck. "Does she 'ave 'er own printing press?"

Horace shook his head, "I told you she was a money magnet. She's alw-w-ways going on about how she doesn't need the stuff." He checked the envelope and pulled out another two twenty pound notes. Setting them on the floor he read the note aloud, "'My darling Horace. W-w-while I have no respect for the enclosed, I am aw-w-ware that it is important to the youth of today,'" he groaned and was about to discard the note but Harriet insisted that he finish reading it, "'You now have the most w-w-wonderful w-w-woman in your life and I absolutely insist that you give her the very best of everything. The enclosed should help you make sure that you do so. Perhaps...'" he stopped reading and started blushing.

"What?" Harriet demanded.

Knowing that he had little choice in the matter, Horace continued, "'Perhaps if the ointment doesn't w-w-work, you could take Orchid to a nice hotel. Sometimes just a change of scenery can w-w-work w-w-wonders.'" The rest of his letter reading was drowned out by Harriet's laughter. Despite himself, Horace couldn't help but join in.

When they had themselves under control, they gathered up the banknotes and counted them into piles.

"Whew," Harriet breathed when the last of them had been stacked, "Three grand!"

Horace was shaking his head in disbelief, "You really can have the best of everything now."

"It's yours," she insisted.

"Nope. It never pays to go against the w-w-wishes of my mother. Let's just think of it as ours, okay?"

Harriet shrugged, "Whatever you want, big guy."

"I bet you're only agreeing w-w-with me because I'm rich."

Harriet swatted him on the knee and reached over to hug him, "Don't even think it. I agree with you because I love you, right? And don't forget it!"

Horace kissed her, as happy as he had ever been in his life, "I love you too, Harry," he whispered to her when they parted, "And to prove it, I've even remembered to buy you a present or two. Hang on here w-w-while I go get them."

While he was in his bedroom collecting her gifts, Harriet reached behind the sofa to where she had hidden her own presents to him.

When Horace returned, she stared at the huge bundle of gifts he was struggling with, "They can't all be for me!"

Horace smiled, setting the presents on the floor between them, "Just following my mother's instructions."

"Well, 'ere's yours," she set two packages on the floor, "Open yours first. And before you say it, yeah, I am being a big kid again. I wanna open mine last."

"Little kid, maybe." This earned him another swat on the knee and a glorious giggle from Harriet.

He opened the first of his gifts with considerably more care than he had his mother's and drew out a jet black denim shirt. On the left-hand breast pocket was an "H" embroidered in white silk. "That's fantastic!" he said, delighted.

"I'm glad you like it. I think black suits you, and besides, we don't want to end up wearing the same things, do we?" Her own denim shirts were invariably blue.

"No matching anoraks," Horace agreed.

"I nearly got the woman to put "HW" on the pocket, but then I thought I'd better just leave it at the "H". I know how much you 'ate explaining your surname to people, and if anyone asks you what the "W" stood for, it'd be a real pain, yeah?"

Horace looked at her, smiling broadly, "That's very thoughtful."

"Now the other one."

Horace picked up the smaller present and unwrapped it. Inside was a small red box and he opened it slowly. He looked inside and laughed aloud.

"What?" Harriet asked, concerned, "You do like it, don't you?"

Horace laughed again, "Nothing. And, yes, I do like it. Love it, in fact." He pulled a silver chain from the box and the pendant, a silver "H", dangling from the bottom of it, caught the sunlight. He slipped it over his head and stared down at it, shaking his head slightly. "It's fantastic," he told a puzzled Harriet. "Now your turn. Start w-w-with that one."

Harriet picked up the smallest of the items as instructed and unwrapped it. Inside was a small red box, and, even before she opened it, she began to shake her head. She lifted the lid and burst into gales of laughter.

"Incredible or w-w-what?"

Harriet, still laughing, slipped the chain over her head, and, just as Horace had a few moments earlier, gazed down at the silver "H" dangling against the front of her shirt. "I can't quite believe it," she managed, when her laughter subsided, "Great minds and all that."

"Quite. But I promise I haven't bought you a black denim shirt."

"Don't spoil the surprise," Harriet grinned, "But I must say I'm relieved to 'ear it, though. That'd just be too spooky."

She picked up the nearest gift and unwrapped it to reveal two framed Salvador Dali prints, an artist she greatly admired, "They're wonderful," she said, studying the detail in each of the pictures, "I'll hang them in my bedroom. They'll make me think of you."

"W-w-why? Because the clocks are limp I suppose?"

Harriet laughed, delighted that he had made a joke at his own expense. The blush confirmed it, "I must remember not to put the Tiger Balm close to them though. Don't want them stiffening up."

Horace winced and he handed Harriet another present in an effort to divert her attention.

She opened the wrapping and drew out seven albums, Queen's entire output, "Wow! Oh, Orris, you shouldn't 'ave. These're really expensive you know?"

"Only the best for my little Orchid," he said, grinning at her pleasure.

She swatted him gently and then gave him a quick kiss. Setting the records aside, she picked up a rather badly wrapped gift and struggled to pull the contents free.

"Better be a bit careful w-w-with that."

Harriet adopted a gentler approach and eventually pulled out a large coffee mug. On each side, a cartoon of an orange cat with black stripes and a sour expression, was saying 'I'm a real bear until I have my first coffee'.

"Seemed appropriate," Horace said.

She gave him a mock-scowl and then laughed, "'E's great. Who is 'e?"

"Apparently he's called Garfield. He's a massive hit in the States."

"Love 'im." Harriet picked up her next to last gift. This proved easier to open and she quickly pulled out a large T-shirt. On the front, the same cat was pleading to the heavens "Why Me?". She laughed delightedly.

"Good job you like him," Horace said.

"I really do. And this'll be great to wear when I get up in the mornings. If you're a really good Orris, I might even let you see me in it."

"I'll be good."

Harriet picked up the last present and unwrapped it slowly. Inside a large white teddy bear was holding a small red silk heart with the words "I Love You" embroidered on it.

"Oh 'e's so cute," Harriet squealed and hugged the bear.

"Not too cute?"

"Not at all. 'E's adorable, just like the guy who bought 'im for me." She set the bear down beside her and hugged Horace again, "Everything's just perfect. A bit spooky with the cards and the pendants, but perfect anyway."

"That's w-w-what I thought, but anyw-w-way, that's the lot."

Harriet pulled back, "Actually, not quite. But that's gotta wait until later."

"W-w-what has?"

"Never you mind. It's just one last thing, and, like I said, it's gotta wait until later."

"Give us a clue."

Harriet laughed and shook her head, "I guess you could say it's not much, not very big, anyway."

"Oh, come on!"

"Enough! If you keep pestering I won't give it to you at all."

Horace shrugged, grinning, "Okay, then. Just one more question though. Can I wear it?"

Harriet laughed and slapped his thigh, "No, but that's the last clue. Anyway, the Crown should be open in a few minutes, and I'm gasping."

Horace looked at his watch, surprised to find that it was almost midday, "W-w-wow. I'll grab my jacket."

"I'll just pop back to the flat," Harriet said. She rose and picked up the kaftan from the sofa, "Back in a minute, I'm just going to change."

"Oh no, not the kaftan. Please?"

Harriet giggled and dropped it back on the sofa, "Just kidding, H. I'm only going to get my jacket."

While she was gone, Horace slipped out of his shirt and put on his new black one. Checking himself in the mirror, he was surprised to find that black really *did* suit him. All in all, everything had gone pretty well.

13

They returned to the flat at eleven, having spent lunchtime in the Crown and the afternoon mooching around the local shops and drinking coffee in the local café. They had gone back to the Crown in the evening and spent a fortune assassinating little green men, as well as toasting Stephanie and Matt in champagne when the couple announced their impending engagement.

The combination of alcohol and the party atmosphere, and possibly the after-effects of the previous day, left them feeling more than a little tired and they slumped gratefully onto Horace's sofa as soon as they got into the flat.

"Coffee?" Horace yawned.

"Not sure if I could stay awake long enough."

"Me neither. One last House of W-w-weird brandy then?"

Harriet giggled softly, "Good idea, big guy. I'll sleep like a log."

"W-w-we don't have a fireplace," Horace said, pouring two shots of his mother's potent brew.

"Funny guy. But talking of your mother-"

"Must w-w-we?" he interrupted, handing Harriet one of the glasses.

She took the drink and swatted his thigh gently, "No, we don't 'ave to, but I reckon it's in your interests."

Horace sat beside her and shrugged, "W-w-whatever you say." A thought occurred to him, "W-w-what about my other present?"

"Well, if you'd just listen up a minute, you might find out something."

"All ears," Horace confirmed.

Harriet waited until she was sure Horace wouldn't interrupt again before continuing, "The two things are sorta related in a way," she said, "But 'cos it's so late, I reckon it better wait until the morning."

"Tease."

"Hmm. At this rate, I'm not gonna give it to you, so just behave, okay?"

Horace's grin broadened, "Behave w-w-well or behave badly?" He tickled her under the ribcage.

Giggling and trying not to spill the potent brandy, Harriet pulled back, "Definitely the morning. But there is one thing I've gotta do now. Promise you'll be a good boy for two minutes at least?"

"Yes, miss."

Harriet gave him a mock-scowl and took a sip of the brandy. Shuddering, she set the glass on the coffee table and stood up, collecting the kaftan on the way, "I believe you where thousands wouldn't," she grinned. "Now, you stay right 'ere for a minute while I pop into the bedroom, okay? And no peeking!"

Horace looked up at Harriet and then down to the kaftan she was holding in her left hand. He gulped, "F-f-fashion show?"

Harriet blushed, "Only if you promise to be good."

Horace, blushing himself, nodded vigorously, "Absolutely. Totally."

She kissed the top of his head and made for the bedroom, pulling the door firmly shut behind her. Horace sat nervously, taking a couple of small sips out of his glass. It was less than a minute before Harriet reappeared, standing shyly in the doorway of his bedroom, "What do you think?"

Horace stared. She had removed her jeans and shirt and replaced them with the pale blue kaftan which billowed around her, reaching down to just above her bare ankles. With the light from a bedside lamp behind her, Horace could see that the kaftan was translucent. He could also see the outline of her panties, a solid colouring against her skin. The ties at the front of the garment started at the waist and rose towards the upper part of her chest. Only the bottom three had been tied, and the neck of the kaftan hung open to just beneath her bust.

"W-w-wow!" he exclaimed softly, "It's fantastic. And you've got legs!" he added, setting the brandy glass alongside Harriet's.

Harriet giggled and twirled around, "Feels great, too."

"I b-b-bet it does."

Harriet, a smile on her face accompanying a rare and gentle blush, crossed the room and sat beside him, "Since you seem to 'ave been a good boy, I'll let you check it out for yourself," she whispered.

Horace's right hand seemed to have already made up its mind anyway and he rested it on her shoulder before stroking it lightly down her arm. The sensation of the silky smooth fabric was electrifying, "You're right. It does feel fantastic. Of course, it helps that it's you inside it."

"Flatterer," Harriet grinned and then sighed deeply as his hand crossed to the front of the kaftan, gently cupping her left breast, "But I'm not complaining."

They kissed deeply, Horace's hand exploring the contours of Harriet's small, perfectly formed body through the smooth material. Gradually they settled back into the comfort of the sofa and each other's arms.

Horace woke first, just after three in the morning. He couldn't remember drifting off but he was glad that he had. They were still locked in a gentle embrace, Harriet's head resting on his left shoulder, her left arm draped across his thighs. His own left arm was almost asleep, curled around her back, and he tried to gently ease it out so that he could attempt to bring the circulation back to normal. As it slid from behind Harriet's neck, she woke and grinned sleepily at him.

"This is nice," she murmured.

"Yeah," he whispered, massaging life back into his limb.

Harriet slowly sat upright, stretching to ease her own cramped form. During their cuddling, before they fell asleep, the three ties on the kaftan had "mysteriously" come undone, and as she now moved, Horace could see the gentle mound of her left breast. He stared at her unashamedly, "You're really beautiful," he said quietly.

Harriet grinned at him after she saw where his eyes were looking. She blushed once again, "Thanks, big guy. Do you..." she trailed off, her blush deepening.

"W-w-what?"

Harriet avoided his gaze as she spoke, "Well, do you think I could, sorta, stay 'ere tonight. I really don't feel like going 'ome now?"

"Of course. I'd love it. You can have the bed, I'll be fine here."

Harriet looked up and shook her head gently, "I'd rather... rather stay with you. If you don't mind?"

Horace looked nonplussed for a moment and then smiled, a blush rising to his own cheeks, "N-n-no. N-n-not at all."

"Promise you'll be a good boy?"

He let the smile fall from his cheeks to show her how serious he was, "I promise. W-w-with all my heart."

"You know? I don't doubt that for a minute," she grinned sheepishly and stood up. "Come on then."

Just as on the first occasion they had met, she held out a hand to him and Horace took it without thinking, rising to join her. She led him into the bedroom, switching off lights on the way.

Horace closed the door behind them and turned to face Harriet who was now standing on the far side of the large bed, "Are you sure..."

Harriet smiled, "Yeah."

"I do promise I'll behave."

"Well or badly?" she grinned.

"W-w-well, rat," he smiled back.

Harriet seemed to take a deep breath and then reached up with both hands, gently tugging the kaftan from her shoulders. She hesitated a moment and then let it slide down her arms. After another moment's hesitation, she pulled her hands free of the sleeves and the garment settled gently on the floor around her ankles. Once again, Horace stared at her in wonder. Her legs, which he had never before seen, seemed to be surprisingly long and completely smooth. Her hips were almost boyishly narrow and the white cotton panties seemed to emphasise her youth. "Like I said, you're really beautiful."

Her nerve failing her, Harriet dived into the bed and pulled the duvet up to her neck, "Thanks, big guy. Now it's your turn."

Blushing furiously, Horace pulled off his shirt and with trembling hands, undid his jeans and pulled them down to his ankles. He sat down on the edge of the bed and pulled his feet free, his socks remaining inside the cuffs of his jeans. Dressed only in his boxers he stood quickly and attempted to pull back the duvet so he could dive into the bed and cover himself. Harriet stopped him.

"Fair's fair," she grinned, staring up and down his body. "Well cute," she informed him at last and let go of the bedcover.

Blushing, he dived gratefully under the cover and reached across for Harriet without thinking. His hand brushed across her small breasts before gently grasping her right arm. She rolled onto her side to face him, blushing nearly as much as he was, "You will-" she began.

"I promise."

Harriet smiled and snuggled closer, pulling Horace into her. Horace tried to keep his erection away from her but she tapped him lightly on the shoulder and then tugged harder at his hip, "Don't worry, big guy. I think of it as a compliment. Just make sure the ferret doesn't escape, okay?"

He snorted laughter into her ear and let his body ease up against hers, "The door's bolted." His left hand traced the curve of her back and then rose over the firm mound of her right buttock. The skin was smooth and bare under his fingers, the panties, he realised, being of the tiny and skimpy variety. His erection became, almost inconceivably, even harder.

"I love you, big guy," Harriet told him.

"I love you too."

Once again they drifted into a peaceful sleep, their bodies locked together.

When Horace woke, sunlight was streaming into the room. During the night they had drifted slightly apart and Horace almost jumped as his hand touched bare flesh. It had seemed all too much like a dream, but now he realised that Harriet really was there beside him, that they had actually slept together in the same bed. He opened his eyes carefully and looked across the pillow.

Harriet was already awake and was smiling down at him, "Hiya, sleepy."

He grinned, "You're not a dream then?"

She laughed, "Dreamboat, maybe."

"I'll go along w-w-with that." He raised himself onto his right elbow. As he did so, the duvet slipped down both their bodies and Harriet's small breasts were exposed. He stared at them for a moment and then made to pull the duvet up to her shoulders.

Harriet stopped him. She was blushing furiously now, "Don't like the view?" she gave him a half-smile.

"L-l-love it," he stammered, his own blush blooming on both cheeks.

Harriet reached forward and kissed the tip of his nose, "Love me?"

Horace nodded vigorously, "You bet."

They smiled at each other from a distance of no more than an inch. Horace lifted his left hand from the edge of the duvet and ran it lightly over Harriet's right breast. She sighed and lay back. Horace continued to caress her gently, occasionally kissing her. When his lips found her erect right nipple and drew it into his mouth her sighs became groans. As he released the pliant flesh she rolled onto her side and pulled him tightly to her.

He could feel the hard points of her nipples pressing into his chest and he groaned himself. He let his hand wander over Harriet's naked back and then onto the firm mound of her bum, pulling her harder into him. They began kissing, harder than usual, tongues probing each other's mouths, teeth occasionally clicking against each other.

After a couple of minutes, Harriet pulled back slightly, sweating, colour high in both cheeks, "I think," she grinned, panting heavily, "That there's an escaped rodent on the loose."

Horace realised it was true. His boxer shorts had proved to be no longer up to the task of containing his monumental erection, and he could now feel the bare skin of Harriet's thigh touching the stiff member, "S-s-sorry-" he began to stammer, but stopped as Harriet shook her head.

"Don't be," she whispered. "Besides, I'm not even sure it is a ferret." The colour in her cheeks deepened appreciably and Horace held his breath as he felt her right hand slide down the length of his chest before it paused briefly.

"I love you, H," Harriet whispered.

Her hand continued its downwards progress and before she gently grasped his rigid member. Horace wasn't sure who groaned the loudest.

"Yep," Harriet breathed heavily, "That's a ferret."

"Better p-p-put him b-b-back then."

Harriet smiled and then shook her head, "Well, it is Christmas. Let's let 'im play out for a while, eh?"

Horace stared at her dumbstruck, the feel of her hand on him as deliriously wonderful a sensation as he had ever experienced, "If you're s-s-sure?"

"I'm sure," she whispered, "But it seems a little unfair."

"W-w-what?"

"Well… you seem a little under-dressed compared to me," she whispered.

Horace felt her hand let go and then held his breath as Harriet gently pulled the waistband of her lacy panties down her right thigh. He moved his hand from her bum so as not to impede her progress, and Harriet rolled quickly onto her back before tugging the garment all the way down her legs. As she kicked it free, the duvet moved with her motion and she lay before him, completely naked under his eager gaze. Between those narrow hips was a light, almost perfect, triangle of curly blonde hair. Without realising what he was doing, Horace let his hand slide down her belly and trail through the triangle. Harriet parted her legs slightly and his hand continued down between them.

He could feel the heat even before his finger found its target and he gently eased it between her moist, warm lips. Harriet groaned loudly and bucked slightly under his touch. The feeling for Horace was almost as violent, the softness, warmth and wetness beyond anything he had ever experienced.

"Y-your turn," Harriet breathed heavily at him.

He looked uncomprehending for a moment and then realised what she meant. He withdrew his hand and quickly pulled off his boxer shorts, his erection, now totally freed, springing up before him. He had imagined that he would be embarrassed if anyone saw him this aroused, but he found to his astonishment that this was completely untrue. As Harriet gazed down at his body, he felt himself becoming even more excited. His heart rate seemed to be in the four figure region and he was panting heavily, every part of his body vibrating.

"Come 'ere," Harriet whispered, holding her arms wide.

Horace hesitated, "I'm not s-s-sure... You know? The p-p-promise?"

Harriet looked deeply into his eyes, "Horace," she whispered, for once pronouncing it correctly, "I don't know why it is, but it is."

"Is?"

"Is right. I love you, H, and I'm not gonna take the chance that it's not you."

He shook his head, "N-n-not me?"

Harriet smiled, "That extra present I told you about? Well, it's me. If you want me, that is?"

"You m-m-mean...?"

146

Harriet nodded, "The vow's off. If you want?"

"Of course I w-w-want you. But…"

"I'm sure," Harriet smiled, replying to his unspoken question.

"W-w-what about, you know?"

"I'm on the pill," she said, "There might 'ave been a vow, but you never know these days, do you?"

Horace shook his head in response. He wasn't really sure what the question was but he didn't care anyway. Gently, his breath coming in short gasps, he edged across the bed until their bodies touched. He leaned forward and began to kiss her gently, "I love you, Harry," he whispered into her mouth.

Both her hands began to roam across his back as he caressed her breasts. Horace could feel Harriet panting heavily beneath him and he could also feel the gentle pressure she applied to his back. Following her guide, he eased himself between her legs as she spread them wider. Because of the difference in their height, he could feel the tip of his erection already pressing at the warm, moist, inviting centre of her. This was it, he thought, this was really it. "Are you s-s-sure?" he asked gently, pulling apart from her, so that he could see her eyes.

Harriet, panting, nodded, "Y-yes," she managed. "Just, you know? Be gentle?"

Horace nodded and bent back down. They kissed deeply once more and then Horace felt her buck very slightly, raising her hips to his own. The head of his erection slipped smoothly into her and she gasped loudly in his mouth, "Okay?" he whispered.

Harriet nodded vigorously, despite there being no room between them. She gently pulled at his back.

As slowly as he could, Horace eased himself into her until, after a moment of resistance he had slid the entire length of his erection into her warmth. It was like no sensation he had ever experienced and he knew that he would remember this moment for the rest of his life. They clung tightly to each other that way for a full half minute before he pulled back slightly. Once again, he slid slowly deeper and they both groaned in pure ecstasy. He pulled back once more and repeated the process, both of them savouring each tiny movement. Gradually the pace quickened, their kisses deepening, and Harriet began to buck harder beneath him.

As the pace quickened, so too did their breathing. Horace could feel the sweat mingling between them, lubricating their skin as they slid together. Harriet raised her knees either side of him, pressing her groin hard against his with every thrust he made. Her groaning increased in intensity and he could feel a tightening inside her. He could also feel his balls begin to tighten and realised that he was rapidly approaching orgasm. Gasping for air, he pulled back slightly from her, "I l-love you," he panted.

Her gaze was intense, almost rapturous, as she smiled and gasped up at him, "You too, big guy."

He kissed her once more and clung to her as the shudders began to rack his body. With one final thrust, he climaxed explosively, the feeling lasting for what seemed like an eternity, his body almost going into spasms as he filled her.

Harriet's own muscles began to convulse and she cried out once in what seemed almost like surprise as the intensity of the convulsions increased. Shortly after Horace's, Harriet's own orgasm shook through her body and she cried out again, clinging tightly to his back.

As their passions subsided slowly, they held each other tight, Horace still deep inside her, their faces buried in each other's necks. They stayed that way, silent, for a full five minutes before Horace pulled back sharply. He had felt something tickling his neck. He gazed down at Harriet, worry creasing his features, "W-w-what's wrong? You're crying."

148

Harriet laughed and sobbed at the same time, "Nothing's wr-wr-wrong," she grinned through her tears, "I'm just so 'appy, that's all."

"Sure?" he asked, still concerned.

She nodded firmly, sniffing back a tear, "Positive."

Horace nodded. He felt a little like crying himself. "That w-w-was truly w-w-wonderful."

Harriet smiled, "And they say the first time's never any good."

"I'm not sure I could stand it if it w-w-was any better than that," Horace grinned. Something, he felt, had changed inside him. He could have sworn he almost felt like a real man. He lifted his hand and gently fondled Harriet's small breasts. They both felt a small stirring inside her.

"Very fit ferret you've got there," Harriet grinned.

"Randy, anyw-w-way."

Harriet smiled ruefully, "I would love to encourage 'im, but to be 'onest, I'm a little bit, sorta, sore."

"I'm really s-s-sorry, but I did t-t-try to be gentle."

Harriet laughed, "You were gentle. It's just the first time and all that."

"If you're sure?"

"I'm sure. Maybe later, okay?"

"Of course, I guess I'd better, er, round up the rodent," he grinned as they both felt the distinct stiffening sensation.

Harriet grinned back, "Yeah, I think you'd better."

Gently, Horace eased himself out of her, his eyes widening in surprise as the relatively cool air greeted his semi-tumescent member. He glanced down at himself and winced as he saw some blood spread on Harriet's thigh and his near-erection. "Sorry," he said quietly.

"Don't you dare be. At least you know it really was my first time."

"I never doubted it."

She pushed herself up from the pillow, "Good," she said, kissing him gently, "Now, you've 'ad your present, where's my coffee?"

He laughed and climbed off the bed, "Coming right up."

"I said maybe later."

"W-w-what? Oh! I mean, coffee's coming right up."

"Get to it, big guy."

On his way to the kitchen, Horace turned on the shower. When the coffee was brewing he poked his head back round the bedroom doorway, "Shower's hot if you w-w-want wh-wh-wh-one."

Harriet stood up and looked down at her body, still covered in sweat, "I guess we could both do with one." She crossed the room to where he was standing and hugged him, "But I think the ferret should 'ave a cold one," she giggled in his ear.

"G-g-good idea."

By the time Harriet emerged from the steamy bathroom, Horace had poured their coffee, and while she went into the bedroom to dress he took her advice. As he soaped himself under the cool jet of water he felt himself relax and by the time he emerged, the towel that he had wrapped around his waist only stuck out three inches or so.

From The Diary of Horace Wilt

"Thursday, 28th December, 1979

Dear Diary,

I'm still finding it hard to believe what happened this morning. It was the most magical, amazing, wonderful and incredible moment of my entire life. Harry's extra present for me turned out to be Harry, herself - the vow, in other words, no longer applies. I've actually, really and honestly, finally made love to a woman - a very beautiful woman who I love more than life itself.

It's been a really amazing few months since I started at college - but this was the most amazing thing of all. I'd love to be able to describe it; record every tiny memory of it for posterity, but... it seems wrong, somehow. I'll never, ever forget it anyway.

I'll close now - because Harry's waiting for me in the bedroom..."

Chapter 3

1

For Horace, that first term at college finished on a high and the year of 1979 on an even greater high. To cap it all, during the New Year's Eve celebrations at the Crown, there was even a heavy flurry of snow which for a few hours covered the greyness of London in a pristine white shroud. As he and Harriet walked slowly back to their flats, kicking up small clouds of sparkling snow with every step, Horace could finally believe that the torments of his youth were past.

Their lives together grew even closer and it was only Harriet's insistence that she needed the occasional space on her own to study that prevented her moving in with him on a full-time basis. This did not, however, prevent them from spending a large proportion of their time when they were alone together making love and making plans (although the plans took a back seat).

On the last Saturday in January, Stephanie Jameson and her boyfriend Matt threw a party at the Crown to publicly announce their engagement. Horace and Harriet arrived late, having drifted off to sleep during the afternoon following another energetic bout of love-making, and the party was already in full swing.

Stephanie waved them over as soon as she saw them, "Hiya guys. Glad you could make it."

"W-w-wouldn't have missed it for the world," Horace assured her, grabbing two glasses of champagne.

"Too true," Harriet agreed, grabbing two glasses herself. She and Horace looked at each other, realising that they had played copy-cat with the champagne, and burst out laughing, "Not again!" Harriet protested.

Stephanie shook her head and sighed, "If it weren't for the fact that Horace is taller, I'm pretty certain I couldn't tell you two apart."

"Taller and cuter," Horace corrected her.

"And more short-sighted," Harriet agreed.

Stephanie groaned, "I'm not sure whether you two are a match made in heaven or a match made in hell."

"A bit of both, I would 'ave thought," Harriet replied. "I'm an angel and 'e's an 'orny little devil."

Despite blushing furiously, Horace grinned, "Not so much of the little."

Harriet winced, "That's true, anyway."

"Oh, please!" Stephanie laughed, "You're making me jealous."

"Jealous?" Matt asked, joining them.

"Just, er, talking about their flats," Stephanie said quickly, her eyes flashing a warning to Horace and Harriet.

Matt hadn't noticed, "Yeah, I can see why you're jealous. Lovely places you two have got. Steph's hoping that you'll move in together so she can grab the one that's left free."

Horace still couldn't see why Matt was so possessive and jealous, but he came to Stephanie's rescue anyway, "Funny you should mention that," he said, "Only the old girl upstairs, the one in the flat above Harry, is moving out next month. If you like, I'll have a w-w-word w-w-with Penny; she's the estate agent handling them."

Harriet snorted, "I bet you will," she grinned. "She's got these long legs and wears next to nothing at work. Every time Orris goes to pay the rent, 'e comes back and pretty much jumps on me. And it's definitely not brass in his pocket," she added in reference to the Pretenders' track that was currently booming out of the speakers.

Horace blushed once again, "That's n-n-not true! W-w-well not much, anyw-w-way."

Stephanie laughed, "Well, whichever one of you talks to the lady with the legs, I'd be really grateful. There's not enough room to swing a cat in my place."

"No problem," Horace said, "I'll go and see her first thing on Monday."

"Yeah," Harriet agreed, "No problem. But *we'll* go see 'er."

"Cheers guys," Matt said, "I haven't had a chance to swing a cat for months now."

Stephanie smacked him gently on the arm, "Don't tell everyone you like to tie me up and whip me."

Matt's smile turned into a frown, "Enough of that, Steph."

She blushed and shrugged an apology to her friends, "Sorry, guys. Just my tongue running away with me. Anyway, enjoy the party, we'd better circulate."

As Matt led Stephanie away by the arm, Harriet frowned after them, "I'm really not sure about that guy. I'm sure Steph can do better than 'im."

"Definitely," Horace agreed, "She's a lovely girl."

"Not too lovely, I 'ope?"

"N-n-no! Not nearly as lovely as you."

"Pass a bucket," Snoopy Fellows commented, passing them.

From The Diary of Horace Wilt

"Saturday, 27th January, 1980

Dear Diary,

I'm beginning to think that starting every entry with "Dear Diary" is a little bit childish - after all, I'm very much a real man now, thanks to my beautiful little Harry. Must remember to stop it in future.

Just back from Stephanie and Matt's engagement party. Don't know what to make of Matt - he seems a bit odd about some things and Harry and I both think that she could do a lot better than someone like him. Still, I suppose it's her choice. My choice would definitely be Harriet, but I guess it's too early to start thinking about things like engagement just yet. One day, perhaps..."

2

They rose early on the Monday and were waiting downstairs when Penny Marchant, the estate agent, arrived, "Hello, you two," she said with a smile. "Come to pay the rent?"

Horace nodded, "And to ask you a favour." He trailed after her into the office and explained Stephanie's request.

When he had finished, Penny shrugged, "I don't see why not. If she's twice the bother you two are, it still won't be any trouble, and it'll save us advertising the vacancy. Tell her to come in and see me later today if she can."

"That's great," Harriet said, "And thanks."

They left her and returned to Harriet's flat where they had spent the night together. "We'd better go in to the lecture today and tell Steph the good news," Harriet suggested.

"In a w-w-while," Horace nodded, grinning mischievously.

"What are you up to, big guy?"

Horace grabbed her around the waist and dragged her into the bedroom, "Your fault," he said, "After all, you w-w-were the wh-wh-wh-one that told Steph that I alw-w-ways jump on you after I meet Penny," he dropped her on the bed. "And in case you didn't notice, you could clearly see her nipples through that blouse she w-w-was nearly w-w-wearing," he pulled his sweatshirt over his head and jumped onto the bed beside her.

"Trust you to notice," Harriet grinned.

Forty minutes later, Harriet rolled out from under Horace's outstretched arm, her body still slicked with sweat, "I'm glad you don't 'ave to pay the rent on a weekly basis," she told the contentedly grinning Horace.

"Maybe I should pop downstairs and suggest it to Penny?"

Harriet giggled and threw his sweatshirt at him, "No chance, animal. We'd better get to college and tell Steph the news."

"Must w-w-we both go?"

"Yes! And before you say anything, I know why you don't fancy turning up for the Red Setter's lecture today."

"Really?" he asked as innocently as he could.

"You still 'aven't completed your latest assignment, right?"

He nodded unhappily. In fact he hadn't completed the last three assignments, "W-w-well, course w-w-work doesn't count for much at the end of the day."

Harriet sighed and shook her head, "Twenty percent. And you're impossible. Now, get dressed, we're both going to the college today."

Horace stuck out his tongue as Harriet went into the bathroom.

"I saw that!" she called back.

Horace grinned and, shaking his head, pulled on the sweatshirt.

Stephanie was delighted with the news when Harriet told her after the lecture while Horace was trying his hardest to explain his latest failure to Guy Pink, "That's fantastic!" Stephanie exclaimed, "I'll go straight up there after I grab some lunch," she paused for a moment and then shook her head. "On second thoughts, I'll go up there right now. I don't wanna miss out."

She had left by the time Horace, shame-faced, joined up with Harriet in the Student Union, "How did she take the news?"

"As you'd expect. How did Guy take the news?"

Horace frowned, "As you'd expect."

3

Three weeks later, Harriet and Horace helped Stephanie move into the second floor flat. When the two dozen boxes and bags had been ferried up the four flights of stairs, the three of them collapsed gratefully onto the thickly-carpeted floor.

"'Ow on earth did you get all this stuff into your old place?" Harriet asked Stephanie, panting heavily.

"Don't ask. That's the main reason why I wanted a place this size." She gazed around happily at her new, airy apartment. "I can't wait to get unpacked."

"We'll 'elp if you like?" Harriet offered.

"Oh, I couldn't ask-" Stephanie begun, but Horace interrupted her.

"Nonsense. It w-w-won't take us long and then w-w-we'll buy you a flat w-w-warming drink at the Crown."

Stephanie shrugged, "Tell you what? You help me unpack and I'll buy the drinks."

"Deal," Harriet nodded, and looked around at the boxes. "What goes where?"

Stephanie pointed out the various items, "All the bags in the bedroom plus those two boxes. Those three in the kitchen, that one in the bathroom and the rest in here. How about me and you doing the bedroom and the bathroom and Horace doing the rest?"

"Good idea," Harriet agreed, "I don't want my Orris rummaging through your undies."

"Heaven forbid," Stephanie laughed as Horace blushed. She stood and pulled Harriet to her feet. "Let's get to it then, I'm gasping for that drink."

When the two girls had ferried the relevant items out of the living room, Horace began to open the remaining boxes. The first three contained lamps, ashtrays, candles, an ornate middle-eastern hookah, a stereo and stacks of cassette tapes. He distributed the items around the room in what he hoped were appropriate places and then turned his attention to the remaining boxes. These were all larger than the others, but much lighter.

He opened them and drew out the contents which turned out to be a vast collection of prints, watercolours, and drawings. He carefully separated the reproductions and originals into two piles and then began to stack the drawings in a third. These latter items turned out to be nudes of varying degrees of skill and he scanned each one briefly before settling them onto the rapidly growing pile. The last five caused him to stop and spread them out; he recognised the model immediately.

Although none of the figures had clearly defined heads, the body was obviously the same in each of them – it was, he knew, Stephanie herself. He was just about to gather them together and bury them within the rest of the drawings when the featured model came back into the room, along with Harriet.

"Oh, I'm glad you've found those ones," Stephanie said as he hurriedly gathered the five images together.

"They w-w-were the l-l-last wh-wh-wh-ones," he blushed furiously.

Harriet looked quizzically at his florid features, "Not like you to be so shy about a few nudes," she commented, looking at the pictures as Stephanie took them from him.

Stephanie laughed, "You might not recognise the model, but our Horace does."

Harriet looked from the top drawing to Stephanie and then down at Stephanie's body. Light dawned, "Oh, I get it; these're all of you, right?"

Stephanie nodded as Horace blushed even deeper, trying to ignore the two girls, "Quite. And that's why I'm glad Horace found them. If Matt ever saw them, he'd go loopy."

Harriet had taken them from Stephanie and was looking through them, "I can't see why; these're really good, aren't they, H?"

"Um, er, w-w-what? I didn't, er, r-r-really notice."

The two girls laughed, "Yeah, right," Harriet said. "Stop fretting. Art's art, even when you do know the model."

"And sneak into their changing room," Stephanie added with a giggle.

"That makes me f-f-feel a lot better."

"I still don't see why Matt doesn't like this sort of thing, though," Harriet persisted, "I mean, I'm not sure I could ever pose like that, but I don't think Orris would mind, would you?"

Horace, knowing that this conversation wasn't going to end quickly, resigned himself to taking part, "N-n-no. I mean, I'm sorta p-p-proud of the w-w-way you look," his blushed burned fiercely, "And as you say, art is art."

Stephanie shrugged, "I don't know why he objects, he just does. He's very…" she paused for thought, searching for the right word, "Possessive, I guess."

Harriet nodded, "Thought so. If you like, we could always take them downstairs for you. I'm sure Orris would be 'appy to 'ang them in 'is bedroom."

"Harry!"

Stephanie laughed, "Better make it your bedroom, Harry. Matt won't ever go in there."

"Deal," Harriet nodded, grinning at Horace. "And Orris spends plenty of time in there so we won't be depriving 'im."

He groaned and hung his head, "How about that drink now?" he suggested desperately.

The two girls laughed, "I guess you deserve it," Harriet agreed. "If you're sure you wouldn't like a cold shower first?"

"Just the drink," Horace sighed in resignation.

From The Diary of Horace Wilt

"Monday, 19th February, 1980

DD (At least it's an improvement on "Dear Diary")

Helped Stephanie move into her flat this morning. Between her and Harry, I ended up really embarrassed - again - when I found some drawings of Steph without clothes on. 'Cos of Matt, they're now hanging in Harry's bedroom and I must admit, they're pretty good. As you know, I used to love to draw and paint, and I'm wondering whether maybe I should start it up again; Harry almost said as much that she wouldn't mind posing for me like that..."

4

Despite Stephanie's presence in the flat above Harriet's, and despite her presence on the walls of Harriet's bedroom, she had no real effect on Horace and Harriet's lifestyle. The passions that they had discovered on their own private day of Christmas celebration did not abate, and in fact, became more intense.

Harriet's innate shyness had disappeared completely by the Easter holidays and she surprised both of them by buying a short skirt and wearing it to the Crown on the first really warm day of the year. On the Easter Monday morning, in bed in his flat, Horace surprised her with a small drawing.

"What's this then?" Harriet asked as he handed her an envelope.

Horace was blushing, although not nearly as fiercely as he would have been a few months before, "Just s-s-something I've been w-w-working on."

Her curiosity roused as much by his blush as the contents of the envelope, Harriet quickly opened the gift. She stared down at it, her mouth hanging open.

"Do you, er, l-l-like it?"

The picture was drawn in ink. It was of her, in a pose similar to that in Stephanie's drawings, and like Stephanie, she was depicted naked, "It's brilliant!" she exclaimed when she finally found her voice.

Horace breathed a sigh of relief, "Good. I just thought it w-w-would b-b-be nice to have a picture of you l-l-like that. I mean, Stephanie's okay but y-y-you're beautiful and…" he stammered to a halt.

Harriet reached out of the bed, put the picture on her dressing table and then turned back to hug him, "It's a lovely thought. And it's really very good, too. When did you do it? Come to that, *'ow* did you do it? I've never posed for you."

Horace winced, his blush deepening, "W-w-well... s-s-sometimes w-w-when you're asleep, I sort of like to l-l-look at you," he said sheepishly. "I did the outline stuff wh-wh-wh-one night a w-w-week or so ago."

Harriet laughed, "That's lovely. But I still didn't know you could draw."

Relieved that Harriet didn't mind his nocturnal spying, he shrugged, "I've alw-w-ways enjoyed it."

"Since you're that good, I'll pose for you anytime."

He cleared his throat noisily, "That'd be, er, n-n-nice."

"I must show this to Steph. Perhaps she'll pose for you as well."

"N-n-no! I mean, no to the posing, but, w-w-well... I guess I don't mind her s-s-seeing it, the drawing."

"Matt too?" Harriet teased.

Horace stared intently at her, "I m-m-meant w-w-what I said about you. I'm really p-p-proud of you, of the w-w-way you look. So, yes."

Harriet smiled, shaking her head, "I guess you mean it." She glanced at the drawing, "I'll see if I can pluck up the courage."

"W-w-whatever. It's your choice."

"Yeah. And right now, my choice is that you jump on me," she paused and shook her head. "On second thoughts, I'll jump on you." She wriggled across his thighs and sat up.

"P-p-posing already?"

163

"Maybe. But you won't 'ave a chance to draw much with what I've got in mind." She lifted his hands to her breasts and groaned.

"Don't w-w-worry. I don't think I'm in the mood for drawing just now, anyw-w-way."

5

Matt had returned from Durham for the holidays, and the four of them spent the Monday lunchtime in the Crown, discussing the latest trends in music.

"Well I still reckon that it's derivative rubbish," Matt insisted after Stephanie had claimed that Blondie were one of the most innovative groups around. Their latest single, *Call Me*, was being played at that moment.

"Never," Harriet shook her head.

"No w-w-way," Horace added.

Matt snorted his contempt, "You're all just so retro. You should be looking at all these New Romantic groups; that's where it's at."

Harriet groaned, "Well I still think Queen are the greatest. And I come from a long line of music lovers. Actually, I come from a long line of 'ungry music lovers. 'Ow about some grub?"

Everyone thought that this was a good idea, and they left the Crown in search of a restaurant open on a bank holiday, finally settling on the Indian close by their flats.

After gorging themselves for an hour they returned home for a much needed rest and congregated in Horace's flat, the two girls curled on the sofa, Matt in the armchair, and Horace propped on one elbow in the middle of the carpet. The conversation was idle and mercifully relaxed after the earlier tension.

"Did the big fella buy you a nice egg?" Stephanie asked Harriet.

"Must we talk about food?" Matt complained.

Harriet laughed, "No 'e didn't, thankfully. I can't stand chocolate."

"Lucky you," Stephanie grumbled, "I love it but my diet doesn't allow it."

"Diet? You don't look as if you need it."

"Quite. But that's only because I'm on one."

Harriet shrugged and then remembered Horace's gift to her, "I'll show you what 'e did get me though," she said, blushing slightly. She glanced at Horace for permission and, although he too was blushing, he just shrugged, indicating that it was her choice. She took a deep breath and stood up, "'Ang on a second, it's in the bedroom." She crossed the room quickly.

"What is it?" Stephanie asked Horace while she was gone.

His blush deepened, "Er, nothing m-m-much."

Harriet returned and quickly handed the drawing to Stephanie, "Good, isn't it?"

Stephanie's eyebrows rose, "Wow! That really *is* good. Who…" she began and then glanced over at Horace who was busily studying his favourite part of the ceiling. "Horace did this?" Harriet nodded. "Well, there's a surprise. I mean, a nice surprise. This is really good Horace."

"Er, thanks."

"You should take up art," Stephanie enthused. "In fact, I'm amazed you're not on the course at the college." She turned back to Harriet. "Mind if I show Matt this?"

Harriet shrugged, blushing harder, "I guess not."

166

Stephanie handed the drawing to Matt who had been following the conversation with a quizzical look. He stared down at it and then straight at Harriet.

"Good isn't it?" Stephanie asked.

Matt coloured slightly, "I guess so," he coughed to clear his throat, "I mean it's a good likeness," he handed the drawing back to Stephanie. "Just don't let me catch you posing like that."

"Oh don't be silly," Stephanie protested, "It's only art."

"Not when it's you. And don't forget it."

"Well I like it," Harriet insisted, more angry than embarrassed, "And I think it's a lovely thought," she directed this comment towards Horace but made it clear to Matt that she meant what she said.

Horace muttered a small "thank you" as Matt grunted, "Each to their own."

Stephanie sighed and rolled her eyes, "Have you got no romance in your soul?"

"Romance, plenty," Matt replied, "But I still won't let you go around flashing yourself like that."

"Let me?" Stephanie growled. She realised that the tension was escalating towards another argument and forced herself to stop. "Oh, never mind," she muttered. She turned to Harriet. "Sorry about that. Anyway, I guess we'd better get going and leave you two in peace. We'll maybe see you at the Crown tonight?"

Harriet smiled at her gratefully, "Yeah, I'm pretty sure we'll be there."

Matt had already stood up, grabbing his jacket from the floor beside the armchair. Unlike Stephanie he did not look at all embarrassed, "See you later," he said quickly, and then to Stephanie, "Come on then."

She trailed him out of the flat, stopping briefly on the way to bend down and kiss the top of Horace's head when she was certain Matt wasn't looking, "It's really lovely," she whispered.

He nodded his thanks.

When Stephanie and Matt had gone, the sounds of their voices rising towards an inevitable argument, Horace got up and crossed to the sofa where Harriet was gazing down at the drawing, "Sorry about all that."

She lifted her head sharply, tears standing in her eyes, "You're sorry! You do something lovely like this, and that… that *pig* makes such a scene! And anyway," she sniffed, "It's probably my fault. I shouldn't 'ave shown it to them."

Horace hugged her tightly, "It's not your fault. And I guess it's not mine either. And you're right," he added, "Matt is a pig. At least I'm only a rat."

It brought a teary giggle from Harriet and she returned his hug, "A lovely rat, though."

From The Diary of Horace Wilt

"Easter Monday, April, 1980

DD,

That Matt really is a pig like Harry says. Harry showed him and Stephanie my drawing of her (which she really loved!!!!!) and he went into one of his moody sulks and began rowing with poor Steph. Felt a little guilty at first but I shouldn't, 'cos it really is just him being a prude. I hope Steph manages to get shot of him somehow; she's far too nice to have to put up with someone like that. I know she really used to intimidate me, but I guess I've got rather fond of her.

Not nearly as fond of her as I am of Harry, though. Not only did she like the drawing, but she's agreed to pose properly for me!!!!"

6

During the remainder of Matt's stay, the arguments that could be heard emanating from the flat upstairs increased in both frequency and volume, and it was hard to say who breathed the loudest sigh of relief when Matt returned to Durham a couple of days early.

Stephanie knocked on Horace's door after she had seen Matt off and followed Harriet gratefully into the flat when she answered it, "I'm sorry about all that," she settled onto the sofa.

"Don't be," Harriet chided, "It sounded as if 'e was making all the running anyway. And I probably didn't 'elp things with that drawing the other day."

Stephanie snorted, "Don't be silly. He's just such a pig at times."

Harriet blushed to hear her own views being echoed, "Still, 'e's gone for a while now."

"Yeah. Last night I nearly came down and got those drawings of me from you. Perhaps that'd send him away for good."

"Do you really mean that?" Harriet said. "I mean, you seem so 'appy with 'im normally, and you're engaged and all that."

Stephanie laughed, "To be honest, Harry, I'm not that sure anymore. Anyway, enough about the pig. Where's your other half today?"

"Still in bed. 'Is mother sent us another couple of bottles of her home-made brandy at Easter and poor Orris drank the best part of one last night. 'E probably won't be up for another couple of 'ours. That stuff can strip varnish. Literally," she added, pointing to the series of concentric rings that had now been burnt into the top of Horace's desk.

To prove her wrong, Horace entered the room groaning loudly, "Morning," he mumbled, his eyes closed.

Harriet burst into fits of giggles, "M-m-morning," she managed as he winced at the laughter, "But I really think you should put some clothes on."

Horace's eyes shot open and he saw Stephanie sitting on the sofa in front of him. His hands flew down to cover his groin and he backed out of the room at a trot, "S-s-sorry," he called from the bedroom.

Stephanie burst out laughing as well, "Oh well, at least I know why you call him 'big guy' now."

They were still giggling when Horace came back into the room fully dressed, "Oh, please!" he implored. "I don't feel too good as it is."

"Poor baby," Harriet sympathised through her giggles, "I think maybe we'd better get you down to the Crown for a 'air of the dog."

"The entire pelt might not do it."

"Oh dear. Tell you what? Grab yourself a mug of coffee and a Paracetamol sandwich or something. I'll just pop and 'ave a shower. You want a coffee, Steph?"

"Please," Stephanie replied, smiling from ear to ear. For her at least, life was already getting back to normal.

Harriet disappeared into the bathroom and Horace fetched two mugs of coffee from the kitchen after washing down four painkillers, "I don't know how long it's been brewing, but at least it's hot."

"I'm sure it's fine," she took the proffered mug. She sipped it and grimaced. "Not too bad, anyway."

"Sorry about, er, appearing like that."

"Don't be. I should say sorry for laughing, but to be honest, that was the first time for days I've actually laughed at anything – I mean, anyone," she hastily corrected herself, "*About* anything!".

Horace gave her a rueful grin, "W-w-well at least some good came of it. But, seriously, it is nice to hear you laughing again." He coloured slightly as he sipped at his coffee.

Stephanie shook her head, a smile playing at the corners of her mouth, "You really are so kind, H. I've told you before; Harry's a lucky girl."

Horace's face reddened considerably, "Thanks," he muttered, unable to meet her eyes.

The final term of Horace's first year at college seemed to last forever, and each time he drew another sketch of Harriet or dabbled with some watercolours he felt more and more certain that he had picked the wrong course. On the other hand, he kept reminding himself, if he hadn't selected business studies, he would never have met Harriet.

As the term wore on, it became clear to Harriet that Horace's heart wasn't exactly in his course work and as they approached the final weeks of the term she began to coax him into working harder.

"Come on big guy," she goaded one Saturday morning, "It's about time you at least *looked* at those assignments you 'aven't done yet."

Still swaddled in his dressing gown, Horace looked up from behind the *Times* and frowned, "There's plenty of time yet."

Harriet sighed, "No there isn't. There's exactly three weeks and two days – and you 'aven't even started on your year one thesis."

"It w-w-won't take long," Horace replied airily, "I'll copy most of it from Guy's book. He's already said he appreciates people doing that."

"Well, why don't you at least start doing that?"

"I thought you w-w-wanted to drag me round the shops this morning?"

"And that's another thing. For a start, I'm not 'dragging' you anywhere, and if I can go for a change of image, why don't you?"

Horace groaned. It was true that Harriet's recent conversion to skirts and silky blouses had been a most pleasant revelation, but her increasingly frequent attempts for him to try a new look were beginning to get under his skin, "I'm quite happy the w-w-way I am."

It was Harriet's turn to groan, "You can be impossible sometimes." She searched for another reason why he should change his image. She was reluctant to use the only one that she had so far not used, but her frustration dictated that it was time for the heavy artillery. "Maybe, just maybe, a new look would stop 'alf the guys at college calling you 'Wilted' all the time."

"It's not so much of a problem."

"It's not much fun for me either, you know?"

This got his full attention and he stared hard at her for a moment, "Is it that bad?"

Harriet's shoulders slumped. She was already regretting this tactic, "It can be a bit, you know? Annoying?"

Horace sighed again and shook his head, "Look. I'll think about it, okay?"

"Really?"

"Really."

In an effort to appease her, Horace stayed home while Harriet went shopping and managed to make a start on the thesis. When she returned two hours later he had completed the introduction and showed it to her as proof of his commitment.

"Happy now?"

Harriet grinned ruefully, "Well, I guess it's a start."

"I'll make you a deal," he said, "If you don't moan w-w-when I skip the lecture on Monday, I'll go down to the market and by the time you come home, I'll be a new man. How about it?"

To his surprise, she agreed, "That's a deal. Anything to get you to do it."

"Anything?" he asked, gently fondling her breasts.

She wriggled against him, groaning softly, "I think you should take that bloody ferret to the vet while you're down the market." She groaned louder as he slid a hand under her blouse. "On second thoughts, forget the vet."

From The Diary of Horace Wilt,

"Saturday, 28th June, 1980

DD,

Problem. Have told Harry that I'm going to change my image on Monday (at least I get to skip Guy's lecture which is probably a very good thing given the state of my latest assignments), but I haven't got the faintest idea what sort of image to adopt.

Spent most of the afternoon making love. Still can't believe this is all really, actually happening to me!!!!"

8

Harriet made sure Horace was wide awake before she left for college on the Monday morning, "You won't 'forget' or anything, will you?"

Horace shook his head, "As soon as I've had my coffee, I'll go straight there. Promise."

"Really, really promise?"

"Really, really."

"You'd better," she grinned, "Or I 'really, really' will take the ferret to the vet."

Horace winced, "I might even skip the coffee before I set off."

"Okay then, I believe you. Now remember, I'm hitting the library after the lecture and you're to meet me in the Crown at six, yes?"

"I'll be there. Even if you don't recognise me."

After she left he took a leisurely shower and settled at his desk with a coffee. He had every intention of keeping his promise but he also had a problem; he didn't have the faintest idea of what sort of "new look" to try out. He reached forward and switched on the radio where the Undertones' *My Perfect Cousin* was soon replaced by what, according to the disc jockey, was a new wave classic, the Stranglers' *No More Heroes*. Horace couldn't fathom how such a recent release could be termed a classic and was about to change the station when a thought struck him. Harriet wanted him to have a *new look*, and for the last three or four years the music scene had been dominated by *new wave* and the whole punk scene.

This was it; the perfect idea. Horace resolved to turn himself into the archetypal punk in just seven hours. If anyone can do it, I can, Horace told himself.

He had thought that it would be the simplest thing in the world to wander down the local market and find all he needed for the transformation, but the majority of the stalls seemed to be stocked with fancy, frilly shirts in every imaginable pastel shade. He had walked almost the entire length of the street before he finally found what he thought he was looking for. A row of three shops behind the market stalls had been vacated, and an entrepreneurial type had opened up the middle one and set up four trestle tables on which his wares were displayed.

Horace wandered into the gloomy interior and began poring through the contents of the makeshift displays. He had just picked up a pair of leather trousers which had been carefully ripped, together with a fluorescent green tie-dyed T-short (also ripped), when a rough voice startled him.

"Wotcha after, guv?"

When Horace's gaze finally settled on the source of the enquiry, he was amazed that he hadn't noticed the man before. Six foot tall, dressed in ragged leathers much like those in Horace's hands, and with a bright blue Mohican haircut adorning a head variously pierced with safety pins, this guy was the very essence of punkdom.

"Oh, er, Hi," Horace said. "Actually I w-w-was looking for something like this," he held up the jeans and T-shirt, "In fact, I w-w-want to change my, you know? Image?"

The guy chuckled, "Well if you wanna stand out in the crowd, you've certainly come to the right place."

"I do," Horace insisted.

"So, exactly wot sort of fing are you after?"

"I guess I w-w-was hoping for something like, w-w-well, like your look, I suppose."

"You sure?"

"Absolutely."

"'Air an all that as well?"

Horace hadn't really considered this but decided that if he was going to have an image change, he might as well go the whole hog, "Oh, yeah, of course." He hoped he sounded more positive than he really felt.

The guy gave another throaty laugh, "I guess it's your lucky day then, squire. Me girl's in the back," he pointed over his shoulder towards a graffiti-covered door, "And she can do all that "air stuff and the pins and fings. Let"s see wot we can do wiv you.'

Horace felt a sense of relief. Knowing himself, if he was left to his own devices he was bound to get things wrong. But now he was among experts.

The punk looked Horace up and down and then rummaged through the items on the trestle nearest to him, plucking out half a dozen garments, and then motioned for Horace to follow him through to the back of the shop.

The back room was lit by a bright spotlight positioned above a rust-speckled mirror which had been leant precariously over a sink. On the room's only item of furniture, an ancient armchair shedding its stuffing, was the punk's 'girl'. Like the guy himself, she was the classic punk; ripped clothing, bright yellow hair in a crazy series of gelled curls, enough safety pins to equip a large maternity unit, and a necklace of what looked suspiciously like real razor blades. She was busily rolling an enormous joint and barely glanced up when they entered the room. The Sex Pistols were apparently still calling for *Anarchy in the UK*, the punk anthem blaring from a small tape player.

"Got one for ya, Doll," the guy said.

She finished twisting the ends of the reefer and then gave Horace an appraising look, "I guess I could do summink wiv 'im," she said at length. "Wot you after then?"

"The works," the punk said before Horace had a chance of replying.

"Er, yeah, that's right," Horace agreed.

The girl shrugged and set the joint on the floor beside the chair, "Okay, then. Get yer kit off an' we'll see wot I can do."

"Er, w-w-what?"

"Yer kit, yer gear. Get it off and we'll see wot new gear looks best on you for a start," she explained as if to a child. "It's only after we get the right gear on you that I can work out wot sort of 'airdo and stuff goes wiv it."

"Oh, er, right," Horace nodded. He pulled his sweatshirt over his head and folded it carefully before placing it on the least dirty-looking section of the grubby floor. He stood upright and waited for the next move.

"Shy one, yeah?" the girl grinned. She pointed to his jeans. "Them an' all."

Horace looked alarmed, but decided he'd better co-operate if he was to go through with this. He unbuckled the jeans and kicked off his trainers before stepping out of both. He felt highly self-conscious standing in just his boxers.

"Still shy?" she grinned again. "Shorts as well, guv."

"W-w-what?!"

The punk guy gave his customary throaty chuckle, "They'd show fru the jeans, guv," he explained, "And don't worry about Doll, she

179

won't grab yer cock and start suckin' it or anyfing. Cut it off, maybe. Just kiddin', just kiddin'," he added quickly when Horace began to bleat.

Horace stood there wracked with indecision. He thought of Harriet and his promise to her and then finally, with utmost reluctance, sighed and quickly pulled his shorts to the floor. He kicked them to one side and covered his exposed groin.

"'E's a big one," the punk guy commented, as Horace's blush quickly accelerated through the red part of the spectrum. The punk held up one of the three pairs of trousers he had brought into the room with them and discarded it, "Better not try that one," he explained cheerfully, "Can't 'ave you wandering round wiv yer cock 'anging out, can we?"

"Er, no," Horace agreed sheepishly. He was beginning to doubt the wisdom of this enterprise.

"Anyways up," the guy went on, "I'd better get out there an' make sure no-one 'alf-inches the gear. Doll'll sort yer out alright."

"You're going to leave me alone in here?"

"I promise she's 'armless mate. See yer in 'alf an 'our, okay?"

Horace guessed he really didn't have much of a choice. If he was going to become a punk, he'd better just go along with everything, "W-w-well, I suppose so."

"Come on then, big guy," she said to Horace coincidentally mimicking Harriet's pet term for him, "We'll start with the trousers." She held each of the remaining pairs up to the light and opted for the less ripped pair. Horace went to take them from her but she waved his hand away, "Let me put 'em on yer," she said, "Only for the first couple of times it ain't that easy, see? Yer keep putting yer feet through the tears an' that."

"Oh, er, okay."

She gathered up each leg of the trousers and then knelt at Horace's feet. He looked down at her to see which leg they would start with and then drew in a deep breath. Her ripped t-shirt was far too large for her small frame and he could clearly see down the front of it – to where her small breasts were completely open to his gaze.

"Come on then," she said with a hint of impatience, "Right leg first."

Horace automatically lifted his right foot and despite his fervent desire not to, continued to stare down at her small bare breasts which jiggled as she slid the trousers over his raised foot. The exercise was repeated with his left foot and she began to work the leather legs up to his knees.

"It gets a lot easier once we're past these," she said, tapping his left knee.

As she straightened, the t-shirt slipped down her right shoulder a few inches and her breast was now fully exposed. She glanced down at herself but made no effort to cover it, "Oops," she grinned, "But I s'pose fair's fair, right?"

Horace couldn't speak. To his further horror, his ferret was becoming rather interested in the view.

She pulled the trousers up his thighs and stopped when they reached his hands, "Come on then, I can't get these all the way up wiv yer 'ands there, can I?"

"I, er, it's just-"

He had been about to explain his predicament but wasn't given a chance. Sighing, the girl pulled his hands away and then laughed as his half-erect member sprang forward, "I'm not sure I'll be able to get them up anyway," she grinned.

"S-s-sorry," Horace stammered, his cheeks a bright vermilion, "It's just, y-y-you know?" he glanced back down at her bare right breast.

She laughed and pulled the t-shirt over it, "I take it yer like girls wiv small tits then?"

"Yeah," Horace muttered miserably.

"Don't fret, luv. I guess it's a bit of a compliment, right? Anyway, if that don't settle down in a couple of minutes, I'll give you a quick blow. That should sort it out."

"W-w-what? No! I mean, th-th-thanks and all that, but…" he trailed off.

The girl got to her feet and grinned, "Just teasing yer. Forget about it for a minute or two an' you'll be okay."

"Forget about it!" Horace groaned. A sudden thought struck him. "What if he," he pointed at the door, "Comes back in?"

"Don't fret. 'E's got a sense of 'umour." She looked back down at Horace's groin, "See, there you go. While you were panicking you kinda relaxed."

Horace realised with relief that she was right and he hastily pulled the trousers up to his waist, "Thank god for that."

The girl helped him fasten the safety pins that served as a fly and then pulled a fluorescent green T-shirt over his head before adding a studded, sleeveless, leather jacket to complete the ensemble. She stood back and appraised her work, "Yeah," she nodded finally, "This might just work. Course, you'll need some DMs to finish the gear off. What size d'ya take? I'll get Dave to grab a pair for yer."

"Tens," Horace told her, happy to be fully dressed once more – if the term "fully" could be used for garments with this many rips and tears in them. "I'll get some cash." He rummaged in his own jeans and pulled out a roll of banknotes, handing the girl a twenty.

She went through to the front of the shop and returned almost immediately, "Okay, then, let's ave a look at yer barnet."

By the time Dave had returned with a pair of blood-red Doctor Martens, Horace's hair was a wild shade of blue and sporting two bright green horns which the girl had gelled into place.

"Looking good," Dave said admiringly. "Nice job Doll."

Horace stared at his reflection in the speckled mirror. He nodded happily; no-one could say that he hadn't changed his image now.

Doll also nodded happily, "A couple of pins an' an earring and I reckon 'e'll be ready to face the world as a proper punk."

Horace winced at the thought of the safety pins, but guessed that the transformation wouldn't be complete without them and besides, if he had had to suffer, then Harriet would no doubt be even more impressed.

Dave returned to the front of the store after handing the boots to Doll who quickly threaded laces through the bottom two eyelets in each boot, "Ever worn these before?" she asked Horace.

He shook his head.

"Then I'll show you 'ow to lace 'em proper." She dropped to her knees.

Horace was glad that he was now wearing trousers as Doll's t-shirt gaped open. He had almost decided not to look down, but reckoned that maybe it was time for some payback after his earlier embarrassment. He followed her directions as she instructed him to lift each of his feet in turn, watching, a little guiltily as her small breasts moved inside the t-shirt. His reverie was suddenly interrupted.

"Oi," she was grinning up at him.

He immediately turned scarlet which almost completed the colours of the rainbow on his newly decorated head, "S-s-sorry."

She laughed and shook her head, "Just makes you a typical guy, so don't worry about it. Anyway, I'm more interested in findin' out whether you're followin' me instructions than followin' me tits."

"W-w-what? Er, yes, er sort of…"

She laughed again and undid the lace he had barely registered she had been doing up, "Start again, shall I?"

"P-p-please." This time he followed every instruction and only briefly glanced down her t-shirt.

"Well, you've 'ad yer eyeful," she grinned when she'd finished, "Now it's time fer yer earful," She rummaged in a box and drew out a tray of silver rings.

"W-w-will this hurt?"

She shrugged, "Not a lot," She rummaged again and brought out a small bottle of rubbing alcohol and a cork with four large pins sticking out of the top of it.

Horace watched her with mounting fear as she carefully sterilised one of the pins and then poured a little alcohol onto a ball of cotton wool.

"It's not that bad," she reassured him when she noticed his slightly panicked features. "'Ere, you'll like this," She held up the cotton wool ball. "I went into the chemist to get these this morning and I says to the guy behind the counter, 'You got cotton wool balls?' and 'e says 'Wot do you fink I am, a fucking golliwog?'"

Horace laughed despite himself, "Good wh-wh-one." He was beginning to quite like Doll. He briefly wondered what she'd look like out of all that punk gear and hoped fervently that she didn't notice the blush that the idea brought to his cheeks.

If she did, she evidently put it down to fear and quickly went about her business. She rubbed the alcohol into both sides of his ear and then gripped the lobe firmly between her fingers, "Feeling a bit numb?"

"Yeah," he said, taking a deep breath and holding it.

In the event, he hardly felt the needle slip through the flesh of his ear and was surprised when Doll told him that she was finished. As she released his ear he could feel the strange sensation of weight dragging at it, "That w-w-wasn't so bad."

"Told ya. Now let's get yer nose done." She picked up the discarded needle and sterilised it again before selecting a large safety pin which she was evidently intent on sticking through his nose.

Horace felt a moment of panic – along the lines of "What the hell am I doing?" – but before he could voice any of his fears, he was sporting a new nasal accessory.

"Well, wotcha fink?"

He looked in the mirror at the re-born Horace. No doubt about it now, he was one hundred percent punk. He nodded thoughtfully, "Looks right."

"Reckon you want another pin?"

He shook his head, delighting in the movement of new facial ornamentation against his skin, "I reckon that'll do."

"Yeah, I reckon so an' all. So there you are done. I'll find a bag fer yer old stuff."

Horace shuddered as he considered the prospect of walking out of the shop in his new punk regalia but nodded, "Thanks. How much do I owe you?"

"What wiv the change from the DMs I reckon another twenty oughta cover it."

"Only twenty?"

"Yeah. Most of the gear's second 'and, 'cept the earring. And anyway, you're an okay sorta guy."

Horace smiled and realised that he hadn't even blushed at the albeit small compliment. Perhaps this new image might work on his self-confidence a bit, "Thanks. But I'd feel better if you'd take this," he handed her another two twenty pound notes.

She tried to refuse but he was insistent. Reluctantly she pocketed the notes, "Nice of yer."

He decided to test out his new-found confidence, "And I'm sorry I looked at your," he hesitated and pressed on, the tiniest of blushes rising on his cheeks, "At your, you know, tits." There, he'd finally said the word out loud to someone.

She laughed, giving him a quizzical look, "No problem, big guy. Besides, I'd hardly wear somefink like this if I cared whether guys got the occasional peek, would I?" She pulled the front of her t-shirt away from her neck.

From Horace's elevated position he could once again see the rise of her small breasts. Confidence surging through him he nodded, "I guess not. They're really nice."

She laughed again and let the t-shirt fall back into place, "Thanks," she paused and gave him another quizzical look. "You're not normally like this, are yer?"

Horace sighed. Was he that transparent? "Not really, I guess I'm kind of shy."

Doll smiled at him, "Well, keep up the new image, big guy, you're okay. And if you're ever in the Draughtsman, come over and say hi, will yer?"

He nodded happily, "I w-w-will."

Doll looked at a watch that was sitting on the arm of the chair, "Talking of the pub, fancy a beer? Only thanks to you, I'm loaded."

Horace thought for a moment. He definitely fancied a beer, and, if he went somewhere with Doll, at least his first steps on the street as a punk wouldn't be lonely ones. He was about to say yes when he realised something else, "What about Dave? I mean, he said you w-w-were his girl?"

She laughed, "I just work for 'im, I'm not 'is *girlfriend.* Besides, 'e'd probably reckon it'd be good fer business."

"I guess that's a yes then."

They left the dilapidated shop together and Horace took a deep breath of the June air, "I really do feel like a new man," he told Doll.

"Me too."

On the way to the pub Horace noticed that people seemed to give them a wide berth and he was quite enjoying the feeling until Doll asked him what his name was. "Er, Horace," he mumbled.

"Did you say 'Horace'?"

"Er, yes," Horace mumbled again. To his surprise she found this great news.

"That's perfect for a punk," she said.

"Horace?"

"Yeah. All you gotta do is shorten it a bit, make it 'Hor'."

He shrugged. No-one had ever shortened it before and he supposed having a name that sounded like 'whore' wasn't so bad – if you were a punk, anyway, "I guess so."

"It's a bit like mine," Doll explained, "I mean not 'whore', before you say it. My real name's Dolores, so it's easy to shorten it to Doll, like that punk guitarist."

Horace decided to try out his new found confidence again, "Yeah, I see w-w-what you mean. And you look like a real Doll."

He was rewarded with a slap on his rump and a laugh, "Keep it up, Hor. I'm getting to really like you."

They arrived at the back-street pub and Doll led them into the dingy interior. The bar was dimly lit and not one that Horace had ever been in before; he was vaguely aware that it had a bad reputation. Inside, half a dozen other punks, three girls and three guys, were crowded around a small table in the corner, plastic beakers of beer arrayed on its stained surface. The air carried a distinctly herbal scent, reminding Horace of his mother's house.

Doll crossed the short distance from the door to the table, Horace following happily, glad to be among his 'own kind'.

"Hiya guys," Doll greeted them, "This 'ere's Hor."

The six faces turned towards Horace and he smiled at them as they nodded, a couple of them giving him a brief "Hi". He was really enjoying this.

"You should see the size of this guy's cock," Doll went on, mainly to the other three females, "'E's 'uge."

Horace nearly choked but, since he doubted anyone could see his blush, he decided that, as a punk, he should brave it out, "Yeah, w-w-well," he shrugged as nonchalantly as he could.

"Anyway," Doll said to him, "These are Phlegm, Smeg, and Razor," indicating the three guys, "And Blow, Titsy and Dog," turning her attention to the three females.

Horace didn't think he'd have much trouble remembering the second girl's name.

Doll went to get everyone drinks after further extolling Horace's virtues by adding his generosity to her earlier observation, and returned with eight more plastic tumblers of beer, expertly – if not very hygienically – carried in one go.

Horace found them stools and they took their places with the others. Doll rummaged in her enormous bag and withdrew the joint she had been rolling when Horace had first seen her.

"Who's gotta light?" she asked.

Horace looked on in amazement as the guy he believed to be Phlegm handed Doll a Zippo, "Doesn't he mind?" he asked, nodding to the bar where a grizzled old man, evidently the landlord, was busy topping up a Bells whisky bottle with one bearing the label 'Tesco Own Brand'.

Doll laughed, "Old Joe? Shouldn't 'ave fought so, Hor. 'E's the one wot supplies the gear." She put the joint in her mouth and spun the Zippo into flame. Inhaling deeply, she lit the joint, holding the smoke in her mouth for twenty seconds before taking it down. "Christ, that's better," she exhaled deeply. She took another, shorter, drag and then held the joint in front of Horace's face.

"I, er, don't sort of, actually…" he trailed off. He had never even smoked a cigarette, much less a joint. As far as he was concerned, smoking was the single leading cause of statistics.

Doll laughed, "Go on, Hor. It'll do you good. Really good gear this."

Shrugging, he accepted the roll-up and tentatively put it between his lips. He took an experimental suck and, remembering what Doll had done, held the fragrant smoke in his mouth for a few seconds before drawing it down his throat. He coughed it out violently and continued coughing while Doll patted him on the back, "Touch of asthma," he managed by way of weak explanation when he could finally speak.

Doll laughed again, "Yeah, right. Well this is good stuff for asthma, ain't it, Titsy?" The girl in question had taken the joint from

Horace's unresisting fingers while he had been coughing and was inhaling deeply.

"Oh yeah," she replied after exhaling, "I used to be chesty all the time."

"And you're not now?" Razor laughed, lifting her t-shirt to reveal her massive breasts.

Horace should have been shocked, but for some reason he wasn't. In fact, it all felt very natural, very relaxed, "Nice," he commented to his own surprise.

"Ta," Titsy said with a grin, tugging the t-shirt back over her bust with considerable difficulty.

When the joint made it round again to his position, he decided that he'd better have another try. This time he barely coughed at all, and he was sure he could feel the smoke drifting throughout his head, "You're right," he nodded to Doll, "This is good stuff."

"Told you."

He handed the joint on to Titsy and was about to offer to buy refills of drinks. He was just turning back towards Doll when he found her face inches from his own. Before he could react, she closed the gap and planted her mouth firmly over his own. He knew this was wrong. Absolutely, definitely wrong. Her tongue probed gently between his lips and eased into his mouth. Totally wrong. Just think of Harriet, he told himself. Well, she does *look* like Harriet himself replied. And why spoil the relaxed mood? Horace gave in and returned the kiss.

It seemed to last forever and he was nearly breathless when she finally released him. He glanced around at the others to see what they had made of it and was not unduly surprised to see three pairs of punks doing exactly what he and Doll had been doing. With the exception of Razor and Titsy. Razor was kissing her once-again bared breasts. "W-w-wow!" he muttered. "I guess the landlord doesn't mind this sort of thing either?"

Doll laughed, "Nah. Reckons it adds to the character of the place."

Horace looked hard at her, "I really shouldn't, you know? I mean, I've sort of got a girlfriend."

Doll raised a quizzical eyebrow, "Still, if it's only "sort of" I guess it's okay then."

Horace knew this was wrong as well, but as he looked down at Doll, leaning forward on the stool, her small, firm breasts once more visible to his eager gaze, he felt himself drifting into an area where he had little control, "If you really think so?"

She smiled, "I do. Wanna go through the back?"

"The back?"

"Yeah, the back room. It's a bit more private, like."

"I, er…" he began, but Doll took this for a 'yes' and grabbed his hand, pulling him to his feet.

"See ya later, guys," she offered to the others.

Horace let himself be led through a door at the back of the bar and found himself in what had once been a second bar. Half a dozen armchairs and two overstuffed sofas were now the only furnishings in sight. Doll closed the door behind them and pushed a bolt into place, locking them in.

She turned to him and smiled, "You're great, you know that?"

Horace shrugged, he was desperately trying to clear the cotton wool out of his head, "W-w-whatever."

Still smiling, Doll dropped her hands to the bottom of her oversized t-shirt and in one fluid movement pulled it over her head, dropping it across the nearest armchair.

Horace stared at her small, half-naked form in wonder, a certain ferret reacting instantaneously, "W-w-wow!" She stepped forward and before his conscious mind could stop him, he had raised his hands to cup her firm breasts. Horace thought afterwards that if she hadn't groaned as he did so, and if that groan hadn't sounded exactly the same as the one Harriet always gave, anything could have happened. As it was, at the sound of her pleasure, his mind cleared. "No!" he exclaimed, as much to himself as to Doll. He dropped his hands to his side.

"What?" she asked, perplexed.

"It's not you!" Horace explained, not wishing to upset his new friend, "It's just, my girlfriend, you know?"

Doll sighed, and for a moment, as she struggled for words, Horace thought that she was going to scream at him. Instead, she seemed to recover her poise, "The faithful type, yeah?"

"I'm s-s-sorry, I didn't know w-w-what you had in mind," he said miserably.

To his relief, Doll smiled. "Faithful and pretty innocent, I reckon. I guess that's not such a bad thing."

"You don't mind too much?"

She shrugged, "I can't really, can I? But promise me one fing?"

"W-w-what?"

"If you and your girl ever split up, come and find me, okay?"

Horace sighed in relief and pleasure, "Count on it."

She nodded, satisfied with his answer, "I reckon you will an' all. Now, just one last kiss an' I'll let you out." She reached up and kissed him once more, Horace unresisting. After a minute their lips parted and Horace took a step back.

His new-found confidence was riding high again, and he deliberately let his gaze wander over her small body, "You're really cute."

"Thanks," Doll replied picking up her t-shirt. "'Ad enough of a butcher's yet," she added with a grin.

"I doubt it, but I guess I'd better say yes."

Doll laughed and pulled the t-shirt over her head, covering her nakedness, "Whatever you say, big guy. Now, 'ow about I buy you another beer before you run off?"

Horace wasn't sure it was such a good idea, but on the other hand didn't want to offend her any further, "Yeah, that'd be good."

9

Horace left the Draughtsman at five, much later than he had intended, and his head was buzzing pleasantly. He'd taken another couple of drags on passing joints and he was now feeling carefree, confident, and at peace with the world. Also hungry.

He stopped at a burger van halfway up the market and couldn't decide whether he would prefer a Hamburger, Cheeseburger or Hot Dog. In the end, he opted for all three and gorged himself on the junk food on a bench near the bus station. Unusually, none of the local tramps seemed inclined to settle themselves next to him and ask for a bite. This new punk image had lots of side benefits, he told himself.

After finishing the last of the burger, he threw the greasy wrappers into a bin and decided to head straight for the Crown. He was really looking forward to meeting Harriet and showing off his new image, so he didn't want to risk being late.

He arrived there at five-thirty and went around to the back of the pub, letting himself into the back-bar by the doorway reserved for known regulars. Behind the bar, Flat-foot Fred, the short-sighted, sixty-something barman-cum-potman, was busy polishing glasses.

"Evening, Fred."

Fred looked up at the newcomer. He gave a load grunt, "Get out."

"Pardon?"

"I said, get out," Fred repeated reasonably. "No punks allowed."

"But Fred! It's me, Horace!"

Fred took another look, "So it is. Sorry, didn't recognise you there."

"That's okay, then," Horace breathed a sigh of relief.

"Go on then."

"Er, go on w-w-what?"

"Get out."

"But it's me!"

Fred tutted, "Look sonny, I don't care if you was the fucking pope. Rules is rules. No punks allowed. Now, go on, scarper."

"Since w-w-when are punks banned?"

"Since last weekend, that's since when. Ever since we got that new regular band in."

"W-w-what's that got to do w-w-with anything?"

Fred shrugged, "Apparently, their fans are all New Romans or something. And that lot don't exactly get on with punks, see? Iain don't want no trouble."

"But I'm *never* any trouble!"

"Might be if them New Romans started having a go. You might even *make* them start having a go."

Horace cast around desperately for an argument, "But, I'm supposed to be meeting Harry in here at six."

"You'll just have to meet her outside then, won't you? Now 'op it."

"But-"

195

Fred interrupted him, "Do yerself a favour, son. Just go quietly."

Horace's shoulders slumped. The new-found confidence was taking a bit of a knock, but he decided he should at least offer a passing shot, "All right, then. But w-w-we'll just take our custom elsew-w-where."

"You'll have to if you want a drink," Fred agreed, reasonably.

Horace trudged outside and tried to work out what to do. Harriet really liked the Crown and if he wasn't allowed in, he doubted that she'd be very happy with him. There again, this new image thing *had* been her idea in the first place. He decided to wait outside the back door, and explain things to her when she arrived.

10

It was ten past six and there was still no sign of Harriet when Horace suddenly realised that she wouldn't be using the back door of the pub – that was only used outside of official opening hours. Cursing his lack of forethought, he dashed around the side of the building and almost ran into Godfrey who was just about to enter the bar.

"Oi, watch it!" Godfrey protested before doing a double-take. "Horace?"

"Yeah. Look, can you do me a favour Godfrey? Only I w-w-was supposed to meet Harry inside at six and Fred w-w-won't let me in. Can you ask her to come outside a minute?"

"It is you," Godfrey went on, oblivious to Horace's pleadings. "Fuck me."

"Please?" Horace begged the grinning Godfrey, "Just don't tell her about, er, this," he pointed down at his clothing, "I w-w-want it to be a surprise."

"That it will be. Hang on, pal, I'll go get her." Still grinning Godfrey disappeared through the doorway.

Two minutes later Harriet appeared at the door. She stopped and looked round, confused. Her gaze travelled past Horace before stopping and slowly returning. Her jaw dropped as she stared first at his hair and then at his clothing.

"Er, hi," Horace greeted her, "The all-new Horace here."

Harriet's jaw snapped shut and she shook her head in wonderment, "This," she told Horace slowly and quietly, "'Ad better be some sort of joke."

"Joke? But you said I should get a new image."

"Oh my God! You're serious, aren't you?"

"You did s-s-say and all that," Horace pleaded.

She shook her head again, "You know something, H? I didn't think that even *you* could be so, so..." she struggled for a moment, "Stupid!"

"But-"

"Look at you! What a bloody mess! Jesus H Christ, it's not even as if being a punk is fashionable. You look ridiculous!"

"Not fashionable?"

"No, *not* fashionable. These days, in case you 'ad't noticed, everyone's getting into this New Romantic stuff," she explained icily.

"But I w-w-was w-w-with some punks earlier."

"Well, at least you'll 'ave someone to be with in the future then," Harriet snapped.

"W-w-what do you mean, in the f-f-future?"

"What I mean, Orris, is that I would not be seen dead going around with such a... a... a pathetic looking excuse for a 'uman being. If you want to look like something out of a freak show, that's fine. Just count me out!"

Horace stared, dumbstruck, as Harriet marched back into the bar, "But it w-w-was your idea," he said miserably.

He was still standing there minutes later when Godfrey came back outside, "Er, Horace?"

"But…"

Godfrey sighed, "I reckon your best bet would be to go home, mate. Maybe she'll cool down a bit in a while."

Horace looked at him with pleading eyes, "Do you really think so?"

Godfrey shrugged, "Actually, not from what she's saying in there at the moment."

"Oh God."

"Lay low for a while, uh?"

"You sure she's not coming out?"

"For your sake, pal, right now I'd pray she didn't – and I'm an atheist."

Horace winced, "Okay then," he said, resigned, "I'll get back to the flat. Just do me wh-wh-wh-one last favour?"

"Whatever you like, pal."

"Tell her I still love her," Horace said, tears beginning to press at his closed eyelids. Without waiting for a reply, he turned and dashed off, heading for the relative quiet of the back streets.

11

Horace wandered around for an hour, trying to work out where he had got things so terribly wrong. After all, it had been Harriet's suggestion that he change his image in the first place. He couldn't remember for certain whether he had made that point in their brief discussion outside the Crown and he decided that it would be best all round if he made sure that she had heard that argument. He resolved to head back to the flats and wait outside her door until she arrived.

He hurried back to Church Hill Buildings and scampered up the stairs. Of course, he reasoned, for all he knew, she could already be back at her flat. He knocked loudly on her door but got no reply, which he hoped was a good sign. If she was still at the Crown, then he might have more time while she cooled off.

The afternoon's beers coupled with the few drags he had taken on the joints had left him feeling a deep need for a drink. He dashed into his flat and returned to the landing with an unopened bottle of his mother's home-made paint stripper. Resolving himself to making sure that he didn't miss Harry when she came back, he sat on the stairs leading to the second floor and unscrewed the top of the bottle.

It was half empty when the downstairs door opened at eight. Although he didn't feel at all drunk, he reeled alarmingly as he stood up and only the banister rail stopped him from pitching down the last five stairs to the landing below.

Harriet came into view a moment later and he lurched in front of her, "Look, Harry-"

Her snort of contempt cut him short, "Orris, I told you earlier. I'm not 'aving anything to do with someone that looks like you do," she paused and sniffed. "And you're pissed again."

He was at a loss for words as she pushed past him, fumbling her keys into her door, "But…"

"Forget it, H," she said over her shoulder. "If you want to talk to someone, go find some of your own kind. You know, other wimps who 'ide behind stupid masks?"

He looked on dumbstruck as she opened her door, and barely flinched as it crashed shut behind her. He shook his head in disbelief.

His addled brain managed to remind him about his side of the argument and he quickly rapped on her door.

It swung open immediately, "Orris," she said menacingly, "I'll say this one time and one time only. Leave me alone, okay?"

His head nodded involuntarily. Harriet nodded back, once, firmly and then went back inside her flat, the door closing behind her.

This, Horace thought, *cannot be happening*. Everything had been going so well! His legs seemed to decide that they'd had enough exercise for the day and before he knew what was happening he was sitting beside Harriet's front door. Shaking his head, hoping for some explanation to pop into it, he picked up the bottle and raised it to his lips, taking a long swallow.

He followed it with another, barely noticing the brandy's fiery passage down his throat.

He started awake sometime later, the now-empty bottle falling from his grip, "W-w-what's happening?"

"I said, get the fuck out of here!" A raised, angry voice told him.

He looked up and tried to focus.

"Oh Jesus," The voice dropped to a normal level. "Is that really you, Horace?"

"Shteph?"

Stephanie was staring down at him with a mixture of horror and disbelief, "What on earth have you done to yourself?" She stared down at the blue hair and the green horns, one of which had crumpled while he had dozed against the wall.

"Harry don't think itsh sho good," he nodded miserably.

"I'll bet," Stephanie tried to hide a grin.

"She called me a wimp!" Horace protested, drunkenly.

"I hate to tell you this, H, but I think I might have done, as well."

"Oh, thanksh," he hiccupped.

Stephanie shook her head, "Oh, Horace. What are we going to do with you?" She stepped forward and held out a hand. "Come on. Let's get you inside your flat and see if we can do something about all... this. I've never seen you this drunk before."

He struggled to focus on both her hand and her words. At the third attempt he grasped the hand. At the fourth he grasped what she was saying, "I'm not sho think ash you drunk I am," he said, "Itsh no ushe. She don't w-w-wanna know me."

Stephanie hauled him to his feet where he swayed gently, "We'll see."

She led him inside and straight through to the bathroom, propping him upright between the sink and the shower stall where it was impossible for him to fall down. She began to run hot water into the sink and then turned back to him, "For a start, let's get rid of those ridiculous clothes."

Horace made a couple of attempts at pulling his t-shirt upwards, before Stephanie tutted and helped him pull it over his head. He squawked as it snagged on his safety pin, and again as Stephanie extracted it from his nose. The earring followed and then she began to unpin the front of the torn leathers. "I hope you're wearing something under these," she said as she tugged at the waistband.

"Can't remember."

Stephanie tugged them downwards, "Oh well, it's not as if I've never seen it before," she shrugged, "And I'm pretty certain you're in no state to use it." She pulled the leathers down his legs and, after a brief struggle, off his feet.

"I can remember now," Horace said, "You're the shame ash Doll." He nodded and almost lost his balance.

"Doll?"

"She shaw me like thish today, too," he nodded again.

Stephanie sighed, "I haven't got the faintest idea what you're on about, H, but if I was you I wouldn't mention that little gem to Harry."

"She won't talk to me," Horace's voice dropped back to full-blown misery.

"Come on, let's see what we can do." She guided him into the open shower stall, leaning him against the back wall. She picked up a pint glass by the sink, emptied the toothbrushes it contained onto the shelf and then filled it with the warm water.

"Close your eyes," she instructed Horace stepping into the shower stall. When she was happy that he had, she tipped the water slowly over his multi-coloured head. Although the water was warm, Horace reacted as if it was freezing, gasping and going rigid, "C-c-c-cold," he managed.

"It's not. Stop being such a baby. You do want me to help, don't you?"

"Don't shee much point," Horace mumbled.

Stephanie ignored him and refilled the glass. She poured the second one over his head and was rewarded with a drenching when Horace shook his head, dog-fashion, "Oh, thanks, H!" She looked from Horace's shoulders, which were beginning to turn blue, to her damp sweatshirt and groaned. "If this stuff really is going to come out of your hair, I'm likely to end up with a multi-coloured sweatshirt," she said, more for her own benefit than the now shivering Horace's. She stared hard at him and, when he failed to focus on her gaze, shrugged. "I really don't think you're capable, but no funny business, right?"

The swaying Horace didn't seem to be able to focus on the question, "No funny bish... what you shaid."

"Turn round, then," she instructed. When this met with no response, she grabbed his shoulders and turned him to face the back of the stall. After satisfying herself that he wasn't about to fall over, she let go and quickly pulled off her sweatshirt, jeans and pants, "It's a dirty job," she muttered, stepping back into the shower, "But somebody's got to do it." She picked up a bottle of shampoo, and turned on the shower jet, hoping that the temperature regulator was accurate.

It was and she stepped under the stream of water, manoeuvring Horace backwards until it cascaded over his head. She poured some shampoo into her hand and began to massage it into Horace's blue and green scalp.

"Thatsh nishe," he murmured.

"It's not supposed to be nice. By rights I should have just shaved it all off."

"Shorry," he said child-like.

Stephanie grinned, "Okay. Now just hold still, will you?" His swaying was become more pronounced and his back was brushing her breasts as he reached the outermost point of his arc. She steadied him and poured more shampoo onto his head. The water cascading down his body was now much darker, and Stephanie began to believe that she could get most of the colour out of his hair.

Another ten minutes of shampooing, massaging and rinsing, and the water was running clear. "I guess that's as much as we can do," she told Horace.

"Whatsh it like now?" he managed, his first fully aware comment since Stephanie had found him.

"Let's get it dry and you can see for yourself," she replied, guiding him backwards out of the shower stall. She picked up the largest towel she could see and draped it over his head, rubbing hard and ignoring his complaints. When she was sure his hair was as dry as it could be, she let go of the towel, leaving it draped over his shoulders, "You can do the rest of you yourself," she instructed, quickly rubbing herself down with another towel.

"'Kay," he muttered and began wiping haphazardly at his damp arms and chest.

"Oh really," Stephanie moaned, "You'll never get dry like that." She took the towel back from him and vigorously dried him off, avoiding only his groin. "That bit you do yourself, okay?"

"'Kay," he muttered again, taking back the towel.

Stephanie picked up her own and finished drying her legs. She draped the towel over the edge of the bath and grabbed her clothes, dressing quickly while Horace was still fumbling at his groin. Amazingly, and for a change, Horace hadn't seen her nakedness. "Finished?"

He nodded, "Can I shee it now?" he asked miserably, trying to peer at the mirror above the sink.

"Of course," she grinned, "But we'd better use the mirror in your bedroom, this one's too steamy." She looked around and saw a large towelling dressing gown on a hook behind the door and after another brief struggle, managed to get Horace inside it. She led him into the bedroom and sat him on the edge of his bed, facing the mirror. The light was better there and she was relieved to see that his hair wasn't too bad. The ridiculous green horns had completely disappeared, and his hair, overall, seemed to be a very dark shade of blue.

"What do you think?" she asked.

"Shtill blue."

"Not very," she wondered just how blue it would look in daylight, "But I've got a good idea, anyway. In the morning I'll grab a bottle of black hair dye. Your hair's pretty dark anyway, and even if it's got a slight bluish tint, I doubt whether anyone will notice. You'll be pretty much back to normal."

"Really?" Horace asked, a ray of hope lightening his tone.

"Really. Now I reckon you could do with some sleep, don't you?"

Horace yawned and hiccupped, "Too misherable to shleep."

Stephanie shook her head and grinned, "It'll all look better in the morning. And the sooner you get to sleep, the sooner it'll actually *be* morning."

"'Kay then." Horace rolled onto his side and began to try to get the duvet out from under him.

Groaning, Stephanie pulled him upright and managed to persuade him to stand up long enough for her to pull back the cover. When she was ready he collapsed back into a sitting position, before rolling onto his side once more, this time struggling to get his arms free of the dressing gown. Another intervention by Stephanie and Horace was finally tucked into his bed, his eyes drooping closed almost as soon as his head rested into the pillow.

Stephanie stared down at him, a fully-fledged adult who had been reduced to a child in just a couple of hours. She smiled and reached down to peck the top of his head. As she did so he stirred briefly, "Thanksh, Shteph."

"It's okay," she whispered back.

She stood up and switched off the lights, retreating to his living room. She wasn't too happy about leaving him alone while he was that drunk. Sighing, she made herself a much needed coffee and after drinking it slowly, returned to the bedroom. She gently eased herself onto the bed and moved over until her hip was resting lightly against Horace's back, "Goodnight, H," she whispered to him.

His reply came in the form of a snore.

12

The first thing Stephanie felt when she woke in the morning was an overwhelming sense of disorientation. She was certainly not in her own bed. The second thing she felt was a hand resting on her left breast. It was certainly not her own hand.

She opened bleary eyes and looked around. Of course – she was in Horace's bedroom, and, looking down to confirm the fact, the hand was his. At some point during the night, he must have rolled over and the fact that his hand was where it was, she was almost certain, was pure chance. She gently removed the offending mitt and pulled her sweatshirt back down to her waist. She wondered briefly what Harriet would have made of *that* little scene had she found them. Come to that, she wondered what Matt would have made of it!

She eased herself off of the bed, leaving the gently snoring Horace to sleep on. He was going to feel bad enough when he woke up, and there didn't seem any point in disturbing him before absolutely necessary. She checked her watch, surprised to find that it was almost nine, and hastily scribbled a note for Horace should he wake up before she returned.

Stephanie went up to her flat, taking a more conventional shower than the previous night's, and then dressed quickly. On her way out of the building she stopped at Harriet's door and tried to rouse her. Either she was already out or she wasn't seeing anyone, and after a couple of minutes, Stephanie gave up.

Using Horace's own keys, she let herself back into his flat and checked that he was still snoring. Happy that he was, she left the building, returning five minutes later with two bottles of black hair dye and a two pairs of rubber gloves. She made a pot of strong hot coffee and then returned to the bedroom.

Wincing at the prospect, she gently shook Horace's bare shoulder, "Horace, it's me, Steph. Time to wake up, big guy."

He slowly opened an eye, "Steph?" he asked, confused.

"Sure am. How do you feel?"

Horace opened his other eye and them snapped both of them closed, "Oh God."

"That bad, huh?" Stephanie couldn't help but grin. "Well don't worry. Coffee's ready and the Paracetamol are waiting."

Horace struggled to a sitting position, one hand clamped to his forehead. "Oh God," he groaned again and then paused, the memories of the previous evening – or at least, the early part of it – flooding back. "Tell me that w-w-was all a dream?"

"'Fraid not, H," Stephanie said, "But there is hope. Do you remember me from last night?"

Horace, his eyes now partially open, thought hard, "Something about a shower?"

"Very good," Stephanie grinned. She explained what had happened.

A look of relief mixed with gratitude settled on Horace's pain-stricken face, "That w-w-was really kind of you."

"What are friends for?"

"Good friends," Horace nodded, wincing as his brain rattled against his skull, "I had some really w-w-weird dreams last night," he added thoughtfully.

"Oh?"

Horace nodded again, this time less enthusiastically, "Yeah. Wh-wh-wh-one I remember w-w-was w-w-when I thought Harry w-w-was in bed w-w-with me. But something w-w-was wrong. She w-w-was much too big or something."

Stephanie suppressed a laugh. Given where Horace's hand was when she woke this morning, she didn't think an explanation would help him any, "Well, dreams can get like that when you've had a load of grief the evening before."

"Not to mention mother's home-made brandy. Let me at those painkillers." He threw the duvet back and then hastily recovered both it and his own nakedness. "Er, s-s-sorry."

This time Stephanie couldn't help but laugh out loud, "H, I could hardly have showered you without taking off those rotten things you were wearing yesterday."

"I guess not," he muttered, blushing.

Stephanie handed him his dressing gown, "I'll be in the kitchen pouring the coffee."

He joined her after a short trip to the bathroom and gratefully accepted a coffee after first dry-swallowing four Paracetamol. They drank their coffees to the background of *Xanadu*, ELO's latest release which seemed to fit the rather strange mood. He wondered if he would ever have another early morning coffee with Harriet after the previous evening. He told Stephanie of his fears.

"I doubt whether you've got too much to worry about," she said, "And after you've finished that, I'll get to work on your hair."

"Thanks."

By eleven o'clock he looked more like his normal self although his hair was now nearly jet black. Somehow, the remnants of the blue colouring actually leant it a more natural look.

"Not bad at all," he said, inspecting it in his bedroom mirror. While Stephanie had been about things, she had also trimmed his hair and restyled it, "I never realised you w-w-were good at this sort of thing."

"My mum's a sort of hairdresser," Stephanie said, "And I guess it runs in the family. Anyway, I'm glad you like it. Now we go on to stage two of the plan."

"Stage two?"

"Yep. This was all about you getting a new image, right? Well, what I reckon is that I accompany you to the shops and we'll see what we can find for you. Someone had better keep an eye on you or you'll probably end up dressed as a Red Indian or something."

Horace grinned despite himself, "That's really good of you, Steph, but you've done enough already."

She wouldn't take no for an answer and half an hour later they were in the market. En route, Stephanie had explained about the latest fashion trends and seemed intent on getting Horace into the New Romantic look, but he demurred.

"That's just another sort of mask," he insisted, "It's one of the things I can remember Harry saying last night. I've got to find something different."

In the event, and despite Stephanie's early protests, he *did* find something different. They returned to the flat laden with bags and Horace took them into his bedroom, arraying the contents across the duvet. Every item was either black or white and even though most of the shirts were full, there was no way they could be referred to as typically New Romantic. He dressed in black chinos, a black silk shirt, white leather tie, white socks and black sneakers. On top of this, he pulled on a black cotton jacket, the long sleeves rolled up.

"What do you reckon?" he asked Stephanie when he stepped back into the living room.

"Wow!" she exclaimed. "That really suits you."

Horace smiled, some of the misguided self-confidence he had felt the day before returning, "Thanks."

"One last thing and I reckon you'll be ready," Stephanie added.

"Oh?"

"I think we'd better disguise those holes you had bored into you yesterday."

He winced, "You're probably right."

Stephanie went up to her own flat and came back with a make-up bag and a small box. She used the make-up on his nose and then put a small silver ring through his left ear.

"Won't Harriet object to the earring?" he asked.

"Not at all. And it goes really well with the black."

Horace checked his looks in the mirror for the tenth time, "I guess it does look okay. And thanks again-"

"Don't say it!" Stephanie interrupted, "That must be the thousandth time today. Just get yourself in the right frame of mind to meet Harry."

Stephanie had telephoned the college while Horace was trying on his new clothes and, after reassuring her that he was no longer a punk, Harriet had reluctantly agreed to meet Horace at the Crown.

"Are you sure about that?" Horace asked.

Stephanie sighed and shook her head, "For the last time, yes. Stop fretting."

"And you w-w-will come w-w-with me?"

"Yes!" She checked her watch. "And while we're on the subject, it's quarter to six. Time to leave."

13

Harriet arrived just after six and peered cautiously around the bar before spotting a very nervous Horace and groaning Stephanie. She looked again and was amazed at the transformation; Stephanie had been right – he actually looked rather good. She walked over to them.

"Hi, big guy," she smiled sheepishly.

"Hi, Harry," he replied, in an even more ovine manner.

"Look, about yesterday-" Harriet began.

"I'm really sorry-" Horace started at the same moment.

Harriet smiled and shook her head, "Looking good, big guy."

"Thanks. You should thank Steph as w-w-well, though."

"This gear all your idea?" she asked Stephanie.

"Actually, no," Stephanie explained that it was mostly Horace's and that she'd only helped out with the hair. She didn't explain the exact circumstances, reasoning that it was better kept quiet; it's rather hard to explain how you showered naked with someone's boyfriend before sleeping next to him all night.

Stephanie left the pair of them alone after it became clear that they had made up and were once more the item that had been the most constant feature of everyone's first year at college.

From The Diary of Horace Wilt

"Tuesday, 2nd July, 1980

DD,

What relief!!!! I'm not going to go into too many embarrassing details right here in my very own diary, but I screwed up big time. Went down to the market in search of a new image yesterday and found what I thought was the ideal thing - punk gear. A really cute little punk girl called Doll helped me dress in the new stuff and then dyed my hair and stuck a pin through my nose. Went to a rather dodgy pub called The Draughtsman afterwards and, well, had a few beers and so on. I reckon I could have got a bit further with Doll if I'd wanted to, but, of course, Harry was at the front of my mind at all times.

When Harry saw the gear she went ballistic, and I thought it was suddenly all over between us. I was rescued, though, by Steph - who I'll never be able to thank enough - I guess I was a bit drunk when she found me, but she sorted me out this morning and now I'm pretty much back to normal, and Harry's forgiven me. Thank God!!!!"

Chapter 4

1

Life soon returned to normal – involving considerable nagging on Harriet's part in order to get Horace to complete his end of year thesis. She finally managed to persuade him by refusing to have sex with him until it was complete. He finished it by the end of the week, and even threw in one of his missing assignments as a gesture of good faith.

On the last day of term the Red Setter threw a party in the student union and wished everyone a happy holiday. For reasons neither of them could fathom, neither Horace nor Harriet had made any sort of holiday plans and they left the bar in search of a travel agent, desperate to get away from the normal British summer before they caught pneumonia.

Harriet decided that she favoured somewhere a little exotic, maybe India. Horace, who had never travelled further than Paris was dead set against the idea, citing a desperate need to simply put his feet up for a couple of weeks and turn a funny shade of brown.

"I can't even speak a foreign language," he complained.

"Typical," she smiled, "If you speak three languages, you're trilingual; if you speak two, you're bilingual, and if you speak one, you're English."

Despite Harriet's grumblings about his lack of adventure, she eventually relented and they booked themselves a three week stay in the South of France.

"Why book first class, though?" she asked as they left the travel agency.

"If God had w-w-wanted us to travel tourist class, he w-w-would have made us shorter and narrower."

When they returned to the flat Horace discovered – to his horror – that they had visitors. Stephanie had found them outside, let them in, and was entertaining them in her own flat. She intercepted Horace and Harriet on the stairs and beamed from ear to ear, "Visitors, guys."

Horace raised an eyebrow, "For us?"

"Oh, definitely."

"I'm not sure I like that grin," Horace said, "Who is it?"

Stephanie didn't need to answer.

"Darlings!" his mother's voice trilled from the top of the stairs. It was followed by the sound of a rapid descent.

"Oh bugger," Horace muttered, "Hello, mother."

She embraced both of them, cooing over Horace's new, improved, appearance and complimenting "Orchid" on how wonderful she was looking, "I suppose the Tiger Balm's working then?" she enquired.

Both Horace and Harriet immediately blushed. "Mother!"

"Such shy things, aren't they?" she said to Stephanie, indulgently.

Stephanie, already quite confused by Horace's mother, could only nod.

They were joined by Maisie Briggs, her considerable bulk slowing her descent, "Hello, dears," she greeted them, "So nice to see you again. You're looking lovely Orchid," she added, already ignoring Horace.

"Thank you, er, Starchild," Harriet replied.

"Still as polite as ever, she's such a dear isn't she?" Maisie asked the assembled company.

"And so lovely with it," Horace's mother agreed.

"Oh, please, you're embarrassing me," Harriet protested half-heartedly.

"Me too. Anyw-w-way, w-w-what brings you here?" He unlocked the door to his flat and shepherded them inside.

"Great news," his mother enthused, "We're setting up a proper cult."

"A w-w-what?"

"A cult, darling. You know, a little bit like a club."

Horace shook his head, stifling a groan, "And w-w-where are you setting up this cult?"

His mother trilled a laugh, "At home, silly. We've acres of space there."

"Betw-w-ween the ears, maybe," Horace muttered.

"What was that dear?"

"Nothing mother, just w-w-wondering w-w-what the neighbours are going to make of it. How many members w-w-will this cult have?"

"Oh, there won't be too many of us," she assured him, "And anyway, Sandra from next door is going to join up as soon as she manages to get Bert out of the house."

"Sandra and Bert are splitting up?"

"Oh, yes," his mother confirmed, "I managed to persuade her to see the light. That was quite a little party the three of us had, wasn't it Starchild?"

"W-w-what!?" Horace squeaked.

His mother smiled indulgently at him, "So shy and innocent, as I said before. But Sandra - she's calling herself Jade now – was ready to be persuaded. Amazing stuff that brandy we make."

Horace was staring at his mother, horrified fascination taking over from common sense, "You're not saying that she's a… w-w-well, you know, like you?"

"Lesbian, dear? Oh, yes. Well she is now, anyway."

"Mother!" Horace protested again, "You can't just go round…" he searched for the right word, "*Seducing* the neighbours!"

"I don't see why not," she looked bewildered by her son's attitude, "And I have always rather fancied that Theresa at number eight."

"Mother! Anyw-w-way, I thought you and Maisie w-w-were, you know, an item?"

"That's the beauty of our new cult, dear," Horace's mother explained, "It's a very permissionable one."

"Permissive," he muttered absently, rolling his eyes.

"I thought you of all people, a student, would understand. I'm sure you two girls do, don't you?"

"Oh, er, yes," Stephanie agreed, stifling giggles.

"Absolutely," Harriet joined in, her shoulders quivering. "Can I get anyone a drink?"

"Not the brandy!" Horace snapped.

His mother laughed, "Don't panic, darling. I'm not here to try to prise Orchid away from you," she turned to face Harriet, "Although you would always be welcome. You too, Stephanie."

"I don't think my boyfriend would like it very much," Stephanie said.

"Mine neither judging by the steam coming out of 'is ears," Harriet added.

"Oh, well. Do let me know if you ever change your minds. And as for the drink, I'm afraid we can't stop. Lots of things to sort out. And Horace," she added, "That wasn't a very nice thing to whisper about your mother. Don't think I didn't hear you."

Horace refused to look shame-faced, "You know, mother? You never cease to amaze me."

"She is rather wonderful, isn't she?" Maisie agreed. "Anyway, Moonflower, we really must go. It's a pity you two young things didn't come home earlier. We could have had a nice cosy chat. Well, with Orchid, at least," she concluded a little frostily.

"I'm so sorry," Horace said sarcastically, "But w-w-we'd better let you go then."

Horace's mother sighed, "Men!"

"Absolutely," Harriet agreed.

"Always a nuisance," Stephanie nodded.

Harriet and Stephanie accompanied the two women as far as the front door while Horace collapsed onto the sofa. They were both giggling when they came back.

"Your mother's quite amazing," Stephanie observed.

"Don't remind me."

He and Harriet told Stephanie about their holiday plans and asked whether she would mind watering Harriet's vast collection of plants while they were away.

"No problem," she said, "And if I'm not here for any reason, Matt will be." She left them soon afterwards on the grounds that she had to make her own flat presentable for Matt when he arrived that weekend.

"I really quite like your mother," Harriet told Horace after Stephanie had departed.

"I really can't believe w-w-we're related. She w-w-was a little bit mad before, but now she seems to have turned into some sort of sex maniac!"

"And you can't believe you're related?" Harriet grinned at him mischievously, unbuttoning her blouse.

The holiday proved to be every bit as relaxing as Horace had hoped, and they extended their stay for an extra ten days after checking with Stephanie that it was okay with her. Their goodbyes to the hotel staff were reluctant, and they boarded the coach that was to take them to their flight from Nice airport with even greater reticence. Seven hours later they emerged from the Walthamstow Central railway station into typically English summer weather.

"Should've brought an umbrella with us," Harriet complained as her thin sundress absorbed the grimy rain.

"My tan's going to w-w-wash off at this rate," Horace grumbled beside her.

They ran the short distance back to Church Hill Buildings which proved to be a pointless exercise as it took Horace nearly five minutes to find their keys. They were drenched but laughing when they finally reached the sanctuary of Horace's flat.

"I'll put the coffee on," he said after they had dumped their cases in his living room. "The Crown w-w-won't be open yet."

"Good idea, H. I need something to wash away the taste of that airline food. I'll just pop over to my place to make sure everything's okay. Back in five minutes."

"All in order?" Horace asked when she returned.

Harriet shrugged, "Yeah, I guess so. Everything that should be green still is, but I'm sure something's different in my bedroom."

Horace poured the coffee, "Perhaps Stephanie moved the plants around or something?"

"Yeah, could be. I'll pop-up and see her after this," she took a mug.

Horace gathered the small heap of post from the surface of his desk and opened anything that didn't look like junk mail.

"Anything interesting?" Harriet asked.

"Not w-w-what *I* w-w-would call interesting," he replied, grimacing over one particular letter. "My mother's 'cult' is apparently up and running and she's got eight members now. She's calling it the Cult of the Natural Cycle, and she w-w-wants both of us to visit her so she can show off the range of products they've started making. I knew w-w-we shouldn't have come back."

Harriet laughed, "Cult of the Natural Cycle? Sounds a bit ominous."

"Reminds me of that Queen video you like, you know, *Fat Bottomed Girls*? Can you imagine Maisie cycling round the garden starkers?"

"I'll tell your mum you said that," Harriet threatened, laughing, "It's not nice."

Horace grinned, "Oh, so you *can* imagine it then?"

Their laughter was interrupted by a knock at their door.

"Come in, it's open," Horace called.

A moment later, Stephanie appeared in the doorway of the living room, "Hi guys," she said quietly, "I heard the laughter so I knew you were back."

Both Harriet and Horace stared at her, open-mouthed. Her normally fine features seemed to be slightly out of true. A rainbow coloured bruise covered much of the left side of her face and they could see the dark tufts of medical sutures at the corner of her mouth. Both her lips were swollen and the stitches pulled her mouth out of true as she attempted a smile, "Not such a pretty sight as usual, hey?"

"Oh my God," Harriet groaned, finally finding her voice. "What on earth 'appened? Who did it to you?" She rose and crossed the room.

Stephanie hugged her, wincing as other bruises were compressed. Tears had formed at the corners of her eyes and as she held on to Harriet, they spilled down her cheeks.

"Who w-w-was it?" Horace asked quietly, although he thought he already knew.

Stephanie, still clinging to her friend, sniffed loudly, "Matt. He… found something. Got upset."

"The fucking bastard!" Harriet snarled.

Her unusual use of an expletive seemed to shock all three of them into silence. After she regained her normal composure, she eased herself away from Stephanie, and led her to the sofa, sitting down beside her, "What on earth got 'im this upset?"

"It was my fault really," Stephanie explained after dabbing gingerly at her tears with a tissue, "I forgot about them, see?"

Harriet looked at her quizzically, "Forgot what?"

It was Horace who answered, "It w-w-was the drawings, w-w-wasn't it Steph?"

She nodded miserably as light dawned on Harriet's face, "Shit! Oh, Steph, I'm so sorry. I forgot all about them. I never thought Matt would ever come into my bedroom anyway, but I guess he did the plant watering, yeah?"

Stephanie nodded, "I'd forgotten all about them too. Asked him to cover for me when I went to visit my aunt a week or so ago. He was waiting for me when I came back. Threw them in my face and just laid into me. Called me all sorts of names – bad names – he just wouldn't stop. I tried to tell him they weren't of me but that only made it worse. He said that I couldn't possibly have seen *what* he'd thrown at me so I must have known what was on them – must have known because it *was* me. Apparently he even phoned someone at the college and found out about the art class thing. And he just wouldn't stop hitting, punching me," her voice rose to a wail as she finished her explanation. "It's all my fault!"

"No it's not," Harriet said sternly, "I hope you called the police?"

Stephanie looked away, embarrassed, "No. I was too… ashamed, I guess."

"It's probably not too late. When did it 'appen?"

Stephanie shrugged, "About a week and a half ago, I guess, but I still don't want the police involved."

"'E didn't do, you know, anything else?"

"No, thank God," Stephanie breathed a sigh of relief, "I'm not sure I could've handled that as well."

"That's a relief," Harriet agreed. She paused. "'Ang on, a week and a 'alf ago?" Stephanie nodded, "I thought you sounded a bit odd when I phoned."

"Yeah," Stephanie sniffed, "It happened the day before."

"Oh you silly cow! Why didn't you tell me what 'ad 'appened? We would 'ave been straight 'ome!"

"There wasn't much you could have done anyway. And I didn't want to spoil your holiday."

Harriet shook her head in disbelief, "After all you've done for me and H, you still don't rate us as good friends then?"

"Of course I do!" Stephanie protested, close to tears once more.

"I'm sorry," Harriet breathed, "It's just the thought of you 'ere alone after all that, and there's us 'aving a ball in France."

Stephanie smiled tearfully at her, "To tell the truth, I was really sorry I didn't tell you almost as soon as I hung up. I was scared he was going to come back."

"Where is he now?" Horace asked levelly.

The two women looked over to him and it was hard to say who was more surprised. His face looked like thunder.

"He's gone back to Durham. I checked with one of his mates up there."

"Just as well for him," Horace said, "I'm really sorry for our part in all this, Steph," he added in a more normal tone of voice. Harriet noticed that Horace hadn't stuttered once when he had spoken of Matt.

"It really isn't your fault," Steph said. She nodded at him, feeling an almost telepathic link between them. "And really, thanks for your concern. Nothing's been permanently damaged; I didn't even lose a tooth. The bruises'll fade soon enough. In fact you should have seen them a week ago!"

Horace let out a sigh, "Oh w-w-well," he smiled, "At least you'll be an ideal model for the surrealist classes."

"Orris!" Harriet protested, but Stephanie burst into laughter.

"Oh, thank God you two are back. That's the first time I've laughed since it happened."

"Sure you're okay?" Harriet asked, giving the sheepish-looking Horace a stern look.

"Yeah, positive. I went down to the college for a check-up. That's where I got the stitches," she paused and pulled her lower lip down, displaying the full extent of the damage to her mouth, causing the others to wince. "I told them I'd been mugged in the market. I don't suppose they believed me, but at least at the college they don't ask too many questions."

Harriet nodded, "Okay then. I guess you're sure. Now, 'ow about coming down to the Crown for a beer; I wouldn't mind betting you could use one?"

"I'm not really sure I want to be seen out looking like this…"

"You look better like that than Orris did as a punk, and I seem to recall 'e was proud of it at the time," Harriet said. "If anyone asks, I'll just tell them that you let one of me prize plants die when we was on 'oliday, and that was my retribution."

Stephanie laughed again, "Well, okay then. I guess I could do with a pint or two."

"I thought you w-w-was drinking vodka these days?" Horace asked.

"I am," Stephanie replied with a smile.

From The Diary of Horace Wilt

"Monday, 8th September, 1980

Got back from holiday to find poor Stephanie all beat up. Apparently Matt saw the drawings of her in Harry's bedroom when he came to water the plants and went crazy. Steph looks a real mess now and this happened ten days ago, so God knows what she looked like then! Matt was rather lucky that he'd gone back to Durham; I swear I would have killed him.

On a much lighter note, I've finally decided (thanks to tons of pressure from Harry and Steph) to take up art lessons this coming term. At least I'll have one thing to look forward to!"

3

The rest of the holiday passed without incident and Stephanie looked almost normal by the time the new term started. Despite Horace's protests, she and Harriet managed to convince him to take up the art classes and this represented the only change to the routine established during the previous college year.

During mid-October the subject of Horace and Harriet's birthdays arose. His was on the twenty second and hers the twenty eighth, so they decided to have a single celebration on the twenty fifth, the Saturday in-between.

The day before his twentieth birthday, Horace's mother paid them an unexpected visit and left him one large envelope which contained, she said, her gift to him, another containing more banknotes, and three bottles of home-made paint stripper. She also left four large packages for Harriet, instructing her not to open them until her birthday. With a final flourish she swept back out into the street, her kaftan billowing behind her.

"Well, what's in it?" Harriet asked Horace as soon as his mother had left.

"Big kid," Horace grinned, "Anyw-w-way, it's not my birthday until tomorrow."

"But she didn't make you promise not to open yours."

Still grinning, he tore open the envelope and extracted its contents.

"Well?"

Horace shrugged, "I did tell you she w-w-was w-w-weird, didn't I?" he said, handing her a single sheet of paper.

Harriet read it eagerly, but by the time she finished she was none the wiser, "It's just your mum rattling on about apartheid in South Africa and telling you to go to London zoo and ask to speak to a guy there. What's that all about?"

"Search me. And w-w-why on earth w-w-would I need to take identification with me?"

"It's all a bit mysterious, isn't it? When should we go?"

"Go?"

"Yes, go," Harriet insisted. "It's supposed to be your mother's gift to her son on his twentieth birthday. You've got to go."

"I'm not sure. This all smells very fishy to me. You know how w-w-weird she is."

"Don't be a wimp. This sounds like fun."

"I still don't see how you can use the w-w-word fun in any connection w-w-with my mother, but I suppose I should go and find out w-w-what this is all about."

"Absolutely. Let's do it now."

"But the Crown'll be open in ten minutes," Horace complained.

"You shouldn't be drinking lunchtimes during the week anyway," Harriet beamed back, "Come on, big guy. My curiosity's aroused, grab your jacket."

Reluctantly, knowing that she would simply pester him until he relented, Horace pulled on his jacket and trailed out into unseasonably warm October morning sunshine. He insisted that if they really must go on this wild goose chase then at least they would go by taxi, and they arrived at Regent's Park in less than forty minutes. He paid the driver and they made their way through the park until they reached the zoo.

After paying their entrance fees he asked the woman behind the ticket counter where he could find William Banks, the man mentioned in his mother's letter. They were handed a map with the route clearly marked and set off, Harriet almost dragging Horace behind her in her eagerness to have the mystery solved.

William Banks turned out to be an elderly man, sporting a long, white, flowing beard and London Zoo sweatshirt. He listened carefully as Horace explained his mother's message and then handed over his passport.

The old man looked at it for a second and then smiled, "Oh, right! Now I know who you are."

"And? I mean, w-w-what's this all about?"

William Banks laughed the laugh of a lifelong smoker, "All about raising awareness of apartheid in South Africa," he said, gesturing for them to follow him, "So, concerned citizens have been given the chance to adopt one of our South African animals. What you get, see, is a plaque on the side of their cage, or wherever they're kept, and you get to name the animal an' all. Next to the plaque, there's all this bumph about the apartheid business."

"Oh, er, I see," Horace said, suspiciously, "And I suppose, I'm now the proud adoptive parent of an animal, is that w-w-what you're saying?"

"That's right," William agreed happily.

"What sort is it?" Harriet asked excitedly.

"You'll soon see."

"I'm not sure I w-w-want to!"

"Don't be mean," Harriet chided, "I think it's a lovely idea. And in a good cause, too. I 'ope it's a lion or something like that."

"I doubt it," Horace sighed, looking down at her. He nearly walked straight into the back of William Banks, who had stopped and turned to face them.

"Here you go then," he gestured behind him and, in a loud voice, announced, "Master Horace Wilt, meet your adopted animal, Horace the Aardvark!"

"Horace the Aard…" Horace nearly choked as several children nearby giggled. This couldn't be happening, he thought. He looked downwards, towards where William Banks was gesturing, and, sure enough, he was face to face with his namesake. The plaque on the cage said so. "Oh bugger," he muttered.

"'E's lovely!" Harriet squealed, staring at the ugly-looking brute, "Just like you," she added, grinning at Horace.

"He's a young 'un, too," William said. "You'll have your name immortalised here for years yet."

"Somehow, I just knew you w-w-were going to say something like that."

"You can go in and pet him, if you like," William went on, oblivious to Horace's discomfort, "He's a friendly one, and they don't bite or nothing."

"Oh, can we?" Harriet pleaded as Horace tried to frame a polite refusal.

"Remind me never to have children," Horace muttered, ignoring a young boy who was trying to find out if Horace was "the guy that ELO sing about". He sighed and looked back into the small cage, "W-w-why not?"

They spent ten minutes inside, Harriet cooing over the small animal and Horace reluctantly deciding that, all in all, he was quite a nice little creature, if somewhat ugly. When they finally left the aardvark in peace, Horace read the notices outside the cage. Apparently he was a victim of the 'Adopt an Aardvark' campaign.

He was also rather grateful that his mother hadn't opted for the 'Adopt a Dik-Dik' option; Horace the Dik-Dik would have been one humiliation too far.

After Harriet had waved goodbye to her 'other Orris', they thanked William and decided to tour round the zoo for a while on the grounds that they had, after all, paid the entrance fee. They spent a long time outside the enclosure where three tigers were feeding and Horace mentioned that he absolutely adored the large cats.

"Do you like small cats as well?" Harriet asked.

"I w-w-would have loved a cat at home w-w-when I w-w-was younger, but I w-w-was afraid my mother w-w-would eat it," he replied, smiling.

"Orris! That's not very nice. Especially after she dreamed up that wonderful present for you."

"I guess it w-w-was…" he searched for the right word, "Unusual, anyw-w-way." Secretly, he had decided that he might pop back from time to time to see how his namesake was getting on.

Later, back at the flat, Harriet asked, "Where did you get to yesterday afternoon? I thought you promised to do some study work in the library after the lecture?"

"Oh, er, yes, I do seem to recall saying something like that. Must have slipped my mind," Horace replied as innocently as he could. He was already three assignments behind for this term.

"Hmm, I suppose I'd better take your word for it. But, anyway, that wasn't intended as a nag. It's just that I've got some good news – I meant to mention it last night, but it was late when you got back from the art class. 'Ow was it, by the way?"

"Er, fine." It had been the first life-class he had attended, and he could, if he had wanted to, have assured Harriet that all of Stephanie's bruises had cleared up. "W-w-what's the good news?"

231

Harriet narrowed her eyes. She always knew these days when Horace was avoiding a subject, "It's about that nude you painted last night," she grinned, "Stephanie?" she went on when she received no response.

Horace cleared his throat, "Thought I recognised her. I w-w-was right at the back of the room. W-w-what about her?"

Harriet giggled as he blushed, "If it's a good painting or drawing or whatever, I reckon we should put it in my bedroom."

Horace cleared his throat again, "Er, w-w-well, I guess w-w-we could. W-w-when it's finished, anyw-w-way. But w-w-what if Matt should come back?"

"'E won't," Harriet said. "But that's the good news. Steph's got a new boyfriend."

"Oh? First I heard of it. Who is he?"

"A guy called Alan. Apparently 'e's in your art class."

Horace thought for a moment, "Oh, yeah, Alan Wright; tall blonde guy. Never seems to mix much. W-w-well, I guess he w-w-won't be complaining about her posing, anyw-w-way."

Harriet laughed, "'Ardly. Anyway, she's gonna bring 'im to our do on Saturday, so I guess 'e'll be doing a bit of mixing."

There was something about Alan that Horace didn't like. He'd only spoken to him a couple of times, but the guy was pretty stand-offish – he didn't join any of the others in the student union after class, for instance – and he seemed to have an air of general dislike for students, despite being one himself. Perhaps, Horace thought, he was just shy, "I guess w-w-we'll see w-w-what he's like on Saturday, then."

4

Saturday arrived and Horace went over to Harriet's flat to see if she was ready for the party. He found her in her bedroom, clothes strewn all over the place.

"'Elp," she whimpered when he came in.

Horace laughed, "It's all very w-w-well changing your image, but it can be a real pain w-w-when you've got so many clothes to choose from, right?"

Harriet groaned, "You're not wrong, H. I've tried on just about everything I've got and I still can't make up my mind. What do you reckon?"

"Come as you are," Horace grinned. Harriet was naked except for a small pair of flimsy knickers.

"Very funny. Come on, though. Seriously, what do you suggest? And stop that," she added as he stood behind her and began to fondle her breasts, "We 'aven't got the time."

He reluctantly dropped his hands to her hips, "How about the short white skirt and that dark-blue silk blouse you bought the other day?" He loved the feel of Harriet's body through silk blouses.

Harriet grunted. It had been the first combination she had tried on; she had specifically bought the items for the party after all. "If you're sure?"

"Absolutely. You look w-w-wonderful in them. Of course, you look even more w-w-wonderful out of them."

She gave him a black look and quickly pulled on the clothes he had chosen. She looked at herself in the mirror and nodded. He'd made the right choice – as usual, "Okay then, I'm ready."

Horace laughed, "It's taken you two hours to choose and ten seconds to dress. Is that some sort of record?"

Harriet stuck her tongue out at him, "I guess it might be easier to let you choose in future."

"Before you get too carried aw-w-way, remember w-w-what my first choice w-w-was."

She swatted his rump, "Time enough for that later. If we don't get a move on, we'll be late for our own party."

They hurried out of the Buildings after collecting Stephanie, and arrived breathlessly at the Crown's function room just as the first of their guests were arriving.

The evening passed in a blur, drinks arriving at their table in copious quantities, and they talked themselves nearly hoarse above the background noise of their favourite music.

Alan arrived half an hour into the celebrations and immediately latched on to Stephanie's arm. Although he seemed somewhat reserved, he chatted with Harriet and Horace whenever prompted, and even posed one or two questions. Horace put his earlier reservations about the guy down to shyness. Whatever else he might be, he was certainly no Matt, and for that, both he and Harriet were grateful.

Alan left them at eleven o'clock, explaining, embarrassed, that his parents exercised a strict curfew. Horace reasoned that if his parents were that strict, then a degree of shyness and reserve were likely to go hand in hand. Alan pecked Stephanie on the cheek and said a few quick 'goodbyes' before hurrying out of the pub.

"Seems nice enough," Harriet commented to Stephanie after he had left.

"Yeah. He's quiet, but, you know? Nice. It makes a real change."

"Wh-wh-one for the better."

Stephanie beamed, "Glad you both like him. It also makes a change not to have a guy pawing me every few minutes."

"I'm not sure I'd like that," Harriet giggled.

"Not every one's a little nympho like you," Horace laughed.

Harriet pulled a face, "Any more cracks like that and I know one guy who won't be getting any for a while."

Horace grinned, "You couldn't stop yourself, let alone me."

"True," Harriet realised that she was tipsy, "I think I'm a little drunk."

"You are," Horace agreed. "A little drunk nympho."

She slapped his thigh, harder than intended, laughing as he yelped.

Stephanie grinned at the pair of them, shaking her head, "You two are terrible."

"Who's the w-w-worst?" Horace asked, pointing at Harriet who bit his finger.

"Nothing to choose. And even if there was, I wouldn't tell you. I like both of you just as much as each other."

"Or in other w-w-words, she means you," Horace told Harriet.

"That reminds me!" Stephanie exclaimed, before Harriet could tickle Horace, "I've got a birthday surprise for you both."

"Oh?" Horace asked, "I thought w-w-we told everywh-wh-one "no gifts" or anything?"

"Okay then, a thank you surprise."

"That's okay then," Harriet beamed, "And goody, I love surprises. What is it?"

"She really is just like a big kid, isn't she?" Stephanie grinned at Horace.

"Don't you start! I 'ave enough trouble with this big lug."

"Sorry, couldn't resist," Stephanie said. "Blame it on my first proper drink of the evening."

"Your first?" Horace asked. "But w-w-we put a fortune behind the bar so everywh-wh-wh-one could enjoy themselves."

"Alan's not really into that sort of thing. And I don't mind. I probably *do* drink too much anyway," she ignored Harriet's frown and hurried on. "Well, as I said, I've got a surprise for you." She set her large vodka and black on the table and picked up her handbag, rummaging through it for a moment before drawing out an envelope. "Who wants it?"

"Me!" Harriet giggled.

She took the envelope and quickly tore it open. She withdrew the contents and stared at them for a moment, her jaw dropping. Leaping to her feet, she hurried round the table and hugged Stephanie tightly. "Oh thank you, thank you, thank you!"

"Somewh-wh-one mind letting me in on the secret?"

Harriet disentangled herself from Stephanie and rushed to him, sitting herself on his lap, "Look!"

He stared down at the two tickets in her hand. A smile spread over his face, "How on earth did you manage to get hold of these?" he asked Stephanie. Harriet was holding two tickets for a Queen concert at Wembley Arena scheduled for December 9th. He had tried

236

everywhere to get tickets after hearing that his girlfriend's favourite group were going to be in London later that year, but to no avail.

"My mother," Stephanie said. "Remember back when I did your hair?"

"Yeah. But w-w-what's that got to do w-w-with Queen tickets?"

"I told you my mum was a 'sort of hairdresser', and she is," Stephanie said, "She does hair for one of the band, has done for years. She never has any problem getting tickets."

"You never told me your mum them!" Harriet said excitedly.

"I didn't realise you were that keen on Queen."

"Keen!" Horace groaned. "They're never off my record player."

Harriet rose shakily and hugged Stephanie again, "You're the best. I mean the tickets are fantastic, aren't they H?"

"Sure are," he agreed. Privately he wasn't too sure about the merits of attending a rock concert. He'd heard all sorts of stories about damage to hearing and that sort of thing.

"You'd better sit down," Horace advised, delighted by his girlfriend's joy, "And w-w-while you're at it, you'd better close your mouth, the 275 bus is due any minute."

"Er, what?" Harriet asked, returning from whichever planet her brain had disappeared to.

Horace laughed and shook his head, "Come here." He hugged her tightly as she babbled on about her 'favourite rock band in all the whole wide World', alternating those sentiments with a thousand thanks in Stephanie's direction.

5

As far as Harriet was concerned, the six weeks between their party and the concert passed as slowly as six years. On the Sunday, two days before the concert, Horace was close to despair, retreating to the Crown as soon as it opened to get away from the incessant, excited babbling that trailed him around his flat.

"I'll be glad w-w-when it's all over," he told Flat-Foot Fred, sipping his first Guinness.

"The concert?"

Horace couldn't believe there was anyone left in London who didn't know that he and Harriet were going to see Queen the following week, "Absolutely."

"Don't hold with 'em meself," Fred said, "All that loud noise. Then there's the drugs and stuff."

Horace nodded, he still wasn't entirely happy with the idea himself. He'd said as much to Harriet in a desperate attempt to reduce her level of enthusiasm, but she had just accused him of being wimpish and not wanting to try anything new. She had even compared his attitude with that of Stephanie's boyfriend, Alan, who, it was becoming clear, would never earn the title Mr Personality. Horace didn't know what Stephanie saw in him.

He took his pint to a nearby table and spread out his Sunday Times. Unusually, he checked the Reviews section and found a review of Queen's first London concert the previous evening. If the reviewer was anything to go by, he might just enjoy it after all. Harriet, as she had promised, didn't arrive until one o'clock.

238

"Only fifty-four hours to go now," she told Horace by way of greeting.

He groaned, "Any chance of giving it a rest for a w-w-while?"

Harriet stuck out her tongue, "Oh alright then. Just one last thing, though. I don't reckon I'm gonna be able to sleep tomorrow night."

"If you don't, you'll probably doze off during the concert," Horace said, resigned to another few minutes of Queen-mania.

"No chance," Harriet sipped her vodka and black. "I'm gonna 'ave loads to drink tonight and sleep most of tomorrow. That way, if I really can't sleep tomorrow night, it won't matter too much, will it?"

Horace raised an eyebrow, "Sleep most of a Monday? You, my little sw-w-wot? Actually, planning to miss a lecture?"

She swatted his thigh playfully, "Unlike some students I could mention," she stared pointedly, "I'm not weeks behind with my assignments."

"I got good marks on my thesis."

Harriet grunted, "I keep telling you, you can't rely on just the theses."

"Yes, you *do* keep telling me," Horace grumbled, secretly happy that Queen hadn't been mentioned for at least a minute.

"Somebody's got to remind you," Harriet grinned. "You seem to spend more time painting ladies with no clothes on than you do on business studies."

"There's only two ladies," Horace said, "And I'm not sure either of you could really be termed 'ladies'."

Harriet swatted his thigh again, "I'll tell Steph."

"Tell me what?" Stephanie asked as she arrived at their table.

"Michelangelo 'ere don't reckon that we qualify as ladies," Harriet said smugly as Horace blushed.

"Not nice, H," Stephanie scolded, still smiling. "Retract that scandalous statement or I won't let you paint me anymore."

"You have to pose at the classes anyw-w-way," Horace muttered.

"I meant at home," Stephanie grinned at his discomfort. "After all, you did say that you wanted to try a composition with the two of us in it," she indicated Harriet.

"Yeah, you did say that," Harriet unnecessarily reminded him.

Horace blushed harder. "Er, yes, w-w-well..."

"I think it's a great idea, don't you Harry?" Stephanie asked, the pair of them intent on getting as much mileage from this as possible.

"Definitely, Steph. I remember thinking when the big guy 'ere said that the contrasts in our shapes and sizes was intriguing that 'e was dead right."

"Me too. I'm really looking forward to this."

Horace cleared his throat, "How long to the concert now, Harry?"

6

That evening, Harriet kept her promise about the drinking and they left the Crown after one in the morning, Horace almost carrying the giggling Harriet all the way back to Church Hill Buildings. At least, he sighed to himself, she was in no state to keep wittering on about Queen.

He took her into his own bedroom and sat her on the edge of his bed before easing her clothes off. As he took off the last item, her right sock, she collapsed backwards across the duvet, giggling quietly. He stood and stared down at her naked form, feeling a stirring in his groin; her perfect little figure never failed to make him, or rather, his ferret, respond. He realised that she had stopped giggling and was staring up at him.

"What're you thinking?" she smiled, "Ash – *as* – if I can't guess?"

"Just how lovely you are."

"That's nice," she yawned, "I think I could sleep for a week."

Horace laughed, "You'd miss the concert."

"Sorry about that," she said, her smile slipping.

"Er, w-w-what?"

"About rabbiting on about it."

"Don't be. And now, you'd better get some sleep. I promise I w-w-won't w-w-wake you in the morning."

"You're great, you know that?"

Horace smiled, "You too. Now, climb in and snuggle down. See you w-w-when I get home tomorrow."

Harriet struggled to sit up and awkwardly pulled the duvet out from under her. Eventually satisfied, she lay back on the bed, her long blonde hair cascading over the pillow. She pulled the duvet up to her chin and turned onto her side, closing her eyes. "Night, H," she whispered, "Love you."

"Love you too." He turned off the lights and left the room, a contented smile on his face.

He slept that night on the sofa, not wishing to disturb Harriet (although privately doubting that a nuclear strike would wake her) and, for a change, left for college in the morning. The Red Setter hassled him after the lecture but after promising that he would have at least two assignments ready the following week, the last of the term, he managed to escape to the Crown.

He got back to his flat at three o'clock and went straight into his bedroom. Harriet was yawning, only just awake.

"Hiya, Harry. How are you feeling?"

She sat up and stretched. A surprised look came over her features, "Believe it or not, I feel absolutely fantastic!"

"You look it, too," he grinned.

"Ta. Now, where's me coffee?"

He groaned and retreated to the kitchen and filled the machine. He heard Harriet go into the bathroom and, a couple of minutes later, the sound of the toilet flushing. He had expected her to come through to the kitchen, but she clearly wasn't ready to join the world of the upright yet. He carried her coffee through to the bedroom and set it on the bedside table. Harriet had retreated back under the cover of the duvet.

"Going to stay there a w-w-while longer?"

242

She smiled lazily up at him, "Maybe just half an hour. I reckon it's the most comfortable place to thank you for the coffee." She pulled back the duvet, a mischievous grin on her face.

The coffee was cold by the time Harriet's gratitude had been sated and Horace was dispatched back to the kitchen for more. He prised his t-shirt from under Harriet where it had somehow got lodged and pulled it over his head as he left the room. "Oh yuck!" he moaned in the doorway.

"What's up?"

"W-w-well, you know how you moan about getting to sleep on the w-w-wet patch?" he asked, grimacing.

"Yeah, so what?"

"You've never suffered until you've had to w-w-wear it!" He quickly pulled off the garment and left her giggling.

7

They went to the Crown early that evening and returned relatively early as well, picking up a takeaway on their way back.

"Reckon you'll sleep?" Horace asked Harriet after they finished the last of the chapattis.

Harriet yawned, surprising herself, "Yeah, I guess I might."

Ten minutes later they were snuggled together in Horace's bed, and Horace was already fast asleep. Harriet dozed for a few hours, waking at six in the morning – an hour she had only seen recently when she'd been on her way *to* bed. Being careful not to disturb Horace, she slipped out of the bed and padded, naked, into the kitchen.

She closed the door behind her so that the noise of the coffee machine wouldn't disturb Horace, and pulled on her Garfield t-shirt. She filled the machine and switched it on, already feeling a hoard of butterflies rampaging in her stomach at the thought of the concert later that day. She looked around for something to divert her attention.

Horace's battered old radio stood to one side of the sink and she reached over and switched it on. She groaned aloud as the thumping bass line of *Another One Bites The Dust*, Queen's most recent hit, echoed around the room. She almost switched it off as the DJ's voice faded in over the last few bars.

'And that's the number one in America this week,' his voice, Harriet thought sounded very downbeat. Perhaps he didn't like Queen very much?

'And of course,' the DJ went on, *'For anyone who hasn't heard yet, America is the scene of one of the saddest stories to hit rock*

music in years. Over to our news desk for more information.' His voice faded out and a short jingle announced that this was Capital News.

'Sad indeed,' the newsreader intoned. Harriet's heart began to flutter a little. *'In the most tragic fashion, the life of John Lennon was brutally ended last night outside his apartment in New York. The thirty-nine year old former Beatle was returning to the Dakota building when he was accosted by a young man asking for an autograph. As Lennon complied with the young man's request, the man drew a gun and fired it at Lennon from point blank range. Lennon died soon after....'*

The newsreaders voice seemed to fade into the background as the shock of what she had heard hit Harriet with the force of a runaway truck. Surely she couldn't have heard right, could she? She forced herself to return her attention to the sombre tones of the newsreader.

'.... Harrison said he was totally devastated by the news. Police have arrested Lennon's murderer and he is currently being questioned....'

It was true then. Harriet was surprised to find her hands shaking as she poured herself a mug of coffee. Trying desperately to believe that she was still asleep, that this was just a dream and that John Lennon, one of Horace's musical heroes, was still alive and living his unconventional lifestyle in America, she slopped hot coffee over her wrist. The pain let her know as much as anything else that this was no dream.

"It can't be true!" she whispered aloud, much as she had as a small child when their family's pet cat had been run over in the street outside their home. She had thought that, maybe, if she just wished hard enough, the truth would go away; be replaced by the version of things that *she* wanted. "It just can't be true," she repeated, louder as the shock and surprise pressed home.

"W-w-what can't be?" Horace yawned in the doorway.

"S-s-sorry," she stammered. "I didn't see you there."

245

Horace yawned again and tried to focus his sleep-filled gaze on Harriet, "Heard you yell out," he mumbled.

It was probably as she spilt the coffee, Harriet thought, but she didn't realise that she had made any noise, "S-s-sorry…" she began again before a lump in her throat forced her to stop.

"'S alright," Horace tried to smile.

"No it's not!" Harriet wailed, crossing quickly to him and holding him tightly, tears now pouring from her eyes.

Horace tried to pull back and look at her when he felt her hot tears on his chest, "W-w-what's up?"

"It's John Lennon," Harriet managed through her sobs.

"W-w-what about him?" Horace asked her gently. He could feel a sense of dread beginning to overwhelm him, dark wings of fear battering at the inside of his skull.

Harriet's sobbing increased. It was all Horace could do to make out the words 'dead' and 'murdered'. "Oh no…" he muttered, his mind racing. Like Harriet before him he uttered the words that should mend everything but never, ever do. "It can't be true."

They held each other tightly in the kitchen doorway for what seemed like an eternity. In the background, the radio repeated its tragic story a couple more times before they finally parted, sitting mutely at the small table in the kitchen.

"I'm so sorry," Harriet sniffed after a few minutes.

"Me too," Horace said quietly.

"I mean, I've been going on and on about Queen these last few weeks and then one of your heroes goes and dies like that!"

"Hey, don't w-w-worry," he said, his mind still numb from the shock, "It's hardly your fault is it?"

"We can't go to the concert now can we?" she asked miserably.

He looked at her in surprise, "Can't? Of course w-w-we can! W-w-we must. To celebrate music if nothing else."

Harriet looked up, her tears subsiding, "Are you sure?"

"It's the only thing *to* do. I've never seen John Lennon live in concert and now I'll…" his voice hitched, "N-n-never be able to. You've got to see these guys w-w-while you can," he tried to smile.

Harriet rose and then settled on his lap. The first light of dawn was streaming through the windows before either of them moved.

8

In the Crown where they ate a lunch that neither of them really fancied, the talk was of nothing else but Lennon's murder, and it was a relief when they finally left and made their way back to the flats.

At six, Horace telephoned for a taxi and they joined the milling throng outside Wembley Arena an hour later. Although there was a buzz of excitement in the air, there was a muted quality to it. Fifteen thousand music lovers were together to share in the experience of hearing their heroes perform live. They were also there to mourn a tragic loss.

The concert started an hour late and by then the excitement had mounted to fever pitch. As the first chords crashed through the speakers, the entire Arena seemed to roar; people flew from their seats cheering, whistling and clapping. The stage, dark until that point, suddenly lit up as bank upon bank of coloured lights burst into brilliant life.

Horace and Harriet were seated as close to the stage as it was possible to get, and they joined the thousands of others on their feet, yelling for all they were worth.

The music swelled and Horace's earlier fears dissolved. This was music.

The first few tracks were frenetic, upbeat numbers that had the entire crowd keeping time with their feet, hands and even the plastic seats. After the fourth track, every light in the Arena went out, leaving them all in total, inky darkness. As one, the crowd seemed to hold its breath. After a few moments, Horace began to whisper to Harriet, asking her if she knew what was going on, when a single, piercingly bright white spotlight lit a small circle on the centre of the stage.

Freddie Mercury stood within its glow and looking up he started to sing very gently. '*Imagine there's no heaven....*'

The audience, released now from those long moments where time had seemed suspended let out a roar that must surely have been heard across the entire capital. Mercury's voice went silent as the crowd cheered and cheered.

Horace could feel every single hair on his body erect, electricity coursing across his skin. He looked round and every face he saw held similar expressions; a cross between pure joy and the most terrible mental agony. Most people that he could see close by him had tears coursing down their faces and he suddenly realised that he, too, was crying. He looked at the stage, where Freddie Mercury was standing motionless and saw the bright sparkle of the great singer's tears. He glanced at Harriet and she seemed to feel his gaze. She turned towards him, her own eyes full of tears, and smiled, shaking her head.

Horace had heard the term 'mass-hysteria'. He had now witnessed it first hand, and he doubted he would ever be able to describe that feeling to anyone else.

After two, five, maybe even ten minutes, Freddie Mercury's voice rose once more, and the entire crowd joined him in a momentous tribute to one of the greatest musicians of his, or any other era.

Whatever had happened after Freddie had started the first line of *Imagine*, it seemed to act as some form of catharsis and the rest of concert became a joyous celebration. After their third encore, the strains of *God Save The Queen* announced that the entertainment was finally over.

House lights went up and the crowd, many still singing and cheering, began to make their way out of the stadium. A steward had told Horace and Harriet that they should wait in their seats until someone came and saw them and ten minutes after the group had left the stage, a young woman with a clipboard sidled along the row of seats and introduced herself.

"Hi guys, I'm Lynn and I'm here to present the young lady – Harriet, is it? – with some goodies. As long as you've got your passes, anyway."

Horace realised that his hearing capacity had dropped noticeably. He wondered for a moment whether this might be a permanent effect and then decided he didn't care, "Hi," he replied, his voice hoarse, "I'm Horace and this is Harriet. Here are the passes." He had been holding on tightly to them ever since they arrived.

"That's great," Lynn said, taking the passes and then handing them back, "I guess you"ll want these as souvenirs too, yeah?"

"Oh, yeah," Harriet nodded firmly, taking them.

"Okay, then. Here you go." Lynn had handed Harriet a bulging bag.

Horace took Harriet's hand and felt her trembling almost violently, "Promise you w-w-won't pass out on me?"

Harriet laughed nervously, "No chance, big guy. This is amazing."

An older woman joined them then who neither Horace nor Harriet had noticed before. It was clear who she was though, the likeness between herself and her daughter very close indeed.

"You must be Mrs Jameson," Harriet smiled at her.

"Sheila, please. And you two must be Steph's best friends."

Horace nodded, "Thanks ever so much for helping organise this," he said, sincerely.

She waved away his and Harriet's gratitude, "It's nothing. And besides, it sounds as if you're very good friends with my Steph."

"We are," Harriet agreed. She suddenly yawned, surprising herself. "Oh, excuse me! I think maybe all the excitement's catching up on me."

"It is half past midnight," Horace agreed, "I suppose w-w-we'd better make a move. I'll call a cab. W-w-we're only going as far as W-w-walthamstow."

"Nonsense," Sheila said, "Stephs insisted I organise a final little treat and I'll sort out a driver for you right now." Ignoring their half-hearted protests she scurried off with Lynn now in tow.

Harriet called her thanks after them, then peeked inside the bulging bag. It was crammed full of T-shirts, sweatshirts, records and photographs. Her jaw came extremely close to hitting the floor, "Oh this is just so wonderful."

Sheila returned and told them that Tom, one of the band's personal drivers, was waiting for them outside in the 'big white job'. She also warned them that there were thirty or forty autograph hunters out the back and that they should go straight to the car or risk getting mobbed.

After another round of 'thank yous', they were led to large doors at the very back of the Arena. Harriet offered another half-dozen exclamations of gratitude and, taking Horace's hand, they sprinted into the night. The 'big white job' turned out to be a Rolls Royce, its windows darkly tinted, and they were both grateful to dive into the back of the vehicle, shutting out the cheers and camera flashes.

"Where to, guys?" the driver, Tom, he told them, asked them when they had managed to edge through the press of the crowd.

"Walthamstow, please," Harriet replied, happily.

Tom nodded and switched on a cassette player. The unmistakable sound of Queen filled the car and Harriet grinned at Horace, "What a night!"

Horace grinned back, "The best."

"There's champagne in the fridge in front of you," Tom told them as they rolled almost silently through the Wembley streets, "Help yourselves."

"W-w-why not? Thanks."

A few minutes later, something that had been puzzling Harriet became clear. "Tom," she began, "I've never heard some of these tracks before. Are they from a new album or something?"

Tom laughed, "Nah. The guv'nor's a bit of a perfectionist, if you know what I mean? These are some of the studio stuff that never made it onto the albums." He leant forward and switched off the tape player, ejecting the cassette. "If you promise not to copy this and hawk it round the markets, you can have it," he offered, holding the cassette up.

"Really?"

Tom nodded, "If you promise."

"I promise," Harriet said firmly.

"She does," Horace added.

"There you go then," Tom grinned at Harriet in the rear-view mirror.

Harriet took the cassette from him, reverentially, and stared at it in awe, "Oh, thanks," she whispered.

"No problem."

"Any more nice surprises tonight and I think I'll just float away," Harriet sighed.

They reached their flats all too soon, and thanked Tom profusely before reluctantly climbing from the comfort of the Roller. They were surprised by three quick flashes and looked round to see Stephanie holding a camera and grinning at them from the doorway.

"Hiya, guys," she called, "Mum called and said you were on your way back, so I thought I'd capture it for you on film."

They waved goodbye to Tom and followed Stephanie up the stairs.

"Wanna tell me all about it?" Stephanie asked when they reached the first landing.

Two hours later, yawning heavily, she excused herself and made her way up to her own flat.

From The Diary of Horace Wilt

"Wednesday, 10th December, 1980

DD,

The Queen concert yesterday was the most amazing thing I have ever seen in my life. I'll never, ever forget Freddie Mercury singing Imagine, *and the presents Harriet got after the show were out of this world. Harry's been sleeping pretty much ever since, the poor little thing. She must have played the tape Freddie's driver gave her two dozen times already.*

I was wrong to worry about the dangers of rock concerts - they're just so unbelievably great! Off now to get a Standard *and see if there's any more coming up soon!"*

9

The Queen experience turned Horace into a concert animal and he spent most weekends scouring the newspapers to see who was performing where, sometimes attending two or three concerts in a single week. By March, even Harriet, the music lover, was beginning to tire of the constant round.

"Oh, not again," she moaned one Monday evening in her flat when Horace began extolling the virtues of yet another forthcoming event.

"I thought you liked concerts?"

"Moderation in everything. And anyway, you've got at least four assignments to finish. You don't 'ave time for all these concerts."

Horace groaned, "Please don't nag. I've already told you that I'll get round to them soon."

"Yeah, yeah." Harriet gave him a contemptuous look and rose from the sofa, "I'm off to bed. Go and do something useful, like a bit of course work, okay?"

"Can't do that in bed," Horace grinned.

Harriet stared at him. "I know," she said, no humour in her voice. She turned and marched into her bedroom, pointedly closing the door firmly behind her.

Horace stared at the closed door, not unduly surprised. This sort of thing was happening more and more often. He sighed and got to his feet, "Bugger," he muttered and left Harriet's flat for the relative warmth of his own rooms.

The following weekend Harriet told him that she had been asked to go and visit her family over the Easter holiday and that she had decided to take up their offer.

"How long w-w-will you be gone?" Horace asked, not bothering to hide either his disappointment or disapproval.

"Just the weekend, Friday to Tuesday."

"I'll miss you," Horace said, "And that's a very long w-w-weekend."

"Go to a concert or something," Harriet snapped.

The fateful day arrived far too soon for Horace's liking, his suggestion that she could at least come back to the flat each night having had no impact on Harriet's decision.

"It'll do us good," she reasoned. "We've virtually been living in each other's pockets for the last eighteen months."

"Seventeen. And anyw-w-way, I *like* living in your pocket."
"Well I for one need a bit of space for a couple of days."

"Call me every day then?"

"It's supposed to be a bit of a break, you know?" she explained, much as she would to a child.

Horace, much as a child would, sulked for the rest of the day.

Harriet knocked on the door of his flat at five, a small suitcase in hand. "I'll see you Tuesday," she said when he opened the door.

"Are you sure you w-w-won't change your mind?"

"Oh, for goodness' sake! 'Aven't you worked it out yet? It's just this sort of behaviour that makes me *want* to get away for a while."

Horace shook his head. He was all out of ideas, "See you Tuesday then."

Harriet sighed, letting the tension out, "Yeah, big guy. See you then." She reached up and kissed him briefly. "I gotta go. Brenda's due to pick me up any minute."

Horace just nodded and, shrugging, she turned and made for the stairs. He stood there, listening to her footfalls. "I love you," he called as she reached the bottom of the flight. Harriet said something in reply, but Horace couldn't hear it. Sighing deeply, he turned and went back into his flat to get his jacket.

Eight hours later, he returned from the Crown, drunker than usual and feeling extremely maudlin. He slept fitfully and didn't rise until ten on the Saturday morning, when the telephone began to ring.

He dashed through to his living room and snatched the receiver up, "Hi. I've been missing you!"

"Really?"

At first Horace couldn't place the voice. Finally the penny dropped, "Oh, it's you, Alan."

"Charming," Alan muttered.

"Sorry. It's just that I w-w-was expecting somewh-wh-one else."

"Whatever. I was just calling to see if you were going to be at that pub lunchtime."

Horace looked at the receiver, puzzled. Was he hearing the teetotal Alan right? "The Crown, do you mean?"

"That's the only place you ever drink, isn't it?" he replied testily.

"Guess so. And, yeah, I probably w-w-will be there."

"About one o'clock?"

Horace checked his watch, "Yeah, I'll be there. W-w-what's this all about?"

Alan snorted, "I'll tell you when I see you. Later," he finished, and hung up.

Horace replaced the receiver and made his puzzled way into the kitchen. Oh, well, he shrugged to himself; he had been planning on being there for the duration anyway.

In the event, Horace arrived at the Crown just as Iain McHay, the manager, was opening the back doors.

"Early for a Saturday," he commented.

"Nothing else to do," Horace trailed Iain into the bar.

He settled himself down with *The Times* and a pint of Guinness. He guessed that he really should take the drink a bit easy after his heavy session the previous night, but somehow, without Harriet around, the little resolve he did have was weakened still further. By the time Alan Wright arrived Horace was feeling distinctly light-headed.

"Hiya, Alan," Horace called when he saw the young man crossing the bar towards him.

Alan frowned and nodded a curt greeting, "Hello, Horace."

"W-w-what can I get you?" Horace asked, draining his pint.

Alan shrugged, a look of distaste on his face, "An orange juice, please. No ice."

Horace made his way, a little unsteadily, to the bar. He returned a couple of minutes later, setting Alan's orange juice in front of him and slopping some of the Guinness onto the *Review* section of the newspaper as he re-took his own seat.

"So w-w-what brings you here?" Horace asked, "Meeting Steph?"

"Stephanie," Alan corrected, "And no. I was just wondering how well you know her."

"Steph?" Horace asked, taken by surprise. "W-w-well, she is our neighbour. And, let's face it, I've seen quite a lot of her at the art classes." He grinned.

"Please don't talk about her like that. And I'm more interested in what you know of her... well, social habits."

"I don't follow you."

Alan took a deep breath. This was clearly not going to plan. "Well, for instance, does she smoke? You know, drugs?"

Horace looked quizzically at the earnest young man sitting opposite him, "Don't you know?"

"She *says* she doesn't, but I'm not one hundred percent positive."

"You don't trust her, then?" Horace's tone became more serious.

"It's hard to trust anyone," Alan shrugged. "What about drinking; does she drink?"

"Only fish don't drink," Horace said levelly. "I really don't see w-w-what this has to do w-w-with me."

"You're her friends, right? You and Harriet? I just need to know if she's the right sort of woman for me. You'd know things about her that I don't."

Horace was beginning to lose his temper, "You're trying to employ me as a spy, then?"

"I wouldn't put it quite like that..."

"So, anyw-w-way, how do you know that you can trust *me*? Trust w-w-what I say?" Horace pressed him. "My mother's alw-w-ways saying you can never trust a man w-w-with testicles."

"You're Horace. Everyone *knows* you're trustworthy. From what I hear, you're not even capable of deceiving people; far too… well, *soft* to do that sort of thing."

Horace tried to keep both his amazement and anger in check. "A trustw-w-worthy and soft spy?"

"I know it doesn't sound too good when it's said like that, but, well, basically, yes."

"W-w-why not ask Harriet?"

Alan smiled, the first time since he'd entered the pub, "Well, clearly, Harriet and Stephanie are both females. They do tend to hold onto their little secrets, women, don't they? I mean you've at least already told me that Stephanie drinks; it's because you're male. No secrets between men, right?"

"Oh yes," Horace agreed, hoping that the level of sarcasm wasn't too obvious. He nodded to himself. He paused to drain half of the pint of Guinness. Then he sighed deeply – it was, after all, a waste of good beer, but what the hell? He stood up and stepped around to Alan's side, leaning forward as if to whisper in his ear.

When Alan tilted his head obligingly to one side, Horace poured the remaining half pint of Guinness over it. "You are a self-righteous little prick," he said, reasonably. "Now, please leave me in peace."

Alan gasped as the cold, dark liquid coursed over him, "What the…" He stared up, dumbstruck, Guinness staining his shirt and pooling in his lap.

"Bit of an accident here Fred," Horace called over to the bar, "I think this guy's had enough."

Flat-Foot Fred appeared at a trot, "What's all the fuss?"

Horace explained that the young man had bumped into him and made him spill his beer. Alan, still staring in amazement said nothing. He still hadn't said a word as Fred led him out of the bar.

"Kids today, huh?" Horace grinned at Fred as he ordered another Guinness. He was feeling rather pleased with himself.

The rest of the Saturday passed in a blur for Horace and he was almost surprised to find himself back in his flat when he woke the next morning, his head full of molten lead and his stomach of sulphuric acid. He groaned his way through to the kitchen and set the coffee machine gurgling in sympathy with his belly.

A shower, four Paracetamol and three mugs of coffee later, he was ready to face the world. He bought the *Sunday Times* and strolled to the Crown, enjoying the unseasonably early warmth of a fine Spring morning. He was now almost halfway through the enforced separation.

Bryan Ferry was whistling his way through *Jealous Guy* when Horace settled himself with his pint and paper and, by coincidence, was whistling it once more when he left, three hours and seven pints later. He made his way back to the flat after picking up yet another takeaway and mooched around for the duration of the afternoon, glancing at the stubbornly silent telephone every few minutes. When it had still not uttered a single noise by six o'clock, Horace decided that he might as well return to the Crown.

Like the previous two days, the consumption of large quantities of alcohol helped him forget about his separation and he was whistling happily to himself as made his slow way back to the flat at eleven, his progress hampered by his inability to walk in a straight line.

He fumbled the key into the downstairs door and made his way slowly and carefully up towards his flat. As he approached the top of the stairs, a noise slowed his progress even further; it sounded for all the world as if there was someone very miserable just a few feet away – he was sure he could hear sobbing. Taking a deep breath, suddenly scared that it might be Harriet, he forced himself onwards.

Stephanie was sitting at the foot of the stairs opposite him wrapped in a dressing gown, tissues clasped to her face. She didn't appear to have heard Horace's cautious approach.

"Stephanie?"

She raised her head slowly and Horace stared at her, horrified. Her hair was a tangled mess and her eyes were like some sort of poor imitation of Alice Cooper's; mascara streaked haphazardly in all directions. The tissues she had been holding to her face fell away as her hand dropped into her lap, and he could see lipstick smeared along her left jaw.

"Horace?"

She was drunk, Horace realised, and clearly distressed. "Yes, it's me," he tried to smile. He crossed the landing and crouched in front of her. "W-w-what's wrong? W-w-what's happened, Steph? Are you hurt?"

Stephanie struggled to focus on Horace's face, "Not hurt," she managed at last and then burst into tears.

In normal circumstances, Horace would have been at a complete loss; not knowing how to respond, but a combination of alcohol and the fact that Stephanie was his friend – one of his few friends – cleared his mind. He sat beside her, putting an arm around her heaving shoulders and hugged her tightly. He whispered comforting words to her, words that he could not remember later and which probably didn't matter anyway; any soothing words would have done. She buried her head under his chin, her tears dampening the front of his shirt, and slowly, very slowly, her sobbing subsided.

When Horace felt that Stephanie was under control, he gently pulled her to her feet and, taking her arm, led her into his flat. He was making a monumental effort to sober himself up, wondering if this was a reversal of the incident the previous summer when Stephanie had found *him* sitting, drunk and miserable, on the landing. He guided her onto the sofa, pulling the dressing gown she was wearing tighter around her; partly for the sake of modesty and partly for the sake of the comfort the feel of it might give her. "Settle here for a minute," he said gently, "I'll get some coffee on."

He checked on her constantly while he waited for the coffee machine, watched her sitting in his living room, her gaze almost vacant, the occasional tear running through the ravaged make-up. He brought them two mugs of coffee, adding some cold water to Stephanie's so that she could drink it as soon as possible. "Drink this. It'll make you feel better." He sat beside her in case she was going to drop the mug.

Stephanie seemed to act on auto-pilot, sipping at the drink whenever Horace prompted her. When she had drained the last of it, he took the mug from her and set it on the coffee table. "How are you feeling now?"

Stephanie struggled with her focus for a minute and finally settled her eyes on Horace's. She tried a brave smile, "Think better... think I'm a bit better."

"Ready to tell me w-w-what's wrong?"

Stephanie's eyes began to fill with tears and she reached out for him, burying her head once more on his shoulder, "It's Alan," she wailed.

"W-w-what's he done?"

At first Horace thought that she wasn't going to answer, but then the story come pouring out of her, her words a little slurred, muffled in Horace's shirt. Apparently, Alan had called on Stephanie the previous night and had started accusing her of binge drinking behind his back, how she seemed to revel in showing herself off (echoes of Matt, there) how she kept bad company. She had protested and he had left in a vile temper, saying that he would be back the next day, today, to talk to her again. She had decided to try to appease him by dressing nicely, almost provocatively, doing her hair, taking time with her make-up. He'd arrived earlier that evening, taken one look at her and began to lay into her once more; not like Matt before him, but with words. He had called her a slut, a lush, a fool. Stephanie didn't know which hurt the most.

Horace was glad that Stephanie couldn't see his face as she told her story; he could remember only too well Alan's appearance in the Crown the previous afternoon, and he felt a horrible sense of responsibility settling over him.

"Oh, Steph," he sighed when she had run out of words, "I'm so sorry." He hugged her harder, "I think maybe this is my fault."

"Of course it isn't," Stephanie protested feebly, miserably.

"I saw Alan yesterday," Horace explained, still holding her tightly so that she couldn't see the shame written on his face. "He w-w-was… asking questions about you. Personal stuff. I told him to get lost, poured a drink over him. I might even have said something about drinking; I think I probably did."

Stephanie struggled out of his grasp, sitting upright and struggling once more to focus on him, "What?"

Horace told her, as best as he could remember, all that had happened, his eyes locked on his lap. When he had finished, he looked up at her as she swayed beside him, "So, you see, I'm really sorry."

Stephanie stared at him for a moment more, "What a pig."

"I know. I'm really, really sorry Steph... Stephanie."

To his amazement, she laughed, "Not you, shilly… silly. Him. Alan, the pig."

Horace looked up at her again, surprise written all over his features, "Him?"

Stephanie nodded, almost swaying onto the carpet as she did so, "Yeah, him. Did you really pour a drink over him?"

Horace smiled at the memory, slightly shame-faced, "'Fraid so."

Stephanie gave another laugh, despite fresh tears forming in her eyes, "I'd love to have seen that. And it's definitely not you who should be shorry... sorry, it's me. There just seems to be something wrong with me. All the guys I end up wiv, end up with... I mean, end up thinking I'm awful, some kinda tart..." she trailed off as more tears spilled down her cheeks.

"Oh no, Steph! You're not. You're nothing like that."

"What is it about me? What's wrong with me?"

Horace reached out for her and pulled her to him, holding her tightly, stroking her hair, "There's absolutely nothing wrong w-w-with you. You're lovely. Beautiful and kind and w-w-witty. You've just been unlucky w-w-with these last two guys."

She couldn't be pacified that easily, "Yeah, s-s-sure. Beautiful, yeah. Even you prefer Harriet's looks-" she stopped suddenly. "Oh, I'm so sorry, H. I didn't mean that. You see? I'm horrible."

Horace hugged her even tighter, "You're not. And you *are* beautiful. Harry's my first girlfriend, remember? Yes she's lovely, but you're beautiful. I mean it," he finished, gently but firmly.

"Really?" Stephanie asked in a small pathetic voice.

Horace manoeuvred her back so that she could focus on his eyes, "Yes, really," he smiled and a blush appeared on his cheeks, "Sometimes it's difficult to hold the brush or the pencil steady in the art classes w-w-when you're posing, you know? Hell, sometimes it's difficult to stand close to the easel!"

Stephanie paused a moment, trying to process the information, then laughed, "Oh, Horace, you're wonderful." She hugged him tightly, "Why couldn't I have got to you before Harry, huh?" She was crying again, but softly now.

Horace shook his head and hugged her back. They sat that way for a few minutes, Horace listening as her quiet sobs gradually petered out, feeling her breathing slow. His own consumption of alcohol was beginning to catch up with him and he could feel his eyes growing heavy, "Steph?" he whispered.

She had been on the verge of sleep, "Yeah?"

"I think I'd better get you upstairs to your bed. I reckon you could do w-w-with a good sleep."

She stiffened in his grasp, "I… I don't want to be alone," she whimpered. "Can I sleep here? On the sofa? That flat up there seems to be full of horrible memories at the moment."

Horace could well believe it, "Of course you can. You can have the bed; you'll sleep better there." Stephanie began to protest, but he quietened her, stroking her hair and telling her that everything would be better in the morning.

When she finally acquiesced, he led her through to the bedroom. He stood her by the dressing table and turned back the duvet when he was sure she wouldn't fall over. She let him sit her on the edge of the bed and he left her for a moment, his full bladder making its presence felt. When he returned from the bathroom, she had taken off her dressing gown and was curled on her side under the covers, facing the door.

"Thanks, H," she whispered.

"It's no problem. Good night." He made to turn off the bedside lamp. Stephanie stopped him.

"Please don't. Sounds silly, but whenever I'm upset, I really hate the dark."

"Okay," Horace smiled. "If you need anything, just yell, all right?"

"Thanks. Good night, H."

Horace kissed the top of her head and left her to sleep off her misery and the drink.

He stripped off in the living room, but then decided that he'd better keep on his boxers. If Stephanie did need anything in the night, he didn't think that his naked form would be the ideal sight to confront her with. He climbed into the sleeping bag he had laid out on the sofa and settled his head on a makeshift pillow of cushions.

He had thought that he would be asleep in seconds, but he was still tossing and turning when he heard sounds from the bedroom. Stilling himself he listened hard; Stephanie was sobbing quietly and the sound sent a wave of pure misery through him. He could feel a lump forming in his throat; Stephanie of all people didn't deserve that sort of anguish.

Shaking his head, he rose and padded through to the dimly lit bedroom. "Steph?" he called softly.

Stephanie had rolled onto her other side and now rolled back so that she could see him, "I'm sorry, H," she said, "I didn't mean to disturb you."

He crossed to the bed and sat on its edge, "Don't be silly," he tried a smile, stroking her hair, "I can't bear the thought of you so miserable."

For some reason that seemed to bring more tears, "S-s-sorry," Stephanie hiccupped. "Horace…" she began, then stopped.

"W-w-what?"

"Please… will you hold me? I feel so lonely."

"Of course."

He rose, meaning to make for the other side of the bed where he could lie on the unoccupied expanse of duvet, but Stephanie gave a shake of her head. She scooted backwards, making room for him and then held the duvet up so that he could climb underneath it, with her, "Please?"

Horace couldn't help but stare for a moment at her naked form. This probably wasn't the greatest idea ever, but he simply couldn't refuse her. He turned and climbed into the bed, facing her.

"Thank you," she whispered and moved forward, her arms slipping around him, pulling him tightly to her.

Horace returned the hug, once more feeling her tears on him. Also feeling her body against him, firm breasts against his chest, the gentle tickle of hair against his belly above the waistband of his boxers. It was Horace's turn to apologise as he felt a certain stirring, "S-s-sorry," he tried to ease his hips backwards, "But I did say that I really did think you are b-b-beautiful."

"Then don't be sorry," Stephanie whispered. She pulled him back to her, hugging him fiercely.

They held onto each other for what seemed to Horace to be hours but was, given their earlier consumption of alcohol, probably no more than five or ten minutes. They fell asleep.

11

It was still dark outside when Horace woke, a moment's disorientation followed quickly by realisation when he heard the gentle sobs from close by him. He glanced at the clock and realised that he could only have been asleep for an hour at most. He rolled over to find Stephanie facing away from him, her shoulders heaving with each of her near-silent sobs. He put a hand on her neck, "Steph?"

She turned over. "Sorry," she whispered.

He slid a hand under her armpit, feeling the firmness and weight of her left breast as he did so. She moved into his embrace. "I can't believe how anywh-wh-one could treat you bad," he whispered, "I'd never, ever do that."

Her hold on him tightened, "I know you wouldn't," her sobs receding once more.

Once again, there was no point in him trying to hide the fact that he found her attractive, or more accurately, arousing, "You're really beautiful."

She pulled back so that she could see his face, "And you're the nicest guy I ever met." Her words were still slightly slurred. "Really wonderful." She leaned her head forward and kissed him gently. "Thank you for everything," she said when she parted the kiss.

Whatever alarm bells were ringing in Horace's mind, he must have blanked them out, "You're so very w-w-welcome." He leaned forward himself and kissed her.

It started as a gentle kiss and became something more when Horace whispered "beautiful" into Stephanie's mouth. Horace's last ounce of resistance drained away as Stephanie's tongue flicked lightly across his lips. His free left hand moved up her back to her shoulder, paused only briefly and then slid gently down her front, cupping Stephanie's right breast. He squeezed gently and both of them groaned.

Horace pulled back, "Really beautiful."

Tears were still present on Stephanie's eyelashes. Horace kissed them away.

"Am I?"

Horace nodded slowly, "Can I show you?"

Stephanie stared up at him, "Please" she said in the quietest of voices.

Horace pulled the duvet back. He eased her shoulders back onto the mattress, stroked her hair, her neck, her breasts, teasing gently at her now-erect nipples. He kissed the same, lips and tongue and teeth. Slowly he sat back, pulling his shorts down his thighs, his eyes taking in every detail of Stephanie's naked body. Then he eased himself forward.

"You're rather beautiful yourself," Stephanie whispered, her breaths coming quickly.

"Not a patch on you," he smiled back, every nerve in his body seeming to tremble as he gently moved onto her. And then into her.

They made love twice, the first full of passion, pure lust, the second slowly and leisurely, for Horace a celebration of Stephanie's beauty external and internal; for her something similar and maybe a reaffirmation in something that she thought was lost. It was four o'clock before, sated, they fell asleep once more, tangled in each other's sweat-soaked arms and the sweat-soaked duvet.

12

Horace woke to sunlight streaming through the open curtains. The room was warm, the duvet bunched at the foot of the bed. The events of the previous night slowly permeated his fuzzy brain and he started fully awake. Could it really have happened? He looked quickly to his right but the bed was empty – no clues there.

He swung his legs out of the bed and pulled on his discarded boxers, hopping around in his haste. He scurried through to the kitchen. It must have been true; Stephanie was sitting at the kitchen table in her dressing gown, a mug of coffee between her hands. She looked up as he entered.

"Hi, H," she hardly dared meet his eyes.

"Er, hi," he responded, equally embarrassed, "How are you, er, feeling?"

"Like shit," she said, nodding as if they both expected that answer, "Want a, er, coffee?"

"Er, w-w-what? I mean, yes… please."

Stephanie rose and poured him a mug, "I hope you didn't mind?" she asked, nodding at the coffee machine.

"No, of course not," Horace took the mug, "Thanks."

Stephanie finally met his eyes properly, "It should be me thanking you. For last night," she stared levelly at him. "For everything."

"Er, yes, er, w-w-well…"

Stephanie smiled, "I guess we shouldn't have gone that far really, but…"

Horace could see that she was feeling guilty. He was feeling guilty himself, come to that, "W-w-well, circumstances and all that. I'm s-s-sorry."

Stephanie stared at him, "Don't be. It was wonderful. You were wonderful. I guess it's what I needed more than anything else at that time."

"I told you how b-b-beautiful you w-w-were."

"Thank you. And I promise I won't tell anyone, huh? Our little secret?"

Horace nodded, relieved and embarrassed at the same time, "W-w-well, if you're sure?"

Stephanie closed the distance between them, taking the mug from his hands and setting it behind her on the small table. "I feel a bit guilty as it is," she assured him, "But there's no way I'd come between you and Harriet. Not deliberately. Let's just put it down to circumstances and the fact that you're just so wonderful, okay?"

"Okay."

"And thanks again," Stephanie hugged him tightly.

Horace was glad that Harriet wouldn't return until the next day. He wasn't sure he could face her just yet. He hugged Stephanie back, relieved, grateful, confused. He let her go quickly when he realised that he was also becoming aroused.

"N-n-not again," he stuttered, his blush returning.

Stephanie laughed, a hint of sadness in her tone when she said, "I guess not." She turned back to the table, handing Horace his coffee once again. "The Crown'll be open in ten minutes," she said, quickly changing the subject, "And I'm a free woman again. One with a hangover and a friend who's probably got one as well. What say we shower and make for the pub? I reckon I owe you a drink?"

"Good idea," Horace agreed, equally happy to change the subject.

From The Diary of Horace Wilt

"Monday, 13th April 1981

DD,

Something very... unusual happened last night. I came back from the Crown to find Steph on the stairs, really upset because she and Alan have split up - in a big way, thanks to the little bastard. I fed her coffee and comfort and then let her sleep in my bed. I guess you could say one thing led to another, and I ended up in bed with her - and I really mean with her.

I never thought I could ever be unfaithful to Harry - and as far as Steph and I are concerned, I haven't been. But, well, she's very beautiful, is Steph, and I'd do anything for her. It's made me realise that there might be a life without Harry - not that I want that - and it's also made me wonder about what would have happened if Steph and me had got together before Harry. I'm really confused about it all, but I can't shake the feeling that everything's okay. I just don't know what I'm going to say to Harry when she gets back."

13

By the time Harriet returned on the Tuesday evening, Horace had resolved that he wouldn't tell her anything about what had *really* happened on the Sunday night. He and Stephanie had agreed that it would be best if they both described the events up to the point where she had gone to bed – that way, nothing could slip out by accident – but Horace had wondered whether he might come clean after all. It was only the thought of maybe alienating Harry and Stephanie, causing Stephanie to lose another one of her friends that stopped him.

In the event, Harriet was somewhat cold and distant when she found him in the Crown, and their conversation was stilted, centred round her myriad family members; a safe, neutral territory. It suited Horace perfectly.

After that weekend, things began to return slowly to normal, neither Harriet nor Horace able to get a fix on what had gone wrong between them. Horace harboured his dark secret as month blurred into month but, to his amazement, felt more comfortable than he had expected when he and Harriet were in Stephanie's company. The only change he noticed in Stephanie was that she stopped referring to him as 'lover-boy', and, very occasionally, he would catch her staring in his direction, a quizzical look on her face.

Although his relationship with Harriet improved, it never reached the dizzy heights of their first year together, and Horace couldn't help wondering whether his night with Stephanie had anything to do with it. No matter that he didn't really feel terribly guilty, he could never quite dismiss what happened, and it hovered over him, over Harriet as well, although she never knew about it.

And as far as Harriet went? He disappointed her when his second year thesis didn't get the marks he thought it should have been worth, and again as his dress-sense seemed to desert him. By the Christmas of their third year at college, they spent much less time together; Harriet working hard in her studies, Horace drinking hard in the Crown, watching concerts by ever-more obscure artists, and occasionally making mysterious trips on his own. Horace the Aardvark was doing very well, and would now eat out of Horace's hand when he went into the cage.

It was as Horace was returning home after one such clandestine visit, early in the March of his final year at college that he realised how little he had worked towards his degree. Whenever Harriet had mentioned the subject, Horace's ears seemed to stop functioning. In the back of the taxi he stared at the date on the top of the newspaper he had been browsing: March 1982 - his finals were now just three months away!

"Oh bugger," he muttered.

"What's up guv?" the driver asked.

"Nothing much," Horace said with a scowl. "It's just that I've suddenly realised that my girlfriend has been right these last few months."

"Ouch! Never a good thing, that is, guv," the driver commented cheerfully.

Too true, Horace thought. They had been arguing – again – about the very subject only the previous evening. That and the planned trip to India that Harriet had organised for the students in their year, commencing two days after the finals. It was yet another subject on which they seemed to disagree, and Horace had only agreed to take part in order to keep Harriet off his back for a while. He really didn't want to go.

He sighed and sank back into the seat, staring gloomily out of the window. He knew he should start getting his life in order, knuckle down to the work that was needed for college, sort things out with Harriet, get his hair cut, drink less.

Oh well, one out of four was at least a start, he thought to himself as he paid the taxi driver outside "Hairs and Graces".

The following Monday he surprised Harriet by walking with her to the college, his battered attaché case under his arm and a purposeful look on his face.

"Good God!" she exclaimed. "Not actually taking my advice, are you?"

Her disappointment with him emerged as sarcasm, and Horace wondered what had happened to the sweet little Harry he had first known.

"Very funny," he muttered, "But, for your information, I'm taking my own advice. I told you I like doing things my own w-w-way."

She nodded, sighing, "Of course. Silly me. Anyway, it's good to see you actually making an effort about *something*."

The emphasis on the last word had clear import, but Horace couldn't be bothered to find out what it was, "W-w-whatever."

"They'll carve that on your ''eadstone," Harriet said with a rueful smile.

They walked on in an uncomfortable silence, Horace wondering just where they had got it all wrong, Harriet knowing, but still hoping that the India trip would rekindle whatever was lost. She was also regretting her earlier sarcasm; it really *was* good to see Horace making an effort.

In early May, Harriet began to nag Horace about the inoculations he should get for India, but by then Horace was trying to find a way to get out of the holiday. He couldn't see what was so fascinating about the place; hot, dirty, streets full of beggars, sleeping under the stars, easy targets for bandits, disease ridden. What could *anyone* find fascinating? He secretly believed that this was just one of those "student things", something that had to be done, some rite of passage between the student years and the adult life to follow.

He prevaricated, citing the studying that he so desperately needed, occasionally slipping up by suggesting that they forget about it for a while and go to the Crown for a pint or two. Another two weeks of near-constant pestering and Horace began to get desperate. So desperate, in fact, that he decided to visit his mother for some assistance.

He had visited his former childhood home only twice since the Cult of the Natural Cycle had been set-up. The eleven women that now lived there made the place intimidating, and judging by some of the looks they gave him, he was fairly sure that if he hadn't been 'Moonflower's' son, they would be quite happy to tear him limb from limb – or sacrifice him to some female deity. He still hadn't quite worked out what was really going on there – much as when Harriet nagged him about something, his ears seemed to shut down automatically whenever his mother discussed the subject – but he guessed it was something about "female self-help" – and possibly self-worship. What he did know, was that the place seemed to be rolling in cash; his mother was talking of expansion.

When he arrived, he was greeted at the door by a plump, middle-aged woman; the incongruously self-styled Willow. Her naturally cheerful features turned sour when she saw who it was.

"Oh, it's you."

"Very astute," Horace replied.

He was led through to what had once been the kitchen, but was now known as the "Heart Room". Given the women's pulse-and-fibre diet, Horace thought that they had only got the name just a little bit wrong. His mother was sitting at the head of the vast table that occupied most of the floor-space.

"Darling!" she trilled when she saw him, "What a lovely surprise!" She rose and, kaftan flapping, hurried across to the doorway, hugging him tightly. "Do come into our Heart. Would you like some nice herbal tea?"

"Hello, mother," he sighed. This could turn out to be a terrible mistake. "Actually, if you've got any of your brandy?"

"Of course," his mother tutted, "I should have known."

She poured him a large glass, a smaller one for herself, and sat back in her chair, "So, what brings my errant son to the Heart? And where is your lovely Orchid?"

"Ah. That's really the point," he said awkwardly, "It's sort of a related matter."

His mother nodded sagely, "Just as I thought."

"Oh?"

"Orchid came to see me last week," his mother said, ignoring Horace's choke of surprise. "She said you were being impossible again, and was wondering what she might do to actually get you moving."

Horace sighed. There was some sort of conspiracy going on here, "That's the trouble. I don't really *w-w-want* to get moving."

"It's always been your trouble," his mother said in a matter-of-fact tone, "And I suppose what you're really saying is that you don't want to visit the ancient and mysterious land, isn't it?"

"Ancient, mysterious, disease-ridden etc. land, yes."

His mother sighed, "You really don't know how lucky you are, do you?"

He was treated to a ten minute eulogy on his fortune, the wonders of the Asian Sub-Continent, and the missed opportunities of her own youth.

"But that w-w-was *your* ambition," Horace complained when she finally finished, "I just don't w-w-want to go! I w-w-was hoping you could sort of, I don't know, maybe explain things to Harriet for me. She never seems to listen to me."

"Do your dirty work for you, you mean?" his mother asked, a resigned smile on her face.

"If you w-w-want to put it like that, then yes."

His mother sighed deeply, "I was really hoping that college would make a man of you, but I suppose I should have known better."

"Mother! It's not like that. It's just, w-w-well, because it's Harriet, I suppose."

His mother softened, "Oh, you poor thing. It's not going so well, these days, is it?"

"No, I guess not."

"Well," his mother became more business-like, "As far as I'm concerned, you've made your bed and you'd better make it." She ignored his automatic correction and went on. "You just have to steel yourself and tell her you don't want to go."

"But I don't know how!"

"I thought that's what you'd say. Okay then, mummy to the rescue it must be."

Horace looked up, a glimmer of hope appearing on the horizon, "You'll tell her for me?"

She ignored him for a moment, "Are there any other spare places on this little adventure apart from the one you'll leave?"

"Four at the last count, why?"

His mother smiled, "Starchild!" she trilled, ignoring Horace's question once again.

Maisie Briggs appeared in the doorway, "Yes, Moonflower?" she asked pleasantly, ignoring Horace altogether.

"The trip's on. And apparently, five of us can go. Be a sweetheart and go and tell Elspeth that there'll be room for her as well, will you."

"W-w-what?! I mean, w-w-what's going on here? And w-w-who's Elspeth, come to that?"

"Well," his mother explained, "When Orchid visited last week, she told us all about the trip and how you were behaving. I put two and two together and asked Orchid whether it might be possible for one or two of us to go with them. On the condition, of course, that you decided not to go; it would look silly for your mummy to be on the trip with you, wouldn't it? Oh, and Elspeth's our newest member. She's a white witch."

Horace sat and stared. Did he actually hear all of that right? His mother and Harriet conspiring behind his back, seemingly knowing his every thought? White witches? "I, er, w-w-well…" He gave up trying to form a coherent sentence and took a large swallow of the home-made varnish-remover.

"And talking of Elspeth, here she is. Elspeth, this is my son, Moonchild – or Horace as he prefers for some weird reason. Horace this is Elspeth."

Horace turned towards the doorway and nearly sprayed brandy all over the newcomer. Elspeth was about his own age, tall and slender with jet black hair, eyes heavy with kohl, lips a dark purple. The effect was striking, but not nearly as striking as her mode of dress. She was wearing, if that was the right word, a dark, diaphanous robe which clung to every inch of her body. Through it, Horace could clearly see her perfectly-formed breasts and the dark thatch of her pubic hair which was an almost perfect diamond shape.

"I'm very pleased to see you, Horace," she said in a dark, husky voice.

Horace, after a brief struggle, managed to raise his eyes to her face, "I'm, er, pleased to see you. Meet you I mean!" he blushed furiously.

Elspeth smiled, and it was all Horace could do to keep a grip on his brandy glass, "You're every inch your mother," she said and then glanced down at his lap, "And more, maybe?" she raised an eyebrow.

"I, er, thanks," Horace said through a throat that had almost closed. He spun back around in his chair, praying that the ferret wouldn't try to tip over the table.

"Elspeth," his mother addressed the vamp, "Good news. Apparently the India trip is on."

"That's wonderful," Elspeth breathed behind Horace. He was wondering just how heavy the table was.

His mother explained to Elspeth what had happened and, after replying once again that it was wonderful news, Elspeth left them to "return to her crystals".

"Beautiful young thing, isn't she?" his mother asked him when they were alone.

"Lovely," Horace managed to squeak. A thought occurred to him. "Is she, er, you know? Like you?"

"A lesbian?" his mother grinned at his discomfort, "Actually no. She's completely celibate."

"A case of 'w-w-what a w-w-waste' all round then," Horace said, his mind not really concentrating on what he was saying.

"Oh, darling! Not a very good thing to say out loud around here."

"Sorry, just slipped out."

"Yes, well. Now, I'd better call Orchid for you, hadn't I?"

Horace nodded and poured himself another brandy while she was out of the room, sipping it nervously. She returned, smiling, after a few minutes and told him that everything was settled. She also told him that "Orchid" was less than delighted with the news, and suggested that he might like to stay over for the night until she had calmed down.

"That bad?"

"You didn't really expect anything else, did you?" she said, not unkindly.

He refused her offer of a bed for the night – the place scared him during daylight hours – and finished his brandy in a single, painful swallow.

"I bet you wouldn't have refused if I told you you'd have to share with Elspeth," his mother teased.

"Mother!" The woman could be so infuriating sometimes. Especially when she was right.

"And don't tell me you're not all male through and through. Orchid said that was the one thing about you that she'd never change. Apparently you're a fantastic lover."

Horace groaned. Was nothing sacred? "I'd better call a cab."

"Oh, no need for that, darling. We've two cars between us here now. I'll get Elspeth to run you back."

"No!" Horace exclaimed, before lowering his voice. "I mean, er, no, that's okay. The cab w-w-will be fine."

"Don't worry, darling. Elspeth doesn't dress like that when she's outside. Or, at least, when she isn't attending a ceremony."

It wasn't just her mode of dress that induced Horace's panic. Celibate or not, she scared him in a very sexual way. "I'll call a cab."

14

Harriet was waiting inside his flat when he got home after a detour to the Crown for some Dutch courage. Half an hour later, Horace was once more single, his ears ringing from her words, his shoulders slumped in defeat. He had meant to spend the rest of the evening studying, but returned instead to the Crown, drowning his sorrows and boring Flat-Foot Fred senseless.

He woke the next day and was surprised that he didn't feel a lot sadder than he did. He was also surprised that he hadn't shed tears over the loss of Harriet. Somewhere in his mind, there was a tiny, tiny trace of relief that things were over. There was also a trace of guilt. It hadn't really been Harriet's nagging that had been annoying him, he guessed, it was more likely to be *himself* that had been annoying him.

Stephanie knocked on his door later that morning and she joined him in a mug of coffee while he explained what all the shouting had been about the previous evening. She commiserated with him at length, offered him her sympathy, offered him a drink in the Crown. He accepted all gratefully.

That evening he almost asked her whether she would, maybe, like to, sort of, go out somewhere with him, but, just as he was seriously considering this, a wave of sadness overcame him.

He had lost Harriet. As much through his own... what? Stupidity? Wiltedish-ness? Lack of attention? He didn't know, and right now didn't care. There would be time for other girls later. In the meantime, he had to work out exactly where it had all gone wrong; he had to study as well, and study he did. He would ask Stephanie out *after* the finals.

15

It was two days after the finals when he came to regret his decision. Regret it with all his heart.

He had waved Harriet off, wishing her a wonderful trip and actually meaning it. She had sighed, shaking her head, and wished him a happy holiday in return. They had started speaking again in the weeks before the finals and she had even helped coach him in some of the more esoteric areas of their course. All of that was good at least.

An hour after she had left, Horace was rinsing mugs in the kitchen when the telephone rang. He sighed and sauntered through to the living room.

"Hello," he said, picking up the receiver.

A woman's voice he didn't immediately recognise, clearly upset, answered him.

"Is that Horace?"

"Yes," he replied slowly, "Who is this?"

"Sheila. Sheila Jameson. Do you remember me?" the woman said, her voice catching slightly.

"Sheila… Of course, Stephanie's mum, yes?"

The woman paused a moment before answering, the sound of a quiet sob escaping her, "Yes," she said, quietly, "Or rather, I was. Oh, I'm so sorry, Horace, but I've some terrible news."

Horace hadn't realised that the expression 'his blood ran cold' could be so accurate. "W-w-w-hat is it?" he asked, his voice full of dread.

"H-h-…Horace…" the woman paused, swallowing hard, "I'm… She's dead, Horace. Last night. A car crash."

Horace's head swam. He nearly dropped the receiver, nearly passed out, "Oh no," he muttered, "It's… I can't…" he trailed off in despair.

He didn't remember a single word of the rest of the conversation and hung up still shaking his head in disbelief, in shock. He sat heavily on his sofa, put his head in his hands and cried himself hoarse.

From The Diary of Horace Wilt

"Wednesday, 21st July, 1982

DD,

The most horrible thing that could possibly happen has happened. Stephanie's mother, Sheila, called a couple of hours ago and told me that poor, beautiful, wonderful Stephanie was killed in a car crash last night. I just can't believe it; can't stop crying. You've no idea how much I wish that I'd told Steph what I really think of her; just how much I'd grown to love her. Now I'll never have the chance. Never.

Poor, poor Stephanie. Can't write any more now. Too upset, too heartbroken."

16

If the trip to India was the rite of passage for many of Horace's classmates, Horace's own was Stephanie's funeral. It took place on Tuesday, August 3rd, a warm, sunny summer's day; a total contrast to the moods of those present.

Horace had sent flowers from himself and on behalf of the absent Harriet, and from the rest of Stephanie's absent friends. He arrived at the crematorium, just outside of Stephanie's hometown of Brighton, dressed entirely in black, sweating profusely in the heat. Stephanie's mother, Sheila, was already there, standing by the door of the small chapel, and she gave him a desultory wave when she spotted him amongst the arriving mourners. He crossed the gravel of the small car-park reluctantly; he had no idea what to say, how to react. He'd never been to a funeral before.

In the event, words weren't really necessary, it was clear from their mutual looks of grief that they shared emotions, and, indeed, the only words they exchanged were identical: "I'm so terribly sorry". The ceremony was, for Horace, painfully brief, doing nothing to capture anything of Stephanie's real, vivacious, caring character, and he could barely bring himself to glance in the direction of the white coffin in which his friend's body lay.

He surreptitiously glanced around during the short service, surprised that there were so few people there, surprised, also, that Stephanie's mother seemed to be her only relation present. After the coffin had made its sedate, horrific, journey through the purple velvet curtains and the priest, vicar or whoever he was, had said a few final words the small congregation rose and followed Sheila Jameson back into the sunlight outside.

She spoke with each of the mourners as they passed her in the doorway and Horace hung back, half-hoping that he wouldn't be required to say anything; his throat felt half-closed and he could feel the insistent prickle of tears in the corner of his eyes. When it became clear that Stephanie's mother was waiting for him before she moved off, he steeled himself and stepped forward.

"Thank you for coming, Horace," she smiled.

"I had to, really," he responded quietly.

She seemed to understand what he meant, nodding, "And thank you for the flowers, they're beautiful."

Horace swallowed heavily, "So w-w-was Stephanie."

Sheila bit her lip, closing her eyes for a second, "Thank you, yes, she was," she paused for a moment. "Just one question."

"W-w-whatever."

"The inscription. What does it mean?"

"I had a friend, a Spanish friend, w-w-when I w-w-as younger," he explained. "It's a traditional Spanish saying. It just seemed so appropriate…" he trailed off.

"What is it?" Sheila asked again, quietly.
"Nos ha dejado a todas heledas," Horace replied, his voice barely a whisper, "It means 'She has left us feeling like ice'."

Sheila stared at him for a moment, taking in his words, and then nodded vigorously, her eyes filling with tears, "Yes, you're right," she struggled to say, "It's very appropriate. Thank you again, Horace."

His own tears were creeping from his eyes and he couldn't find his voice no matter how hard he tried. Instead he acted on pure intuition, spreading his arms and then hugging the now-sobbing woman.

After a while, they had both regained some semblance of control, and they separated. "Horace, will you come back with the others to the house?"

"I'm not sure I'd be such great company. Besides I'm not really good around strangers and I don't know anywh-wh-one here except you."

Sheila seemed to understand. Maybe Stephanie had told her how shy he was. "Okay, then. Can't say I blame you. I'm not exactly looking forward to this myself. But promise me one thing?"

"Anything."

"Promise me you'll come back and see me in a few days. I'd love to hear about what she was like when you knew her."

"Of course."

Sheila fumbled in her black handbag and produced a business card, "That's my address; the place is in the middle of the town. My phone number's on there as well. Give me a call whenever you're free, I really would like to see you again."

Horace took the card, holding her hand for a moment, "I promise I'll call. And soon," he added.

Sheila nodded, satisfied, "Thank you again, Horace."

They joined the other mourners, now poring through the arrays of flowers, and Horace stayed for a few minutes, chatting quietly to anyone who spoke to him, explaining three times what the Spanish inscription on his own vast arrangement meant. As soon as he politely could, he said a few goodbyes, the last to Stephanie's mother, and then walked slowly away, his footsteps crunching on the gravel.

17

During the next few days, Horace went to work at his easel, taking an earlier portrait of Stephanie and duplicating it in loving detail. The original had depicted her from the waist upwards, naked, but the duplicate covered her upper torso in a dark-blue, flowing, silk blouse. If anything it was better than the original, highlighting her green eyes and straw blonde hair. When he was happy with the result, he made the promised telephone call to Sheila Jameson and arranged to travel down to Brighton the following Tuesday.

He arrived just after midday and strolled from the station to the address she had given him. Stephanie had once told him that she and her mother had lived above the hairdressers that her mother had owned, and which was now just a sideline since she had begun working in the music industry.

The 'few' rooms turned out to number twelve, the apartment vast and rambling above not one, but three shop fronts. Sheila met him at the entrance and led him up a steep flight of stairs, settling him on a sofa in the vast living room that looked out towards the sea.

"W-w-what a lovely place," Horace said.

She nodded, "It is rather, I'm always glad to get back here after a tour. Now, what can I get you to drink, coffee? Beer? Something stronger? And, before you reply," she smiled, "I'm having something stronger."

"Perhaps a vodka?"

"It's yours."

She poured drinks for both of them and then settled in an armchair close by Horace's side, "So, tell me, what's in that large case you've got there."

Horace took a deep breath, "W-w-well…I, sort of, painted a bit at college and Stephanie w-w-was good enough to pose for me…"

"She used to for the art class as well, didn't she?" Sheila's mother laughed. "Don't worry, Horace, she told me all about it."

Relieved Horace went on, "W-w-well, yes. But she also agreed to pose for me as w-w-well, back at the flat." He paused and unzipped the case, "I thought that, w-w-well, you might like this." He extracted his duplicate oil.

Sheila took it from him and gazed down at it for a full minute before she spoke, "Oh, Horace. It's absolutely beautiful. But I couldn't take something as good as this from you-"

"Please!" Horace interrupted, "I'd really like you to have it. Stephanie w-w-was such a good friend to me, to us that is, Harriet and me, and you w-w-were so kind about the concert."

Sheila stared at him for a moment, and Horace thought that he could see a tear forming in her left eye. Then she blinked and nodded, "Thank you, Horace. And I can promise you that this will be framed and take pride of place in this very room," she nodded towards the wall on their left, "It's really so very good."

"Thank you," Horace smiled, blushing. "I w-w-was hoping you'd like it."

They fell silent for a moment or two and Horace sipped at his icy drink. He had been half-dreading this meeting – and half-needing it. Now he wondered just what they could talk about.

In the event, he needn't have worried. Although the conversation was a little stilted at first, they were soon gabbling away; Sheila telling him all about Stephanie's girlhood, the scrapes she had got herself into. Like the time she had made her own hair-ribbons out of pieces of liquorice and had to have six inches cut off her precious locks; the time she had 'borrowed' her cousin's motorcycle and had promptly ridden it into a swimming pool; countless others. Horace told her about Stephanie's life at college and even surprised himself by relating his first meeting with her, in the changing rooms by the gym, and the incident in Room 21.

There was a great deal of laughter and a few tears, and it was four o'clock before they seemed to run out of words.

"So, I guess I could say that you really liked my daughter then?" Sheila smiled.

Horace paused a moment. He had never felt so relaxed with someone that he barely knew, the shared knowledge of Stephanie, the shared grief at her passing, seeming to strip away his normal reservations. "I think… No, I *know*, it w-w-was more than that."

"She would have been very happy to hear that, Horace," Sheila said.

Horace shrugged, "I think she, kinda, knew."

They chatted for another half an hour, about Horace's plans, about Sheila's adventures on tour, before Horace checked his watch and gave a wry smile.

"I'd really better get going."

"You can stay here tonight, if you like?"

Horace thanked her, but declined. Today had been a sort of catharsis, maybe for both of them, but he didn't think his presence would help Sheila very much, and for his own part, her uncanny resemblance to her daughter wouldn't rest easy in his mind. He thought he detected similar sentiments in Sheila when she shrugged and said "Well, if you're sure?"

She led him back to street level with his now-empty portfolio case, and they hugged briefly, awkwardly, on the doorstep, their earlier intimacy already slipping away.

"Thank you ever so much for coming," Sheila smiled, "And for that wonderful painting. You've got quite a talent there. Come and see me whenever you're in the area."

"And thank you," Horace smiled back, "For the hospitality… for everything. And, if I'm passing, I'll be sure to look you up."

He walked away, feeling relieved of a burden that he hadn't been aware that he carried, turning once to wave at Sheila who was still standing in her doorway, watching him go. She returned the wave and retreated back into her apartment.

From The Diary of Horace Wilt,

"Tuesday, 10th August, 1982

DD,

Just got back from Brighton where I saw Sheila Jameson. She really liked the painting of Steph and she was really kind and nice. I guess I feel a bit better now; less alone, somehow. Maybe I can start getting my life back in some sort of order. I seem to have lost everything that was precious to me, but maybe - just maybe - I can move on a bit. I'll try to imagine that I'm doing it for Steph, as much as me. Perhaps that will work."

Chapter 5

1

The next few days took Horace by surprise. After all that had happened in the past few months, the sudden lack of anything to do left him feeling slightly frustrated, slightly bored. Most days, at a loss for anything better to do, he retreated to the Crown, sipping a pint or two, reading newspapers, playing video games, marking time.

The examination results were not due until mid-September, and without knowing how he fared, he didn't feel inclined to start the onerous task of job-hunting. Horace didn't really consider that he had many friends as such, and most of his acquaintances were in India. Even Godfrey had disappeared for the summer, an extended honeymoon after his sudden marriage to his long-time girlfriend, Mandy.

One afternoon at the end of August, in complete desperation, he even tried phoning his mother.

"Cult of the Natural Cycle, may our Mother bless you," a husky voice intoned when his call was answered.

Horace shook his head. He had just been about to hang up, realising his mother was absent only after he had finished dialling her number, but the voice sounded familiar, "Elspeth?" he asked after a moment's thought.

"Indeed. And you are Horace, yes?" she breathed.

"Er, yes. I thought you had gone w-w-with my mother?"

Elspeth chuckled, forcing every hair on Horace's body erect, "Last minute complication with my passport." she explained. "Why were you calling?"

"Believe it or not, I'd forgotten about the India thing. I just w-w-wanted a w-w-word w-w-with my mother."

Another throaty chuckle ensued, and it wasn't only the hairs on his body that were becoming erect, "Will I do?"

"W-w-will you do w-w-what?" Horace squeaked.

"For the word you wanted, of course," the silky voice explained, "Or anything else for that matter."

"I, er, no. That is, I d-d-don't think so."

"Well," Elspeth went on, "If you ever want anything from me... anything, do please call me."

"That's, er, very kind. I'll bear it in mind... I mean I'll *keep* it in m-m-mind!"

"Good," Elspeth breathed, "Well, I'll see you sometime then."

"Yes," Horace gulped, "I'm s-s-sure you w-w-will." He rang off gratefully.

He stood for a moment, staring at the telephone. If that woman was celibate, Horace would eat his ferret.

2

After he recovered, he began to realise why he might be feeling so bored and frustrated. There was absolutely no-one in his life at the moment with whom he could be in *any* way intimate. What had he been thinking of, slumming it in the Crown every day? What he could really do with was a new girlfriend.

He felt happy with his reasoning for all of two minutes, before he realised that it was all very well to resolve himself to his problem, but who the hell did he know that could possibly fit the bill? Nearly every female he had ever known was in India, with the exception, of course, of Elspeth, and he was fairly sure that he wouldn't survive a single night with her. Sighing deeply, he pulled on his jacket and left the flat; he would just have to go back to slumming in the Crown.

It was as he was passing the top of the market when a thought struck him. Okay, so it had been two years, but he couldn't help wondering whether the punk girl, Doll, was still around. After all, she had told him to come and find her if he was ever a single guy again, and he couldn't be more single now if he tried. He glanced at his reflection in the window of the carpet shop at the top of the street. Despite the heat, he had dressed from head to toe in black. It wasn't exactly punkish, but there again, he wasn't wearing frilly shirts and mascara as half the young guys seemed to be.

He took a deep breath and began to make his way down the market. He reached the shop where he had first met Doll and her boss, Dave. They were, of course, no longer there and Horace hadn't really expected them to be. He shrugged, and began to make his way towards the only other place he could think of to look for her, The Draughtsman.

He arrived outside five minutes later and hesitated. The only other time he had been in there he had been dressed from head to toe as a punk – as had every other customer – and he wasn't sure how his current gear would go down. Then he thought of another two hours in the company of Flat-Foot Fred and marched quickly through the open door into the dingy interior.

Other than half a dozen youths dressed in denim and leathers sitting at the back of the room, the place was devoid of life – human life anyway. Oh, well, he told himself, it was a bit much to ask anyway. He was about to retreat back to the market when the door behind the bar opened and a short, skinny, old man shuffled in.

"Morning, squire," the old man breathed whisky fumes over Horace, "What can I do you for?"

"I w-w-was just…" Horace began, but then shrugged, the long walk in the bright sunshine had left his mouth feeling dusty. "A pint of Guinness, if you do it, please."

"Don't do much else," the old man coughed, picking up a plastic pint cup and holding it under the counter where the taps were situated. "Bleedin' typical, that is," he rumbled on, "First stranger we get in 'ere fer weeks, 'an 'e drinks bleedin' Guinness 'an all."

"Sorry-" Horace began, but he was interrupted by another phlegmy cough which could, depending on your strict definition of the term, be called a chuckle.

"Don't bleedin' fret, squire," the old man said, "It's probably the wisest choice in 'ere anyway. Wouldn't drink the other crap meself. S'why I stick to the whisky, see?"

Horace shrugged and fumbled in his pocket for some change, "Er, how much is it?"

"Eighty pee or a quid for cash," the old man gave another chuckle. He set the plastic pint on the scarred counter. "What brings you in 'ere anyway? Bleedin' lost or summink?"

Horace handed him one of the new pound coins and shrugged, "Keep the change. Actually, I w-w-was sort of looking for a girl."

"Ta," the man said, pocketing the coin, "But we're not that sort of place, squire."

"Not that sort...Oh, no! I meant a particular girl."

The old man's chuckle turned into a coughing fit. "Christ you're easy to wind up," he told Horace when he recovered his breath. "What's this bird's name then?"

Horace took a cautious sip of the Guinness before replying. His eyebrows rose in surprise and he took a larger swallow, "This is really good. The girl's name is Doll-"

He was interrupted by the old man's chuckle. "Well, fuck me sideways," he wheezed. Horace tried to ignore a mental image that his mind was trying to play to him. "As in, short fer Dolores Mercer, would that be?"

"W-w-well, yes. Or at least, the Dolores part. I never knew her surname."

"Sounds a familiar story," the old man grinned ruefully, flashing teeth that would make a baby grand jealous. "Quite a bleedin' coincidence though."

"Er, w-w-what is?"

"Well, squire," the old man's grin broadened, "The fing is, you're talking to Jim Mercer. Doll's my girl, see?"

"Your daughter?"

"Well, I'm not 'er bleedin' 'usband, am I? We only moved back 'ere six weeks ago."

"She's 'ere – I mean here – then?" Horace asked, delighted.

"Yeah. Sitting upstairs readin' a bleedin' book or summink. Don't know wot she's sees in 'em meself, but there you go. She know you then, does she?"

"She might remember me. W-w-we w-w-were sort of friends a w-w-while back."

The old man looked him up and down and then shrugged, "Yer look like an alright sort," he said at length. "I guess I don't mind if yer wander up an' say 'ello."

Horace didn't catch his meaning for a moment, "You mean…"

"That's it, squire. Come through 'ere and I'll let you up the stairs. Yer can't miss 'er. She's sprawled out in our front room. It's right at the top of the stairs."

Whatever Horace had been expecting, it wasn't this, "Oh, er, thanks," he set the Guinness on the bar and made his way to the door.

"No funny business, mind," the old man advised.

"Of course," Horace nodded vigorously. "And thanks."

He found himself at the bottom of a steep flight of stairs. He climbed them slowly, wondering whether his courage was deserting him, and whether it might not be better just to return to the bar and say it was a case of mistaken identity or something. He thought once more of another lunchtime making small talk with Flat-Foot Fred and continued up the stairs.

He arrived in what the old man had called the front room. It took him a moment before he spotted the woman lying face down on the sofa, a book propped on the arm.

"That you, pa?" she asked without turning round.

"Er, actually, it's not," Horace said sheepishly.

The woman flipped over, "I 'ope fer your sake 'e let you up 'ere." She glowered.

For a moment, Horace didn't recognise her, thinking that it really *was* a case of mistaken identity. Instead of the multi-coloured dress and make-up of the typical punk, the young woman was wearing smart black jeans and a tight white T-shirt over her lean body. Her hair, now ash blonde, was cascading below her shoulders, her face devoid of make-up, not a safety pin in sight. "Doll?"

The girl sat up, a quizzical look on her face, "Yeah… And I know you from somewhere, don't I?"

Horace tried to smile, "I w-w-was hoping you w-w-would."

Doll frowned at him for another few seconds and then he saw recognition in her eyes, "Bugger me," she breathed. "That stutter gives you away, mate. It's…" she struggled for a moment, and then beamed, "It's bleedin' Hor, ain't it?"

"Horace, that's me."

Doll laughed delightedly, struggling to her feet, "What the fuck brings you 'ere?"

"W-w-well, you did say…" Horace began.

Doll's jaw dropped open, "You mean, after all this time, you still remember that offer?"

"You're hard to f-f-forget."

She laughed again and, dropping the book – The Cherry Orchard, Horace noted to his surprise – rushed across the room, launching herself at him at the last moment.

Horace caught her and, despite her light weight, nearly toppled backwards down the stairs, "I take it you're glad to see me," he said, still in a state of shock.

Doll hugged him, "Course I am! I'm not the sort to go round makin' empty promises, you know? I fink it's bleedin' magic!"

Horace set her on her feet, "You're looking a bit different these days," he said, barely able to contain his delight at her enthusiastic greeting.

"You too, mate. Black really suits yer, you know?"

"Thanks," Horace grinned, "And that really suits you."

"Reckon?"

"Really."

Doll's smile slipped, "What brings you 'ere, anyway?"

"You, I guess."

The smile returned, and she looked amazed, "This is *so* weird. I mean good type of weird, not weird type of weird. We've only been back 'ere a few weeks."

"Your dad told me."

Doll frowned, "I'd better 'ave a word wiv 'im, an' all. Letting you up 'ere like that. You could've been anyone."

"I'm glad he did."

Doll wrinkled her nose, "Yeah, I s'pose so." She stopped again and gave him a quizzical look, "Are you, like, single these days, then?" Horace nodded. "This ain't one of those rebound fings is it?"

"Not at all. W-w-we split up months ago."

Doll nodded, her broad smile returning, "Well, fuck me!" Horace enjoyed this image much more than when her father had said something similar. "Me and my guy split up a couple of months ago as well, so that's alright all round, then. So, what are we gonna do? Fancy a beer? We've got loads of news to catch up on, I reckon."

Horace couldn't really remember anything about Doll anyway, but he was more than happy to agree, "Yeah, w-w-why not?"

"Not downstairs, though," Doll said firmly. "Me old man'll be 'overing round us like an asthmatic bat. 'Ow about your local, wherever that is?"

"Suits me."

"Great! I'll just get me jacket." She rummaged behind the sofa and pulled out a fine leather jacket. "Come on, mate. This 'as really made my day."

"Mine too," Horace agreed, following her down the stairs.

Doll said goodbye to her father while Horace drained his Guinness and she grabbed his hand as soon as he'd put the "glass" back on the counter. With Doll dragging him, they ran out into the street.

During the fifteen minute walk to the Crown, Horace calculated that Doll must have said something in the region of six thousand words – to his own twenty or so. This was partly due to her natural exuberance, and partly because Horace was having a great deal of trouble trying to believe his luck.

When they stepped into the back bar of the Crown, Doll stopped and stared around her, 'Bit bleedin' bright in 'ere, innit?" she remarked cheerfully. She was about to say something else when she caught sight of the yawning figure behind the bar. "Fuck me! It's Uncle Fred. Do they still call him Flat-Foot?" she asked Horace.

"Er, yeah," he replied after a short pause, surprised to find that his mouth could still function.

Doll dashed over to the bar, still dragging Horace by his hand, "Wotcha, Unc!" she called over to the nearly comatose Fred.

He looked up slowly, "Christ almighty," he breathed, a smile spreading over his features. "What are you doing here, Doll?" he came up to the bar and leaned forward, proffering his slightly stubbly cheek for a kiss.

She pecked it, jumping onto the brass foot-rail in order to reach, "Charmin' bleedin' greetin' I must say," she grinned, "But if you must know, my old mate Hor – Horace – 'ere came and found me." To Horace's delight, the aitch in his own name seemed to be the only one she ever bothered with.

"Small world, innit?" Fred nodded happily, and to Horace. "I didn't know you knew my niece."

"Nor me," Horace grinned.

"I keep meanin' to pop down and see me brother," Fred told Doll. "Tell 'im I asked after 'im, will you, girl?"

"Course, Unc," She turned to Horace. "Well, what about that drink then, mate? I reckon I owe you one."

"Guinness, please."

"That's two pints of Guinness, then, Uncle Fred," Doll beamed at her relative.

He frowned a moment, "'Ere, are you sure you're old enough?"

"Course I am! It was me eighteenth back in May. You wouldn't 'ave refused me anyway, though, would you?"

Fred snorted, "Since when 'ave I ever been able to refuse you anything, eh girl?" He took two pint glasses and began to pour their drinks.

Horace had been doing some quick mental arithmetic, "By my calculations, you was only just sixteen then w-w-when I met you?"

"Yeah, coupla weeks past me sixteenth, I s'pose. Why?"

Horace winced, "Actually, I thought you w-w-were about twenty or something."

Doll laughed, "That's what all that war-paint does fer yer." She went to pay her uncle for the beers, but he refused.

"Call it a belated birthday present," he smiled. This was two firsts in one, in Horace's experience; Fred buying a drink *and* smiling.

He and Doll retreated to a table in the far corner of the room and chatted animatedly. Or at least, Doll chatted animatedly and Horace occasionally grunted through his grin. A couple of hours later, Doll announced that she was ''ungry', and after a quick goodbye to her uncle, they left the pub, blinking in the bright sunlight.

"W-w-what do you fancy?" Horace asked as they strolled through the crowds of shoppers.

"Anyfing. I'm not fussed."

They settled on a takeaway Chinese and Horace suggested that they take it back to his flat for a bit of comfort.

Doll hesitated before nodding slowly, "Alright then. But remember what me dad told you, eh? No funny business."

Horace grinned at the memory of her in the disused back bar of the Draughtsman, "Of course."

"'Ere, what's so funny?" she asked, frowning and smiling at the same time.

"Er, nothing," Horace managed not to laugh.

Doll stopped in her tracks, "Oh, right. I remember," she gave him a rueful grin, "'Ere, I 'ope you didn't get the wrong idea, mate. I weren't really like that, you know? Whether you believe it or not, you was the first guy I ever took back there."

Horace couldn't stop himself from looking surprised, "Really?"

Doll's look was a mixture of hurt and humour, "Yeah. Up till then anyway. You know wot it's like when you're a kid an' 'angin' out wiv an older crowd. "'Ave to impress them 'an all that."

"Yeah. Sorry. I sort of, well, you know? Assumed?"

"Not your fault. I'm not that 'appy about it meself. It's one of the reasons I dropped all that punk stuff. People sort of expect it. It can get you in some right scrapes, I'm telling you."

"I bet," Horace nodded, remembering his own nightmare that followed that fateful afternoon. "Anyw-w-way, I promise you're safe w-w-with me."

Doll looked at him and then nodded, her natural smile returning, "I don't know what it is about you, mate…" she trailed off blushing.

"W-w-what?"

Doll cleared her throat, "Nuffin'," she said as innocently as she could. "Come on, I'm starvin'."

When they reached his flat, Doll stood in the middle of his living room and turned a full circle, her jaw hanging open, "Bleedin' 'ell, this place is fantastic!"

"W-w-well I like it," Horace called from the kitchen, where he was busy ladling fried rice onto two plates. He brought them through and indicated that Doll should sit on the sofa, "Chopsticks or fork?"

"I reckon I'd better stick wiv a fork," Doll looked aghast at the two sticks. "Never could get the 'ang of them fings."

Horace laughed, "It's pretty easy really. I'll show you if you like?" He was determined to get a little control over *something*.

"Be it on yer own carpet."

It took them thirty minutes to clear their plates. It's not easy to eat while you're giggling hysterically.

When they'd finished, Doll insisted on taking the plates through to the kitchen to at least rinse them. Horace gave up the protests and settled back into the comfort of the sofa, his belly full, his inner-self happier than it had been for weeks.

"Where'd you get them paintings?" she asked when she returned, drying her hands on a tea-towel.

Horace looked up, puzzled, "Paintings?"

"The nudes on the kitchen wall."

"Oh, them. Actually, they're mine."

"I know that, silly, I meant where did you buy 'em?"

Horace smiled self-consciously, "I, er, didn't. W-w-when I said 'they're mine', I meant I painted them."

"Wow. They are seriously fucking good. Who are they?"

Horace shrugged. It wasn't a subject he wanted to get into, "Just a couple of girls from the college. I w-w-went to some art classes there; they posed for me." It was pretty much the truth.

Doll smiled, "Full of surprises, you are. College, art; any other 'idden talents?"

"None at all," Horace smiled back. "And I'm not even at college any more. I'm just killing time until the results come through."

Doll sat back beside him, one leg crossed under her so she could face him. She paused a moment, biting gently at her bottom lip, "Can I ask you summink?"

"W-w-whatever,"

306

"Look, I don't really know 'ow to say this," she paused again and then seemed to reach some sort of decision. "Wot it is, like, is, well… Do you reckon me and you could, sort of, go steady or whatever the right word is? I mean, I'm not really good at all this stuff, you know? I've only ever 'ad one proper boyfriend. I mean I've 'ad a couple of guys, but only one proper boyfriend, like…" she trailed off, blushing in a way that would challenge Horace's own powers of self-embarrassment.

Horace couldn't help but smile, "I don't think there's anything in the w-w-world that I'd rather do."

Doll let out a deep sigh, "Christ, I'm bleedin' glad that's over wiv!" She giggled, as much to herself as for Horace's benefit, and then leaned forward and kissed him.

The kiss went on for a minute or two before Horace gingerly raised his hand to Doll's shoulder, letting it slide down her arm, his thumb trailing across the side of her breast. He felt her stiffen slightly and pulled his hand away, breaking the kiss.

"S-s-sorry."

Doll shook her head, her face serious at first, before she gave a smile, "No, don't be. It's just me," she didn't meet his gaze.

"W-w-what is it?" he asked gently, "Had some sort of guy trouble before?"

Her head snapped up, a surprised look on her face. She stared at him for a moment and then nodded slowly, "Something like that," she said, her broad cockney tones disappearing for the present. "How did you know?"

Horace shrugged. To be honest, he wasn't really sure, "W-w-women's intuition?"

Doll giggled, a lot of her tension slipping away, "You're silly."

"W-w-want to tell me about it?"

Doll began to shake her head, but then stopped. She paused for a while before answering him, "I promise I *will* tell you. I mean, if we're gonna be, sorta, an item, I guess I'll 'ave to, but... it's all a bit too recent right now, you know?" Horace nodded. "It's not you, I promise you that," Doll went on, her mind playing back a memory, a small grin appearing on her face, "An' I'm, like, sorry if it's a pain an' all, but-"

Horace stopped her protestations and apologies with a kiss, "Don't worry. It's not a problem. For me, anyw-w-way."

"Sure?" Her half-smile giving away just how much she wanted to believe him.

"Absolutely."

She breathed out a sigh of relief, "I reckon I was right about you. You really are an okay sorta guy."

"Thanks, I think. W-w-what w-w-would you like to do now?"

Doll giggled, blushing.

"W-w-what?"

"Nuffin'," she replied, still grinning, "I was just finking. About them paintings, you know?"

"W-w-what about them?" Horace asked, confused with the direction of the conversation.

"If I could pluck up the nerve, d'you reckon you could do one of me?"

"I'd love to."

"Not yet, I mean," Doll went on quickly, "I mean, when we get to know each other a bit better, like..." she trailed off and giggled again. "Christ, what do I bleedin' sound like? I mean, the first time I met you, you was 'alf naked inside ten minutes, getting a right old

308

eyeful of my tits! And yet 'ere I am now, nervous as a fuckin' kitten!"

Horace laughed, "Doesn't seem very likely, does it?"

"What a prat!"

"Me or you?" Horace grinned.

"Now or then?"

They spent another hour in the flat, Doll begging Horace to show her all of his artwork, before heading back to the Crown and more Guinness. At eleven o'clock, Horace insisted on walking Doll back to the Draughtsman and when they got there, she in turn, insisted that he come inside. Like many pubs in the area, the licensing laws were taken as a very rough guideline rather than a hard and fast rule, and the place was more crowded than Horace had ever seen it.

A couple of the regulars called greetings to Doll, and she introduced Horace to them, calling him "her wonderful long-lost boyfriend", before dragging him to the corner of the long bar where they settled onto stools.

Jim Mercer shuffled over when he saw them and smiled at his daughter, "'Ave a good time, luv? This guy treat yer okay?"

"Yes and yes," she grinned, "'E's a real gent."

Jim nodded approvingly at Horace, "About time you got yerself a good 'un. Wot you youngsters 'avin' then?"

They ordered two more Guinness, Jim refusing Horace's offer to pay, "Any geezer that keeps my Doll 'appy is worth 'is weight in Guinness, mate."

They drank happily for another hour before Doll yawned, surprising herself, "Christ, sorry, Horace. Guess all the excitement's catching up wiv me."

He laughed and drained the rest of his pint, "Guess I'd better get going then."

She walked him outside through the back door, a nod in the general direction of the licensing laws, and they stood for a moment, staring into each other's eyes.

"Can I see you tomorrow, then?" Doll asked, shyly, barely able to keep her eyes on his.

"Anytime you w-w-want."

"'Ow about, I come and find you, say, midday?"

"Can't w-w-wait," he leaned down and kissed her gently.

Doll hugged him briefly and then released him, stepping back from the kiss, "Go on then. Get lost before I drag you back inside."

He laughed and nodded, "See you tomorrow then."

"Count on it," Doll called after him as he began his walk home.

From The Diary of Horace Wilt

"Tuesday, 24th August, 1982

DD,

Great news, at last! Guess who's got a girlfriend once more? I remembered the beautiful little punk girl, Doll, and went off in search of her. By the luckiest of coincidences she and her father have recently moved back into Walthamstow and he's the new manager/owner (dunno which) of The Draughtsman!!!

She was really happy to see me and now we're an item! Simple as that.

Finally, things are beginning to look up. She's really cute, as well - a bit like Harry in some ways; and she never stops talking and giggling. Happy days are here again, I guess!!!"

3

As promised, she arrived promptly at twelve the next day – and the next. By the end of the week, Horace once more had a pattern and meaning in his life, and found himself whistling as he doodled over another drawing, or while he paced the flat, waiting for Doll to arrive. His results were due to be released the following Tuesday, and he even found himself forgetting about them for an hour or two at a time.

On the fateful day, Doll got to his flat at eleven, intent on accompanying Horace to the college and, although he had been reluctant to face the results sheets, her enthusiasm won him over, and they raced the half-mile to the college.

Doll insisted on dragging him through the large double doors and then stopped, looking up at him expectantly, "Okay, where are they?"

Horace looked across at a small group of students by the main notice board. He took a deep breath, "I guess it's that w-w-way."

Doll, still holding his hand, dragged his reluctant form to the edge of the small group, "Well?" she asked, grinning from ear to ear.

"You look just like a little puppy."

"Charmin'. Me own boyfriend reckons I'm a dog."

"I didn't mean it like that! As I'm sure you're w-w-well aw-w-ware," he added with a mock-scowl, "It w-w-was a purely artistic observation."

"More like prevarication."

She kept on surprising him with the extent of her vocabulary, and Horace shook his head in wonder, "W-w-why don't you enrol here? You'd qualify, no problem."

Doll wrinkled her nose, Horace not having the nerve to say that the gesture was even more puppy-like, "I don't reckon they'd take on anyone wot sounded like me. And you're still prevaricating. Go find out 'ow you done!"

He hadn't been *entirely* prevaricating, but guessed he'd better do as he was told. He turned towards the board and scanned it for the business studies results. As so often before, he spotted Guy Pink's name before his own, and shuffled sideways to get a better look. He scanned down the list and then let out a massive sigh of relief. He'd passed – a second. It was an average score, but average or not, he was now the proud possessor of a degree. He quickly scanned the other names. Harriet had unsurprisingly got a double first, although Horace couldn't for the life of him remember her saying anything about doubling up the business studies with information technology. Fellows, he was glad to see, had failed. He was about to turn away and tell Doll the good news when his eyes were drawn to Stephanie's name. She'd got a first. He closed his eyes for a second, and then spun round, moving quickly away from the board. In his haste, he nearly flattened Doll.

"S-s-sorry, Doll," he shook his head.

"Oh, Horace," she sighed, sympathy dripping from her. "You did say that you could sit it again, though, didn't you?"

Horace stared at her, confused for a moment before realisation dawned. He shook his head, "No, that's okay. I passed, it's just..."

"Well, that's good, then, ain't it?" Doll asked, confused.

"Yeah, I guess it is, it's something else, that's all."

"What is it?" Doll pressed gently.

Horace closed his eyes a moment and then nodded once, firmly, to himself, "Come on through and I'll tell you," he said, taking her hand.

He led her through to the Student Union, which was unusually busy for this time of year, and settled her at a table. Over a pint of lukewarm lager, he told her all about Stephanie Jameson – everything about her. When he had finished, he finally raised his eyes in Doll's direction, from where they had been studying the worn carpet at his feet.

Her features radiated sympathy and something more complex that Horace couldn't read, "What a fucking tragedy," Doll said quietly, shaking her head.

Horace could only nod.

"I reckon what you should do is go over there to the phone and give 'er mum a call. Bet she'd be really 'appy if it was you wot told 'er. Better than some official envelope coming through 'er door or summink."

Horace gave a start, "Of course," he muttered, cursing his own lack of forethought, "You never cease to amaze me, Doll."

"Go on, then."

He returned a few minutes later, "You w-w-were right, as usual," he gave Doll a half-smile, "Sheila w-w-was really grateful."

"Told you."

"She told me that I w-w-was to go out and get celebratorially pissed, as it happens," Horace smiled at the recollection of her words, "On the grounds that I've got to get pissed for Steph as w-w-well as myself."

"There you go then," Doll beamed, glad that his melancholia seemed to have passed, "I'll give you an 'and then, if you like?"

Horace smiled, "Reckon you can carry me home after?"

"Nah, but I reckon I could put a lead round yer neck an' let you crawl after me."

"Deal. Come on then, let's go and find your uncle."

In the event, it was Doll who was the more drunk when they left the Crown at ten that night.

"I'm not sure w-w-what your dad w-w-will say w-w-when he sees you like this," Horace worried.

"Me neither," Doll agreed, disentangling her sleeve from a privet hedge which had jumped out at her. "Tell you wot, I'll give 'im a bell an' say I'm staying over wiv you. Wot d'ya reckon?"

Horace shrugged. Although he had met Jim Mercer on quite a few occasions, he had no idea what the man might say, "Up to you I guess. But w-w-where w-w-will you stay?"

Doll looked hard at him, confused as well as out of focus, "Well, wiv you, of course-" she stopped, suddenly realising that she hadn't even asked him if it was okay. She clamped a hand over her mouth and giggled. "Horry, Sorace... Sorry, Horace," she giggled again, "I mean, if it's okay wiv you?"

Horace laughed, "Of course it is. You can phone him from the flat. If he doesn't like the idea, I can call you a cab. And I promise to be a good boy."

"'E won't mind," Doll assured him. In fact, her father had been encouraging her to ''ang on to this geezer', and even insisting that she go back on the pill (much to her embarrassment).

They got back to the flat via an impressive collection of hedges, telegraph poles and a flower bed, and were giggling when Horace finally found the right key and let them in. Doll phoned her father when she had regained some semblance of control over her voice, and received not just approval, but some rather crude encouragement.

"Men!" she grumbled, after hanging up.

"W-w-what about us gorgeous creatures?"

"See wot I mean?"

Horace stuck out his tongue, "W-w-women!"

"Anyway," Doll hiccupped, "I bags the sofa for tonight."

"No chance! You'll have the bed. And before you start arguing, just remember I'm bigger than you."

"Who was gonna argue?" Doll grinned mischievously.

He threw a cushion at her and laughed, "Go on through, then. And since you've been such a good girl today, I'll even bring you through a coffee in the morning."

"Lucky me," Doll beamed. She jumped onto the sofa beside him and gave him a long goodnight kiss. "See you in the morning then," she climbed unsteadily off the sofa, "And not too early either. I reckon I'm gonna sleep like a log."

"You'll have a job. There's no fireplace through there."

She wrinkled her nose at him, before stumbling through to the bathroom and then into bed.

"There's a lock on the door if you w-w-want to use it," Horace called through.

"Wot? And miss me coffee in bed in the morning? No bleedin' chance. Night, Horace!"

4

Horace was surprised to find that he felt perfectly fit when he woke the next morning. He was also surprised to find that it was only eight o'clock; normally after a day like the previous one, he would be lucky to see eleven. Making sure that his boxer shorts were decent, he rose and started the coffee machine bubbling away before relieving his distended bladder.

When the coffee was ready, he pressed his ear to the bedroom door. All was silent on the other side and he quickly padded back into the kitchen, intent on waking Doll with the promised coffee. He poured it, added two sugars, and carried it carefully back through the living room.

He opened the door as quietly as he could and stepped inside, stopping abruptly. Doll was standing, naked, by the side of the window, peeping out at the street below. On hearing the door open, she spun around, a little gasp escaping her, quickly covering her breasts with one hand and her groin with the other.

"I'm s-s-sorry," Horace began to back out of the room.

"No, it's okay," Doll stopped him, breathlessly. She gave a nervous laugh, "And, besides, I desperately need that coffee."

Horace gulped and moved quickly to the bedside table, setting the mug down. He looked round at Doll who hadn't moved an inch, trying to keep his eyes focussed on her face, "I'm s-s-sorry. I'll be through in the living room w-w-whenever you w-w-want to come through." He made to leave again.

Again Doll stopped him, "No! Look… it's okay, no need for apologies…" she paused again. "If you really must know," she said, blushing, "I really don't mind you… being in 'ere," she took a deep breath.

"To be 'onest, wot I'm trying to do, right at this very minute…" she trailed off again.

"W-w-what?"

She giggled nervously, "Well, the fing is… Wot I really want to do right now… is, well, put me arms by me sides. They just don't seem to wanna obey me though."

Horace stared, open-mouthed, "You w-w-want to…"

Despite her furious blush, Doll pressed on, "Look, Horace. I really, really like you, an' I really, really wanna, well, get a bit more… intimate, like. It's just… as I said, I'd really love to let you, you know, *see* me, but some'ow me arms don't seem to be working."

"Perhaps they know b-b-best?"

"Nah, don't reckon so," she stared hard at him for a few seconds and then dropped her gaze to the carpet. "Would you… come 'ere?" she asked quietly.

He approached her cautiously until he was standing a foot away.

She raised her eyes from the carpet and stared into his, "Do me a favour?"

Not trusting himself to speak, Horace nodded.

Doll took a deep breath, "Promise me you won't run out on me?"

"Of course I won't," Horace managed, finding his voice, still confused.

At the periphery of his vision, he saw Doll's shoulders move as she dropped her hands to her sides. He realised that he was holding his breath.

Doll giggled quietly, nervously, "Well after all that effort you could at least 'ave a look."

Horace released the contained breath in a single long sigh and gave a chuckle, "G-g-good idea." He let his gaze wander downwards, "W-w-wow!"

Doll had clearly grown in the two years or so since he had last seen her in a state of undress. Her breasts were heavier, although still small, her nipples extraordinarily pale. Her hips flared from her narrow waist and the thatch of pubic hair below was a pale V-shape pointing between her surprisingly muscular thighs.

"Do I take that as approval?"

The ferret was all the answer Horace really needed to give, but he spoke anyway, "You are absolutely gorgeous."

"Thanks," Doll whispered, taking hold of Horace's hands. "Will you do me another favour?" she asked, her shy smile never leaving her face.

"Anything."

Doll took a deep breath, her breasts rising, "I know it's a terrible cliché, but I really mean this… Be gentle with me."

She waited until he nodded before closing the gap between them, pulling him tightly to her. They stayed that way for a while before she eased backwards, tugging on his arm and leading him to the bed.

Horace was as gentle as he could possibly be, his touches light, his caresses lighter. She was already highly aroused, damp and willing, but he took his time, easing himself slowly into her welcoming warmth, moving slowly, aware how small she was.

Afterwards, Doll lay curled against his chest, their sweat gradually cooling and after a couple of minutes, she wriggled backwards so that she could look into his eyes.

"Thanks," she said, a half-smile on her face.

Horace smiled back, "Surely that should be my line."

"No, I meant for being gentle."

"W-w-whatever."

"Only you see," she began slowly, then changed tack. "You remember me telling you I'd had some sort of problem?"

"I remember."

"Well, it was my last 'boyfriend'," she almost spat the word. "Well, 'e *wasn't* gentle. In fact, I didn't really want 'im to do, well, anything at all…"

"You mean he …," he couldn't bring himself to say the word. "You don't have to go on w-w-with this," Horace said, stroking her hair away from her face.

"I do," she nodded, staring up intently, "I guess 'e sort of forced me, but well, I guess I'd led 'im on a bit-"

Horace began to protest, but she stopped him, placing her fingers against his mouth.

"I know, but, well, that's what 'appened anyway," she looked at him ruefully. "Anyway, straight after that 'e just upped and pissed off. Got what 'e'd wanted, see?"

Horace looked at her aghast, "How could anywh-wh-one do something like that? Especially to somewh-wh-one as nice as you?"

"Yeah, well, 'e did. An' that's why I was sorta, well, not really very, well, you know? I mean, with you? Christ, I've *wanted* to be, pretty much from day one!"

Horace pulled her to him, "I told you, it isn't a problem. W-w-wasn't a problem. And if it's any consolation at all, don't w-w-worry, I'm not going to up and leave you now that I've got w-w-what I w-w-wanted."

"Oh," she giggled against his chest, "You did want to then?"

"Didn't it show?"

"Good God! If I'm not mistaken, it's showing again."

Horace felt a warm hand stroke his semi-tumescent member, "Could be," he swallowed noisily.

"At this rate I'll never get my coffee." She rolled Horace onto his back, sat up and stared down, a smile lightening her features. She shook her head once, emphatically. "This is bleedin' weird, mate."

"Oh?"

She nodded, "All this time I've been, well, you know? Sorta scared of well... sex, with you and now..."

"And now?"

She shrugged, swinging a leg over his thighs, "And now, I can't seem to think of anything else. Sod the bleedin' coffee."

5

"Christ almighty I'm sore," Doll grumbled in the Crown that lunchtime.

"You are?" Horace grinned. "The third time w-w-wasn't my idea."

"Hmm," she muttered, darkly. "Anyway, since I need time to recover before we start banging away again, wot are we gonna do in the meantime? Didn't you say summink about job 'untin'."

Horace groaned, "W-w-what if I promise I'll be really, really gentle?"

"What 'ave I started? Not that I'm complainin', mind you. Really though, wot are we gonna get up to?"

"Job hunting for me, I suppose," Horace didn't relish the idea, "And w-w-why don't you go down to the college and see if you can enrol? I mean, you're really fascinated w-w-with literature aren't you?"

"You really reckon I've gotta chance?"

"Absolutely. You're a damn sight smarter than you think – or than you make out anyw-w-way."

"But I ain't got any 'O' levels or stuff…"

"It shouldn't matter these days. Tell you w-w-what, w-w-we'll go down there together and I can probably get the Red Setter to have a w-w-word for you."

"The Red who?"

"Don't ask," Horace grinned.

They had just agreed to leave after their next pint when they were interrupted by a cry that made Horace's blood freeze in his veins.

"Darling! There you are!"

"Oh bugger, bugger, bugger," Horace groaned, ignoring Doll's quizzical look. "Hello mother, w-w-what on earth brings you here? Come to that, how did you know w-w-where to find me?"

His mother swept across the bar, the kaftan having been replaced by a violently bright yellow sari, "Lovely welcome as always," she tutted, smiling at her son. "And to answer your questions in order, Elspeth's car and you surely can't have forgotten that I've just spent eight weeks in India with Orchid. She bet me twenty pounds that I'd find you here. I must remember to post it to her; they go mad for Sterling over there. And who is this lovely little creature?"

As usual, Horace was finding hard to keep up with his mother's butterfly brain. "Harriet's still in India?"

His mother nodded, "She met up with some young men from America, and decided to extend her stay. Now, come on, darling, introduce me."

Horace shrugged, "Mother, this is Doll; Doll, this is, for my sins, my mother."

"Nice to meet you," Doll said politely, through a huge grin.

"Likewise," Horace's mother smiled back. "Are you and my son, shall we say, soul-mates?"

Doll giggled, "You could say that."

"You know," Horace's mother went on, "You do look a lot like his previous girlfriend, Orchid."

"Harriet, that is," Horace explained for Doll's benefit.

Doll shrugged, "I've seen pictures of her. I reckon I'm taller, blonder, and me tits are definitely bigger."

Horace winced; his mother laughed. She gave Doll a thorough once-over, "I do believe you're right," she smiled, "And you're maybe even more beautiful."

Doll blushed, "Ta."

"Mother-"

"Quiet, darling. Have you known Horace long?"

"Either a couple of weeks or a couple of years, depends 'ow you look at it."

"Well," Horace's mother said, "Take my advice. If you haven't got him into bed yet, make sure you do. Orchid reckons that he's quite marvellous."

Doll laughed loudly as Horace groaned, slumping beside her, "As a matter of fact, 'e's bleedin' brilliant. Or I s'pose you could say fuckin' brilliant. More appropriate, innit?"

Horace was whimpering as his mother laughed delightedly, "Glad you approve," she beamed at Doll, "At least my darling offspring has one talent; you might as well make the most of it."

"Please, mother?"

"Oh, I will," Doll said, "And as a matter of fact, 'e's got a couple of other talents too. 'Ave you seen any of 'is paintings? They're bleedin' brilliant. And, of course, 'e's got a degree now. Quite the little smartarse."

If Horace had been in possession of a white flag, he would have been frantically waving it by now, "Anywh-wh-one w-w-want a drink?"

The two women ignored him, "He's still dabbling with art?" his mother asked, surprised. "He used to be mad keen on it when he was knee high to a flea, but I had no idea he was still dabbling. You must let me see some of it. And he actually passed his degree! Quite amazing from what I've been told. Well done, darling. It was a third I suppose?"

"A second, actually," Doll said.

"Will wonders never cease!" his mother exclaimed, with a broad grin.

"Charming. If anywh-wh-one's interested, I'm having a beer."

"What was that, darling," his mother seemed to notice that he was actually present.

"Drinks anywh-wh-one?" he asked again.

Doll nodded and his mother asked for a large gin.

Horace hurried away to the sanctuary of the bar. "Two Guinness and a large gin please, Fred."

"Who's the batty old mare?" Fred asked.

"Unfortunately, my mother," Horace replied darkly.

"Oops, sorry, H."

"I don't see w-w-why *you're* sorry. It's my mother that's the batty old mare."
"She can't really be that bad, can she?"

"W-w-worse," Horace complained, paying for the drinks. "I'll tell you all about her sometime w-w-when I've got a couple of hours to spare."

He left the laughing Fred and carried the drinks reluctantly back to the table. Doll and his mother were giggling like school kids.

"Oh, thank you, darling," his mother said as he handed her the gin, "You've certainly got a wonderful eye for the ladies. There's only one possible name for this little one – Diamond."

"Rough diamond, maybe" Horace gave a mock-scowl in Doll's direction.

"Don't be mean, darling," his mother chided as Doll stuck out her tongue, "And make yourself, useful, dear. Go and see if Elspeth wants to join us for a while, I'm sure she'd be very interested in what our little Diamond has been telling me."

Horace took the time to give Doll a very black look before asking his mother, "Elspeth is outside?"

"I did tell you I came in her car."

"You didn't say anything about Elspeth being in it though. I'd really rather not-"

"Don't be a silly, darling! Sometimes I find it hard to believe that my very own son is the end product of millions of years of evolution. Now, be a good Moonchild and go and fetch her. And before you make any silly comments, she's quite properly dressed."

He winced and made slowly for the door, Doll's questioning voice following him.

"Moonchild?"

It wasn't hard for him to spot Elspeth's car; there were very few hearses parked in this area. He took a couple of deep breaths and approached the midnight-black vehicle. He was about to knock on the window, when the glass slid down silently.

"Hello, Horace," Elspeth breathed.

He swallowed noisily and ducked down to her level. His head clattered against the top of the window frame as he shot upright again. If that was his mother's idea of 'properly dressed' she was even weirder than he'd thought. Elspeth was wearing a long black skirt below a black silk blouse that was open to the waist, her breasts almost completely exposed.

"What can I do for you?" Elspeth asked huskily, a hint of humour in the sultry tones.

"I, er, that is, my mother, w-w-wondered w-w-whether you might like to join us for a d-d-drink?" He prayed for a negative answer.

His prayers weren't answered. "I'd be totally delighted."

He stepped back as the door opened and Elspeth swung her long legs onto the pavement. He couldn't help but stare at her as she slowly stood upright, the blouse gaping open even further. Horace couldn't remember ever seeing naked breasts on a street in Walthamstow before.

"I, er, that is, w-w-well…"

"Yes?" Elspeth asked, one immaculate eyebrow raised.

"Your, er, I m-m-mean…" he nodded at her still gaping blouse, "I don't think that… w-w-well, there's s-s-sort of a d-d-dress code in the bar," he finished lamely.

Elspeth stared down at herself, "How very quaint." She pulled the blouse free of her skirt and held the two front tails in her hands, pausing in the act of tying them under her breasts. "Don't be ashamed to look, Horace," she smiled darkly, "One should never be ashamed of the beauty of Mother Nature's creations. You do think I'm beautiful, don't you? I can… *see* these things."

She was gazing directly into his eyes. Had she been gazing three feet lower, she would have had no need of the question.

"I, er, that is…"

"Well?" Elspeth pressed him, still holding the blouse open.

Horace looked around frantically, praying that no-one was close enough to witness this, "I, er, w-w-well, yes you're, er, very b-b-beautiful," he said desperately, hoping that his agreement would hasten the cover-up.

Elspeth nodded, satisfied, and very slowly tied the two tails of her blouse tightly, "You really must come and see me at the Heart," she told the blushing Horace.

"I, er, oh, w-w-whatever," he managed, resolved to yet more embarrassment, "C-c-come on then." He walked quickly back to the bar, desperate to put plenty of space between them. He certainly didn't want anyone to think that she might actually be with him.

The next two hours passed extraordinarily slowly for Horace, even though he spent most of it standing at the bar, for once grateful for Flat-Foot Fred's conversation.

"I drink, therefore I am," Fred said at one point.

"How about, 'Beauty is in the eye of the beer-holder'?" Horace countered.

"My favourite," Fred laughed, "Is that old Dean Martin one – 'You're not really drunk if you can lie on the floor without holding on'."

"Good wh-wh-one." Horace looked over to the table and saw his mother beckoning him. He wandered over reluctantly. "I can't tell you how much this reminds me of Macbeth; act one, scene one," he commented grumpily.

His mother and Elspeth both looked blank, but Doll gently slapped the back of his thigh, "Not nice, H."

His mother gave him a frown before shrugging, and getting around to the subject in hand, "I know it's a bit of a delicate subject, darling," she began, Horace's groan starting some limbering-up exercises, "But we have a little problem at the Heart, and you might be in a position to help us."

Horace stared back dubiously; he couldn't possibly see how he might be able to help them with any problem they might have, and, for that matter, couldn't imagine wanting to, "Yes?"

"Well, the thing is, darling, we're running desperately short of space, and until we finalise the deal on the mansion-"

"W-w-what!? I mean w-w-what mansion?"

"Didn't I tell you, darling? We're buying an old place a few miles from town. More space you see – and more privacy come to that."

"Sounds like a good idea." The further away they were, the more it suited him.

His mother gave him another frown but continued anyway, "Well, as I was saying, we're very short of space at the Heart and we've decided that it might be best if one or two of us moves out for a few months until the mansion is ready. That's where you come in."

Horace's smile slipped away faster than a politician's manifesto promise, "Oh, no! The flat's not a bad size, but it's not nearly big enough for lodgers."

His mother trilled a laugh, "Of course, darling. Besides, with the reputation you've got for the ladies, I'm not sure it would be safe for them anyway." She ignored his spluttered protests, "But, well, this is the delicate bit, you see? I know you were good friends with Stephanie, but her flat is, well, unoccupied, so to speak, and we were wondering whether you could maybe have a word for us?"

Horace began to shake his head. The thought of someone taking Stephanie's flat didn't unduly bother him. What bothered him was any closer association with his mother's lunatic cult, "I really don't think that w-w-would be a good-"

Doll interrupted, "Don't be mean, H. I think it's a great idea. I know if I 'ad a flat there, I'd be really 'appy to know who my new neighbours were."

"That's just the point," Horace continued, "I really don't know anywh-wh-one at the cult. Other than mother, Maisie and Elspeth, that is."

"There you go then," his mother beamed, "You see, Elspeth has volunteered to move out for a while, haven't you dear?"

"Oh, yes," Elspeth breathed, her eyes locked on the hapless Horace, a small smile playing around her purple lips.

"Oh, no!" Horace objected, "No! Definitely not!"

"Whyever not, darling?" his mother asked.

Horace avoided looking in Elspeth's direction as he tried to form a cogent argument, "W-w-well, I mean, she's... W-w-well, the, er... dress for one thing. I mean it's a v-v-very respectable address-"

"Oh, I shall be very discreet," Elspeth promised.

"Of course you will, dear. Now, don't be a silly, darling. Will you put in a word for us?"

"'E will," Doll told them over Horace's further splutterings, "I think Elspeth's great. And it'll be nice for you to 'ave someone of yer own age upstairs. I mean, the last thing you want is an OAP or summink, innit?"

Horace thought that an OAP would be perfect and was just about to say so, but he was stopped by Elspeth.

"Horace, really," she breathed, "I'll be on my best behaviour. My very best."

Horace, panicking, turned to Doll, "Listen!" he whispered fiercely, "You don't know w-w-what she's really like. She's a, a, vampire!"

Doll laughed, "Yer mother's right, H. You really are a silly. Now, be a good boy and tell them you'll do it."

Horace groaned. He always prided himself on getting on well with women; probably something to do with being brought up as a single child by his single mother, but there were times when they frightened him half to death. Elspeth could do it on her own, and here he was now, faced by three of them ganging up on him.

"Come on, darling," his mother encouraged. "You've already offended Elspeth enough. Now make it up to her by helping us out with our little problem."

Despite thinking that 'little problem' was litotes taken to its extreme, Horace knew when he was beaten, "I really don't think…" he began before trailing off, his shoulders slumping. "Oh alright," he muttered under his breath.

"What was that, darling?"

"I said 'alright'."

"Good boy," Doll grinned.

"Very good," Elspeth added, smiling broadly.

"Well, go on then," his mother prompted.

Horace looked at her blankly.

"No time like the present," his mother said. "It's only five minutes up the road, but I'm sure Elspeth would give you a lift if you wanted, wouldn't you dear?"

Elspeth didn't have time to respond before Horace jumped to his feet, "No! I mean, er, no, I guess I could do with some fresh air after a shock like this. I'll go and see Penny then. If you're sure this is a good idea…"

"Of course it is, darling," his mother said firmly. "Now off you go."

Summarily dismissed, Horace drained the last of his pint and trudged across to the doors. When his back was turned towards the women, he allowed himself a grin. Just because he was going to *ask*, didn't mean the answer would be 'yes'. And of course, should he happen to forget to ask… well, who was to know?

The grin disappeared as a voice at his shoulder said, "Don't mind if I come with you, do you darling? Only there's one or two things I need to tell you in private."

"Mother!" Horace protested, but she was in no mood to be denied.

"And besides, son of mine," she gave him a knowing smile, "You were brought up by a devious woman and I do believe some of it has rubbed off on you. I think it might be sensible if I come along just to make sure you don't 'forget' anything."

Horace left the pub with his mother hanging on to his elbow, a thoroughly beaten man.

6

Despite his fervent prayers, Penny was more than happy to issue a four month contract on Stephanie's former flat – especially when Horace's mother paid everything in advance. His mother then insisted that they popped upstairs for five minutes so that she could give him something, and he trudged after her, thoroughly demoralised.

"Well, that was all nice and straightforward, wasn't it, darling?"

"Oh, just *perfect*."

"Elspeth's a really lovely girl when you get to know her. And I don't see why you object to her, shall we say, leisurely dress sense after seeing that young woman downstairs." True to form, Penny had been wearing a micro-mini and a distinctly see-through blouse – although "wearing" was probably too strong a word.

"W-w-whatever."

"Anyway," his mother continued, business-like. She handed him an envelope, "I just wanted to give you this, dear. I suppose you'll be looking for a job soon and I thought it might come in handy."

Horace shrugged and tore it open. Inside was a small blue booklet, a gold crest on its front cover. Raising an eyebrow he opened the book and stared down at the two lines of type that had been added to the first pale-blue page:

'Wilt, H: Account No. 5434322-1216HWPIM

Credit – 14-09-82: 40,000.00'

Horace stared at the final figure for another ten seconds, trying to work out whether what he was seeing was true.

"But that's f-f-f-"

"Yes, darling, I know. Now that you'll be looking for work, you'll need to get yourself a few things, a decent wardrobe, for instance."

"For this much I could get a whole house, never mind a w-w-wardrobe!"

"Well, whatever you feel like, darling. I just wanted to make sure you'll be okay after we move out to the wilds of Kent."

Horace stared at her in amazement, "W-w-where on earth do you get all this money from?"

His mother laughed, "Well we do seem to be canning it at the cult," she ignored his correction as usual and smiled broadly at him, "But as it happens, that little sum has been waiting for you since before you were born, darling. One of the suspected fathers signed it over to me."

Horace frowned at his mother, "You never have told me who the suspects w-w-were."

"True. But let's just say that neither of them would benefit from the knowledge being made public. One of them has even built his career around the concept of celibacy, but I`m probably saying too much already."

Horace stared at his mother, a mixture of horror and wonder on his face, "You don't mean-"

"Anything at all, darling," she interrupted. "Now, we'd better be getting back to the girls with the good news."

Horace stared after her as she bustled out of his front door, sari shimmering in the afternoon sunlight. Could she really have meant...? He shook his head and trailed after her.

Elspeth was delighted by the news and even more delighted when Horace told her that the flat was ready for occupation. Elspeth decided that she would move her things in on the Thursday, declining Doll's offer of assistance. "I've only a handful of things, dear. And apart from my crystals, there's nothing that weighs more than a few ounces."

"Certainly true of her clothes," Horace muttered as he made his way to the bar with another drinks order.

From The Diary of Horace Wilt

"Tuesday, 21st September, 1982

DD,

Talk about a day of contrasts! Doll and I made love this morning!!! That was wonderful, marvellous and beautiful. This afternoon, though, my rotten mother arrived at the Crown with Elspeth (who actually flashed her breasts in the street!!!!) and somehow managed to persuade me to get Penny to lease Steph's old flat to her.

I just hope and pray I can stay out of Elspeth's way; I'm convinced she's got designs on my body. Now that things are progressing so wonderfully with Doll, that's the last thing I need! I've got to take steps to make sure nothing goes wrong."

7

The start of the job hunting and the promised trip with Doll to the college were postponed until the following day on the grounds that it was after five o'clock when his mother and Elspeth left the pub. Horace and Doll decided that an early night would be a good idea for both of them, and Horace walked her back to The Draughtsman at eight.

"I w-w-wish you could come back w-w-with me," he said outside after a night-cap at the bar.

"I'd like to, but I s'pose it'd look a bit odd after comin' back 'ere."

"Tomorrow night?"

"Yeah, why not," Doll cuddled up to him, "Dad'll be glad to get me out from under 'is feet."

"And the night after?" Horace smiled down.

"If you can put up wiv me?"

"I can. W-w-what about Friday night, too? And Saturday. And Sunday."

Doll pulled back so she could read his face, "'Ere, are you suggestin' wot I fink you're suggestin'?"

"That you move in w-w-with me?" Horace grinned. "If you'd like to, then yes."

"I…" Doll trailed off, a surprised look on her face. "You know, mate, I said I'd never sorta move in wiv anyone…" She continued quickly when a disappointed look come over Horace's face, "But, as

I've said before, there's something different about you. So, if you really mean it, I guess the answer's 'yes, please'."

Horace hugged her tightly, "That's such a relief."

"You reckon I'd say no then?"

"I w-w-was a bit concerned. But now that there's going to be two of us there at night, I w-w-won't be too w-w-worried about the vampire upstairs."

Doll thought about this for a moment and then smacked his rump as hard as she could, giggling at the same time, "You can be really 'orrid sometimes. But I guess I'll let you off this once. Come on, mate, let's go tell dad the news."

Horace wasn't too sure about that – about how Jim Mercer would take it – but was dragged into the bar anyway.

The job hunting and visit to the college had to be postponed until the Thursday, after the all-night party in The Draughtsman left neither of them in any state to face the world on the Wednesday.

8

The visit to the college coincided with Elspeth's arrival – to Horace's immense relief – and he chatted happily with Guy Pink after the lecturer had taken Doll along to the faculty of Literature, introducing her to the senior tutor there.

The Red Setter expressed more than a little surprise at Horace's degree pass, but also offered him some guidance for the job-hunting.

"Your best bet, old boy, is to go into any branch of a High Street bank and just ask to see a personnel officer. A couple of years in a bank and you can either decide to press on with it as a career, or branch out into some other related business; you'll get a fairly wide range of experience at the ground level that way."

Horace nodded, it sounded plausible and he had been dreading visits to employment agencies, "I might just do that."

"Good man," Guy said, "And, by the way, make sure you wear a suit when you go in; makes it look as if you're serious."

"I'll go and buy wh-wh-one as soon as w-w-we leave," Horace promised.

They were interrupted by Doll's return. She was beaming from ear-to-ear, "I don't bleedin' believe it!" she squealed delightedly.

"I take it Barbara was suitably impressed?" Guy smiled.

"Yeah. She said she was gonna give me an 'attitude test', and of course, me an' my big mouth, I says, 'Don't you mean aptitude?' Well I reckoned I'd blown it right there and then, but she just gave a silly laugh and said 'Congratulations, that's the first test passed'!

Couldn't believe it! Anyway," Doll babbled on, "I sit down an' go through the test; she marks it straight away, and as long as I can stump up three 'undred quid, I can start in two weeks on a proper, no nonsense, degree course."

"You'll qualify for a grant, as well," Guy said.

"That's fantastic, Doll," Horace beamed, "And don't w-w-worry about the money. I'll make sure it's all okay."

Her smile slipped, "I'm sure me old man would-"

Horace put his finger to her lips, "I said, don't w-w-worry. Remember how much my mother gave me?" he had shown an incredulous Doll the building society book that morning.

"Well, if you're sure?" Doll's smile returned to full strength.

"I am."

Doll shook her head in wonder, "This is just so fuckin' incredible!" she squealed and then covered her mouth with her hand. "Sorry," she said to Guy, "I mean, it's just so, well, *very* incredible."

Guy laughed, "Don't apologise, dear. You're about to embark on a course of English Literature, and you'll be absolutely amazed at how, shall we say, Anglo-Saxon, Shakespeare could be."

"Yeah, I guess so."

She and Horace bade Guy a happy farewell and danced out into the sunlight.

"We should go an' celebrate," Doll told Horace, "Everything's comin' out really good, innit?"

"Definitely. And w-w-while w-w-we're on a roll, there's something I'd better do before a drink." He told her about Guy's suggestion, and they made for the nearest tailor. Half an hour later, Horace emerged in an immaculate three-piece suit, high-collared white shirt, dark tie and black brogues which reflected the late-morning sunlight.

"Bleedin' 'ell," Doll breathed approvingly, "You really look the part."

"Sure that's not 'the prat'?" Horace asked, running a finger under the unfamiliar collar.

"Definitely not!"

Horace's luck really did seem to be well set. He walked into the nearest bank and, after asking a teller if he could have a word with the personnel officer, he was shown through to a brightly lit office and told to relax until Mr Graham arrived.

A young man entered the room a few minutes afterwards. "Mr Wilt?"

Horace gave his customary wince and then nodded, "Horace."

Mr Graham introduced himself and then chatted for a while about employment options, Horace's academic record and, inconsequentially, rock music. Ten minutes into the conversation he appeared to be satisfied and asked Horace to complete a three page application form while he 'stepped outside to see what we have'.

Horace had just completed the form when Mr Graham returned.

"Well, Horace," he beamed, "I've some good news for you. There's a grade three post coming up at our Hackney branch in the first week of December. You seem to be ideal and so," he paused dramatically, "The job is yours if you'd like it."

Horace stared in amazement, "J-j-just like that?"

"As Tommy Cooper would say," Mr Graham nodded. He handed a sheaf of papers to Horace, "In there you'll find all you need to know about us and about what your work will entail. And this will be your starting salary, subject to review after a six month probationary period, of course." He scribbled a few digits on the pad in front of him, turning it round so Horace could see it.

Horace hadn't known what sort of salary to expect, but this exceeded his wildest dreams, "That's, er, very good."

"Splendid," Mr Graham said. "Well, that's all there is to it. We'll send your contract in the post." He rose and offered his hand across the desk.

Horace, still shell-shocked, rose and grasped the proffered hand, "Thank you." He tried to cover his amazement with a smile.

"Thank *you*," Mr Graham beamed back, "And welcome to our happy little family. I also cover the personnel requirements in the Hackney area, so no doubt I'll see you after you start."

Horace was shown out of the office by a pretty young woman, her name tag bearing the legend 'Donna'. "I take it that you'll be joining us?" she asked.

Horace nodded, "December. The Hackney branch."

"Oh, good," the girl smiled, "I'm starting down there myself in a couple of weeks. Look forward to seeing you there then."

Horace nodded again, "Yes. At least I'll recognise wh-wh-one person w-w-when I start."

Donna left him at the door and he hurried outside to Doll, who was finishing the last of a hot dog.

"Well?" she swallowed hard.

"As of December, I'm employed," he beamed.

She stared at him open-mouthed, "You mean, just like that?"

"As Tommy Cooper w-w-would say," Horace nodded, wiping a trail of mustard from Doll's chin.

She let out a whoop of joy and flung her arms around him, "Well done, H! Wot a fuckin' fantastic day, eh?"

Horace nodded happily and kissed the top of her head, "Not bad at all. Now, how about that drink?"

From The Diary of Horace Wilt

"Thursday, 22nd September, 1982

DD,

Well that was easy! Time spent job hunting: 1 hour. Number of jobs obtained: 1. I'm going to be starting at the Hackney branch of my bank in December as a grade three - whatever that might be. I can't believe how simple it all was - must remember to ask Doll to thank Guy for me (she's starting at the college in a couple of weeks; and it was Guy that recommended the course of action).

Let's just hope that I like the job - I've got rather used to bumming around the flat all day. Mind you, with Doll at college, I guess I won't have much else to do."

9

To Horace's surprise, Elspeth didn't start causing problems from the very first day, his purchase of a string of garlic cloves proving to be overkill. Other than occasionally popping into the Crown for a quick Bloody Mary (What else could it have possibly been? Horace thought), Elspeth kept herself to herself.

Doll spent the two weeks before her course started in a state of high excitement, buying, after encouragement from Horace, a complete new wardrobe for her role as student. She had moved the last of her things into his flat the day after her visit to the college, and life had quickly settled into a comforting pattern.

On the weekend before she started her degree, Horace finally managed to persuade Doll to pose for him – if nothing else, to take her mind off college for a while. Despite her earlier misgivings, Doll was soon giggling as she lay back, naked, on the sofa, and it was all Horace could do to hang onto the brushes as he began to capture her on canvas. After two hours Doll became restless and wanted to see what progress Horace had made, but he refused, hastily covering the easel and chasing her into the bedroom.

"'Ere, I've gotta complaint," Doll giggled as they wrestled on the bed.

"Not catching, I hope."

Doll poked her tongue out, "Nah, silly. But you said you was gonna paint me in the nude."

"Yes?"

"Well, you've still got yer clothes on," Doll giggled.

"Not exactly original," Horace replied, "But we can soon change the situation."

It was another hour before Horace resumed his artwork.

10

Horace finished the painting during Doll's first day at college, relishing the now-unfamiliar peace and quiet, and, satisfied with the result, he took it down to the market in the afternoon so that Pete Baker at *The Artful Artist* could frame it.

Horace had just finished hanging it in the bedroom when Doll let herself into the flat, scampering through to find him, already babbling excitedly about all that had happened at college. She stopped in her tracks as she caught sight of the painting. Horace had made her promise not to take a peek at it until it was finished, and he could see from the look of surprise and delight on her face, that she had kept the promise.

"Wow," she breathed, staring at her image.

"Like it?"

"Like it!" Doll exclaimed breathlessly, "It's fuckin' brilliant!" She quickly covered her mouth with her hand. "Sorry, I know I did promise not to swear so much, but, well, wot else could I say? It's really fantastic! Do I really look that nice?" she blushed as she asked the question.

"It's very life-like," Horace assured her, delighted with her reaction, "So don't question my artistic talents. You're beautiful, you know?"

Doll hardly noticed the compliment, "And you framed it beautifully."

"Ah! Actually, I don't trust myself to do the framing; I, er, know a guy in the market who does it for me."

Doll turned to him, "You mean that you took that painting down to some guy in the market?" she asked, her smile slipping.

"W-w-well, er, yes. As I said, I didn't w-w-want to go and ruin it by being my usual clumsy self."

To his surprise, Doll's smile returned, "I'm not sure I could look the guy in the face, but, well, you know 'ow shy I am an' all that? Well, this is sorta different, some'ow. It's such a fu... bleedin' good painting, and I guess I *do* look pretty good in it..." she trailed off.

Horace had raised an inquisitive eyebrow, "Not so shy now, w-w-when it comes to art?"

"Yeah, I reckon you were right all along. It's like I said; it's different some'ow."

"W-w-want me to hang it in the living room, then?"

Doll blushed, "You reckon it wouldn't look out of place?"

Horace had a number of paintings hung on the walls, including a couple of Stephanie and one of Harriet, "It should take pride of place," Horace assured her.

"And I guess we could always, sorta, 'ide it if anyone comes and I lose me nerve, I s'pose?" Doll's blush deepened.

"That's settled then," Horace smiled and took down the painting. He carried it through to the living room and hung it there to the background noise of Doll's account of her first day at college. After agreeing to help her with the book hunting needed for her Literature course – if he had thought his own reading list was long, this one seemed endless – they retired to the Crown to celebrate Doll's start on the road to education.

The first person to see Doll's painting was Elspeth who had popped down to Horace's flat a few days later to borrow some honey. She was chatting with Doll in the living room while Horace rooted through his kitchen cupboards, and spotted the painting as she glanced around the room.

"Well, well," she said after doing a slow double-take between the painting and Doll, "It would seem that Moonflower was right about her son's talents. That's a fantastic image of you."

"Ta," Doll grinned. "It is good, innit?"

"Very," Elspeth agreed as Horace returned from the kitchen, wiping the outside of a honey jar with a damp cloth.

"Bit sticky, I'm afraid," he looked up at Elspeth.

She took the jar from him and slid it into a plastic bag, "Thank you, Horace. I was just telling Diamond that you possess a great talent."

Horace looked confused, "Talent?"

Elspeth nodded in the direction of Doll's picture, "You've not just captured her likeness, you seem to have somehow captured the very essence of her character. It's a truly remarkable piece."

"It's, er, w-w-well, thank you."

"Perhaps," Elspeth smiled, "You would do me the honour of capturing me? I'm not without vanity, as you know."

"I, er, that is…"

"Yeah, go on, H," Doll nodded.

"I will, of course, pay you for your efforts."

Horace tried to explain that this might not be a very good idea, but the combined persistence of the two women finally got him to make a vague promise that he "w-w-would think about it".

"I really don't like the idea," Horace told Doll when Elspeth had retired to what Horace referred to as 'The Belfry'.

"Don't be daft. You're really good at it, *and* she offered to pay you. You never know, you might be able to make a few bob on the side with this art stuff."

"Yes, but you know w-w-what she's like."

"She's perfectly okay," Doll said, "And besides, she even said that I can be there if it makes you feel any 'appier."

Horace grunted. It was true that Elspeth really *had* said that – to his surprise – and it was also true that, from an artistic point of view, Elspeth was an interesting character; all dark shadows whereas his three other life models had been fair, both in hair and features, "W-w-well, I suppose, if you promise to stand guard…"

"Good boy," Doll grinned, "And while we're on the subject of your artistic talents, I told Marva about it. She'd like to come and see it, if you don't mind?"

"Marva?"

Doll sighed, "I'm sure you don't listen to a word I say when it comes to college. Yes, Marva. She's the black girl on the same course as me. We went to junior school together, years back, remember?"

Horace nodded vigorously, "Of course." In fact he could only remember the names of a couple of Doll's classmates, and Marva certainly wasn't one of them. "Anyw-w-way, w-w-why's she interested?"

Doll giggled, "Well, see? Christmas is coming up, an' she wants to give 'er boyfriend a surprise. Apparently, 'e's been on at 'er fer months to 'ave a, sorta, few photos done, but she's too shy," Horace shrugged as Doll paused to make sure he was listening. "Anyway, I told 'er about 'ow good you were, an' about this painting, an' she reckons that she might be able to pluck up enough courage to, like, sit for you – if you don't mind, that is?"

Horace grinned, shaking his head, "That's definitely wh-wh-one of the things I love about you."

"Wot's that then?"

"Encouraging me to spend hours looking at naked ladies."

"And gettin' paid for it, don't forget. I reckon, by rights, I should be getting' a commission 'ere. Anyway, wot do you reckon about Marva?"

Horace shrugged. Once again, from an artistic point of view, the idea appealed; he'd never painted a black person before. He also remembered his long-held desire to try out a composition using two contrasting characters, something that he had never got round to with Harriet and Stephanie, "Sounds as if it might be okay," he said and then grinned. "Tell you w-w-what. I'll do a deal w-w-with you?"

"Oh?"

Horace told her about his idea of a composition of contrasts, "So, if you agree, then I could probably do both in wh-wh-one or two sittings."

Doll wrinkled her nose, "I'm not sure, H. I mean, me posing wiv someone else."

"W-w-why not? After all, she is a w-w-woman?"

Doll giggled, "A *big* woman, mate. For a start, you probably won't get both of us on a single canvas."

"W-w-well, think about it," Horace grinned back.

"Christ, the things I do fer you. Tell you wot? I'll invite 'er over on Saturday. I mean, I don't even know if *she'll* pluck up the courage yet, let alone me."

"W-w-whatever."

"Anyway," Doll said brightly, "I'm off upstairs to tell Elspeth you'll do 'er. The painting that is.' Horace's smile slipped off his face. Doll grinned at his discomfort. "And before you ask, there's no fuckin' way that I'm gonna pose with our resident vampire, so don't even think it!"

Horace, for some reason, had never given the matter a moment's thought. He was subconsciously scared that Elspeth would eat Doll.

11

Logistical difficulties meant that Horace wasn't able to start on either painting before he started work at the bank and as the day approached he realised that he was becoming increasingly nervous about the prospect. He had never liked meeting new people and also he'd never had a job before.

He had sent the signed contract to the bank in mid-November and had received in return the bank's booklet detailing the rules, regulations, pay-scales, and holiday entitlements. The Friday before he was due to start, he picked up the booklet and began to read it. By midday he had finished and was becoming depressed. Apparently, his duties would be mainly associated with the back-room, finance, side of business, but even going in as a grade three and a graduate, he would have to take his turn on the floor of the bank and in the post room. He would also have to be referred to by his surname at all times.

Downhearted, he was about to make his way to the Crown when there was a knock on his door. Shrugging into his thickest jacket – the weather had turned arctic over the last few days – he called for whoever it was to "w-w-wait a minute", and put his bulging wallet in the front pocket of his jeans. Satisfied he was ready to leave, he opened the front door.

"Hello, neighbour," Elspeth greeted him huskily.

"Oh, er, Hello, Elspeth." Although she had behaved impeccably since she arrived, there was always something that troubled Horace when he was around her. Today it was the fact that she seemed to be wearing nothing more than a purple silk dressing gown two sizes too small for her, and only held shut by her arms, crossed under her breasts, "W-w-what can I do for you?" he asked, trying to keep his eyes focussed on hers.

"A small favour on Tuesday fortnight," Elspeth smiled, "If it's not a problem?"

Horace did some quick mental arithmetic, "The, er twenty-first?"

"Quite so."

"Er, w-w-what sort of favour?"

"Well," Elspeth smiled, "Firstly you know about my beliefs, don't you?" Horace nodded. "You must also appreciate that my apartment is on the other side of the building to yours, yes?" Horace dutifully nodded again. "So, I have a small problem."

"W-w-which is?"

"I cannot clearly see the sunrise from any room in my apartment," she said. "It's important to my beliefs and so I was wondering whether I might be able to make use of your apartment?"

Horace did some more quick calculations. The only room that directly faced the sunrise this time of year was his bedroom and he started to protest before he realised something else. "W-w-what t-t-time does the sun, er, rise?"

"A little after eight fifteen."

Horace breathed a sigh of relief. By eight fifteen, he would have left the flat to get to the bank in Hackney. "I guess that'll be okay then. I'll leave the door on the catch if Doll's not going to be here."

Elspeth looked surprised, "Why, thank you, Horace. That really is most extraordinarily kind. Are you sure you cannot join me for the ceremony?"

"That's okay, and, I'm afraid not; w-w-work you see?"

"As you wish, Horace. Anyway, I must let you go now, I can see you are on your way out. By the way, is it still on for the sitting on Saturday week?"

Horace's light-hearted feeling rapidly put on weight, "Er, yes, I, er, guess so."

"I can't wait," Elspeth grinned, the white of her teeth just visible between lips that were painted the darkest shade of red.

"Me n-n-neither," Horace managed.

Elspeth stood back from the doorway to let him out and he gratefully pulled the door closed behind him, locking it more out of habit than necessity.

"Oh, by the way," Elspeth stopped him as he made for the stairs, "Do you think a small crystal in my navel will spoil the effect of your composition?"

Horace shrugged, "I don't see w-w-why; if it detracts in any w-w-way, I can alw-w-ways paint it out."

"Only, I've just bought this beautiful Amethyst," Elspeth grinned again, her green eyes narrowing slightly, and pulled apart the dressing gown.

Horace gulped noisily, staring momentarily at her proud breasts, the near-perfect diamond shape of her jet black pubic hair, and the glittering purple crystal in her navel, before snapping his eyes back to her face, "That's, er… it'll be f-f-fine. And really, Elspeth, I do w-w-wish you w-w-wouldn't do things l-l-like that. W-w-what if old Mr Benjamin sees you?"

Elspeth laughed, and pulled the robe shut, "Oh, Horace. Diamond's quite right, you are a silly. And, for your information, Mr Benjamin is visiting his relatives in Australia. There's only the two of us here."

Horace found this in no way comforting, but at least it explained why he hadn't heard Terry Wogan's dulcet tones drifting through his kitchen ceiling recently, "Yes, w-w-well, I'll see you later then." He hurried to the stairs before his resident vampire could reply.

12

Horace hardly slept a wink the night before he started work and as he rolled over, mumbling to himself for the hundredth time, Doll sat up beside him and switched on the bedside lamp.

"Oh, you poor thing."

"Just for wh-wh-once, I *feel* like a poor thing," Horace groaned, also sitting up.

"Come 'ere," she whispered, tugging gently on his arm.

Horace let himself be drawn across the broad bed and lay back beside her.

"Perhaps this'll take your mind off things," Doll suggested, a mischievous grin on her face. She began to run her hands down his chest, a gentle, circular motion. Horace felt some of the tension draining out of him. It began to pour out as her hands slid ever-lower, finally grasping his now-erect member.

He swallowed noisily, "That's nice."

Doll stretched her leg over his thighs and eased herself into a sitting position above him. "I bet this feels even nicer," she whispered, raising her hips and moving forward.

Horace groaned with pleasure as he entered her, Doll letting out a deep sigh at the same time.

"Sorry to be such a pain," he whispered.

"Can't say this is much of a pain, mate," she grinned back, beginning to ride him.

Whether through residual tension, or simply the passion of the moment, it seemed to go on forever and it was Doll who climaxed, noisily, first. Horace, almost delirious with pleasure soon followed, and they collapsed, panting and sweating, side by side.

"Th-th-thanks," he gasped in her ear.

"Uh, huh," Doll shook her head, "Thank you!"

"Thank us!" they said in unison, laughing.

"I really needed that," Horace panted. "It took my mind off things for a w-w-while."

"Glad to 'ear it. But it won't be so bad. After all, at least your first week will be a short one."

"Pardon?"

"Well, wot wiv you not startin' until the Tuesday," Doll explained, confused.

"Tuesday! W-w-what do you mean, Tuesday!?" Horace sat upright, panic creeping into his voice.

"Well, you start in the morning, right?"

"Yes," Horace said slowly, trying to calm his racing heart.

"And it's now four-thirty on Tuesday morning. You start today."

"Tuesday morning!?" Horace screamed. "But, but, yesterday w-w-was Sunday, w-w-wasn't it?"

Doll shook her head, "Monday the sixth, 'onest."

"But you weren't in college!"

"I told you on Friday," Doll shook her head, "Barbara cancelled yesterday's lecture because of some conference. You really don't listen to a word I say about college, do you?"

"But, but…" Horace trailed off. He groaned even louder than he had been doing for much of the last forty-five minutes, "I w-w-was supposed to start yesterday!"

"Oops," Doll couldn't stop a giggle escaping. "Well at least you needn't worry about bein' sacked on yer first day – you weren't even there."

Horace groaned again and shot out of bed, grabbing his new suit off of its hanger.

"Where on earth are you off to?" Doll called after him as he made for the bathroom at a run. She sighed, grinning to herself, and padded through to the bathroom door.

"Horace!"

"W-w-what?"

"Well, I may be wrong 'ere," Doll grinned at the closed door, "But I don't reckon they'll still be waitin' for you to turn up at five in the morning."

The sounds of frantic activity behind the door ceased and Horace slowly pulled open the door. "I guess not," he sighed.

"Come back to bed. Just make sure you're there on time this morning. They're bound to understand. You could tell them that you was on 'oliday last week or summink; say yer flight back was delayed."

"That might just w-w-work."

"What would you do wivout me, huh?"

Horace sighed and settled back into the rapidly cooling bed. "I honestly don't have a clue."

"Never a truer word," Doll grinned.

13

Horace was standing outside the bank by quarter past eight, thirty minutes early, despite Doll's protests that he would 'freeze yer nuts off', and it wasn't until twenty to nine that he spotted two men who were clearly employed there. He stepped forward as they approached, laughing loudly between themselves.

"Er, Hello?"

The younger of the two noticed Horace, "Ah!" he said cheerfully. "You must be our new recruit. Wilt isn't it? We were expecting you yesterday, old bean!"

"Yes, er, that is, I'm the new recruit." Horace explained quickly. "S-s-sorry about yesterday, but, w-w-well..." Although Doll had given him a potentially viable excuse, Horace's natural honesty got the better of him, "Actually, I got confused w-w-with the days," he confessed, blushing brightly in the frosty air.

To Horace's surprise, the man laughed, his older colleague also grinning, "Well, never mind, old bean. Just as long as you don't think every week's a four day one, what?"

Horace laughed himself, relief pouring through him. He reminded himself to tell Doll that honesty really *was* the best policy, "I'm really terribly sorry."

The man waved aside his efforts, "Anyway, old chap. Let me introduce ourselves. I'm Richard Devlin, officially known as the Loans Officer, but more normally referred to as the Lone Arranger, what?"

Horace laughed again, his relief sending a rush of blood to his head, "And you must be Tonto, right? A little bit older than I expected…" he trailed off as the older man's smile froze, to be rapidly replaced by an intimidating scowl, and Richard Devlin's laughter dried in his throat.

"Actually, Wilt," the older man said slowly, levelly, "I am Mr Edwards. People generally refer to me as just that. Alternatively, of course, they can refer to me as 'The Branch Manager'."

"Oh bugger," Horace's face went from a light pink to a deep scarlet in a nanosecond. "I'm s-s-so s-s-sorry! It's just, w-w-well, nerves I guess."

Devlin clapped him on the back, "Never mind, old bean. A bit of 'Foot in Mouth' disease, what?"

Edwards gave a 'harrumph' and left Devlin and Horace on the pavement while he made his way through the security systems and into the interior of the bank.

The rest of the first day was little better. He was assigned to tea and coffee duties in the morning, managing to forget Mr Edwards altogether until the manager located him in the kitchen, reminding him of his presence by pointedly banging his mug on the counter. Later, in the post-room, Horace managed to unravel a continuous print-out of seven hundred customer statements, delaying the other post-room staff's tea break for more than half an hour. His only bright spot during the bleak day was when he met Donna, the girl he had seen in the Walthamstow branch, as she was leaving the strong room.

"Oh, Hi!" she greeted him cheerfully. "You're Horace, right?"

"Hello, Donna," he smiled shyly.

"So how's your second day?"

He explained that it was his first day and that it had been a total disaster from start to finish – he had just knocked over a bucket of water the cleaner had set on the floor in the corridor – and was surprised to find more sympathy in Donna than hilarity.

"Oh you poor thing. Look on the bright side, though. It's all up from here."

Horace gave a rueful smile, "I certainly hope so."

Although his various confusions with the tea and coffee orders, coupled with the post-room disaster, should perhaps, have alienated him from many of his colleagues, he was surprised when he was invited along with them for an "after-hours" beer. He began to demur, dreading what new faux-pas he might make in a pub, but was finally persuaded by Donna.

"It'll only be for an hour," she said, "And if anyone deserves one today, I reckon it must be you."

"W-w-well, okay then. I guess I could use wh-wh-one."

The hour passed surprisingly quickly, and for Horace, surprisingly pleasantly. He was asked several times to repeat his story about how he had called "Old Edwards" Tonto, and even began to enjoy the notoriety.

He arrived home, exhausted, at eight, and, declining Doll's suggestion of a beer down at the Crown, ate quickly and was in bed before nine-thirty.

From The Diary of Horace Wilt

"Tuesday, 7th December, 1982

DD

What a disaster! Not only was I a day late for my first taste of the life of banking, but the first person I speak to I manage to insult - and he was the bloody branch manager! The whole day was a disaster from start to finish - don't even know if I can pluck up the courage to go in tomorrow. Bed now. Knackered."

14

The rest of Horace's first week proved little better, but at least he managed not to upset too many people (in fact, only Edwards' secretary, a grossly overweight middle-aged woman named Beryl, had any real cause for complaint – and how was Horace to know that someone so large had managed to appear silently behind him as he tossed a paper cup full of water over his shoulder into the what had been intended as the sink, but was in fact her cleavage).

"At least I'm sleeping better at nights," he sighed that Friday evening in the Crown.

Doll laughed, "It's seemed a bit odd this week. You never seem to be awake."

"At least w-w-we'll have the w-w-weekend to ourselves."

"Not all of it, we won't. In case you've forgotten, you're s'posed to be capturing a vampire on canvas tomorrow."

Horace groaned; he'd forgotten all about it. "I reckon she only w-w-want's it done because she can't see herself in mirrors."

"Not nice," Doll chided, grinning. "True, possibly, but not nice."

"You do promise-"

"I promise!" Doll interrupted, "I'll stand guard over your neck at all times. And you can borrow my silver cross, if you like?"

"I like!"

"And Marva will be comin' over on Sunday," Doll added.

Horace groaned before draining the last of his pint. He stood wearily, "I don't know about you, but I could murder another pint."

"Count me in. All this literature at college does wonders fer yer bleedin' thirst."

"If not your vocabulary," Horace grinned.

15

Saturday morning dawned too early as far as Horace was concerned, and it was only a great deal of coaxing by Doll, and the smell of freshly brewed coffee, that finally persuaded him out of the warmth and comfort of his bed.

He had been even more reluctant, the previous weekend, when he finally agreed that Elspeth would sit for him in her own apartment, and only then on purely artistic grounds. He had set foot in the place only once since Elspeth had moved in and had been both shocked and a little annoyed by the flat's transformation. Where once it had been a light and airy place, totally in keeping with its previous occupant, it was now distinctly dark, almost sinister – totally in keeping with its current occupant, he supposed.

Just after ten, he trudged wearily up the stairs with Doll in tow. Before he had a chance to let Doll past him so she could knock on the door – Horace being laden down with an easel and artists' materials – Elspeth opened it and smiled a welcome.

"Good morning, Horace, Doll," she breathed, "Please do come in, I've been so looking forward to this."

"Morning Elspeth," Horace yawned, "And, of course, so have I." His sarcasm didn't seem to register with Elspeth, although Doll gave him an admonitory poke in the back as they walked into the living room.

The pale pastel curtains, with which Stephanie had highlighted the room's large windows, had been replaced by velvet drapes in the deepest shade of purple. Where there had been flowers and plants dotted around before, there were now scores of candles – dark blue, dark red and some even jet black. Several of these were now lit, and although the heavy drapes were drawn open, the room still seemed gloomy. A totally fitting environment, Horace thought.

Elspeth offered them coffee and although Doll declined Horace accepted – anything to delay matters.

"You're prevaricatin' again," Doll whispered while Elspeth was in the kitchen.

"Do you really blame me?"

Elspeth returned before Doll could respond, and handed Horace his coffee. "Well, Horace," she smiled, "How would you like me?"

Horace had several answers to the question but, after a warning look from Doll, settled for the artistic response, "Er, w-w-well, I w-w-was thinking that since you're, er, rather tall and, w-w-well, shall w-w-we say, rather dark and mysterious…" he looked up to see if Elspeth was taking any offence, or even any notice, before he continued, "Perhaps standing – maybe in front of the drapes, although I w-w-was thinking of something a little more… natural as a background?"

"I'm completely in your hands, Horace. But you'll have to be patient with me; I've never done this sort of thing before."

"This is fascinating," Doll commented as Horace began to unpack his things. "I mean, I know I was the subject once, but seeing it done from a, sorta, third-party view, it's all a bit different."

"It alw-w-ways seems it to me," Horace said absently, adjusting the easel's height.

Elspeth had crossed to the drapes, un-tethering one so that she had a reasonable amount of background material around her. Horace nodded to himself. If she hadn't done anything like this before, he would eat his brushes.

When he had everything settled, he crossed to where Elspeth was – the word "hovering" came to mind – standing, "I think it w-w-would be best if you w-w-were standing facing slightly aw-w-way from me, say twenty degrees or so, and then turn your head tow-w-wards me. It might get a little uncomfortable after a w-w-while, but just say if it does and w-w-we can take a break, okay?" He was being determinedly business-like in an effort to distract himself from what was going on.

"As I said, Horace, you're the boss. Shall I take my robe off now?" She smiled at him intently.

"I, er, that is, w-w-well, er, yes, er, please," he managed, not nearly so business-like.

Elspeth gave a throaty chuckle, "A definite first; Horace actually asking me to uncover."

Doll giggled in the background as Horace blushed furiously.

"Yes, w-w-well, it is rather necessary, isn't it?" Horace crossed to the easel and took up his position. "Just try to get yourself comfortable," he told Elspeth as she took her pose, naked, in front of the drapes.

"This seems fine," she said after a few minor adjustments, and Horace once again had the impression that she was no novice in these matters. Elspeth turned her head to face him. "Okay for you?"

"Perfect," Horace nodded, glad that he had no reason to manoeuvre her in any way, "Just let me put a couple of markers down and w-w-we can get started."

"Markers?" Doll asked from behind him.

Horace nodded, crossing the room with a roll of gaffer tape, "If Elspeth needs to take a break, it helps get the pose right w-w-when w-w-we start again."

"Clever stuff," Doll remarked as he bent over and began tearing strips from the roll.

"Don't w-w-worry about the carpet," Horace told Elspeth without looking up, "This stuff comes off easy and doesn't leave a mark."

"Very thoughtful," Elspeth said.

He went back to the easel and took up his own position.

"What sort of look should there be on my face?" Elspeth smiled across as Horace started some basic texturing of the canvas.

"A snarl with the fangs showing" had been the thought that came immediately to Horace's mind but he managed to stop himself saying it, "Actually w-w-we don't need to w-w-worry about that for a w-w-while," he said instead, "But w-w-when it comes to it, I rather thought a direct stare – pretty much expressionless – maybe, w-w-with your lips just parted a little. You've got, er, very nice, er, t-t-teeth."

Elspeth smiled as if rehearsing, "Sorry, Horace, dear. I don't think I quite caught what you just said, 'I have very nice tits', was it?"

"No! Teeth! Teeth! Stop giggling, Doll." He took a sip of cold coffee and began mapping a general outline of Elspeth on the canvas. Actually, he thought, her tits aren't 'very nice'; they're absolutely fantastic.

To his surprise, Elspeth was able to comfortably hold her pose for two hours before she asked whether they could break for a couple of minutes, and even then, that was only so that she could go to the bathroom. Horace had initially thought that she had been pulling in her belly, but after half an hour had realised that it really was slightly concave.

Just after one, Horace began to work on her face and was surprised once more. Most people's faces are far from symmetrical but Elspeth's was almost perfectly so. Lost in his work, he mentioned the fact.

"Is that good?" Elspeth purred.

Horace looked up from the canvas, "Oh, er, w-w-well it's certainly unusual. I'll show you w-w-what I mean w-w-when I've got a little time to spare."

"It's really weird," Doll told Elspeth. "He draws 'alf of yer face, and you fink, 'Yeah, that's about right', and then, instead of drawing the other 'alf as normal, 'e just draws a mirror-image of the first 'alf. You look totally different." Doll giggled, "The other day, 'e drew my face three times, side by side, like, first using a mirror of one side of me face, then the other side, then as it really is. Identical twins look more alike than those three faces."

"Sounds interesting," Elspeth said.

"Identical triplets," Horace commented absently, busily applying texture to Elspeth's blue-black hair.

"When will I be able to see it?" Elspeth asked him a few minutes later.

Horace shrugged, straightening a little to ease his back which was becoming stiff; he couldn't imagine how Elspeth kept the pose static for so long, "I've just got about half an hour more to do here and the rest I can finish downstairs. It'll be ready Monday evening, I suppose."

"Fast worker," Elspeth said with a smile.

Horace grunted. He had been prepared to dash off a quick outline and do the rest from memory when he had started, but, as so often happened when he had brushes in his hand, he found himself more intent on producing a good piece. He could honestly say that he was, for the first time, totally comfortable in Elspeth's company – and she was stark naked.

So much so that when the doorbell rang downstairs and Doll trotted down to answer it, he hardly noticed, and was not in the least bit concerned. He vaguely heard voices but they didn't register.

Doll trotted back up the stairs, "Er, Horace," she called from the doorway.

"Yes?" he muttered, still busily engaged in his work.

"It's me dad," she said, "Come to see 'is little girl. Alright if I take 'im into your flat?"

"Of course. And that's 'our' flat. I'll be down in ten minutes or so, nearly done here."

Behind him, Doll smiled and shook her head, amused to see him so at ease after all he had said about Elspeth, "See you in a while, then."

"'Kay."

Five minutes later, he dropped his brushes into the spirit bottle hanging from the base of the easel and let out a sigh, "That's about it," he told Elspeth. He stretched his back again, grimacing as a series of pops and clicks echoed around the room.

Elspeth took a deep breath and stepped forward with no obvious stiffness.

"I don't know how you managed to pose like that for so long," Horace said.

Elspeth chuckled, "Among my many practices, I meditate and do some yogic exercises. You really should try it, it works wonders."

"I just might," Horace looked up at her, still grimacing. "Er, that's finished then."

"And?"

"W-w-well, you can, er, put your robe back on now."

She laughed "Amazing, isn't it? As soon as it's no longer art, you're immediately uncomfortable with my body."

"W-w-well, I, er," Horace cleared his throat, "Yes, or rather, you're, w-w-well, a little intimidating."

She laughed again, "I do try so hard not to be. But if it makes you feel happier…" she picked up her robe and slipped it on, tying it very loosely. "Better?"

Horace gave a rueful smile, "Yes, although I guess you're right; I shouldn't be so, w-w-well, embarrassed."

"There's hope for you yet," Elspeth smiled, not unkindly, "You're not at all like your mother, you know?"

"Oh?"

"She so… at one with nature; so elemental."

Horace snorted, "I don't think you need the 'ele' bit."

Elspeth chuckled again, "You're not very nice sometimes, Horace, but most of the time you're very sweet." She took a couple of paces towards the canvas. "Can I see the work in progress?"

Horace put a defensive arm in front of her, "No! I mean, no," he repeated, dropping the level of his voice. "It's a, sort of, superstition, I guess. I never let anywh-wh-one see."

"You? Superstitious?" Elspeth teased.

Horace shrugged, "Artist's habits are alw-w-ways a little w-w-weird."

She chuckled and stepped back while Horace carefully covered the painting with a drape cloth, "So, Horace, do you think I make a good subject?"

"Very good."

"I'm very pleased to hear it. But is that because of my beauty? My looks? Or are we talking about my… essence?"

Horace quickly slid his palette into its case and looked up sharply, "W-w-well, I guess you are…"

"Say it, Horace," Elspeth insisted, a slight darker edge to her already husky voice.

Horace began to blush, "Yes, w-w-well, you are b-b-beautiful. And you also, er, pose very w-w-well," he finished quickly.

Elspeth chuckled, stepping around the easel as Horace bent to pack the last of his things into their case, "Horace?" she murmured, close behind him.

"W-w-what?" Horace straightened quickly, unnerved that she had appeared so silently beside him.

Elspeth's smile was slow and somehow sinister, "You do realise, don't you, that I would be yours whenever you wanted me?"

"P-p-pardon?" Horace squeaked.

Elspeth held his gaze with her green eyes, "Horace, you have a very delicate side to you; it's probably why you get on so well with women – you're in touch with the female side of yourself," Horace made to protest but was quietened by a single, slow blink of the green eyes. "It's a very good thing, Horace," Elspeth's voice seemed to be growing lower, almost hypnotic, "And I am, shall we say, a little darker. Female through and through, but also aware of the maleness within me. We would make the perfect partners, you know?"

The mesmeric quality of her voice reduced Horace's near panic to something more manageable, "It's, er, very nice of you, but, w-w-well, there's Doll for a start and… and…"

"And?"

A sudden thought struck Horace, "But, hang on a minute. W-w-when I first met you at mother's she said that you w-w-were, er, that is, w-w-well, not like, er, them."

"You asked, did you?"

"No, er, that is, I think my mother just told me," Horace stammered. "She, er, said you w-w-were celibate, actually."

Elspeth chuckled, "Surely you know your mother's slight confusion with words by now, Horace? It's true I'm not a lesbian as such, but I think the word your mother was trying to use was bisexual. I told you, I'm very much aware of the man within this female form."

"I w-w-was right, then," Horace muttered to himself.

"You were?"

Not only has she got cat's eyes, she can hear like one as well, Horace groaned to himself.

Elspeth wasn't finished with him, "And as for Doll, I find her… earthiness such a wonderful contrast to her fair beauty. She fascinates me almost as much as you do, Horace. Besides, I believe that monogamous relationships aren't very natural."

Horace's blood pressure was reaching a critical level, "I, er, w-w-well, that is, thank you and everything, b-b-but I'd really better go; visitor, you know?"

"Of course," Elspeth said quietly, a slight movement of her head freeing Horace from the emerald depths of her eyes, "But remember my offer."

"I'd have a lot of trouble f-f-forgetting it," Horace said, truthfully.

Elspeth's smile seemed to indicate that she was satisfied, "Well off you go, then, Horace. I look forward to seeing the completed masterpiece on Monday evening. Right now, I must have a shower and freshen up. Maybe I'll see you both in the Crown later?"

Relieved to have been freed and still in one piece, Horace nodded almost maniacally, picking up his case in one hand and the easel, gingerly, in the other, "Maybe, yes."

Still smiling, Elspeth untied the robe and let it slide to the floor behind her. Horace, despite every mental effort, glanced quickly down at her near-perfect nakedness.

Elspeth's quiet chuckle made him snap his eyes back up to hers, "Horace, I do believe you're learning."

"I, er, yes, w-w-well," Horace stammered, blushing furiously once again, "See you later, then." He dashed for the sanctuary of his own flat, as fast as a seven foot easel, complete with canvas, would allow. He arrived in his living room to find Doll blushing herself; her father was admiring the painting of her.

"Fuck me sideways if that ain't fuckin' brilliant," he informed Horace as he came into the room.

The particular phrase that Jim Mercer seemed so fond of was beginning to give Horace nightmares. "Er, thank you," he cast a quick look in Doll's direction. "Er, to w-w-what do w-w-we owe the pleasure?"

Jim Mercer turned to face Horace for the first time, seemingly reluctant to stop staring at the painting of his daughter, "Oh, right. Well, see, I've gotta new barman an' I fought I'd grab an 'our off an' come an' see me daughter."

"'E's just bein' bleedin' nosy really," Doll told Horace.

"Charmin', ain't she?" Jim grinned.

"Absolutely delightful," Horace said in a Noel Coward voice.

"She's the sort, you know," Jim explained to Horace in confidential tones, "That you 'ave to take everywhere twice. Second time so that she can apologise for the first." He burst into raucous laughter, Horace chuckling himself.

"An' you call me charmin'!" Doll protested with a smile, "An' anyway, the real reason 'e came round was to offer us the use of the family villa in Tenerife next March. Wot do you reckon, H?"

"That's, er, very kind. I'll have to see w-w-what the holiday situation is at w-w-work, though."

Jim nodded, "Well, son, the offer's there if you want it."

Horace thanked him again and left him to chat with his daughter while he stored his easel in the spare bedroom. By the time he had uncovered the canvas and properly cleaned all the brushes, Jim had yelled a "Goodbye" and departed.

"That was nice of 'im, weren't it?" Doll said when Horace emerged, wiping his hands on an old t-shirt.

"Very. I didn't even know your family had a villa."

"It really belongs to me uncle Albert. But 'e's banged up at the minute. Actually," she went on, "'E's banged up for a few million minutes. Got done for armed robbery a couple of years back; servin' ten to fifteen."

"And he, er, w-w-wouldn't mind?" Horace asked, worried.

Doll chuckled, "'Ardly. I'm 'is favourite niece, see? And you'll be counted as one of the family, these days. Anyway, 'ow did it go upstairs after I left?"

Horace shuddered at the thought, but decided against mentioning Elspeth's little offer – or anything else he had found out about her. "Okay, really. I reckon it'll be finished on Monday."

"It was really looking good when I last saw it," Doll nodded approvingly. "Can I 'ave another butcher's?"

"Of course; it's only the subject that I don't like seeing them before they're finished."

He went through to the kitchen to throw the spirit soaked t-shirt into the bin, and emerged at the same time as Doll did from the spare room.

"It's another fu… bleedin' brilliant one," she said, "An' I see wot Elspeth means when she said you 'captured the essence of someone' or whatever it was."

"It isn't that horrible, is it?"

"Not nice," Doll admonished him, giggling nevertheless, "But I'll let you off if you buy me a beer."

"Good idea."

16

On Sunday Horace was introduced to Marva, Doll's 'shy' classmate. By the time she left two hours later, Horace was beginning to seriously doubt Doll's powers of observation.

"You call that shy?" he asked her incredulously, after the giant of a woman had left.

Doll giggled, "Well, that's wot she told me, anyway."

It had been all Horace could do to persuade Marva not to strip off completely there and then, and as it was, he'd been forced to view the largest pair of breasts he'd ever seen in his life when Marva obligingly pulled up her t-shirt – on the grounds that Horace 'was gonna need a whole shitload of brown to do these fuckers justice'.

"Well, she did agree to it," Doll said. "Fifty quid's a lotta money. Come in 'andy just before Christmas."

"I don't need money," Horace reminded her, "And she was probably right about how much brown paint I'll need. Remind me to stock up on Saturday." Marva had agreed to sit the following Sunday morning when "Winston went round to see his slapper of a mother".

"Don't be mean. An' by the way, you never mentioned anyfing about me posin' wiv her. Why was that?"

"I think you w-w-were right about there not being enough room on the canvas," Horace grinned. "Besides, there are contrasts and contrasts. The wh-wh-one between you two is just too big."

Doll laughed, "Maybe you're right, she makes three of me. Perhaps you could do one of me and Elspeth? You seemed pretty relaxed upstairs."

"I, er, don't think so," Horace said. After his last conversation with the vampire, he was now fairly certain that Elspeth *would* try to eat his girlfriend.

Doll shrugged, "I reckon it'd be great, but I guess it's your shout." She looked down at her watch and reached for her jacket. "Come on, H. The pub's open an' it's our last chance of a lunchtime drink before next weekend."

Horace nodded happily. He had been up early that morning, putting the finishing touches to Elspeth's painting, and after the overpowering Marva, a drink was sure to be the perfect remedy.

From The Diary of Horace Wilt

"Sunday, 12th December, 1982

DD

Finished Elspeth's painting this morning and am dreading giving it to her tomorrow. I'm pretty certain that she still means trouble and am going to have to keep a very close eye on her. Got my first real commission today, as well - Doll's "shy" friend Marva, Talk about a big girl...

Bloody bank tomorrow. I hate the place already! Perhaps the second week will be better..."

17

Horace's second week at the bank seemed to last forever, but at least a routine was beginning to emerge. A boring one, to be sure, but routine nevertheless. He had expected to deliver Elspeth's painting to her on the Monday, but she had left a note in his mailbox for him, saying that there was some sort of 'mini-emergency' at the Heart, and she wouldn't return until the weekend. After his conversation with her in the Belfry, he was more than happy to put off another meeting for as long as possible.

He telephoned his mother from work on the Tuesday to be told that the 'emergency' was actually a week-long celebration of some obscure festival, and politely declined to attend "whenever he and Diamond were free, darling".

When Friday finally arrived, he eschewed the now-normal after hours drinks with his colleagues and hurried back to Walthamstow, intent on making the weekend last as long as possible. It was already going to last three days, since some arcane regulation at the bank stipulated that he must take all of his holiday in the current calendar year and he had, apparently, accrued one day already. He wasn't sure how this was possible in just a couple of weeks, but he wasn't going to argue.

He went first to the flat to change and was further cheered by another note from Elspeth saying that she was sorry, but she wouldn't be home until late Sunday night. Horace was positively whistling by the time he reached the Crown where he had arranged to meet Doll. Even her reminder that he had to go and buy "shitloads" of brown paint the next day couldn't dent his contented mood.

"I seem to spend every weekday working for a bunch of tits and then all weekend painting another bunch," he grinned. "Ready for another Guinness?"

Saturday passed in as relaxed and lazy a way as Horace could devise and he felt refreshed when he rose at nine on the Sunday, an hour after having risen in an altogether more intimate way with Doll.

Marva arrived promptly at ten and bustled into the living room, eager for "some serious nudie action". She and Horace had discussed how she would like to pose when she had come over the previous week, and almost before Horace could direct her, she had stripped off and was laying back on the sofa. Or rather, most of her was.

"Come on then, honey," she beamed at Horace through unnaturally large, and unnaturally white, teeth. "Come show Marva exactly where you want her big brown bod."

Horace approached nervously, ignoring Doll's barely stifled giggles, and pointed at Marva's right arm, which she was currently laying on, "If you, er, just, sort of, prop yourself up on your elbow; maybe put a cushion behind your shoulder for comfort."

"Hell, honey," Marva beamed, "I ain't never done no posing afore, and I sure as shit ain't no contortionist. You's better just push me around 'til you get me where you want me."

Horace winced, but reasoned that, all in all, it probably would be quicker that way and the sooner it was sorted, the sooner he could get finished – and the sooner he could persuade Marva to cover herself up again, "W-w-well, er, okay, then." He picked up a cushion and gingerly dropped it behind her broad shoulders and then, as she raised herself on her elbow, shoved it down until it was supporting much of her vast weight. He stood back, the critical look of the artist taking over. "Perhaps if you just move your elbow a little further back?"

Marva almost fell off the sofa as she moved it a good seven inches, "That's what Marva told you, honey," she sighed, heaving herself onto her elbow once again, "I ain't never done none of this shit before. It'd be quicker if you just push me about."

Horace doubted that he could push her an inch, but with a resigned sigh, crossed back to the sofa and attempted to move her elbow into the position he thought would be best. He was severely hampered by her enormous right breast which he couldn't help but, sort of, move to one side at one point.

"I'm really, er, sorry, but it's w-w-well-"

He was interrupted by a deep chuckle from Marva, which in itself caused more upheaval, "Don't you fret none, honey. You just shift that fucker where you want it," she paused and then gave another chuckle. "Say what, honey? Do you realise, you're the first white boy what's ever had the pleasure of handling Marva's tits?"

"I, er, that's…" Horace trailed off, blushing furiously and at a total loss for words.

This reduced Marva to another bout of throaty chuckles, and the positioning process had to be started all over again. It finally took Horace four hours before he completed as much of the painting as he needed Marva's presence for.

"W-w-well, that's it, then," he told her, "You can, er, get dressed again."

Marva nodded reluctantly, "Shame. It's the first Sunday for years I've been told to climb on a sofa and sit still for a few hours." She chuckled to herself, "Winston'll be wondering where I am. Still, makes a change for Marva to be the one that's late," she paused and chuckled again. "Guess I'd better not tell him exactly what I was up to; I'm not sure what he'd think if I told him some cute white boy had spent half an hour almost buried in here," she pointed down to her enormous cleavage as she sat up.

"I, er, guess I'd rather you didn't either," Horace said.

"Don't you fret none, honey," Marva reassured him, "My Winston's a pussycat. You do a good job on this painting, and like as not, he'll be round offering you some more work."

A tiger could loosely be termed a pussycat, Horace thought, shuddering, "W-w-well, anyw-w-way, it'll be ready Monday evening, if you w-w-want to collect it then."

"Sounds good to Marva," she smiled, heaving her belly into the largest pair of panties Horace had ever seen. She picked up her

Marva-sized handbag and rooted through it before extracting her purse. She opened it and pulled out five ten pound notes. "Guess these are yours now, honey," she offered the notes in Horace's direction.

"W-w-wouldn't you rather w-w-wait until you see the finished article?"

Marva gave another throaty chuckle and crossed the room to where Horace was standing by his easel. Her breasts arrived a long time before the rest of her, Horace noted, "No way, honey. Hell, I'd pay you just to tell me to lie on the sofa for a few hours."

Horace reached forward carefully, and took the notes, "W-w-well, if you're really sure?"

Marva chuckled again, tremors rippling through her, "I'm sure, honey. And if you want a tip, I've got the biggest two you'll ever see," she nodded down at her voluminous breasts.

"No!" Horace squeaked, "I mean, er, no thank you."

"Well don't say Marva didn't offer," she shrugged – no mean feat when you sported breasts that size, "But you ain't gonna find 'em on no scrawny white girls," she grinned at the giggling Doll.

Horace, who had returned to the task of cleaning his brushes, thought that Marva looked all too reluctant when she finally pulled her massive sweatshirt over her head. "Shy my bum", Horace muttered to himself.

"You know something?" he told Doll when she had seen Marva out of the building, "I'm not sure that this art thing is such a good idea."

18

Horace slept until ten o'clock the following morning, all too aware of how few Mondays he would, from now on, be able to call his own, and might have slept even longer had it not been for Doll's grumbling departure for college and the knock on his door a little while after she'd left.

He fumbled his way into his dressing gown and called out for whoever it was that he would be there in a minute. Yawning and rubbing his eyes, he stumbled through the living room and opened the door.

"Good morning, Horace," Elspeth smiled.

Her voice cleared his head in an instant and he was glad to see that she was modestly dressed, one of the cult's kaftans billowing around her, "Mornin', Elspeth." He yawned again. "W-w-what brings you down here?"

Elspeth's smile was turned up a notch, "Why, the painting, of course. I've been so looking forward to seeing it."

"Oh, right, yes. The painting. You'd better come in." He let Elspeth past him and trailed after her, guiding her onto a sofa. "If you can just contain your excitement for five minutes, I'll, er, just, er, that is... the bathroom, and put some coffee on."

"I've been eagerly awaiting this moment for more than a week," Elspeth said, "I'm sure another few minutes won't hurt."

Horace nodded, gave another yawn, and stumbled through to the bathroom. As he stood urinating for what seemed like hours, he realised that he had, maybe, just a tiny bit too much to drink the previous evening; he wasn't sure that his brain wouldn't take another hour or two before it came fully on line. He finally finished, flushed the toilet and washed his hands, checking that his dressing gown was decent before padding back through the living room and into the kitchen. Elspeth, he noticed, was flicking idly through one of his art magazines, taking no notice of his progress. A good sign, Horace surmised.

"W-w-would you like a coffee?" he called from the kitchen when the machine had been set bubbling.

"That's very kind of you, Horace. Yes, please."

Even when she raised her voice, Horace thought, somehow she still seemed to be purring. Deciding that his body might be in need of some fast sugar, he added two spoonsful to his mug when it was ready, and took the drinks through to the living room.

"Thank you, Horace," Elspeth smiled as he handed her one of the mugs.

Horace mumbled 'no problem' and set his own mug on the coffee table, "I'll go get the painting."

"Oh, please, drink your coffee first, Horace. I'm in no rush, and besides, it looks as if you need it."

Horace gave her a rueful smile, "You may be right there, thanks." He sat at the furthest end of the sofa, subconsciously as far away from Elspeth as possible. A thought struck him. "How did you know I'd be here today?"

"I met Diamond on the stairs as she was leaving for college. She said something along the lines of 'it's bleedin' alright for some' and pointed at your front door, so I rather guessed you were still here."

Horace laughed at her accurate impression of Doll, "Very good. Actually, I've somehow already accrued some holiday, so today's a day off."

"Lucky for you," Elspeth said, "And for me too… That is, I'll get to see my painting all the sooner."

The pause as she spoke sent a small tingle of alarm through Horace, but he put it down to too much beer the night before. He picked up his mug and began to sip the still-hot beverage and could have sworn he heard his kidneys' screams of pleasure, "W-w-what w-w-was the celebration last w-w-week? Rather a long wh-wh-one w-w-wasn't it, even by my mother's standards?"

Elspeth chuckled, "Well, it wasn't just a celebration. It was more of an informal gathering, spread over the week because we have so many members now. The sooner we move into the mansion the better."

"How many exactly?" Horace asked. Although he normally had no interest in his mother's weird and wonderful schemes, the cult was beginning to intrigue him.

"It's rather hard to be exact. At the last formal count, there were in excess of three hundred members, but that was three weeks ago, and more and more seem to be joining every day."

"Three hundred!" Horace almost choked on his coffee. "Do any of them know exactly w-w-what the cult's all about?" He, for one, certainly didn't.

"It's most unusual of you to take an interest," Elspeth said with a wry smile, "But I'm pleased that you are. In fact, Horace, the cult has multiple-facets, much like a cut jewel. At one level, we are an organisation of women, for women; offering guidance, comfort, protection from the less savoury type of male," she paused momentarily, glancing up at Horace, "Not that you would ever be considered in that category. At another level, we celebrate the very fact of womanhood," she continued, holding his gaze with her cat-green eyes. "From the very essence of Nature Herself, to all of the beauties and wonders that woman represents in this life. Beyond that, we are what might be termed a cottage industry, making or gathering natural products which we sell through a number of sources ranging from health food shops to mail order companies. There are other aspects, as well, but many of these are private concerns of the cult, and as much as I trust and admire you Horace, my first responsibility is to the well-being of our cult, and so, with apologies, these must remain closed from you. I do hope you understand?"

Her low, husky voice had once again seemed to mesmerise Horace and he was a little disappointed when her lecture ended. It took him a moment or two before realising that it had ended with a question, "Oh, er, of course I understand. Er, thank you for the explanation." He drained the last of his coffee and stood slowly, his back creaking.

"Oh, you poor thing," Elspeth purred, "You really must let me show you how to avoid these bodily stresses and strains."

The previous day's painting session with massive Marva had certainly not helped his condition, "I think maybe I w-w-will sometime soon. But right now, I'd better get your painting."

Elspeth nodded, "Very well."

Horace hobbled painfully through to the spare room, his back slowly easing. Inside, he glanced quickly over the painting of Marva, nodding happily as he noted that there was very little finishing work to do, and then retrieved Elspeth's canvas. Holding it so that it faced his own body, he returned to the living room.

He stood in front of Elspeth and took a deep breath, "W-w-well, I hope you like it." He slowly turned the canvas around to face her, studying her face closely for her reaction.

Elspeth's green eyes widened. Very slowly, her dark lips parted, her jaw dropping; the first time Horace had ever seen her without complete control of her emotions and expression. She seemed to be holding her breath and at first Horace thought that she was disappointed, but then she blinked, once, slowly, and licked her bottom lip, her bright pink tongue incongruous against the purple lip-gloss.

"Horace," she said in barely a whisper, "It's... wonderful!" To his immense shock, a tear appeared in each of Elspeth's eyes. "Do you really see me as being that... beautiful?" her voice was full of wonder.

"I, er, yes," Horace replied, quietly. He had been very pleased with the results of his work, but would never in a million years have expected a response like this from the subject of the piece. "You... like it then?"

With what seemed to be a physical wrench, Elspeth turned her eyes away from the painting and up to Horace's. "Horace, I don't think there are words in any language to describe how much I like it... love it." The tears welled further, twinkling like emeralds in the sunlight for a moment, before spilling over her dark lashes. Elspeth fumbled in the pocket of her kaftan and pulled out a crumpled tissue. "Not such a cool, controlled ice-queen now, am I?" she sniffed, laughing, now staring down at her lap.

Horace was totally perplexed, "I... never really thought you w-w-were."

Elspeth glanced up quickly at him and then back to the painting, "I can see that," she nodded, sniffing once again. The tiny scrap of tissue was already sodden and she held it up to him, shrugging. "Have you a tissue?"

Her question seemed to free Horace from the weird spell brought on by her unexpected tears and he shook himself, "Of course." He carefully set the painting on the floor opposite Elspeth and hurried through to his bedroom where he always kept an enormous box of tissues. It occurred to him that it would be the first time they had ever been used to dry tears.

When he got back to the living room he found Elspeth sitting cross-legged in the middle of the carpet, staring at the painting, her head cocked slightly to one side. He handed her the tissues and knelt beside her, "I'm, er, really pleased you l-l-like it so much," he said as she dabbed at her face.

She turned to him, a watery smile on her face, "It's the nicest thing anyone has ever done for me; ever given to me."

Horace returned the smile, still unsure how to react. He noticed that even her tears seemed to fall symmetrically, and noticed also that even when crying, her face was still stunningly beautiful in its perfection, "I didn't mean for you to be upset."

Elspeth laughed, "I'm not. It was just such a… surprise," she cast her eyes downwards for a moment. "I'd rather thought that there would be something of your antipathy towards me in the painting somewhere, something that maybe tarnished it somehow. Left it as nothing more than a physical representation. But there isn't, is there?"

"No, of course not."

"I'm sorry, Horace."

"Don't be. If anywh-wh-one should be sorry, it's me; for giving the impression that I feel any antipathy in the first place, it's just that you, w-w-well… I feel intimidated by you, I guess."

Elspeth laughed softly, "What I say to you, I pretty much mean. But I guess I do like to hide behind my mask. I prefer the… dominance that it can bring. Still, you've well and truly broken that mask today, haven't you?"

Horace smiled, "It w-w-wasn't intentional. But I'm sort of pleased I have."

Elspeth chuckled, her voice sounding more like normal, "Promise you won't tell anyone? I mean, how I behaved like a little child?"

"Of course. As long as you promise to stop intimidating me."

"That's a deal, then," Elspeth smiled brightly. "Now, let me do something for you. I could never really pay you enough for this beautiful painting, no matter how much hard currency I give you. But there is one thing I could do for you."

"Oh?"

"Your back. Let me ease the current stresses, and then I can show you some exercises that will ensure it stays healthy in future."

Horace straightened, wincing as another series of clicks echoed around the room, "Actually, I think I might just take you up on that offer."

"It's the least I can do," Elspeth insisted, "Now, you'll need to lie flat on something fairly firm so that I can work the muscles loose first. How firm is your bed?"

"Rock hard."

"Perfect."

Horace hesitated for a moment, but another twinge of pain made his mind up, "W-w-well, okay then."

Elspeth rose gracefully, "Come then." She led him through to the bedroom and pulled the duvet off the bed. "Take off your robe and lie face down."

"I, er, are you… sure?" Horace stammered. Elspeth might have promised that she would stop intimidating him, but something about her presence, especially in *this* particular room, nevertheless cowed him.

"Please, Horace, let me at least repay you in part by helping you."

For some reason Horace was certain that Elspeth could ease his pain. It was this thought that overrode his doubts. Shrugging, he turned his back to her and slipped the dressing gown off his shoulders, quickly scooting on to the cool surface of the bed.

He felt her weight as Elspeth climbed up beside him. "Relax as much as you can, Horace," she instructed, "Arms by your side. I know you still find me... stressful, but this will only work if you are completely relaxed." She laid her hands on his shoulders, pressing lightly. "As with most things in nature," she explained quietly, "Your entire body works as a series of conflicting opposites; one group of muscles tense as their counterparts relax." Her fingers began to massage, gently at first, then firmer as his muscles began to ease. Her voice, already low, dropped another few decibels, reaching the mesmeric pitch that so entranced Horace. "What I'm doing now, is letting the muscles rest when they should be tense, easing them slightly away from their normal positions, allowing others to work for them..."

Her voice was equally as relaxing as her fingers and Horace felt himself drifting under her tender ministrations. She worked slowly down the length of his back, his sides, moving onto his legs and even his feet. Gradually she began to work her way back towards his neck, pausing for a moment as she reached his lumbar region. Horace felt her weight shift, and then he felt her thighs on the backs of his legs as she straddled him. Her fingers started their work once more and Horace gave a small groan of pure, unadulterated pleasure as he felt his pains drifting away.

Her voice had become a soothing background hum and he found himself no longer listening to individual words, just enjoying the cadence and tone of her speech patterns.

"Horace," she whispered louder, a few minutes later.

"Hum?" he groaned happily, hoping that this didn't signal the end of her treatment.

"As I've been saying," she said, "All muscles work in groups. For this to be completely effective, I need to work on your chest and stomach."

"'Kay," Horace muttered dreamily.

"Roll over then," Elspeth whispered.

Horace felt the weight of her thighs lift, and without much conscious thought, gently turned himself onto his back, his eyes half-closed. He didn't realise the position he was in until Elspeth reached forward, beginning to work on his pectorals. He gasped as he felt his nakedness matched by her own, his eyes opening slowly.

Elspeth was straddling his thighs, leaning forward, kneading gently. At some point she had removed her kaftan and was naked, her breasts swaying slightly in time with her movements.

"I, er-" Horace began.

Elspeth's smile interrupted him, "Sh! Stay relaxed, stay calm, in a few minutes you'll be feeling heavenly. No more pain, no more stresses."

Her voice was still at that mesmeric pitch, her fingers still working their magic. Horace relaxed, staring up into her green, green eyes. Or at least, most of Horace relaxed. By the time Elspeth's fingers had worked their way down to the upper reaches of his stomach – a place that Horace never realised could be massaged – he was totally rigid, "I'm s-s-sorry."

Elspeth looked into his eyes and smiled, "Don't be sorry," she whispered, "Just enjoy every sensation." She moved backwards, her fingers moving lower.

Horace sighed as her fingers spread across his stomach, and then groaned as they moved on. He closed his eyes, his breath quickening.

"There are muscles, even here," Elspeth whispered a few seconds later.

Her fingers closed gently around his rigid member, lightly stroking. Horace groaned again, louder this time.

"Horace," Elspeth's voice was barely audible, "Will you do something for me?"

"W-w-what?" he managed, his mind reeling. He had never in his life felt this aroused.

"Will you show me, with your body, what you showed me with your painting?"

Horace was having trouble thinking. The question was beyond him, "I, er…"

He felt Elspeth lean forward, further and further, until he could feel the firmness of her breasts pressing against his chest. He opened his eyes, to find hers just a few inches away.

"I want you, Horace," she whispered. He began to slowly shake his head, a last fleeting attempt at denial.

But that's all it was; fleeting. He wanted her more than he could remember wanting anyone or anything in his life. Although her question had fazed him, he now knew exactly what she meant.

"Just this once," she whispered again.

Horace raised his left hand to her shoulder, gently guiding Elspeth onto her back. He slid quickly on top of her, her legs spreading either side of him, her hands behind his neck, urging him on. Horace needed no encouragement. He slid into her easily, deeply, groaning loudly in time with Elspeth's own gasp of pleasure, quickly beginning a rhythmic thrusting; feeling Elspeth's muscles contracting around him in time with each movement.

"Open your eyes," he gasped after a few seconds.

Elspeth obeyed, her dilated pupils turning her eyes into the deepest of greens.

"You'll never have to ask me again w-w-whether I think you're beautiful, w-w-will you?" Horace smiled, the expression at odds with the tremendous passions coursing through them both.

"Never," Elspeth gasped. She pulled him tightly towards her, bucking, now, in time with his every thrust, her entire stomach rippling as her muscles began their inexorable journey towards climax.

As Elspeth climaxed, grunting gutturally, animal-like, Horace let his own orgasm free. It seemed to last forever, each spasm bringing him to higher and higher plains of ecstasy, until, finally, almost thankfully, it subsided.

He collapsed on top of Elspeth, sated, sweating, shaking. He could feel small tremors coursing through her like aftershocks, her breath coming in short pants and gasps. Elspeth clung tightly to him, her face buried in his neck, a constant stream of gentle, meaningless, whispers soft against his skin.

They lay together for minutes, their embrace tight, allowing only the smallest possible distance between any part of them. Finally, Horace moved sideways, almost sliding off Elspeth's sweat-soaked body. He opened his eyes to look at her.

Elspeth was still panting, a half-smile on her dark lips, her eyes gazing steadily at him. "Oh, Horace." She paused and shook her head slightly, "I really didn't mean for that to happen," she whispered, a pleading look coming into her eyes.

Horace looked back, nonplussed, "I don't follow…"

Elspeth smiled, shame-faced, "Please believe me, Horace. I didn't come in here intending to… well, seduce you."

Horace stared at her for a moment and then shook his head, "It's strange," he said, "But I believe you. If it's any help at all, you didn't seduce me."

"Really?" Elspeth's gaze was earnest, desperately wanting to believe him.

"Really."

"I did mean what I said, as well," Elspeth said. She continued when he looked blank, "Just this once."

"I…" Horace began but stopped.

"What?" A frown of concern came over Elspeth's features.

Instead of replying, Horace leaned forward and kissed her deeply. After a few moments, he pulled back enough for Elspeth to see that he was blushing.

She gave a laugh as she began to understand what Horace had meant but not said, "Or maybe not just this once?"

Horace shrugged, his blush deepening. His sexual experience with women was not exactly great, but there was something about Elspeth, something very deep, instinctual almost, that he had always found magnetic. Now that the resistance had been breached, he wasn't sure that he could keep away from her for long, "I… don't know," he replied at length, "There's… w-w-well, there's Doll…"

"I won't tell her," Elspeth said quickly, "Ever. Horace, I promise."

Horace smiled and then let out a short laugh, "I alw-w-ways thought you w-w-were dangerous."

"And when I told you I thought we would be perfect together, I meant it," she nodded. "It must really be true that opposites attract."

"So it seems."

Elspeth sighed, "This really wasn't what I had in mind this morning."

"You told me. I believe you."

"Good," Elspeth's smile broadened. "How is your back, by the way?"

Horace started in surprise. Despite the energetic sexual athletics, his back was without pain for the first time in weeks, "It's... fine!"

"I told you I was good."

"Oh, you are," Horace agreed, his blush returning.

"And at least I know now why the painting is so good. I'll never be able to thank you enough for that."

"I could think of w-w-ways," Horace smiled sheepishly.

Elspeth's jaw dropped open and she gave a throaty laugh, "Well, well," she said, as much to herself as Horace. She shook her head and then changed the subject. "Would it look odd if we appeared together at the Crown? I mean, without Diamond?"

Horace hurried to keep up with the conversation, "I, er, guess not. I w-w-was going to suggest that you might w-w-want to get the painting framed, anyw-w-way. W-w-we could alw-w-ways pop in on the w-w-way back."

"I'd like that. And we could show off your talents at the same time. Perhaps you could pick up some more commissions."

"You'd actually show that painting around the pub?"

Elspeth giggled, the first time Horace had ever heard her do so, "Horace, the way I dress half the time, most of the guys in there have already seen what you've painted."

"True. Silly me."

"But before we go," Elspeth smiled, "Is there any more of that coffee? I'm gasping."

"Me too," Horace agreed. He slid gently off the bed and padded through to the kitchen, collecting the mugs en route. As he stood pouring their drinks he shook his head. He couldn't quite place why, and to be honest with himself, didn't really care, but for some reason he felt no guilt at what had just happened – at what, he thought ruefully, would almost certainly happen again.

Horace's mood remained unchanged throughout the day, and was barely dented when Doll returned from college. It helped that it was her last day of term and had evidently been celebrating in the Student Union – so much so, that even if Horace did act a little strange, she was in no position to notice.

Marva had collected her painting early in the evening, her delighted reaction to it serving to buoy Horace's mood even further, and he was a very happy bunny by the time he went to bed, early, in preparation for work the next day; happy too in the knowledge that he would only have to work Tuesday and Wednesday due to the Christmas holidays.

From The Diary of Horace Wilt

"Monday, 20th December, 1982

DD

A very strange day, and one that I'm finding hard to believe really happened. Elspeth arrived this morning after Doll had left and was absolutely delighted by her painting. She reacted in a way I'd never seen from her before - human, emotional, not in complete control. When she's like that, she's so different - so stunningly attractive. Afterwards, she offered to ease the pain in my back, which she actually did manage through a long, sensuous massage. After that... I just couldn't stop myself; didn't want to. Sex with her is incredible, so... thrilling. I don't know why I was so reluctant before; she's almost unbelievably beautiful. Can't work out where this leaves me with Doll, though..."

19

Despite the early night, he still grumbled and grouched as he prepared for work the next morning, not helped by the fact that Doll barely registered his goodbye kiss, preferring instead, to snuggle further under the duvet, only a few wisps of blonde hair evidence that she was even there.

He left the flat in a hurry, remembering at the last minute that Elspeth would be coming down so that she could witness the sunrise, leaving his door on the latch. He worried about what Elspeth might say to Doll but was comforted at the same time by the promises she had made to him. He dashed out into the street just in time to see his bus pulling away from the stop. Groaning, forgetting about the girls in his haste, he began frantically trying to hail passing cabs.

Elspeth had heard Horace's hasty departure and once she was sure that he had left, she made her way down the stairs. Sunrise was still twenty minutes away, but she wanted to be sure that she was fully prepared. She wore the same kaftan she had donned the previous day, and clutched a book and two small candles in her hands.

She let herself into Horace's flat and padded softly through to the bedroom, smiling as she saw Diamond still asleep. She set the candles on the dressing table at opposite ends of the surface so that they would not interfere with her view of the window, and then quickly pulled the kaftan over her head. As quietly as she could, she climbed onto the bed and settled into the lotus position, smiling again as a small voice muttered something unintelligible from under the duvet.

A couple of moments later, Doll's face appeared, her eyes half-closed against the gentle glow of the candles.

"Elspeth?"

"Good morning, Diamond."

"What's… what are you, er, doing?"

Elspeth quickly explained the importance of the occasion, grinning to herself when Doll grumbled that "Horace never told 'er a bleedin' fing".

"Want me to leave you alone, then?" Doll asked.

"Not at all. All I ask is for silence while I prepare for the ceremony."

"Fair exchange for a warm duvet," Doll nodded, yawning. She was actually quite fascinated by the idea, and sat up against the pillows, pulling the duvet up to her neck; although she was getting quite used to Elspeth's penchant for nudity, she was still shy herself – despite Horace's painting.

Elspeth fell silent, her breathing slowing, her eyes slowly closing. For a few minutes there was absolute silence and then Elspeth's eyes flickered open. She gazed intently at the small fragment of horizon she could see through the window and nodded once. She reached forward, picking up the small battered volume that she had placed before her on the bed, and opened it to a pre-marked page. She waited silently for another few minutes until the first rays of the sun appeared, and then began to read slowly and quietly from the book.

The words were in a language that Doll had never heard before, but something about its cadence made her think that it must be very old.

The first rays of sunlight were making their way slowly down the wall behind Elspeth's back, and whether it was the strangeness, other-worldliness, of the ritual she was witnessing, or whether it was something specific about Elspeth, Doll didn't know, but as the first rays finally lit up Elspeth's raven hair, it was all Doll could do not to gasp aloud.

It took only a couple of minutes before Elspeth was bathed from head to toe in the brilliance of the dawn, a couple of minutes when Doll barely took a breath. She watched intently as it lit every part of Elspeth's near-perfect form, seeming to physically caress the smooth planes of her flesh.

As the sun finally cleared the horizon, Elspeth fell silent and hung her head for a moment, before letting out a long sigh. She turned to Doll and smiled, "Quite moving, isn't it?"

It took Doll a moment before she could find words, "Almost surreal. Sorta *mystical*. What was the language?"

Elspeth explained that it was a form of the very earliest true English, older in many respects than what the scholars refer to as 'Old English'; a mixture of pict and another ancient language, used now only by some Druidic sects and a few of the true Pagans. She also told Doll about the importance of the sunrise on the Solstice, about the rebirth of light, the impending burgeoning of new growth, about how it was a central tenet of the Cult of The Natural Cycle.

Like Horace before, Doll became mesmerised by Elspeth's silky voice, disappointed when her commentary came to an end, shaking her head slightly to dispel the spell. "That's really beautiful," she said when she regained her voice.

"Thank you," Elspeth smiled once again, "You really should consider joining us, you know? You have a very close bond with the most basic of our instincts when it comes to all things natural."

Doll smiled at the thought, "I might like to learn a little more about the beliefs and stuff, but I'm pretty certain I couldn't become a member of the cult."

"And why would that be?"

Doll giggled "Well, I'm not really, sorta, like that. I mean, like you all are, you know?"

Elspeth laughed, "I'm sure you may have been misled in what you believe us to actually "be like". I take it you're referring to the sexuality of the members?"

Doll blushed, "Well, basically, yes."

"Probably Horace's doing," Elspeth's smiled broadened, "Although to be fair to him, he was misled by his mother. You see, as I told him recently, I'm not a lesbian – although many of the members are – and it's most certainly not a compulsory thing."

Doll wasn't unduly surprised by Elspeth's revelation, "I sorta guessed you weren't. But isn't celibacy pretty 'ard to put up with? I mean, I know priests an' nuns an' that are s'posed to be, but, well, wiv your looks it'd be a shame to disappoint all those guys."

Elspeth laughed again, "How very sweet of you to say so, but as it happens, I'm not celibate; another of Horace's misconceptions which I have corrected," she paused, her smile turning inward, "You see, my dear, I'm actually bisexual; I try not to disappoint anyone. Besides, it doubles the chances of a date when I go out."

"Bi… Oh! I, er, didn't know."

Elspeth's smiled returned to its former radiance. During the ceremony, as Doll had become used to the temperature outside the duvet, she had let it fall to her lap. Elspeth now turned her eyes downwards, staring admiringly at Doll's breasts, "You really are quite beautiful," she said, her eyes sliding up to her face.

Doll made to pull the duvet back up to her neck. Elspeth's hand stayed her, "There's no need to hide your beauty."

"I, er, thanks," Doll managed. She began to understand what Horace had meant by 'intimidated', "But, I'm not nearly as beautiful as you," she said quickly, regretting it almost as the words came out of her mouth.

"That's very kind of you," Elspeth smiled, her green eyes locking on Doll's, "But beauty must be *fitting*. It must conform to the person;

their personality, their size, their colouring. In all those things, your looks are close to perfection."

"I, er, don't know what to say," Doll said, for once lost for words.

Elspeth uncurled her long legs from the lotus position and turned on the bed to face Doll, "Sometimes, words aren't a necessary commodity." She paused, gauging Doll's reaction. "Please, dear, relax. I'm not here to cause you any pain or tension. That tension you feel now is quite unnecessary and mars your otherwise perfect beauty."

Doll couldn't see where this was leading, but made an effort to follow Elspeth's advice. She took a deep breath, exhaling slowly, "Okay," she said, her mouth dry.

"It's perfectly natural to fear the unknown," Elspeth continued, her voice dropping to the same mesmeric cadence of the ceremony, "But often – more often than not – these fears are completely unfounded; serving only to deny you experiences and pleasures that you would otherwise celebrate. Close your eyes for a moment and concentrate only on the sensations, ignore the circumstances."

Doll, almost hypnotised, stared back at Elspeth for a few seconds and then, slowly closed her eyes. She gasped as she felt Elspeth's hand close gently over her left breast.

"Keep your eyes closed for a moment or two longer," Elspeth breathed, "Concentrate only on the physical sensations you are now feeling. This is pleasurable at that level, yes?" her hand caressed first one breast then slid smoothly over to the other.

Doll swallowed hard. If she really did ignore the circumstances, then Elspeth was right. But even the circumstances seemed to be adding something to the sensations she was feeling; something about the slight edge of danger, of taboos being broken. "Y-yes," she found herself saying before she realised what she was *going* to say.

"That's very good," Elspeth breathed, her voice barely a whisper.

Doll felt Elspeth's hand slide away to one side, surprised at a sensation of loss, and then gasped again as she felt Elspeth's lips brush across both of her erect nipples. Gently, Elspeth drew a nipple into her mouth, her teeth barely grazing the surface, her tongue flicking gently to and fro. She groaned.

Elspeth drew back, her mouth on Doll's breast replaced by her hand, "Open your eyes, now," she commanded softly. She was smiling as Doll focussed on her. "Why fear pleasure? That was pleasurable, wasn't it?"

"Y-yes, it's just... I..."

Elspeth placed a finger over Doll's lips, "Let me show you something; let me show you how beautiful I think you are," her smile broadened as she remembered her time with Horace the previous morning, "For just this one time. It will be our secret."

Doll, mesmerised, confused, simply nodded.

Elspeth held her gaze for a few moments longer, her smile unwavering, and then leant forward, kissing Doll's mouth; gently at first and then firmer as she felt the tension and resistance begin to drain from her. The kiss deepened, tongues finally flicking against one another, and she gently squeezed Doll's right breast, causing her to groan softly. "Touch me," she whispered into the moist, warm mouth.

Elspeth groaned herself as Doll's hands rose and, tentatively at first, cupped her firm breasts. With her free hand, she eased the duvet away from Doll, and then let her hand slide slowly up the inside of Doll's thighs, pausing for a moment where she felt the heat radiating, before stroking gently at the very centre of her.

Doll's groans became louder, more insistent, and Elspeth broke the kiss, smiling deeply into her eyes before lowering her head. She worked her way slowly down Doll's small, naked form, pausing at each breast to tease and satisfy by turns, before continuing lower, finally taking her gently probing fingers away and replacing them by an eager tongue.

Doll's legs scissored open as she felt Elspeth's tongue enter her, Elspeth's teeth nipping oh so gently. Any misgivings she might have had were now long gone, and she let herself open up to sheer physical joy. Horace had shown her what a pleasure this could be, but by Elspeth's standards he was a novice. Never in her life had Doll felt such pure ecstasy; and she even experienced a sense of slight disappointment as she realised that she was rapidly approaching a tremendous orgasm. It hit her like a tidal wave, breaker after breaker rolling through her body, through her brain. As she lay, panting and gasping in its wake, Elspeth slowly uncurled herself and moved quietly along the bed to lie beside her.

"So what was there to fear?" she asked, smiling.

Doll almost laughed, still half in a state of shock, "Nothing, I guess."

"There is pleasure, also, in the giving."

Doll nodded. She knew that instinctively, right then, more than anything else in the world, she wanted to repay some of the pleasure that Elspeth had given her. Without a word, she sat up shakily, and then slid down Elspeth's perfect form, pausing as Elspeth had done, to caress Elspeth's perfect breasts. When she reached the dark diamond of her pubic hair, she paused for a moment, uncertain of what to do – she had no experience, after all – but quickly realised the answer. It was something her uncle Fred often said: "Do unto others as you would have them do unto you". Smiling to herself, she eased her head between Elspeth's long thighs and began to probe gently. Above her, unseen, Elspeth's face was wreathed in a mixture of pure joy, and absolute triumph.

Elspeth's climax was louder even than Doll's, longer as well, and Doll was surprised when she, too, enjoyed a small orgasm; a ripple to the earlier tsunami, a surprise in that giving such pleasure could bring about its own reciprocal joy. When Elspeth's guttural cries had died down to the merest whimpers, Doll lifted her head, quickly moving back to lay alongside the panting, sweating Elspeth.

"That was incredible," she told her, shaking her head in disbelief.

"And very beautiful too," Elspeth panted back, smiling.

Yeah, Doll thought, *she's right. It was beautiful.*
Elspeth's long arm snaked around Doll's back, pulling her tighter, and she settled comfortably with her head resting on Elspeth's shoulder.

"I'm glad you enjoyed the experience," Elspeth said. "As I said, it's something that every woman should experience at least once."

Doll snorted gently, "I'm not sure I could go through the rest of my life, 'aving experienced that only once," she replied, surprised to find that she meant it – desperately meant it.

Elspeth chuckled softly, the look of triumph burning even brighter in her green eyes, once more unseen by Doll, "In that case, my beautiful little Diamond, I would be honoured to share such pleasures with you again... many times again."

Doll still couldn't work out exactly what had happened. All she knew was that she didn't really care, and as far as Horace went, well, it wasn't as if Elspeth was another guy, was it? She reached across and hugged Elspeth tightly, "Promise me one thing?"

"What is it, dear?"

"Promise me you won't tell Horace?"

Elspeth laughed loudly, startling Doll, "Oh, I can readily promise you that. I don't think a man would understand the sheer pleasure of sexual relations just for the joy of it, would he?" She laughed loudly again, although Doll couldn't see what was so humorous.

They lay together for another few minutes, their bodies cooling except where they touched, until Elspeth, with a strange smile on her face, asked whether it would be possible to have some coffee.

Doll agreed – she was parched herself – and reluctantly rose and made her way through to the kitchen, pulling on one of Horace's T-shirts on the way. When she returned a few minutes later with two mugs, she was disappointed to find Elspeth already dressed, brushing her hair at the dressing table.

By the evening, when Horace returned grumpily from the bank, she had rationalised her behaviour – and the decision to possibly repeat it – to the point where it no longer pricked her conscience. Horace himself seemed to be in a slightly odd mood, more stuttery than usual, a little distracted, and she worried at first that something about her was sending out messages at some unexplained level. When she asked him if anything was wrong, he muttered a few oaths about his job, and took himself off to the Crown, despite having to go to work in the morning.

Doll, having stayed back at the flat ostensibly to tidy up her latest assignment so that she could concentrate on the Christmas festivities, wondered whether to go upstairs and see if Elspeth was at home, eventually deciding that so soon was too soon. She had finished the assignment by ten, when Horace returned in a much happier frame of mind.

20

Despite the early night, he still grumbled and grouched as he prepared for work the next morning, not helped by the fact that Doll barely registered his goodbye kiss, preferring instead, to snuggle further under the duvet, only a few wisps of blonde hair evidence that she was even there.

He left the flat in a hurry, remembering at the last minute that Elspeth would be coming down so that she could witness the sunrise, leaving his door on the latch. He worried about what Elspeth might say to Doll but was comforted at the same time by the promises she had made to him. He dashed out into the street just in time to see his bus pulling away from the stop. Groaning, forgetting about the girls in his haste, he began frantically trying to hail passing cabs.

Elspeth had heard Horace's hasty departure and once she was sure that he had left, she made her way down the stairs. Sunrise was still twenty minutes away, but she wanted to be sure that she was fully prepared. She wore the same kaftan she had donned the previous day, and clutched a book and two small candles in her hands.

She let herself into Horace's flat and padded softly through to the bedroom, smiling as she saw Diamond still asleep. She set the candles on the dressing table at opposite ends of the surface so that they would not interfere with her view of the window, and then quickly pulled the kaftan over her head. As quietly as she could, she climbed onto the bed and settled into the lotus position, smiling again as a small voice muttered something unintelligible from under the duvet.

A couple of moments later, Doll's face appeared, her eyes half-closed against the gentle glow of the candles.

"Elspeth?"

"Good morning, Diamond."

"What's… what are you, er, doing?"

Elspeth quickly explained the importance of the occasion, grinning to herself when Doll grumbled that "Horace never told 'er a bleedin' fing".

"Want me to leave you alone, then?" Doll asked.

"Not at all. All I ask is for silence while I prepare for the ceremony."

"Fair exchange for a warm duvet," Doll nodded, yawning. She was actually quite fascinated by the idea, and sat up against the pillows, pulling the duvet up to her neck; although she was getting quite used to Elspeth's penchant for nudity, she was still shy herself – despite Horace's painting.

Elspeth fell silent, her breathing slowing, her eyes slowly closing. For a few minutes there was absolute silence and then Elspeth's eyes flickered open. She gazed intently at the small fragment of horizon she could see through the window and nodded once. She reached forward, picking up the small battered volume that she had placed before her on the bed, and opened it to a pre-marked page. She waited silently for another few minutes until the first rays of the sun appeared, and then began to read slowly and quietly from the book.

The words were in a language that Doll had never heard before, but something about its cadence made her think that it must be very old.

The first rays of sunlight were making their way slowly down the wall behind Elspeth's back, and whether it was the strangeness, other-worldliness, of the ritual she was witnessing, or whether it was something specific about Elspeth, Doll didn't know, but as the first rays finally lit up Elspeth's raven hair, it was all Doll could do not to gasp aloud.

It took only a couple of minutes before Elspeth was bathed from head to toe in the brilliance of the dawn, a couple of minutes when Doll barely took a breath. She watched intently as it lit every part of Elspeth's near-perfect form, seeming to physically caress the smooth planes of her flesh.

As the sun finally cleared the horizon, Elspeth fell silent and hung her head for a moment, before letting out a long sigh. She turned to Doll and smiled, "Quite moving, isn't it?"

It took Doll a moment before she could find words, "Almost surreal. Sorta *mystical*. What was the language?"

Elspeth explained that it was a form of the very earliest true English, older in many respects than what the scholars refer to as 'Old English'; a mixture of pict and another ancient language, used now only by some Druidic sects and a few of the true Pagans. She also told Doll about the importance of the sunrise on the Solstice, about the rebirth of light, the impending burgeoning of new growth, about how it was a central tenet of the Cult of The Natural Cycle.

Like Horace before, Doll became mesmerised by Elspeth's silky voice, disappointed when her commentary came to an end, shaking her head slightly to dispel the spell. "That's really beautiful," she said when she regained her voice.

"Thank you," Elspeth smiled once again, "You really should consider joining us, you know? You have a very close bond with the most basic of our instincts when it comes to all things natural."

Doll smiled at the thought, "I might like to learn a little more about the beliefs and stuff, but I'm pretty certain I couldn't become a member of the cult."

"And why would that be?"

Doll giggled "Well, I'm not really, sorta, like that. I mean, like you all are, you know?"

Elspeth laughed, "I'm sure you may have been misled in what you believe us to actually "be like". I take it you're referring to the sexuality of the members?"

Doll blushed, "Well, basically, yes."

"Probably Horace's doing," Elspeth's smiled broadened, "Although to be fair to him, he was misled by his mother. You see, as I told him recently, I'm not a lesbian – although many of the members are – and it's most certainly not a compulsory thing."

Doll wasn't unduly surprised by Elspeth's revelation, "I sorta guessed you weren't. But isn't celibacy pretty 'ard to put up with? I mean, I know priests an' nuns an' that are s'posed to be, but, well, wiv your looks it'd be a shame to disappoint all those guys."

Elspeth laughed again, "How very sweet of you to say so, but as it happens, I'm not celibate; another of Horace's misconceptions which I have corrected," she paused, her smile turning inward, "You see, my dear, I'm actually bisexual; I try not to disappoint anyone. Besides, it doubles the chances of a date when I go out."

"Bi... Oh! I, er, didn't know."

Elspeth's smiled returned to its former radiance. During the ceremony, as Doll had become used to the temperature outside the duvet, she had let it fall to her lap. Elspeth now turned her eyes downwards, staring admiringly at Doll's breasts, "You really are quite beautiful," she said, her eyes sliding up to her face.

Doll made to pull the duvet back up to her neck. Elspeth's hand stayed her, "There's no need to hide your beauty."

"I, er, thanks," Doll managed. She began to understand what Horace had meant by 'intimidated', "But, I'm not nearly as beautiful as you," she said quickly, regretting it almost as the words came out of her mouth.

"That's very kind of you," Elspeth smiled, her green eyes locking on Doll's, "But beauty must be *fitting*. It must conform to the person;

their personality, their size, their colouring. In all those things, your looks are close to perfection."

"I, er, don't know what to say," Doll said, for once lost for words.

Elspeth uncurled her long legs from the lotus position and turned on the bed to face Doll, "Sometimes, words aren't a necessary commodity." She paused, gauging Doll's reaction. "Please, dear, relax. I'm not here to cause you any pain or tension. That tension you feel now is quite unnecessary and mars your otherwise perfect beauty."

Doll couldn't see where this was leading, but made an effort to follow Elspeth's advice. She took a deep breath, exhaling slowly, "Okay," she said, her mouth dry.

"It's perfectly natural to fear the unknown," Elspeth continued, her voice dropping to the same mesmeric cadence of the ceremony, "But often – more often than not – these fears are completely unfounded; serving only to deny you experiences and pleasures that you would otherwise celebrate. Close your eyes for a moment and concentrate only on the sensations, ignore the circumstances."

Doll, almost hypnotised, stared back at Elspeth for a few seconds and then, slowly closed her eyes. She gasped as she felt Elspeth's hand close gently over her left breast.

"Keep your eyes closed for a moment or two longer," Elspeth breathed, "Concentrate only on the physical sensations you are now feeling. This is pleasurable at that level, yes?" her hand caressed first one breast then slid smoothly over to the other.

Doll swallowed hard. If she really did ignore the circumstances, then Elspeth was right. But even the circumstances seemed to be adding something to the sensations she was feeling; something about the slight edge of danger, of taboos being broken. "Y-yes," she found herself saying before she realised what she was *going* to say.

"That's very good," Elspeth breathed, her voice barely a whisper.

Doll felt Elspeth's hand slide away to one side, surprised at a sensation of loss, and then gasped again as she felt Elspeth's lips brush across both of her erect nipples. Gently, Elspeth drew a nipple into her mouth, her teeth barely grazing the surface, her tongue flicking gently to and fro. She groaned.

Elspeth drew back, her mouth on Doll's breast replaced by her hand, "Open your eyes, now," she commanded softly. She was smiling as Doll focussed on her. "Why fear pleasure? That was pleasurable, wasn't it?"

"Y-yes, it's just... I..."

Elspeth placed a finger over Doll's lips, "Let me show you something; let me show you how beautiful I think you are," her smile broadened as she remembered her time with Horace the previous morning, "For just this one time. It will be our secret."

Doll, mesmerised, confused, simply nodded.

Elspeth held her gaze for a few moments longer, her smile unwavering, and then leant forward, kissing Doll's mouth; gently at first and then firmer as she felt the tension and resistance begin to drain from her. The kiss deepened, tongues finally flicking against one another, and she gently squeezed Doll's right breast, causing her to groan softly. "Touch me," she whispered into the moist, warm mouth.

Elspeth groaned herself as Doll's hands rose and, tentatively at first, cupped her firm breasts. With her free hand, she eased the duvet away from Doll, and then let her hand slide slowly up the inside of Doll's thighs, pausing for a moment where she felt the heat radiating, before stroking gently at the very centre of her.

Doll's groans became louder, more insistent, and Elspeth broke the kiss, smiling deeply into her eyes before lowering her head. She worked her way slowly down Doll's small, naked form, pausing at each breast to tease and satisfy by turns, before continuing lower, finally taking her gently probing fingers away and replacing them by an eager tongue.

Doll's legs scissored open as she felt Elspeth's tongue enter her, Elspeth's teeth nipping oh so gently. Any misgivings she might have had were now long gone, and she let herself open up to sheer physical joy. Horace had shown her what a pleasure this could be, but by Elspeth's standards he was a novice. Never in her life had Doll felt such pure ecstasy; and she even experienced a sense of slight disappointment as she realised that she was rapidly approaching a tremendous orgasm. It hit her like a tidal wave, breaker after breaker rolling through her body, through her brain. As she lay, panting and gasping in its wake, Elspeth slowly uncurled herself and moved quietly along the bed to lie beside her.

"So what was there to fear?" she asked, smiling.

Doll almost laughed, still half in a state of shock, "Nothing, I guess."

"There is pleasure, also, in the giving."

Doll nodded. She knew that instinctively, right then, more than anything else in the world, she wanted to repay some of the pleasure that Elspeth had given her. Without a word, she sat up shakily, and then slid down Elspeth's perfect form, pausing as Elspeth had done, to caress Elspeth's perfect breasts. When she reached the dark diamond of her pubic hair, she paused for a moment, uncertain of what to do – she had no experience, after all – but quickly realised the answer. It was something her uncle Fred often said: "Do unto others as you would have them do unto you". Smiling to herself, she eased her head between Elspeth's long thighs and began to probe gently. Above her, unseen, Elspeth's face was wreathed in a mixture of pure joy, and absolute triumph.

Elspeth's climax was louder even than Doll's, longer as well, and Doll was surprised when she, too, enjoyed a small orgasm; a ripple to the earlier tsunami, a surprise in that giving such pleasure could bring about its own reciprocal joy. When Elspeth's guttural cries had died down to the merest whimpers, Doll lifted her head, quickly moving back to lay alongside the panting, sweating Elspeth.

"That was incredible," she told her, shaking her head in disbelief.

"And very beautiful too," Elspeth panted back, smiling.

Yeah, Doll thought, *she's right. It was beautiful.*
Elspeth's long arm snaked around Doll's back, pulling her tighter, and she settled comfortably with her head resting on Elspeth's shoulder.

"I'm glad you enjoyed the experience," Elspeth said. "As I said, it's something that every woman should experience at least once."

Doll snorted gently, "I'm not sure I could go through the rest of my life, 'aving experienced that only once," she replied, surprised to find that she meant it – desperately meant it.

Elspeth chuckled softly, the look of triumph burning even brighter in her green eyes, once more unseen by Doll, "In that case, my beautiful little Diamond, I would be honoured to share such pleasures with you again... many times again."

Doll still couldn't work out exactly what had happened. All she knew was that she didn't really care, and as far as Horace went, well, it wasn't as if Elspeth was another guy, was it? She reached across and hugged Elspeth tightly, "Promise me one thing?"

"What is it, dear?"

"Promise me you won't tell Horace?"

Elspeth laughed loudly, startling Doll, "Oh, I can readily promise you that. I don't think a man would understand the sheer pleasure of sexual relations just for the joy of it, would he?" She laughed loudly again, although Doll couldn't see what was so humorous.

They lay together for another few minutes, their bodies cooling except where they touched, until Elspeth, with a strange smile on her face, asked whether it would be possible to have some coffee.

Doll agreed – she was parched herself – and reluctantly rose and made her way through to the kitchen, pulling on one of Horace's T-shirts on the way. When she returned a few minutes later with two mugs, she was disappointed to find Elspeth already dressed, brushing her hair at the dressing table.

By the evening, when Horace returned grumpily from the bank, she had rationalised her behaviour – and the decision to possibly repeat it – to the point where it no longer pricked her conscience. Horace himself seemed to be in a slightly odd mood, more stuttery than usual, a little distracted, and she worried at first that something about her was sending out messages at some unexplained level. When she asked him if anything was wrong, he muttered a few oaths about his job, and took himself off to the Crown, despite having to go to work in the morning.

Doll, having stayed back at the flat ostensibly to tidy up her latest assignment so that she could concentrate on the Christmas festivities, wondered whether to go upstairs and see if Elspeth was at home, eventually deciding that so soon was too soon. She had finished the assignment by ten, when Horace returned in a much happier frame of mind.

21

Harriet only stayed in the Crown for a couple of hours, citing jet-lag and a lack of tolerance for alcohol these days, before returning home. Horace stayed on as usual, reading the Saturday papers, eventually being joined by an exhausted-looking Doll. They, too, returned home early and Horace spent the evening sipping some of his mother's home-made brandy, before dozing off on the sofa. He awoke in darkness and quickly undressed, deciding to settle himself where he was for the night; there was no point disturbing Doll who had evidently taken herself off to bed, and besides, he was finding sleeping next to her increasingly uncomfortable.

He was woken at nine by a gentle tapping on his door. He yawned, stretched and pulled on his dressing gown before padding over to the door. He opened it and was surprised to find Elspeth standing there, a smile on her face, a dark blue silk robe hanging loosely from her shoulders, open at the front.

"Hello, Horace," she whispered.

"I, er, I mean, hello," he whispered back, checking nervously over his shoulder to make sure that Doll hadn't heard the knocking. The bedroom door was firmly closed. "W-w-what are you doing here?" he whispered urgently.

Elspeth stepped forward, her hand slipping easily into the front of Horace's gown, fastening itself gently around his already semi-tumescent member, "I wanted to see you," she smiled as he stifled a groan. She lifted his hand to the firm nakedness of her breasts.

"I, er..." Horace glanced over Elspeth's shoulder to the door of Harriet's flat, realising for the first time that it wasn't just Doll's awareness of the situation that he should be worried about. "You've got to come in," he hissed.

Elspeth released her hold on him, brushing past as she made her way into the living room. Behind her, Horace shut the door as softly as his haste would allow. He trailed into the living room, following his erection.

"W-w-what do you w-w-want?" he asked desperately, glancing between Elspeth and the still-closed bedroom door.

"Quite simply," Elspeth purred, "I want you."

"W-w-what!? Doll's through there!"

"I rather thought she might be. I think you misunderstand me, Horace. When I say I want you, I mean just that. You. All of you, all the time."

"I don't follow-" Horace began, but he was quickly interrupted.

"You and Diamond don't seem to be, shall we say, getting on very well at the moment, do you?" Elspeth asked, her voice a little louder than before, beginning to give Horace palpitations.

"I, that is, w-w-well, no."

"Then I think that it is time for you to request that Doll leaves, don't you?"

"W-w-what!? I c-c-can't just ask her to clear out!"

Elspeth closed the distance between them. She stopped a few inches from him and stared up steadily into his eyes, "I'm sure if I told her what has happened between you and I, Horace, that she would be more than happy to leave."

Horace stared, aghast, "You w-w-wouldn't? You promised!" he cried louder than intended.

Elspeth just smiled, "I really want you very badly."

"But… I c-c-can't just tell her to go!"

"Find a way, Horace… Or I shall."

Horace looked back helplessly, "I…"

"And I would also love a coffee," Elspeth said as if nothing had happened, "While you're making it, I'm just going to pop in and see Diamond; there's something I need to discuss with her in private."

"No!"

Elspeth chuckled, "Don't worry, Horace. I won't mention our little secret. That is, I won't mention it *this* time; maybe tomorrow if you haven't asked her to leave by then. This is purely about arrangements for my lessons in the Pagan arts."

Horace stared, unsure whether to believe her. Doll had said something about Elspeth giving her some guidance in this Pagan thing just the previous day, but after Elspeth's ultimatum, he wasn't sure he could trust her.

In the event he had no choice in the matter as Elspeth slipped quickly past him and opened the bedroom door before he could react. She disappeared inside, closing the door firmly behind her. Horace hung his head and slowly made his way into the kitchen.

22

Doll had still been asleep when Elspeth entered the room and it took her a few seconds before she realised who it was.

"Elspeth!" she whispered urgently when she finally identified the intruder, "What the bleedin' 'ell are you doin' in 'ere?"

"Charming," Elspeth smiled, "But don't fret my dear. Horace knows I'm here. He believes that we'll be discussing arrangements for your introduction to the Pagan arts. Which, in a way, we will." Elspeth pulled back the duvet and laid a hand gently on Doll's right breast.

Doll groaned before gasping and pushing the hand away, "What if Horace comes in?" she whispered desperately.

Elspeth was amused at the similarity between Diamond's reaction and that of Horace, earlier, "He won't. But now you come to mention it, Horace is really what I want to talk to you about."

"Oh?"

Elspeth nodded, smiling, "You see, my dear, I no longer want to share you. With Horace, that is."

"'Ow do you mean?"

"I think it would be better all-round if you left here," Elspeth said, her green eyes locked onto Doll's, "That way, you could visit me without any suspicions, since there would be no involvement between you and Horace. I, also, could visit you, wherever you may be."

"But I can't just walk out on 'im! We're not gettin' on all that great at the minute, but, well, 'e *is* my boyfriend."

Elspeth's stare didn't waver, "I doubt he would object to your departure if he learned exactly what we mean by Pagan arts now, would he?"

"You wouldn't?"

Elspeth let out a chuckle; the similarities really were truly remarkable, "I told you, my dear; I want you all for myself."

"But 'e'll be 'eartbroken!"

"You may be surprised. Remember, I know things."

Doll slumped against the pillows, "But I love it 'ere," she wailed.

"Will you tell him yourself, or would you like me to do it?" Elspeth ignored Doll's pleas, her hand sliding down over Doll's belly, probing gently, bringing forth a groan of pleasure.

"Okay," Doll gasped, struggling upright, determined to break the contact, "You win."

Elspeth withdrew her hand, smiling broadly, "I knew you would see sense." She rose and made her way swiftly out of the room, ignoring the muttered 'bitch; as Doll began to cry.

Horace stared at Elspeth as she entered the kitchen, his anger barely controlled, "This is blackmail, you know?"

"I think it's more to do with the state of your conscience, Horace," Elspeth smiled. "I suggest you take Diamond to the Crown at lunchtime and discuss matters." She stepped in front of him, spreading her robe wide. "This will be all yours. And this, all mine," she added, reaching once more into the folds of his dressing gown.

Horace swallowed noisily, "You really are a bitch, aren't you?"

"The best," Elspeth agreed, smiling to herself at yet another coincidental reaction, "And if you're good, I'll be your very own bitch, to do with as you will." She waited until he was completely rigid in her grasp and then released him. "Don't worry about the coffee. I'm sure you have a lot to think about."

Horace watched as she left the room in a swirl of dark-blue. He stared down morosely. "Harry wh-wh-once threatened to have you taken to the vet," he told his ferret which was still projecting from the gown. "She w-w-was right."

Their lunchtime session at the Crown – their last one together – was an unsurprisingly tense affair, and it was hard to gauge which one of them was the more surprised by the other's ready acceptance of the *fait accompli*. On the way back to the flat Doll was tearful, Horace little better, and when Jim Mercer came to collect his daughter and her belongings early that evening, they hugged each other tightly, neither of them really believing what was happening.

Because of the circumstances, neither could really discuss what had gone wrong and, more than anything else, it was this fact that reduced Horace to floods of tears as he watched Jim Mercer drive away with his Doll.

He spent the rest of the evening pacing his flat, drinking home-made brandy, and cursing his stupidity. He wondered for a while whether he should just phone Doll and come clean, tell her what had really happened, but he couldn't, wimp that he truly was. What he had done with Elspeth was of his own volition, no matter how much he tried to blame the vamp, and even if he *had* been seduced, the fact of his crime against Doll was still there.

Even Elspeth didn't know that another coinciding reaction was occurring just a couple of miles away in a small bedroom above the Draughtsman.

From The Diary of Horace Wilt

"Sunday, 1ˢᵗ May, 1983

DD

This should really be the first of April. I've been the biggest, most stupid, most gullible idiot. Doll's left, and it's all my fault - my fault for trusting Elspeth, the bitch. All this time that I've spent under Elspeth's spell, I'd forgotten how much I really adore Doll; how wonderful she truly is. And for what? Sex with that bloody vampire. Stupid, stupid, stupid!!!!"

23

Horace phoned in sick the following day, his hangover approaching world record proportions, and closeted himself in his living room – he couldn't face the bedroom yet – studiously ignoring both knocks at the door and the telephone, which rang on the hour, every hour.

When he returned to work the next day, he was still morose and was surly with everyone. Even the usually taciturn Mr Edwards noticed and asked Horace what was wrong. When he received no reply other than a simple shake of the head, he shrugged and left the young man to his work. His own son had often gone through these moods and he had found it best to leave him alone to "stew in his own juices".

By the end of the week, Horace's mood had improved little, and so it was a surprise when he agreed to come along for an after-hours drink on the Friday evening. Donna had been volunteered to ask the snappy Horace, on the grounds that she seemed to be the only person Horace could be bothered to be civil with, and after a little encouragement, he finally relented.

As far as he was concerned, the longer he stayed away from his flat the better. He had successfully avoided Elspeth during the week, but was sure that she was plotting something. During the evening, he told Donna something of what had happened – mainly to explain his recent moodiness – and was surprised when this was met with not just sympathy but empathy; Donna herself having gone through a recent and messy split with a long-term boyfriend. Shortly before they left, Horace asked whether they might possibly see each other away from the bank and the rest of their colleagues, but was almost pleased when she told him that she had just started another relationship, and, although she was flattered, and under other circumstances would have been pleased to accept the offer, she couldn't just then. They parted amicably at the station, ignoring one or two ribald comments from colleagues, and Horace found himself all too soon back in Walthamstow.

He had intended going straight back to his flat, tired after another, albeit short, week's work, but spotted a light in Elspeth's apartment and decided that a trip to the Crown would be a better option.

He finally arrived back in his flat after midnight and flopped gratefully onto his sofa, struggling to focus on a note that had been slid under his door. After a few minutes of intense concentration, he worked out that it was from Harriet, and that she wanted to see him over the weekend to tell him something. Shrugging, he made a mental note to call on her in the morning, and staggered through to his bedroom where he quickly undressed and climbed into the comfort of his bed, asleep in seconds.

Sunlight was streaming through the window when he woke the next morning, but it was not the brightness that roused him. It took him a moment or two before he realised that he wasn't alone in the bed, and a further few moments to remember that Doll was no longer living there. Concentrating hard on the situation, he tried to work out who the hell was there with him. Harriet still had a key to his flat and for one moment he thought that perhaps it was her. He was about to whisper her name when the mystery was solved.

"Good Morning, Horace," Elspeth purred.

Horace's eyes flew open and he rolled over to face her, ignoring the dull throbbing in his head, "H-h-how did you get in here?"

Elspeth chuckled softly, "I did tell you that I meant to have you all for myself. And when I mean to do something I always find a way." She quickly pulled back the duvet, reaching down and grasping Horace gently.

"N-n-no, you m-m-mustn't," Horace pleaded.

"Oh, but I must."

Horace had sworn to himself that he wouldn't allow this to happen; couldn't after what Elspeth had done, but as her mouth closed over his stiff member, it was all he could do to mutter a few half-hearted protests, let alone take any actions to stop her. When she left half an hour later, Horace collapsed back onto the pillows, still panting. His eyes stared, unfocussed, at the ceiling as he repeatedly muttered "Bugger".

He had just showered and was sitting morosely on the sofa, sipping coffee, when somebody knocked on his door.

"Who is it?" he called, fearing the worst. His breathed a sigh of relief when Harriet answered.

"Mornin' H," she greeted him with a smile as he let her in. "Bit of a rough night, was it?"

"Not as rough as this morning," Horace muttered, "Coffee?"

"Of course."

He refilled his own mug, another for Harriet, and set them down on the coffee table, "Do I recall a note from you, last night?"

Harriet nodded, "I'm surprised you do judging from the look of you, but yeah, there's something I need to talk to you about. A couple of things, as a matter of fact."

"Fire aw-w-way."

"Well," Harriet sighed, "First of all, I've decided to go back to college after the summer. There's a really interesting computer course, a two year job, at Loughborough University."

"Oh yeah, you took computing w-w-with the business studies, didn't you? I never even realised until I saw your results."

Harriet grinned and rolled her eyes, "I told you about it enough times. Anyway, I applied last week an' I was accepted on the spot," she paused and sighed again, "And that's what I wanna tell you;

Loughborough ain't exactly on the doorstep, so I guess I'll be moving out when I can find a place up there."

"Must you?" Horace asked, crestfallen.

Harriet's half-smile turned sympathetic, "Yeah, H. Look, I really appreciate 'ow you 'elped me with this place, and I really enjoyed all of our time together – well, most of it, anyway. But it's probably for the best all round. Memories everywhere, an' all that."

"I guess so," he tried to return her smile, nearly succeeding. "You must let me know if there's anything I can do to help, I can...." He trailed off. "Oh bugger!"

"What's up?"

"W-w-well, w-w-when you go, and w-w-with old Mr Benjamin off at his relations all the time, that means I'll be all alone here with Elspeth."

Harriet was confused, "What about Doll? And, anyway, I thought you an' Elspeth get along okay; that was the other thing I was gonna tell you. She came down yesterday an' said you'd asked 'er to get your spare key off me so she could let 'erself in 'ere to do a few jobs for you."

Horace grunted. It at least explained how she had come to be in his bed that morning, "I never asked her any such thing."

"Oh Christ, I'm sorry, H!"

He gave a snort of laughter, "Don't w-w-worry, Harry. Elspeth can be very convincing at times; very persuasive. And I guess that brings me to Doll." Horace, never once taking his eyes off the carpet, told her everything that had happened, right up to his surprise bed-mate that morning. He at least owed Harriet the truth. He glanced up at her when he had finished, not unduly surprised to find her jaw hanging open, a look somewhere between anger and outrage on her delicate features.

"The fucking bitch!" she snarled, "I thought about belting you when you started telling me, but I guess she was just takin' advantage of you. What a fucking cow! Mind you, she looks like the type who carries a mattress around on 'er back in case she meets a friend. Likes 'er lovers to be male or female, human and alive – but I'd bet she'd settle for any two out of three. Poor Doll. And to a lesser extent, poor you."

"I should have known better than to trust a w-w-woman that dresses to the left. I w-w-was stupid, w-w-wasn't I?" Horace asked, shame-faced.

Harriet was about to continue her tirade, but stopped herself when she saw his expression, "Oh, Orris! Come 'ere."

He scooted along the sofa and into Harriet's comforting arms, hugging her tightly. "You know something, H?" she smiled down at his head, buried in her shoulder, "I really did love you. And I guess I never really thanked you for all you did for me; all we did together that was so great. So I tell you what, I'm gonna show you 'ow much you meant to me, an' 'ow grateful I am, okay?"

Horace pulled back to see her face, "W-w-what?"

"Well, I ain't about to leave my poor 'elpless Orris 'ere with that vicious bitch," she said, a nasty smile on her face. "If you want 'er out of 'ere, I'll make sure she's gone by the end of the week, okay?"

"I do w-w-want her out," he nodded, sincerely, "But how are you going to do it."

The nasty smile turned nastier, "Play 'er at 'er own game. 'Ere's what we'll do; tell 'er you're gonna come up and see 'er, say... Tuesday evening after you finish work, about eight. Tell 'er you wanna find 'er in bed, ready and waiting for you, okay?" Horace nodded, "Only it won't be you wot turns up, see? It'll be me and a couple of my relations."

"You're not going to... beat her up or something?" Horace asked, not really minding if that *was* what Harriet was planning.

Harriet chuckled, "Oh, no! I said we'll play 'er at 'er *own* game. Trust me on this one, big guy."

Horace nodded happily, "You got it."

24

Harriet still hadn't filled him in on the details of her plan by the time Horace arrived home on the Tuesday, and he was surprised to find two of Harriet's nephews, the very young-looking fourteen year-old twins, Raymond and Roger, quietly sipping Cokes on her sofa. Harriet was busy fiddling with a professional-looking camera, grinning from ear to ear. She finally set the apparatus down by the side of her door and clapped her hands, a General gathering her troops.

"Okay, boys, you both know what to do?"

Raymond giggled, "Sure do, auntie."

"That's 'Arry, not auntie," she grinned back, "Roger?"

"Can't wait."

"Orris, you've gotta come along but you mustn't get in the way. It's only fair you should see 'er get 'er come-uppance."

Horace grinned and shrugged. Whatever the scheme might be, he couldn't see it involving violence, "I guess I'd love to."

Harriet checked her watch, "Okay then, men. Five minutes to Operation *Get the Bitch*. Get yourself ready boys."

To Horace's surprise, the boys began to undress, "Er, w-w-what's going on?" he asked Harriet, concerned.

"Well," Harriet said, a sly smile on her face, "She blackmailed you, right? So, as the saying goes, what goes around comes around."

Horace was beginning to see the picture, "Under age sex, by any chance? A complete set-up job, yeah?"

"Bingo!" Harriet beamed. "Come on guys," she instructed her nephews who were by now only wearing skimpy pants. Judging by a small but nevertheless obvious bulge, Raymond was clearly looking forward to this.

Harriet led them silently out of her flat and up the stairs, stopping outside Elspeth's door. "Okay, guys," she whispered, "Orris, you go in first an' make sure she's in the bedroom. If she is, give us a thumbs up an' then clear out the way. Boys, as soon as you see Orris give the okay, you go quickly and quietly into the bedroom, and onto the bed. I'll be right behind you."

The two boys nodded eagerly, and, grinning broadly, Horace quietly opened the door of the flat, stepping cautiously inside. The living room was lit by a score or more candles and more light was coming from the bedroom. "Elspeth?" he called softly.

"Ready and waiting for you, as instructed," she purred back from the depths of her bedroom.

Horace nodded to himself and turned towards the door, both thumbs raised.

Raymond and Roger scampered inside, barely suppressing giggles, quickly followed by Harriet, her nasty smile firmly in place, the camera already raised to her eye. They paused for a moment outside the bedroom door and then hurled themselves through it, diving for the bed as soon as they had crossed the threshold.

Until their arrival, Elspeth had been laying on top of the duvet, naked, two of her fingers probing deeply inside herself, beginning to groan. The few seconds it took to realise that something was wrong were all it took for Harriet's plan to succeed. Horace, watching from the doorway as the camera's flash strobed repeatedly, could hardly contain his laughter. The eager Raymond had dived for the head of the bed, kneeling with his back to the camera, and had pulled down his pants so that appeared that Elspeth was sucking his tiny dick.

Roger had made for the other end, laying his head between Elspeth's thighs.

As Elspeth realised that something was terribly wrong, she struggled to sit up, trying to push the two giggling boys away from her. Not before, though, the Nikon's motor drive had pushed twenty frames through the body of the camera.

"What the fucking hell's going on here?" Elspeth roared, her normal cat-like tones disappearing under the weight of her outrage.

The twins dived for the safety of the living room as Elspeth began to hurl anything that came to hand, and Harriet followed them quickly, as much to protect the camera as herself.

"W-w-when you've calmed down," Horace grinned at Elspeth from the doorway, "I suggest you pay Harry and I a visit in my flat. W-w-we've a thing or two to discuss w-w-with you." He shut the door quickly as a candle thudded into the frame by his head.

It took just ten minutes for Elspeth to control her anger, and the still-helplessly giggling twins had only just finished dressing when she appeared. It took only another ten minutes for Harriet to explain what would happen if Elspeth chose not to leave the flat upstairs, and just two hours before Elspeth roared off in the hearse, all of her belongings safely stowed in the rear.

The celebratory party lasted until midnight, and was only ended by the arrival of Harriet's aunt Brenda to collect the kids. When they had gone, Horace poured himself and Harriet more brandy and then sat quietly together on his sofa, the occasional giggle escaping one or the other. Harriet reached into her bag and took out the roll of film she had used upstairs.

"You'd better keep this for a while," she suggested. "That bitch might try anything. If she does, give me a call, an' I'll get a girl I know to develop them."

Horace took the plastic container, a small moue of distaste on his mouth, "If you reckon. But I really don't like having these about."

428

Harriet thought for a moment, and then nodded, taking the container back, "You're probably right. I'll 'ang onto it instead. Just call me if she causes any problems, okay?"

Horace nodded, smiling, "Even after you've left?"

"Of course, H," Harriet said, a curious expression on her face. "You'll always be able to call me, you know? We're friends after all, ain't we?"

Horace smiled, "Yeah. Friends."

"Do you have to go now?" Horace asked her a few minutes later, as Harriet made slowly for his door.

She stopped and turned to him, a quirky smile on her face, "I think it's for the best."

Horace nodded, trying to smile, "Okay then."

Harriet crossed back to where he was standing. She slipped her arms around him and hugged him tightly, "Thanks for everything, big guy."

"Thank you," Horace managed, close to tears.

Harriet released her vice-like grip, reaching up to kiss him softly. She broke the embrace after a few seconds and gave him a watery smile, "Take care, H."

Horace watched her quick, tearful exit, with the blood pounding in his ears, tears standing on his cheeks.

From The Diary of Horace Wilt

"Tuesday, 10th May, 1983

DD

The bitch has gone! Harry and her cousins were absolutely brilliant and the set-up worked magnificently. All in all, it was the very least the cow deserved. Had quite a party afterwards and I'll probably be phoning into work sick tomorrow - or rather, today - but I really don't care.

I do care that Harry will be leaving soon, though. I'm going to really miss her - which seems daft given that she's been in India for most of the last twelve months. We had a real long chat after her cousins had left and I wondered for a minute or two whether we might get back together. But Harry insisted that she wasn't "right" for me; not strong enough. And I guess, maybe, I'm not ideal for her either. It's a real shame, but at least we're still friends - the best of friends."

Chapter 6

1

Harriet eventually moved out of her apartment in late August after a party two nights before which had lasted until dawn. They exchanged earnest promises that they would keep in touch, and ritually burned the roll of film in Harriet's kitchen while quizzical looking removal men carried the last of Harriet's possessions down to their van.

Once again, Horace sat at the window in his living room, watching rather sadly as another beautiful little woman left him all alone.

This time he was truly alone, Mr Benjamin having decided to settle with a grandson in Australia, and the flat formerly occupied by Stephanie and then Elspeth, still empty after the latter's hasty departure. His mother had called him a few days after Elspeth's retreat and had demanded to know what he had done to so enrage the 'lovely girl'. Horace had explained in no uncertain terms exactly what he thought of the 'lovely girl' and had subsequently not heard from his mother for some weeks.

Horace gazed around, wondering what to do. He had no intention of 'throwing himself into work' as you were supposed to do at times like this. He hated his job and his boss, although in the latter case, this was a mutual arrangement, and had begun to look round for other things that he might like to do. He was still undertaking a few commissions for paintings, but not enough so that he could forge a career out of it, and turned now to his latest work, a portrait of Marva's boyfriend's sister. He added some texture to the background, and, satisfied with the overall effect, phoned Winston to tell him that it would be ready that evening. He chatted distractedly with the big black guy and then made his was slowly to the Crown, alone except for his thoughts and newspapers.

It was a pattern that he repeated for the next few months, an automatic response as he drifted idly through the rest of the year. Work continued to bore him rigid, and was only made tolerable because of Donna, who was unfailingly friendly with him, even when he was in one of his ever-more frequent bad moods.

As December approached, his relationship with the manager deteriorated even further.

"Wilt," Mr Edwards called one morning as Horace ran into the bank, "You're ten minutes late. Again!"

orace gave him a tight smile, "But just think how early I leave!" He left the manager trying desperately to work that one out.

The bank's Christmas party raced up on him and, despite originally having no intention of attending, Donna managed to persuade him to come. It was to be held in the offices above the bank's trading floor on the last Friday before Christmas.

The day seemed to pass with intolerable slowness despite everyone being kept busy by the Christmas rush, and it was a relief when the clock finally ticked up 17:30. Most of the female staff disappeared in a flash to change into their party gear, and most of the males headed straight for the bar and buffet tables to begin enjoying the bank's generosity. Quite a few people had complained that spouses and partners were not invited, but for Horace this was not a problem. His disastrous dalliance with Elspeth had put him off women altogether and, he reasoned, no partners meant more drinks for the rest of them.

Mr Edwards gave a short speech at seven o'clock which was greeted coolly until he finished by announcing that he was to take retirement at the end of January. When he had returned to his seat, the applause still echoing off the walls, the party began in earnest.

At ten Horace, who had perched himself on a filing cabinet next to the bar, was joined by Donna, her face flushed.

"Having fun?" she asked.

"Only because it's at the bank's expense."

"Sour puss. Come and have a dance with me."

Horace shook his head vehemently, "No w-w-way. I really can't dance."

"Nonsense." Donna giggled, "And besides, the DJ's just said the next one's gonna be a slow one. Everyone can dance to them."

"I don't know–" Horace began, but he was interrupted by the start of 10cc's *I'm Not In Love*, and Donna tugged his arm. He trailed self-consciously after her, trying to hide in the gloom.

She crossed the dance floor until they were in a corner near the door to the administration corridor, and then spun around to face him, "Come here," she smiled.

With a mental shrug, Horace stepped forward into her arms, and they began to shuffle slowly round and round.

"Not so bad, is it?" Donna asked after a minute.

"Not at all," Horace agreed. No-one would have called Donna truly beautiful, but she was tall and slender, and the combination of dark hair and pale blue eyes gave her face an endearing quality. She pulled Horace tighter towards her, until he could feel her breasts being squashed between them. He made to pull apart, but was met with solid resistance.

"I thought you liked me?" Donna giggled quietly.

"I, er, do."

"Well hold on then. And don't worry, no-one can see what we're up to over here."

Horace glanced about and realised she was right. He took a deep breath and did as she had instructed. Donna's hand slid down his back, and then onwards until it settled on his bum, steady pressure ensuring that their hips met. Horace felt a certain ferret, so long dormant, begin to stir. "I, er, s-s-sorry…"

Donna giggled again, "See, I was right when I said you like me, wasn't I?"

"It's, er, hard not to."

"Hard, certainly," Donna said, pressing herself even tighter to him.

Horace was no more than three inches taller than Donna, and as he glanced down, she glanced up, their eyes locking. She broke the eye contact for a second, quickly scanning the room. When she was sure that they were unobserved, she turned back and kissed him.

"That's for Christmas," she said when she broke the kiss.

"I, er, thank you," Horace gulped.

"And what are you gonna give me?"

Their dancing had slowed to a near-standstill, "I, er, guess this," Horace leant forward, his lips finding hers easily. This kiss lasted considerably longer and Horace was breathless when they finally broke the contact.

"Wow, and thanks," Donna grinned.

"The pleasure w-w-was all mine." Horace's self-consciousness was disappearing without trace, "But w-w-wouldn't your boyfriend object?"

"He would if you did that to him. But, anyway, he's not here. And it is Christmas."

"Oh, okay then," Horace whispered, leaning into another kiss.

What started as a kiss, gradually developed into a full-blown, passion-filled embrace, their bodies locked together, tongues darting into each other's mouth, hands caressing backs and bums. Finally, Horace surfaced for air, "I'm really glad your boyfriend's not here," he panted.

Donna's eyes sparkled up at him, "Me too. And I've always liked you, and it is-"

"Christmas," Horace finished.

"Which means there's only one thing missing."

"W-w-which is?"

"Mistletoe. And," she added, "I know just where to find some."

She grabbed his hand and spun round, making for the darkened corridor of the administration block. Horace shrugged and followed. Donna stopped at the door and spun round, scanning the room to see if anyone was watching, and when she was certain they were unobserved, she quickly opened the door and dragged Horace through. The door swung silently shut behind them and Donna let out a giggle in the gloom, "No-one saw a thing," she whispered, beginning to lead Horace down the corridor.

"W-w-where are w-w-we going?"

"You'll soon see." She stopped outside a door halfway down and checked that it wasn't locked. "Here we are."

"You can't be serious?" Horace suppressed a laugh.

"Oh yes I am." Donna swung Mr Edwards' office door wide, "He's the only one that's allowed to put up decorations, and I noticed mistletoe when I was in here on Tuesday."

Horace followed her inside, closing the door behind him. Light from a streetlamp outside was the only illumination, but it was sufficient for Horace to see by. Donna had been right; a large sprig of mistletoe was hanging immediately over the manager's desk. He crossed to where Donna had perched herself against the edge of the desk and accepted the invitation offered by her open arms. Things were, he knew, getting out of control here, but he really didn't care.

Their kisses were passionate, and before a minute had passed, Horace had lifted his hand to Donna's left breast and was fondling her through the thin materials of her dress and bra.

"Christ!" she panted, breaking their embrace for a second, "You've got me as horny as a bitch in heat."

"Likew-w-wise," Horace said, gasping himself.

"Only one cure for this, I reckon," Donna giggled and reached behind her.

Horace held his breath as he heard a zipper being drawn slowly down. Donna manoeuvred him backwards and then let the dress slide to the floor. Under it she was wearing the flimsiest of bra and pants, and it took her just seconds before these joined the dress on the floor. Horace stared at her naked form, mesmerised.

"And before you say it," Donna gasped, "No-one's gonna come looking for us; they're all too busy getting pissed through there."

Horace hadn't actually given it a thought, distracted as he was at the moment, "W-w-whatever," he raised his hands to cup her surprisingly large breasts.

Donna groaned with pleasure, and begun frantically un-tucking Horace's shirt. He reluctantly broke his hold on her to lend assistance and was soon just as naked, a strange thrill coursing through him at what they were doing – and what he now knew they were about to do.

Donna slid off the edge of the desk and sprawled on the floor, dragging the uncomplaining Horace with her. He dropped quickly but gently onto her naked body, and shuffled backwards, "P-p-protection?" he managed through his gasps.

Donna shook her head, "Pill. Now do me before I explode."

"W-w-whatever you say." He moved forward until he could feel her warmth and wetness against his rigid member, and with the minimum of effort, slid into her.

"Now this is what I call a happy fucking Christmas," Donna groaned.

It is fair to say that the first time two people have sex can either be very good or very bad; seldom just average. It is also fair to say that circumstances can dictate which it is to be. It is most definitely perfection to say that if a door opens, a light comes on and someone yells "What the bloody hell is going on here?" just as you're reaching a powerful climax, then 'very bad' is the correct term.

As Horace scrambled to his feet, hands desperately trying to cover his rapidly shrinking erection, and Mr Edwards' shout still echoing around the room, 'very bad' didn't seem adequate. Below him, partially stranded by an orgasm which had begun just a few seconds before the door had burst open, Donna was frantically trying to cover her nakedness with both her hands, and Horace's trousers.

"It's, er, not w-w-what you think," Horace pleaded unrealistically.

"Not what I think!" Edwards' voice was reaching new peaks of fury. "You were quite clearly fuc… fornicating in my own bloody office!" He cast around and came up with Donna's dress, throwing it at Horace. "Now, bloody well get dressed and meet me outside." He turned and stormed from the room.

"Oh buggeration," Horace groaned.

"Thank God we weren't doing that," Donna groaned herself. "I've the horrible idea that we're in the shit here – no pun intended – I've never seen him turn purple before."

"You can say that again!"

He knelt down to begin the search for his clothes and Donna grabbed his arm, "I'm sorry, Horace, but if it's any consolation, you were bloody fantastic."

Horace's shoulders slumped, "Thanks, but there's no need to be sorry. I didn't exactly object, did I?"

Donna giggled and handed him his trousers, "Can't say that you did."

Horace leaned forward and gave her a quick kiss, stopping for just a moment to run his right hand across her bared breasts, "And besides, I didn't like the job anyw-w-way."

Donna smiled, "Me neither. But if we get out of here quickly enough, he might be lenient."

"Edw-w-wards?"

"Ah, I see what you mean."

They dressed quickly and made for the door. Before they went outside to where they could hear the manager pacing up and down, Donna stopped Horace and hugged him, "Thanks again, Horace," she whispered, "And good luck."

Edwards' tirade lasted for a full five minutes which Horace spent blushing and wincing, and Donna spent staring at the carpet. When he finally ran out of steam he stopped shouting and stared at the pair of them with what to Horace felt like lasers. "Very well, then," the manager went on in a more normal tone of voice. "Miss Beckworth, you will be issued with a written warning for violating banking

438

procedures which I hope will serve *as* a warning without giving any indication as to the vile nature of your conduct."

"Thank you, sir," she said in a quiet little voice.

Edwards nodded once, satisfied, and then turned his attention to Horace. "Wilt, you have been nothing but an incompetent nuisance in the year or so you have been here. However, you seem to be well liked by your colleagues," he paused and stared at Donna once again, "Very well liked in some cases, and, whatever you may think of me, I am not an unreasonable man. I recognise that you have your entire future ahead of you and so, if you agree to resign your position with us, I will neither sack you on the spot as I am tempted to do, nor shall I withhold a reference from any future fools that decide to employ you. Is this satisfactory?"

Horace looked hard at Edwards and then nodded firmly, "Very much so, sir," he agreed, secretly delighted that he had found a way out of the bank – and such a pleasurable way.

"That's not really fair, sir," Donna protested.

"It most certainly is, young lady. And that is the end of the matter. Wilt, you may use the secretaries' office to type your letter of resignation which I expect to receive before you leave the building. You will not be required to return to your duties in the New Year. Is that clear?"

"As crystal, sir. Just wh-wh-one thing, though?"

"Well, what is it, man?" Edwards snapped.

"I, er, can't actually type, sir."

Edwards groaned, "God give me strength. Miss Beckworth, I take it you can type?" Donna nodded. "In that case, escort Wilt to the secretariat and type his letter for him, will you?"

"Yes, sir."

Satisfied, Edwards made to return to the party, "Remember, Wilt. I want that letter before you leave here or it's the sack."

"You'll have it, sir."

"Oh Christ, I'm so sorry, Horace," Donna said when they were alone again.

Horace laughed, "Really, don't be. Come on, then. The sooner it's done the sooner I can get back to a proper life."

Donna sighed, "Well, okay then."

They walked together down to the secretariat and Donna switched on a lamp, settling herself in front of a massive electronic typewriter. She threaded paper through the platen and looked up at Horace, "Okay, then; fire away."

Horace smiled, "Here goes then. Dear Horse's Arse…"

When Donna had finished giggling, the letter was typed in seconds and she found Horace an envelope for it. Horace accepted it and shoved it into the breast pocket of his shirt. He crossed to the door and stood there for a moment before he turned and smiled at Donna. "My mother has a saying: 'You might as w-w-well be hung for a sheep as a goat'. She means lamb of course, but then, that's my mother for you," he reached down and quietly turned the key in the door.

Donna's dress reached the floor before Horace reached her.

From The Diary of Horace Wilt

"Friday, 23ʳᵈ December, 1983

DD

440

I'm finally free of the bank! Edwards caught me and Donna Beckworth "fornicating" in his office. At one point I thought that he was going to explode, which, all things considered, might have been nice. What was nice, though, was Donna. It's just a pity that she's got a boyfriend already. Actually, having said that, this has just been yet another example of the trouble I have with women. I guess my New Year's resolution should be to give them up.

Can't believe how happy I am now that I'm a free man once more!!!!"

2

As 1983 ticked over into Orwell's year, Horace made a firm resolution; to avoid females wherever and whenever possible. Had he not been so strongly heterosexual and didn't, anyway, get on well with other men, he might even have considered becoming gay. It was only with the greatest reluctance that he accepted the traditional celebratory kisses from the women in the Crown as Big Ben's chimes died away.

Retreating to the relative safety of the bar, he ordered another pint of Guinness from Flat-Foot Fred, who had recently started talking to him again after his split with Doll, and sipped it thoughtfully, trying to work out what he was going to do with his life. Now that he was once again a free man – no job, no girl, no plans – life seemed even more complicated than usual. He was fairly certain that the last thing he wanted to do career-wise was go after another banking job; the atmosphere stifled him and being addressed loudly as 'Wilt' all day had not helped matters either.

In fact, the more he thought about it, the less *any* nine-to-five, office-based job appealed. He sipped some more Guinness and turned in desperation for help from Fred. "W-w-what career do you think I should take up?"

Fred peered over the counter at him, "I'm buggered if I know," he replied helpfully.

Horace nodded. At least they were of a single mind on the matter, "I think I've decided against an office job, but I don't really know how to do anything else."

"You can paint good enough. 'Ow about a decorating job?"

"It's hardly the same as portrait painting,"

"Well, as I said, mate. Buggered if I know. What I always used to do, though, was sit around and wait for the work to come to me."

Horace nodded. Doll had mentioned that very fact about Fred some time ago. She had also mentioned that Fred once had a tendency to sit around waiting for work for years at a time. Still, Horace reasoned, thanks to his mother, he wasn't exactly in need of cash; didn't actually *need* to work – or at least, not for some considerable time. "I might just do that. I could always use the time to get some more paintings done."

"You know it makes sense, Rodders," Fred said.

Horace grimaced. He had just seen his first episode of *Only Fools and Horses* and wasn't keen on being compared to the hapless Rodney, "Thanks, I think."

"You might think about takin' up a sport or some such."

"Hardly. The most athletic thing I've ever played is chess. I tried golf wh-wh-once, but thought it best to give up w-w-when my instructor kept telling me to shout 'fore' w-w-whenever I putted."

Horace left the festivities at two, sober by his own broad standards, and made his way slowly back to Church Hill Buildings, lost in thoughts of the future. He nearly stepped on the cat as he crossed the road towards his front door, a brief movement alerting him to its presence at the very last moment. It was lying at the side of the road, its tail flicking slowly from side to side, black against the black tarmac, and as Horace bent down to get a better look, it gave a half-hearted hiss.

Cautiously, Horace bent closer, and he realised the cat was injured; one back leg buckled under it at a strange angle. In the yellowish light from the nearest streetlamp, he could see flecks of what was presumably blood along its flank. He gingerly reached out a hand, the cat attempting to lift itself to its feet before collapsing back to the damp road surface, a pathetic mewling escaping through its bared teeth.

"Oh, you poor thing," Horace said quietly, wondering what on earth he should do. He clearly couldn't leave it here to suffer, but had no idea whether a vet, or maybe the RSPCA, would be available during the early hours of New Year's Day. He had also never been particularly keen on animals and, as he had explained so long ago to Harriet, his mother's strangeness included an antipathy to pets of any shape size or form. What he did know, was that an injured cat could become vicious if you try to help it. Horace didn't particularly mind the sight of blood unless it was his own, so he pulled off his jacket and laid it carefully over the injured animal. It let out another desultory hiss, but at least didn't try to stand up this time.

As carefully as he could, Horace slipped the jacket under the animal's limp body, trying hard to ignore its renewed mewling, and gently lifted it from the black-top. The cat struggled briefly before lying still in Horace's arms, only the rapid movement of its chest through the jacket, indication that it was still alive.

Horace carried it to his front door and after a brief struggle managed to get his key in the lock. As carefully as he could, he carried the stricken feline up to his own apartment, and laid it gingerly on the floor next to the telephone. He pulled back the jacket and stared at the animal's injuries. A car was the only thing that could possibly have wreaked such havoc. Not only was the cat's back leg broken, but much of the fur along its flank was missing, the rear quarter a mass of grazes. The cat lay staring at him, bright yellow eyes in a perfectly black face.

"Looks like w-w-we need an expert here," Horace told the cat. It raised one ear and mewled at him.

"I take it that's a yes, then?" He reached for the Yellow Pages and opened it near the back, chancing first time on the section headed 'Veterinarians'. He pulled the telephone towards him, gently stroking the cat's head between its ears.

Forty minutes later, on his twenty-second attempt, a real, live, honest-to-goodness person answered his call.

"Prospect Vets, how may I help you?" a pleasant sounding woman announced.

It took Horace a second or two to realise it wasn't yet another answering machine, "Oh, er, hello. I w-w-was w-w-wondering if you could help me. I've just found a cat, badly injured in the street, and I haven't the faintest idea w-w-what to do."

The woman was immediately soothing and professional, asking him to describe the injuries, how the cat reacted to him and so on. After Horace had finished answering her questions, she let out a sigh, "It doesn't sound good, I'm afraid. I was going to suggest you bring it here, but I rather think that would be a bad idea."

"Oh, no," Horace groaned, surprised that he was upset by this news.

The woman seemed to pick up on the sadness in his voice, "Look, I tell you what I can do. There's two of us on tonight; David's out at the moment, but when he comes back I should be going off duty and if you don't mind waiting up for me, I could pop in on my way home. How does that sound?"

"That w-w-would be w-w-wonderful. If you don't mind?"

"I'm a sucker for the pussycats," the woman said with a chuckle. "Let's have your name and address."

Horace gave them to her and rang off, "Look's like help is on the w-w-way," he told the cat.

Help arrived more than two hours later, in the form of Jane Samuels. She was slightly older than Horace and, surprisingly, she was also taller. Her voice on the phone had led him to believe that she would be a homely, matronly type, but in reality she looked like she had just stepped out of the pages of Cosmopolitan, large white coat notwithstanding.

"Okay, where's our unfortunate feline?" she asked Horace when he opened the door.

"Through here," Horace led her into the sitting room where the cat was settled, still on his jacket, close to a radiator.

The vet set her bag on the floor beside the cat and began to examine it, wincing in sympathy every time the cat mewled pitifully. Finally she sat back on her haunches and looked at Horace.

"W-w-well?" he asked her desperately.

"Not so good, I'm afraid. I rather think that the leg is beyond repair, and the poor thing's in very deep shock. Even if we can patch him up – it's a tom by the way – it'll cost a fortune, and there's no identity tag on his collar. Maybe the RSPCA?"

"I'll pay," Horace insisted. "W-w-whatever it takes."

Jane Samuels tilted her head to one side, "It's really a very expensive procedure. And I don't rate the poor thing's chances any higher than fifty-fifty."

"I don't care. Please, w-w-will you try to help him?"

"It's funny, you know? It's always the men that are the softies when it comes to our furry friends," she said.

"I'm a softie all the time. W-w-will you?"

"Well it is very young, possibly only ten weeks or so, and, as I said on the phone, I'm a sucker for pussycats," she paused and looked at her watch. "Okay, then. I'll take him back to the surgery; we'll see what we can do."

Horace let out a sigh of relief, "Thank you ever so much. I'll get another jacket and come w-w-with you, if you don't mind?"

The vet laughed, "There's really no point. We won't be able to operate until he's out of shock, probably not until tomorrow afternoon. I'll call you as soon as there's any news."

"W-w-well, okay."

446

He helped the vet carry the stricken cat to her car, carefully placing him in a large cage in the back.

"By the way," Jane said as she prepared to drive off, "We'll need to use a name for him. Any suggestions?"

Horace stared for a moment at the poor creature. "How about 'Astrophe'? Astro for short."

The vet laughed, "Catastrophe. Appropriate anyway. Okay then, I'll call you tomorrow when I have some news. In the meantime, try not to worry; I'll promise I'll do my best for him."

"Thanks," Horace smiled, "And good luck, Astro," he called softly after the car as it was driven away.

Taking her advice, Horace tried not to worry, failing miserably. He slept fitfully, starting awake every few minutes, convinced the phone was ringing. Despite not getting to bed until after five, he was up at ten, pacing his living room, waiting for a call he knew would be hours in coming.

When the phone rang just after five, he snatched the receiver off the cradle so fast that the entire apparatus crashed to the floor, "Hello, Horace here," he almost shouted into the receiver.

"Hello, Horace," Jane Samuels greeted him, "And it's good news."

"Thank god for that," Horace let out a sigh of relief.

"Astro looks quite ridiculous," the vet told him happily, "The leg break was totally clean after all, so it was a relatively straightforward repair job, and much of the grazing was superficial. He's now the proud owner of a cast on his leg, much to his annoyance so it seems, and he's totally bald down most of his left side, which he seems to find rather alarming. Other than that, he seems content enough, and he's even had a little food; not too much, of course, because of the operation."

"That's w-w-wonderful news."

"It is. The fact that he's so young probably helped. He doesn't seem to have had any inoculations, so we've given him those as a precaution."

"Marvellous! W-w-when can I come and collect him?"

"Collect him?" the vet sounded surprised. "Do you mean that you want to take care of him?"

Horace hadn't even realised that he'd made the decision – if the cat survived, he would *of course* take him in, "W-w-well, er, yes."

"Normally, we would insist that you – or someone, at least – advertised the fact that the cat was found injured. To try to trace the original owners," she explained, "But to be honest, Horace, just between you and me, he wasn't very well cared for. Since you were clearly so concerned for him, I guess I'll turn a blind eye to our normal procedures."

"That's very good of you," he said.

"Let's just say, I put the cat first in this matter," she laughed. "You can collect him the day after tomorrow. I suggest you bring a cat basket, though, and stock up on some food, milk and so on, before you take him home."

'I w-w-will. And thanks again – for everything."

The following day, Horace went cat-shopping, and by the time Astro came home, there was enough food, milk, litter and cat toys for a dozen Astros. Whether Astro knew, somehow, what Horace had done for him, would remain forever a mystery outside of the feline world, but he took to following Horace wherever he went around the flat, and would sleep nowhere else but on Horace's bed.

One morning, a couple of weeks after Astro's cast was finally removed, Horace woke to find the cat curled on the pillow next to him. "You know something? I used to think that w-w-waking up next to a beautiful w-w-woman w-w-was the nicest felling in the w-w-world. Didn't know w-w-what I w-w-was missing, did I?" Astro began to purr loudly. "Even if you are still half-bald," Horace added. It was best not to let cats get too much praise, he was finding.

From The Diary of Horace Wilt

"Tuesday, 21st February, 1984

DD

I realised this morning that cats are better in every respect (well, nearly) than women. Thanks to my furry friend, I now know that I'll have no trouble keeping my New Year's resolution. One small drawback does occur, though - I really must take him back to Jane and get his claws cut."

3

If Astro was the first nice thing to happen to Horace that year, the second was the arrival of his new neighbour in early March. Penny had come upstairs to ask Horace whether he would mind someone in Harriet's old flat who was a 'bit light up top', Horace only deciding not to take issue with the description on the grounds that whenever she bent over to tickle Astro behind the ears, Horace had a rather fine view of her pert little breasts down the front of her blouse.

After more or less forcing Penny to have a coffee (giving her more opportunities for Astro-tickling), he had told her that he really didn't mind who was to be his new neighbour. Despite Astro's faithful presence, he was beginning to get lonely.

"Well, that's okay then," Penny smiled, making to leave. "He'll be arriving next week," she paused at his door, "And, by the way, I do hope you enjoyed the view." She left Horace blushing furiously.

Dooby arrived the following Tuesday, and Horace greeted him on the landing when he heard someone clumping their way up the stairs, "Hello, you must be my new neighbour."

Dooby was of indeterminate age – anywhere between thirty and fifty – and, despite being only five foot eight, appeared huge. He was thickly muscled, broad-shouldered and, judging by the two enormous cases he was carrying, this was no illusion of strength.

"Mornin'" he returned Horace's greeting with a broad smile, "And I guess that makes you my new neighbour, an' all." He set the cases on the floor and offered Horace an enormous hand.

Horace shook it warmly, surprised at the other's gentle grip, "I'm Horace, by the w-w-way."

"And I do be Dooby."

"Er, pardon?" Horace asked. Had he really said 'Dooby, Dooby'?

"That's what everyone allus calls me," he explained in an accent that seemed to have its roots in every rural part of England from Cornwall to Norfolk. When Horace still looked blank, he gave a chuckle. "Y'see, I always say 'do be', as in 'I do be a window cleaner by trade'. Don't know me real name, and so everyone allus calls me..."

"Dooby," Horace nodded, finally catching the drift. "Makes sense, I guess." Penny's comment that his new neighbour was a 'bit light on top' was, he thought, unfair; although the thick accent and the improbable name might, he supposed, have given someone that impression.

"Anyways," Dooby continued, picking up the bags, "I'd better get a move on. Looks like rain soon, an' all me stuff do be on me cart, see?"

"Oh, right," Horace said, "Please, let me give you a hand."

"That do be mighty neighbourly," Dooby said with another radiant smile, "Now don't you be goin' strainin' nothin', though. They do be sayin' that 'ard work never killed anyone, but I do be figuring, why take the chance?"

"I'll try not to," Horace smiled back before making his way downstairs. Outside, he was surprised to find a genuine cart – two wheels, two long handles, ladders on both sides and an array of buckets and implements hanging from hooks on the underside. The top surfaces were stacked to a height of close on seven feet with boxes, cases and large plastic bags.

Horace was still struggling to take down one of the boxes when Dooby joined him, "You really are a w-w-window cleaner then?" Horace panted.

"That's what I do be saying upstairs, now, isn't it?" Dooby nodded happily. He took the box from Horace with one hand.

"An, er, interesting job, is it?" Horace finally located something light enough for him to carry.

"See some sights," Dooby nodded, gathering a case under his free arm, "An' the pay's a treat."

"Really?"

"The pay do be good enough for this place," Dooby said over his shoulder, "An' I've rented one of them there lock-up places for me cart, so it can't be too bad, now can it?"

Indeed it couldn't, Horace thought, well aware of what the rent was, "Don't tempt me too much," he panted, setting the two large plastic bags down in Dooby's new living room, "I'm looking for something to do myself."

Dooby grinned, "Well, if you've got an' 'ead fer 'eights, this could be your lucky day."

"Oh?"

"My old mate, Leerin' Len, 'e's upped and left for Spain, see? I do be lookin' fer a new lad, right as we speak. Yours if you be fancyin' it?"

Horace looked amazed. He was more than happy with heights and the thought of working outdoors – especially with Spring and Summer looming ever-closer – suddenly seemed to make sense. Perhaps old Flat-Foot had been right about waiting to see what turned up, "I might just give it some thought. If you're serious?"

Dooby laughed, "When you know Dooby a bit better, you'll know Dooby allus says what he means."

All of Dooby's possessions were indoors before the rain began, and Horace walked through the drizzle alongside Dooby as he pushed his cart towards the lock-up. "Don't be likin' the rain," Dooby grumbled. "Can't be doin' no windows, see?"

"Occupational hazard, I suppose."

"It do be 'avin' its upsides, though," Dooby went on, his sunny smile returning almost immediately. "See, if'n yer can't clean no windows, well then, you can 'ave a few beers an' not worry about fallin' off a ladder."

"Good idea," Horace grinned as Dooby settled the cart into its night-time home, "And I know just the place."

Over a few drinks in the Crown, Dooby explained a little about his background; necessarily little, since he knew very little about it himself. He had been found as a stray when he was about seven or eight – to this day, he didn't know his exact age – and he hadn't been able to speak. He had been taken into care after fruitless searches for his parent or parents, and thence into a series of homes and foster care, picking up the name Dooby when he was in his teens.

The State, showing their usual compassion, had turned him out on the streets as soon as they calculated that he might have reached the age of sixteen, and he spent several years touring the country, taking jobs and shelter wherever possible, before moving to London four years ago where he had met 'Leerin' Len'; the nickname, a by-product of his trade as a window cleaner.

Horace was filled with a mixture of horror and fascination as the tale unfolded, and finally, a sense of admiration for the man. Recently, Dooby had even started to learn how to read and write.

"And, so, young Orris," Dooby asked, placing a fresh pint of Guinness in front of each of them, "What do you be reckoning to comin' along with old Dooby? 'Avin' a crack at the old window cleanin' game?"

"W-w-why not?"

4

The following morning, Horace startled Astro by waking at six-thirty and jumping enthusiastically out of bed. The cat watched him trot into the bathroom with a baffled and slightly pissed-off expression – a cat speciality. An hour later, Horace crossed the landing and knocked on Dooby's door.

"All ready," he beamed when Dooby answered.

"So I do be seein'," Dooby beamed back, "Well, let's be getting', then."

They went back to the lock-up and retrieved the cart, Dooby showing Horace how easy it was to push – once you'd got the knack of balancing it correctly – and then he took him to a café under the railway arches, where they breakfasted alongside many of the market's stall-holders.

Not used to physical work, Horace found the first day tremendously tiring; the second, also. When he awoke to the traditional British Springtime sound of torrential rain on the Friday, he sighed contentedly and rolled over; asleep again in seconds.

By the end of the second week, Horace was getting used to the stresses and strains, and the techniques involved in ensuring a perfect job. By the end of the month Dooby was happy to let him loose on his own, and he was even beginning to chat confidently with some of their customers.

He was draining his first pint of the evening in the Crown on a Friday during the middle of May when it occurred to him that he was rather content. He had Astro for company at home, Dooby during the day and Guinness at all other times. The work could be tiring, but fun; he was feeling fitter than he had ever been before in his life, and had even developed a tan.

Stories of window cleaners and bored housewives were thankfully exaggerated. The only problem Horace had faced was Mrs Evans, the young and shapely wife of a local businessman, who seemed to have a habit of 'accidentally' stepping naked into her bedroom while he was cleaning the window, or 'accidentally' letting her towel fall to the ground as she paid him. Thankfully, he was able to persuade Dooby to look after her house; Horace had made his resolution and was determined to stick to it.

In early June he took Astro to the Prospect Vet Surgery for a check-up and a final series of inoculations and was seen by Jane Samuels' brother David.

"Astro's as fit as a flea," David told him, "Although I'm afraid the leg won't get any better than it currently is."

"He doesn't seem bothered by it," Horace said, "But he can't manage the stairs."

"Does he ever go out?" David asked. "Sometimes cats that have been injured on the road get scared of the great outdoors."

Horace laughed, "He's too lazy, anyw-w-way. And besides, w-w-we let him have the run of the first floor flats during the day. Strangely, it's only my curtains that he seems to take out any frustrations on."

"I know what you mean," David laughed along with him, "Jane's got four of the damn things. Aren't you worried about burglars though? Astro's hardly a guard cat."

Horace lifted Astro off the examination table and coaxed him into his basket with one of his favourite treats, "Burglars? No, that's the great thing about our block. I w-w-work w-w-with the guy opposite me, and only wh-wh-one of the flats upstairs is occupied; a girl called Georgina moved in a month or two back, and she w-w-works nights so there's no coming and going during the daytime."

"Lucky man. I sometimes think that Jane's turning our house into an animal sanctuary. Dad keeps threatening to install a revolving door at the front of the place; he reckons it'll speed up the flow of people tramping in and out at all hours."

"Is your Dad a really tall guy w-w-with long grey hair? Only I clean the w-w-windows for a bloke like that called Samuels."

David laughed, "Yes, I know. That's our family house. And I know, because Jane told me that you nearly got an eyeful of her after she came out of the shower a couple of weeks ago. Apparently it was only the clattering of your buckets that stopped her from marching into the bedroom."

"Shame," Horace muttered, then clapped a hand over his mouth. "S-s-sorry," he blushed deeply.

"Don't be. I can hardly object if you indicate that my twin sister's good-looking, can I?"

"I, er, guess not," Horace mumbled, picking up the cat basket and beating a hasty retreat.

Outside, the rain continued to drizzle down and Astro mewled non-stop all the way home; not only was he petrified of the great outdoors, he was also phobic about water, the bathroom being the only room in either his or Dooby's flat that he wouldn't enter.

As he was letting himself into his apartment he heard footsteps on the stairs and looked up, surprised to see Georgina making her way down. A true Celt, she had long red hair and bright blue eyes, but this was the first time Horace had seen her without lashings of make-up and it was this transformation that allowed him to recognise her from college.

"Hi," he greeted her. "It's Georgina Shaw, by the w-w-way, isn't it?"

"Hi, Horace," she grinned, "And I was wondering how long it would be before you recognised me." Her voice had a light Irish lilt.

Astro mewled loudly.

"Hang on a sec, I'd better let the tiger out," Horace grimaced, fiddling with the basket's catches, trying at the same time to avoid Astro's claws.

"He's a beauty," Georgina said as Astro hopped, three-legged into the flat.

"Lovely claws," Horace muttered, dabbing at four scratches on the back of his left hand, "But, yes, I didn't recognise you until just now. It's the, er, lack of make-up." Georgina, he knew, referred to herself as an exotic dancer (Penny referring to her as a "tart"), and Horace thought she looked much better without the greasepaint. Remembering his resolution, he avoided mentioning this fact. "You w-w-were in the art class for a w-w-while, w-w-weren't you?"

Georgina gave a snort which turned into a giggle, "You could say that. I posed for the life class every fourth week."

"Oh, er, right, yes… that's it," Horace blushed, "It, er, slipped my mind." It seemed like every female that ever set foot in this block of flats had been seen naked by him at some point.

Georgina giggled again, "I could take offence at that. But I won't."

"I, er, thanks. W-w-what are you, er, doing home during the day, then?" he asked, eager to change the subject. He immediately wished he hadn't.

"Can't work with the curse, now, can I?"

"Oh, er, right, the, er, dancing."

Georgina gave him an odd look and shrugged, "Horace, I'm not really a dancer."

"Not a…?"

"Don't go spreading it round," she lowered her voice, "But I'm really a prostitute, okay?"

"A… oh."

"Och, I knew I shouldn't have told you-"

"No!" Horace interrupted, "I mean, no. It's okay. Really. Just a bit of a shock. I mean, I've never, er, met…" he trailed off into embarrassed silence as Georgina laughed loudly.

"Well, you have now," she smiled, relieved that Horace wasn't too upset by the news, "So, if you're ever interested, since I know you from the past, I'll even let you have a discount. Oh, I'm sorry, Horace," she went on quickly when his cheeks turned even brighter, "Now, I'm teasing you."

"Yes, er, w-w-well. It's just that I'm, er, off w-w-women at the moment."

"Are you now?" Georgina smiled. "Just for the moment, is it?"

"Absolutely."

"Are we all that bad then?"

"No. Just some of you. And not you personally," he added quickly. Just because he was steering clear of women didn't mean he had to insult them.

"Glad to hear it. And, if you fancy it – just to prove we're not all nasty harridans – why don't you let me buy you a drink somewhere. I hate drinking on me own, you see?"

"I, er…" Horace was torn four ways: Firstly, this was a day off, and he enjoyed a few beers whenever the opportunity presented itself. Secondly, although he didn't care what Georgina's profession was, he rather doubted that he could simply ignore it. Thirdly, his level of trust in women was probably at an all-time low (Mrs Evans had nearly cornered him the day before), and he doubted that his resolution would hold up under a full-on assault by a forceful female. Fourthly, he was beginning to doubt the wisdom of his resolution in the first place; he seemed to be constantly horny these days.

Despite a three-to-one negative call, he shrugged and smiled, "W-w-why not?"

It turned out to be a very worthwhile decision. As soon as they reached the Crown (Horace's suggestion – it never hurt appearances to turn up in your local with a very attractive woman), Georgina reassured him that he was safe with her; she never mixed 'business with pleasure' as she put it, and wouldn't feel comfortable in any relationship what with the work she did. Furthermore, her work was the last thing she wanted to discuss, and so the conversation roamed free. By four, Horace happily realised that he had formed – for the first time – a purely platonic relationship with a member of the opposite sex.

They walked back to the flats together and Horace invited her into his for a coffee, which Georgina gratefully accepted. When he returned from the kitchen with the mugs, she was standing, staring at the array of his paintings.

"Sugar?" he asked.

"Two please." She grimaced. "How come all the thing I like are either immoral, illegal or fattening? But these paintings are excellent. Cheer me up and tell me they're by you; you did say you were still dabbling."

Horace shrugged, "Be happy, then, and thank you, by the w-w-way."

"Say now, would you consider doing one of me?"

"W-w-well, yes, if you'd like." Other than the occasional referral from Winston, he had done next to no life studies in recent months.

"Oh, I would like," Georgina smiled. "You see now, like I said earlier, I work from a couple of houses in the West End – good class ones, mind – and I guess there must be at least two dozen of us. A few high quality paintings of the merchandise, so to speak, would go down a bomb there. You do one of me, and I'll take it down there and see what Mimi reckons."

458

Horace shrugged. He had no intention of asking who Mimi was –
he could guess already – but he was rather intrigued by the idea. It
was only the previous weekend that he had been complaining to
Dooby about the lack of subjects for his art, and the idea that he
might get a few commissions appealed, "That might be nice."
Although he was strictly off women, art was a totally different ball
game, so to speak.

5

They had originally planned to start the painting on the Saturday, but when the next day, Wednesday, dawned damp and drizzly, Horace went upstairs to see whether Georgina would like to bring the date forward. She agreed happily, much like Horace, bored when she wasn't working, and followed him downstairs to where Astro was waiting, his yellow eyes all that was visible in the gloomy stairwell.

Horace draped a length of dark green velvet along his sofa, and Georgina quickly stripped, taking up an archetypal Bordello pose, while Horace retreated to his easel. He looked up as she began giggling.

"W-w-w-hat?"

"You're not going to believe this, but I'm bloody embarrassed!"

Horace laughed, "No need to be. I *have* seen it all before, after all." Now that he had seen her undressed, he recognised her from the life classes. Her pubic thatch was such a perfect bright-red triangle, the art teacher had insisted that the pupils didn't draw it exact – it didn't look natural. "Tell you w-w-what," he suggested picking up an uncomplaining Astro, "Settle him in front of you. He's very comforting – takes your mind off things. Maybe chat about your childhood, or something? Being, er, Irish, did you go to wh-wh-one of those convent schools?"

Georgina accepted the limp, black bundle, and he was soon curled in front of her, purring contentedly as she gently stroked behind his ears. *Lucky bloody cat*, Horace thought to himself as he started work.

While he painted, Georgina gradually relaxed, telling how, when she was a kid, she was really into the church, "I used to pray and pray for a new bike every Christmas," she giggled, "But I never got one. That's the great thing about being Catholic, though; in the end I pinched one and just asked God to forgive me."

"I'm really not sure I believe you," Horace grinned, "But it's a nice tale."

"My uncle Pat's still a right one for the church. Real devout. Me mam reckons he won't be happy until he's crucified. Personally, I'm very much of the 'lapsed' persuasion. I can't help wondering where Christianity would be if Jesus had been let off with ten years in jail and time off for good behaviour. Besides, in Ireland a girl's supposed to only have the choice between perpetual virginity or permanent pregnancy. How about your own beliefs?"

"Typical C of E," he grinned, "Or 'atheist' in other words."

"What about your childhood? I bet you had loads of friends."

"Actually, no. Just two imaginary wh-wh-ones. And they'd only play w-w-with each other."

From The Diary of Horace Wilt

"Wednesday, 6th June, 1984

DD

Georgie's fantastic - it almost seems a pity about my resolution and her work. She was a great model today, and real fun with it. She has the most amazing blue eyes and her figure is totally drop-dead gorgeous (not that I'm supposed to be noticing these things!!!!).

She reckons that she might be able to get me some more commissions from some woman called Mimi; I hope she can, because other than the window cleaning, painting's just about the only thing that I really enjoy these days."

6

July, August and September passed quickly and busily for Horace thanks to the weather clearing, and Dooby's purchase of another cleaning round. His resolution was still intact – aided by the fact that Mrs Evans and her husband were spending the summer in the Bahamas – and his bank and building society accounts were burgeoning. He decided, after prompting from Dooby, to take the first two weeks in October off, and was enjoying a well-earned lie-in on the first Tuesday of his break when he was roused by a knock on his door.

He opened it, still yawning, and found a grinning Georgina – make-up free – standing there.

"Morning, Horace. Got some good news for you."

"Oh," he yawned again, "Come in. I'll put some coffee on."

"You could always put some clothes on, too," Georgina suggested, following Horace into his living room and patting his naked bum.

His relationship with Georgina was so platonic that he sometimes forgot that she was female – thinking of her more as a younger, rather prettier and more effete version of Dooby, "Oh, er, good idea."

After he had pulled on a clean pair of boxers and made coffee, he finally woke enough to remember what Georgina had said in his doorway, "W-w-what's the good news?"

Georgina beamed, "Remember the painting?"

"Oh, yeah, the one I did of you a few months back, w-w-what about it?"

"Well," Georgina giggled, "Mimi's finally back from holidays and when I showed it, went absolutely nuts. Mimi wants you to – get this – do *all* of the girls; same sized canvasses, and then use them as a sort of menu in the reception rooms; you know, rotate them according to who's on duty?"

"All of them?" Horace asked, hardly believing his ears.

"All of them. Thirty-two commissions in one hit."

"Bugger me!" Horace muttered. He had hoped for maybe three of four – but thirty-two!

"No can do, H," Georgina smiled, "I know you sometimes think I'm a bloke, but I ain't really. Anyway, that's not the end of it."

"No?"

"No. Mimi wanted to know how much you charged and so – I hope you don't mind – I took the one of me along to a local dealer. He reckons that sort of quality is worth at least three hundred quid a go!"

"Three hundred!?"

"At least," Georgina beamed, "Anyway, I told Mimi you wanted four, and we agreed on three-fifty each, or three hundred each and free services at the, er, houses."

Horace stared, dumbstruck.

"And," Georgina added the killer blow, "There's a studio standing empty just up the street from Mimi's, belongs to one of the regulars, and we reckon that you can use that when you're working there; saves everyone traipsing over here."

Horace finally found his voice, "You absolute little beauty!"

Georgina giggled, "Did I do okay?"

He crossed the room and picked her up in a bear-hug, swinging her round once full circle, coffee splashing from her mug and narrowly avoiding the still-sleeping Astro. "I take it that's a 'yes' then?" she beamed when he set her down again.

"Oh, yes!" He did some quick mental calculations. "That's more than eleven thousand pounds!"

"I take it you don't want the three hundred plus free services, then?"

Horace chuckled, "Don't tempt me. I w-w-wasn't joking w-w-when I told you the other day how horny I w-w-was getting." The pair of them discussed pretty much everything under the banner of Platonism.

Georgina laughed, "And I said…"

Horace gave a rueful look. What Georgina had said was that, since he was just a friend, purely platonically, she could, maybe, not count as a female if she helped relieve his inner tensions. It was the closest either of them had come to breaking their unspoken agreement over their relationship, and it was difficult to know who had been the most embarrassed by the offer. "Don't remind me, Georgie." She had plagued his more lurid dreams ever since.

They both blushed and strove to change the subject as quickly as possible, "When do you think you could start?" Georgina asked.

Horace shrugged, "I guess it'll take me at least a couple of months – assuming w-w-we can organise all of the, er, girls – so I'd better have a chat w-w-with Dooby. I know it's coming up to the slow season for the cleaning, but w-w-we've had loads on."

"Okay. Well, as soon as you know, I'll pass it on to Mimi. By the way," she added, with a chuckle, "Mimi's simply dying to meet you."

7

In the event, Dooby was more than happy for Horace to start on his commissions as soon as he wanted to.

"I could 'ardly keep you away from two and a 'alf dozen naked ladies, now could I?" he said that evening in the Crown, "And asides, that new lad can cope well enough." The new lad was the sixty-year-old Errol, who had come with the new round.

Georgina, who had joined them for a "quick drink" three hours earlier, was delighted, and left them chatting happily while she called Mimi. She arranged a meeting for the Friday evening, and checked to make sure the studio would be free.

Friday evening arrived and Horace was ready and waiting when Georgina came downstairs to collect him. He did a double take as he opened the door to find her in her full working attire; micro-mini, white silk blouse and about a pound and a half of make-up.

"Not that bad, is it?" she grinned at him through cherry red lip gloss.

"N-n-no," he managed after swallowing noisily, "I'd just, er, forgotten w-w-what you look like w-w-when you go off to w-w-work."

"Well come on then, the taxi's waiting. And close your mouth, you look silly."

The 'house' was situated alongside nondescript but rather grand looking buildings in W1, and Georgina pressed an intercom buzzer to announce their presence. They were greeted by a young girl who gave Georgina a hug and Horace an appraising stare, before leading them through to an office near the back of the vast property. They waited outside while the young girl, Trudi, went in and spoke to Mimi.

"Come in, darlings," a decidedly husky voice called.

Horace shuddered; it reminded him quite a lot of Elspeth's. Shrugging, he followed Georgina into the room, letting the smiling Trudi out first. He hadn't been sure what to expect of Mimi. She was obviously the "Madam", if his terminology was correct, but he had no idea what she might be like. What greeted him was nothing at all similar even the wildest of his private speculations.

Mimi looked like a cross between Liberace and Dame Edna Everage, and clearly had one thing in common with both of those entertainers – male genitalia. Horace's jaw dropped.

"Oh you naughty thing," Mimi chided the grinning Georgina, "You didn't tell the poor boy anything about me, did you?"

Georgina nodded, "There just aren't the right words in the language."

Mimi gave her a playful pat on her rump and then minced over to where Horace was still standing open-mouthed, "You must be the extraordinarily gifted Horace, I take it?" Mimi's teeth dazzled Horace. "My, you're a big one," Mimi added. He extended a hand in Horace's general direction, bearing more jewellery than the average Hatton Garden merchant's safe, and with fuchsia painted nails as long as Horace's pinkie-finger.

Horace made a determined effort to close his mouth and grasped the proffered hand, shaking it as quickly as he thought polite. It was both limp and slightly damp, and it was all Horace could do not to wipe his own hand on his trousers, "That's, er, right," he agreed, although to what, he wasn't sure.

"Well, do come in, you darling boy," Mimi indicated a chair by his desk. "Can I get you a glass of champagne?"

"Er, yes, that w-w-would be very nice," Horace agreed through a suddenly parched throat. He made for the sanctuary of the chair.

"Relax, sweetheart," he was told, a paradoxical instruction if ever there was one. Horace grabbed Georgina's hand for comfort. "Now, darling Horace," Mimi went on after settling into a large leather chair on the opposite side of the desk, "I simply must know when you can start."

Despite the ultra-camp appearance and manner, Mimi was clearly a business man at heart. He had already drawn up a contract for the work, settled the studio fees (which Mimi himself would meet) and organised a loose rota for the girls according to how frequently they worked. He presented Horace with the keys to the studio, a map showing where local art-materials suppliers were located, a cheque for half the total fee, and finally a small envelope which he told Horace was a small bonus, and should be opened later. Finally, Mimi turned his attention to Georgina.

"My sweet little Georgie girl," he beamed, "Since we're talking of bonuses, I have a little surprise for you, my pet." Georgina looked back quizzically. "In recognition of the wonderful discovery you have made with this gorgeous young thing," he paused a moment to give Horace a simmering smile, "I thought I'd reward you with a week off work, my angel." It was Georgina's jaw's turn to drop open, "With pay, based on your average earnings, of course," Mimi went on. "On condition that you make sure our darling young artist has everything that he needs to be happy in his work, and when I say everything, my angel, I mean everything," he finished with another high-voltage grin in Horace's direction.

"Oh, thank you, Mimi." Georgina beamed.

"Such a lovely smile, isn't it?" he asked Horace, "Makes me regret being such a faggot at times. Now off you go, you gorgeous young things; feel free to visit the studio, and, Horace, feel free to pop in and see me at any time, my darling."

"I, er, thank you," Horace gulped.

He was still in a state of shock when they let themselves into the studio a few minutes later, "You might have w-w-warned me!" he protested, grinning at Georgina.

"Now, you wouldn't have believed me anyway, would you?"

"Fair point."

The studio was every artist's dream; clearly light and airy during the daytime; couches, chairs, easels, tidy worktops and a vast array of backdrops, materials and props.

"Like it?" Georgina asked.

"Love it." Horace turned to face her. "You're an absolute angel."

"Oh, don't," she groaned, "You're starting to sound like Mimi already."

"W-w-well, you do thoroughly deserve your bonus, anyw-w-way. And you'll get commission from me as w-w-well."

"That's not-" she began to protest, but Horace stopped her.

"No arguments."

"Well, thanks, then. And, talking of bonuses, what's in the little envelope."

Horace fished it out of his pocket. He opened it and pulled out a small plastic card, bright red in colour, "I'm still none the w-w-wiser."

"Wow," Georgina whistled. She grinned at Horace, "What you have there, H, is one of Mimi's special membership cards. It entitles you to free, er, services, once a month – for life."

"W-w-what!?"

Georgina laughed, "Mimi must have been *really* taken with the painting. Those cards are normally only given to the most senior politicians, law lords and the like. Looks like you're frustrations are a thing of the past."

Horace stared at the card, "I still don't think I could."

Georgina started to say something, but stopped herself, clearing her throat, "Well, anyway," she said instead, "The unbelievable has happened and I'm a free girl – with an escort – what say we check out a few bars while we're here?"

"Good idea."

"Sure you don't mind how I'm dressed?" Georgina asked.

"It's a w-w-while since I've been up W-w-west. But from w-w-what I remember, you'll fit in just fine."

8

They arrived back in Walthamstow at four the next morning and Horace yawned loudly as he paid the taxi driver.

"You really must let me pay you back for at least some of tonight," Georgina insisted as they made their way up the stairs.

"Don't worry," Horace said through another yawn, "It w-w-was my fault that you left your bag in Mimi's office anyw-w-way, leaving in such a hurry like that."

Georgina stifled a giggle, not wanting to disturb Dooby, "At least I know what a 'Bat Out Of Hell' looks like now."

They reached the first landing and stood quietly outside Horace's door, meaning to say goodnight. Instead, Georgina uttered a quiet curse, "Shit!"

"W-w-what is it?"

"My key! It's in my bag!"

"Don't w-w-worry. You can stay in here tonight. W-w-we've got to go over to the studio tomorrow, anyw-w-way, w-w-we can pick it up then."

"If you don't mind?" Georgina sighed gratefully.

"Of course not. W-w-what are friends for?" He took out his key and led them into his living room. "Just wh-wh-one thing though," he added with a half-smile, "Promise me you w-w-won't take advantage of me? My resolve is not so hot at the moment."

Georgina let out a tired giggle and then put on a serious face, "If you *really* don't want me to," she said, blushing, "Then I promise. But…" she trailed off, embarrassed.

"I'm in no position to say just at the minute," Horace blushed himself, "But I guess I'd rather you didn't."

Georgina crossed to where he was standing and took his hands in her own, "Okay, then, H. You've got my word." She reached up and pecked him on the cheek.

"Thanks, Georgie," he said sincerely. "Now, get yourself off to the bedroom, before I change my mind."

"No way. I'll take the couch."

Although Horace protested, she wouldn't be moved, and he only relented when she insisted that if she were all alone in his big bed, she'd get lonely and come and find him.

Horace settled down for his much-needed sleep, happy with himself, and proud of the strength of his resolve.

9

Horace woke at eleven and struggled out of bed and into both boxers and dressing gown, surprising himself by remembering that Georgie was sleeping on his sofa. She was still snoring gently when he crept into the bathroom, and barely stirred as he went into the kitchen to start the coffee machine. By the time coffee had been poured and Astro given his breakfast, there were vague mumblings coming from under the duvet on the sofa.

"Coffee's up, Georgie!"

With a groan, Georgina sat up, "Life saver," she yawned, accepting a mug.

"How did you sleep?" Horace grinned.

"Can't remember," Georgina mumbled taking a sip of the coffee. "'S'good." She yawned loudly and set the mug on the coffee table so that she could stretch, a passable imitation of Astro, who was doing likewise on the floor behind Horace.

"That w-w-was a close-run thing last night," Horace smiled, pulling the duvet back up to Georgina's chin so that her previously exposed breasts offered no further temptation.

"Oops, thanks," Georgina blushed, "And, yeah, you're right. That *was* close last night. Those champagne cocktails sorta dissolved my resolve."

Horace laughed, "I'm sort of glad w-w-we, w-w-well, didn't, you know?"

Georgina giggled, "Me too... I think. But knowing men, I doubt whether we could have got up to too much anyway."

"Oh?"

"I bet you haven't got a single condom in the place. And in my line of work, they're an absolute must. I always keep my supply in my bag, and we know where that is, don't we?"

"Er, actually you're right. Pity you didn't mention it last night, though – I might have slept easier."

Georgina giggled again before picking up her mug and draining it in three long swallows, "Any chance of another?"

"Every chance," Horace nodded, draining his own. He took their mugs through to the kitchen, returning too quickly for Georgina who had been trying to sneak quickly into his bathroom before he came back.

"Tease!" he called after her as her naked bum disappeared around the bathroom door. "And there's a spare robe hanging in there, by the w-w-way."

Georgina returned a few minutes later swaddled in one of Horace's dressing gowns, "Sorry about that," she apologised, blushing. "What are you writing?"

"Don't w-w-worry," Horace grinned, looking up from his diary, "My resolve is back up to full strength this morning." He sat quickly on the sofa, hoping that she hadn't noticed the state of the ferret's resolve. "W-w-what I'm writing is an unauthorised autobiography. Anyw-w-way," he went on quickly, "W-w-we'd better get over to Mimi's so that you can reclaim your bag, and I can start moving some gear into the studio."

"An unauthorised autobiography?" Georgina giggled, "You're a strange one, Horace. But as far as a trip to Mimi's goes, I have a little problem there. My clothes?"

"W-w-what about them?"

"Well," Georgina blushed, "I'm not too happy about crossing town wearing my, er, shall we say 'work' gear during the day," she nodded at the tiny skirt and sheer blouse hanging over the back of the armchair.

"Oh, I see w-w-what you mean. Tell you w-w-what, I'll pop out and get you something a little more revealing. I mean less modest! No! I mean more modest, less revealing."

Georgina giggled, "Read much Freud, have you now?"

"S-s-sorry. Now, er, w-w-what sizes are you?"

"Are you sure, H? You've already been too kind to me."

"Of course I am, and no I haven't. I don't think I'll ever be able to properly repay you for that commission from Mimi."

After a little more haggling, Horace departed with the instruction to bring back a cheap, tracksuit, and a leotard, and returned a few minutes later with the requested items.

"I think I preferred the skirt and blouse," Horace commented when Georgina emerged, showered and dressed, from the bathroom.

"Och, now who's teasing?" She gave his rump a hefty slap.

From The Diary of Horace Wilt

"Saturday, 6th October, 1984

DD

That was a pretty close run thing last night. After all the excitement at Mimi's - now there's a weird bloke - we went out on the town, and when we got back here, Georgie realised that she'd left her keys at Mimi's. Obviously, she had to sleep here and I was really sorely tempted (although apparently it wouldn't have been possible anyway); I guess it's because she's really gorgeous.

She's in the bathroom right at this very minute, and it's all I can do to stop myself walking in there..."

10

The pair spent the rest of the weekend preparing the studio and Horace was ready to start work on the Monday morning, nervous at the prospect. Over the next few days, his qualms disappeared as a procession of girls arrived for their sittings, all of them friendly, and some of them fascinated by his work. An incredibly tall, slender girl named Sam, a Sri Lankan, had been assigned as a sort of go-between after Georgina's week off ended; ferrying messages between the studio and Mimi's. She had been the second girl to sit for Horace, and although she was unremittingly friendly, her unusual skin tone had caused him considerable artistic problems.

"I'm sure you're only pretending to have these difficulties," she teased him one evening, while she was sitting for him for the fourth time.

"Ho, ho," he grinned, "And for your information, you're more trouble than all the rest of them put together." He was totally at ease, absorbed in his work.

By the end of November, thirty of the original thirty two commissions had been completed to a stage where Horace no longer needed the girls to sit for him. He had been working constantly for nearly seven weeks, starting early, finishing late, and it was only Dooby's vigilant presence back at Church Hill Buildings that ensured that Astro was kept fed, watered and cleaned. At nine in the evening, he heard the door to the studio open and called out a friendly "Hi", expecting Georgina to come through as she did most nights before she started work.

"Well, Hello, darling boy," Mimi returned the greeting instead.

"Oh, it's you," Horace smiled up at the, er, man.

"Charmed I'm sure," Mimi flounced onto a velvet-draped sofa.

Horace laughed. In the past few weeks, Mimi had popped in on a regular basis to see how things were progressing, and Horace had begun to enjoy the 'Madam's' company. "Before you ask, I reckon I'll be finished in two w-w-weeks."

"Oh, that's absolutely perfect, angel! Although I'm actually here to tell you a couple of things," Horace nodded, not saying anything; it was easier just to let Mimi have his say. "The first thing is, I might just have upset your schedule a teeny bit darling. You see, I've just taken on another couple of girls; a very special pair, and I was wondering whether you would be an absolute sweetie and squeeze them in, as it were?"

Horace shrugged, "Georgie told me something about some fresh blood. I'd sort of allowed for it. Two more sittings w-w-won't delay me."

"Oh, darling, that's the most wonderful thing, you see. As I said, these are a very special pair. They're twins and they work together, so it'll only be one sitting. I'll adjust your bill, of course."

"No need, Mimi. You've already been more than generous."

"So kind of you to say so, sweet angel, but you just leave the accounts to me. Anyway, perhaps these two might persuade you to actually come and enjoy some of my hospitality; they do re-enactments of some of the more erotic moments in movie history. Apparently they go down – as it were – a bomb with some of my cinema-going regulars."

Horace laughed, "I've told you before, Mimi, it's a very nice offer, but I'm simply too tired to think of anything but bed – my own bed, that is – w-w-when I finish here."

"Oh, yes. You poor little thing. I feel terribly guilty, you know? You had the most marvellous tan when you first appeared in my doorway, and now look at you; quite, quite sallow. And that's the other thing I wanted to tell my little angel. Every year on the Friday before Christmas, we throw a party for our regulars. You said you'd be finished by then, so I absolutely insist that you come along."

"Maybe," Horace shrugged, non-committedly.

Georgina tried to convince him to attend when she arrived at the studio a few days later, her period having arrived "at last", as she put it. "It's really just harmless fun," she said "One or two of the girls entertain their regulars, but mostly it's just drinks and snacks and a rather naughty nativity play. This year the new twins are going to re-enact that scene in *Blow-Up*, where the photographer finds them trying on his costumes and ends up rolling around naked with them."

Horace raised an eyebrow. The twins, improbably known as Suki and Yaki, had been his last subjects, and even if he didn't think it would be a good idea to watch them perform that particular scene, a certain ferret clearly did. "Well, maybe," he shrugged as innocently as he could, blushing when Georgina giggled at him.

Georgina pestered him to come along at every opportunity and he finally, reluctantly, agreed. "But it's on the condition that I don't break my resolution," he said, "And I'll hold you personally responsible to make sure of it."

In the event, he was thoroughly delighted that he had been persuaded. Mimi had spared no expense to entertain everyone in any way they saw fit; champagne flowed, girls danced around the guests, and the twins' routine saw many of the guests disappear immediately afterwards with a girl on their arm. Even Horace had been tempted. As midnight approached, Mimi instructed everyone to gather round, and led them all through to the main lounge, a vast room where clients would normally wait when they arrived, sipping cocktails in anticipation of the delights in store. Up until that point, it had, for some reason, been declared off-limits, and as soon as Horace entered, he knew why.

All thirty-four of his canvasses had been hung on the richly-papered walls, each magnificently framed and with a small spotlight illuminating them to perfection. Horace stopped in the doorway, causing a slightly drunk member of Her Majesty's Government to stumble past him, and his jaw dropped open. He had never been one for self-praise, but as he stared around the walls, he couldn't help but admit to himself that he had produced some very fine work. Somehow, although they were all the same size, the painting of the Sri Lankan, Sam, seemed to draw attention more than the others. It was she who came up to him and led him, unresisting into the centre of the room, kissing him lightly on the cheek and whispering, "Thank, you."

Mimi clapped his hands and, when attention was focussed on him, announced loudly, "Gentlemen, and, of course, ladies, for where would we be without you, I am truly delighted to present to you all, for the very first time, the amazing artworks that have been completed this very week, by our guest of honour, the absolutely wonderful Horace!"

Horace's cheeks burned furiously as the assembled company applauded wildly, a few slightly drunken cheers echoing off the walls; a few calls of 'Speech, speech' being echoed by 'Hear, hears!'

– demonstrating that you could take politicians out of Westminster but not Westminster out of politicians.

The only relief Horace had was that many of the guests were staring happily at his works rather than at his vermilion face, "I, er, that is..." he stammered, having not the slightest idea of what to say.

Georgina came to his rescue, "Our Horace is a typical artist," she announced, "Far too shy and far too modest when it comes to his own talents. But I know our man well," she ignored one or two ribald comments and raised her voice so that she could continue. "And I know he would just like to thank everyone for their appreciation, isn't that right, Horace?"

Horace took a deep breath and let it out in a relieved sigh, "Y-y-yes," he managed, "Thank you all." He turned to Georgina. "And thank you, most of all," he smiled.

She flung her arms round him, hugging him tightly, "You're bloody brilliant, you are. And bloody wonderful as well."

During the next hour or so, a score or more people came up to congratulate him, and many of them asked him for business cards, hopeful that he might consider taking commissions from them. Georgina, clinging tightly to his arm to lend him some moral support, came to the rescue once again. Just as he was about to apologise, she produced some cards from her bag.

"I just knew that this would happen," she whispered, "So I had a few printed."

After the initial hubbub had died down, Horace and Georgina retreated to a quiet corner of the room, he exhausted, she exhilarated, and sat quietly, sipping drinks.

"It's funny," he said after a while, "This time last year – the last Friday before Christmas – I w-w-was at wh-wh-one of those oh-so-sober bank parties, and ended up having sex on the manager's office floor. This year I'm at a, er, brothel, and I haven't even been propositioned."

Georgina giggled, "Disappointed?"

Horace laughed, "No. Just relieved. I take it you w-w-warned them all off?"

"Too true! You were holding me responsible after all. And besides, if you'd changed your mind, I was making damn sure it'd be me."

"*If* I had," Horace said with a smile, "It w-w-would have been."

They finally left as dawn approached, Horace carrying another large check from Mimi – along with a promise of more commissions when new girls joined – and Georgina with her bag firmly tucked under her arm. It was almost full light by the time their taxi arrived back in Walthamstow, and they were both yawning as they made their way up the stairs. Outside Horace's door they paused and looked at each other.

"Well," Georgina sighed, "That was fun, wasn't it?"

"Yeah. Thanks again."

She slapped him lightly on the arm, "Get away with ye," she grinned, deliberately broadening her accent, "And kiss me goodnight before I drag you up those stairs."

He complied. The kiss was tender, almost loving, and he reluctantly broke their embrace. "Goodnight," he whispered.

She stared at him for what seemed the longest time, before nodding, "Yeah, goodnight." She swallowed, once, noisily, and then quickly made her way upstairs.

For a few seconds afterwards, Horace stood there, not knowing whether to follow her or not. Finally, he turned slowly and opened his own door, slipping inside quickly before he could change his mind.

From The Diary of Horace Wilt

"Saturday, 22nd December, 1984

DD

What a night last night was! Mimi surprised me by presenting me and my paintings to the assembled crowd and - get this - they loved them! It was an absolutely fantastic party, and good old Georgie helped me keep my resolution intact. Actually, to be very honest with myself, I might just consider that a little disappointing; she looked absolutely good enough to eat.

With any luck, I'm likely to get a good few commissions out of it all - maybe, just maybe enough to mean I could carry on more or less full time! Once again, who have I got to thank for all that? Georgie, of course. I'm really falling for her... Do I actually mean that?

Yes."

20521609R00271

Printed in Great Britain
by Amazon